DEMON SIEGE

PACTS ARCANE AND OTHERWISE
BOOK 4

JOANNA MACIEJEWSKA

ALSO BY THE AUTHOR:

Pacts Arcane and Otherwise

By the Pact

Scars of Stone

Shadows over Kaighal

Demon Siege

Shadows of Eireland

Humanborn

Myth-Touched

Snakebitten

Other books

Memories of Sorcery and Sand

Collections

Scourges, Spells, and Serenades

To you, Reader.
Thank you for giving this story a chance.

1

Death was never a concern to Veranesh. Those of yalari who had the wits and will to advance above others, to become kanyalari—the most powerful of their own kind—understood that death was a part of the endless cycle. Those who feared death never reached beyond the limits of their own bodies. Veranesh couldn't blame them for being hesitant. After all, no matter how beneficial it could become, death was always a risk, and many preferred to keep their domains intact rather than pursue more power. Back in Yalarethe, he had not died for centuries, as death would bring him no benefit. Already on top, he had nowhere higher to climb.

As his wings carried him across the desert, his shadow skimming through the dunes like a hunting predator, he couldn't help thinking how back then he was convinced there were no more worthy goals to pursue, no scheme big enough to interest him, and no rival powerful enough to threaten him. And then humans started seeking the way to bridge the gap between the worlds, rekindling his ambition. To be the first one to cross meant to seize the opportunities as they appeared, or to learn secrets and ways no yalari had seen before. Others hesitated, sought arguments for and against such crossing, and he was the one to boldly step forward, even though he knew that going to Qinyalarethe, to the human world, ultimately meant death, as humans knew of no way to send a yalari home.

He smiled. Back then, he'd considered himself cunning and knowledgeable, but the events that followed proved him wrong. The mere thought of centuries spent trapped in a crystal brought a grimace to his face, but he didn't let the emotion linger. He was free now. He'd learned his lessons well enough, and the world of humans had indeed presented unexpected opportunities. *Kamira.* A pactee with such promise was a rarity even back when humans practiced arcane arts freely and widely, and many kanyalari would have vied for a pact with her. Instead, she first became his means to an end, and an accomplice later. Now, she could become much more.

Before he could see to his long-term plans, he had to make sure she survived, and along with her, the city for which she cared so much. That meant disposing of those threats she could not face on her own yet.

He looked at the desert below, but so far no place looked suitable for his needs. Not too far to the west, a trace of familiar energies pulled at him. The plateau that saw Uganel's destruction could serve well as another battleground, but Veranesh would have to choose to not destroy his opponent. Otherwise, the power released could reach far beyond the edges of the desert, endangering Kamira's city and other human settlements, possibly stirring the Four in their domain as well. No, the battle had to take place further out into the desert.

Veranesh beat his wings, lifting higher in the air. Flight

in the human world, devoid of any energies that flowed through his home world, came with more strain than back in Yalarethe, so there was little pleasure to it, but it allowed for a better search. Far in the south, a rocky formation jutting out of the sands caught his eye. It was hardly an appropriate place for a battle yalari and humans would talk about for years to come, and at the same time, it was all he needed.

The thought of the upcoming confrontation filled his veins with excitement, countering the cool wind brushing against his body. He used to be one of the most powerful kanyalari, and no one dared to challenge him openly. Even Arujhan, with all his might, resorted to the underhanded means, forging an unlikely covenant with other yalari.

This time the coward would come in person, because in his eyes, Veranesh was without his domain and weakened by centuries of imprisonment, thus an easy prey. If Arujhan backed away or took other yalari along, his own image would suffer, and others would be quick to test his power.

Veranesh couldn't deny that Arujhan had all the reasons to believe in his own superiority, and in the past, the odds of his victory would be clear. Now, with all that transpired— not so much anymore, and Veranesh had learned enough from his pactee about perseverance and facing the impossible to know that he had a chance against his opponent, especially with the tricks he'd learned in the human world.

Yet things could still go wrong, and this battle could be his defeat. Death was never a concern to him, and he would not run when it finally came... But no matter the ultimate outcome, Arujhan would fall before Veranesh did.

~

VEELK STOOD at a distance while Kamira talked to Archmage Irtan. At first glance, she was the same grumpy arcanist he knew, but the subtle differences in her posture, tone of voice, and magic surrounding her signified a deeper change. When he barged in on her confrontation with a Tivarashan priestess, everything seemed familiar enough: the trouble she'd gotten herself into, magic, fighting... But with the battle dust settling came the time for reflections and observations, and Veelk could only hope that there was enough of his true friend left within the first archmage she'd become.

The old archmage gave Kamira a nod and walked away, heading straight for Veelk. "It seems I owe you an apology," he said with a jovial smile that suggested no remorse. "Had the archmage told me she was expecting your arrival, I might have made a different call."

Veelk made a noncommittal grunt of an acknowledgment. Irtan looked and spoke like an old fox, and it left little doubt that his words were but a courtesy. With nothing else left to say between them, Veelk looked over the man's shoulder. Kamira stood alone in the middle of the chamber, her expression hopeful.

"I believe *the archmage* is waiting for me," Veelk said, not bothering with courtesies.

If Irtan took offense, he didn't show. With what could have been a shrug, he departed.

"My quarters?" Kamira asked as he approached. "I'm sure Koshmarnyk would like to hear the news."

"How is he?"

Kamira shifted as if there was something she'd rather not discuss. "He's fine." She glanced up at the shattered dome's edge where Fyertash perched. The demon's eyes focused on them, but Veelk couldn't tell whether he could hear their conversation. "Come, questions can wait."

She led him through the Towers with no less confidence than Atissa did not so long ago. Whenever they came across another person, he or she stepped to the side with a respectful bow and the word "archmage" muttered. Kamira responded to them with polite nods, sometimes addressing them by their names, and their attention didn't seem to affect her at all. At the same time, not once did she put on a smug expression or indulge in the power she seemed to have over others.

They finally stopped in front of a door, plain and unassuming, and as Veelk walked inside, a familiar sight greeted him: a simple room with no superficial furnishing or decorations, much like the room they used to share in the Jagged Swordsman. Two tables were filled with books and blueprints, a bookshelf stood to the side, and only a bed was lacking, but one of the two other doors likely led to a bedroom, and he wouldn't be surprised if it was as sparsely furnished as the main room.

Koshmarnyk was sitting by one of the tables, and Kamira rushed over to him with a huff of displeasure Veelk knew all too well. Archmage or not, her friends—and lovers —still got the caring treatment.

"You should be resting," she said.

"I'm healing just fine without being confined to bed."

He lifted his arm as if to demonstrate. Without delay, Kamira undid one of the bandages, leaning low as if to see his wounds up close. Veelk said nothing, waiting for the end of inspection, but Koshmarnyk sent him a glance over Kamira's bent back. His face bore dark marks of bruises, and the bandages sticking out from underneath his clothes suggested extensive wounds, but he sat up straight and without strain. Perhaps Atissa, unfamiliar with the sight of blood and torn flesh, had exaggerated the adept's injuries in her story.

Kamira was still inspecting Koshmarnyk's arm, and Veelk took a step forward. Surely, such a thorough examination was not necessary…

She straightened up. "They *do* seem to be regrowing," she said with a mix of surprise and approval.

Veelk paused mid-step. "Regrowing?"

"The stones," was all Koshmarnyk managed to squeeze in before Kamira looked at Veelk.

"Your turn. Shirt off!" There was an unyielding demand in her voice, so befitting an archmage, but at the same time, it matched Kamira's familiar stubbornness. "And don't pretend you don't know why. Fyertash told me you were on a brink of death."

With a sigh, Veelk removed his shirt. It seemed that his questions would have to wait until Kamira sated her own curiosity, and he should have known that, just as he noticed changes in her, she'd spot something was different about him. As soon as he sat on one of the chairs, Kamira was by his side, performing an equally thorough inspection. Her fingers skimmed along his forearm and arm, pressing here and there, and once or twice a bite of her nail or spark of magic marked her experimentations.

"It looks like skin. It feels like skin," she muttered. "But it really isn't, is it?"

Koshmarnyk arched his eyebrow, but contrary to Veelk's expectations, he didn't rush in to join the inspection.

"I've been told the burns were extensive," Veelk replied. "The magic from my scars was keeping me alive, but it couldn't help me heal, not that much."

She was so close to him that he could feel her sudden

tension. No matter how much he'd rather *not* tell her that he indeed had been on a brink of death, they never had secrets, and he wasn't about to keep one from her now. Besides, dying was in the past, and it was unlikely they'd dwell on it long.

"The elders decided to apply the blending paste directly to the wounds and let magic work," Veelk added. "You might think of it as one big scar."

"One that's almost the size of you?" she asked with a grimace. Then her expression changed. "You could have died, and I wasn't there to help," she added quietly.

With guilt so clear on her face, it became apparent she'd rather have set out to find him than be an archmage and the ruler of Kaighal. All Veelk's concerns, already fading throughout their conversation, vanished in an instant. This was still the very Kamira he always knew. Now all he had to do was ensure that the "dwelling on the past" part didn't linger.

He huffed. "I could say the same." He reached out and touched her cheek. "You're alive, but you're different as well. What happened?"

"The time in the crystal changed me," she replied.

"Is that why that priestess wanted you dead?"

Koshmarnyk rose from his seat, concern clear on his face. "What priestess?!"

Kamira hesitated, looking between them. "It seems that there's a lot of stories to be told." She walked over to the door. "We have some time, so let me get someone to bring us food and drink, and we can all fill each other in. *Then* we will deal with everything else, including figuring out how to make sure the Four and their priests don't interfere again."

The tone of her voice suggested she was already thinking on how to handle the demons from the north.

Likely a plan Veelk would oppose, but at least he could hope she still followed their rule of survival first and heroics later —if at all. On the other hand, as the archmage, she had the whole city as her responsibility, so things could get complicated.

Koshmarnyk nodded, and Veelk did likewise. "Stories first," he said. "Problems later."

He relaxed. If every other solution for those problems came to naught, his keshal had never failed to get rid of any and all obstacles.

2

Kamira pulled up the hood of her cloak long before she left the Towers. She kept her hands hidden in the sleeves and made her way through the winding stairways and corridors at a quick pace. It was so late in the evening that most students and teachers had already retired, and she could hope that no one would recognize the first archmage in her. Where she was going, no one should know.

Out of the Towers and onto the winding road leading down to the city, Kamira refrained from looking over her shoulder. Even if a spy lurked nearby, ready to follow her, the time to lose any unwanted eyes would be down in Kaighal, among many narrow alleys she knew so well. Regret stained her thoughts. She was the first archmage now, and no matter what the future brought, she would never be free to walk the streets of Kaighal unrecognized and carefree, with Veelk by her side and with their only concern being the destination of their next journey.

She smiled, letting emotions pass. The past was in the past, and she had the present to worry about before she could think of the future, and that required making sure no new trouble stirred. When she'd told Veelk and Koshmarnyk what she had in mind, they both offered to accompany her—and any other time, she'd welcome their presence by her side. But if she wanted to ensure secrecy of her little outing, she had to go alone. Veelk's towering presence would draw too much attention, and even if Koshmarnyk looked less conspicuous than the muscular tribal, Gildya spies might have been keeping an eye on his whereabouts.

When she finally made it down the hill, the city's main streets looked quiet, as they always did. As if people of Kaighal didn't care that the demon army lurked only few days of trek to the south, and the winged higher demons could descend upon them any time. Kamira couldn't decide if it was trust in their archmage's promise to protect the city or a quiet surrender to the unavoidable plight. Every now and then, a group of guards rushed by, paying little attention to their usual marks—pickpockets and thugs—and piles of crates and barrels, conveniently stocked where the streets crossed, suggesting that, despite centuries of peace, the city was preparing a defense, and its citizens were ready to fight for each corner should the demons get through the walls.

That brought an unexpected relief. Even if most of the weight to fend off the demons still rested on the arms of a handful of arcanists and reluctant Gildya adepts, the people of Kaighal were willing to lend a hand as much as possible.

Her destination lay at the edge of the southwestern district of Kaighal, filled with residences of merchants and the city's other wealthy or influential people. Kamira kept to the main street, unwilling to delve into the area where her presence would be easily noticed. In the evening crowd, not as dense as during daytime but still filling streets with pleasure-seekers, retiring traders, and workmen returning home or heading to cheaper taverns by the docks, a cloaked figure raised far fewer questions.

Several times she stopped by inns and still-open stalls, inspecting her surroundings while pretending to decide whether to enter or make a purchase, but it seemed no one was following her.

In the end, though, she had to turn south, into the serene streets surrounded by lavish houses. Few windows shone with lights at that time of night, and the streets themselves were lit with low-glow imbued stones placed mid-height of the stone walls running along it. They provided enough light for the passersby to make their way through but left the rest of the area to the darkness. After all, the wealthy didn't want their slumber interrupted by the outside light.

The gate she stopped at looked like all in the neighborhood, made with thick metal formed into decorative bars, but contrary to others, this one was wide open. The Temple welcomed all their current and future followers anytime they wished to direct their prayers to the Four. An empty sentiment, as far as Kamira considered it, since Kaighal cared little for Tivarashan religion. The city council allowed the Temple to stay only because the priests would pay taxes like everyone else, and having a place of worship encouraged Tivarashan merchants to arrive more often and stay longer.

Kamira took a deep breath and stepped through the gates.

The gardens surrounding what looked like an ordinary, three-story residence were lush and silent. With the night concealing the city and most of its noises, Kamira could almost believe that she stepped into Tivarashan forests, and she had no doubt that priests and Temple workers did their best to maintain such an impression. After all, nothing reinforced faith like reminding followers that their so-called gods reached beyond their homeland and watched over them even in the faithless city and brought comfort to those who missed home.

The building's doorway was wider than an ordinary house's would have been, and as Kamira stepped through, it became obvious that the Tivarashan had made a lot of changes to the building's interior.

What must have been an entrance hall was now the Temple's main room, with proper columns, wooden pews, and gilded candelabra along the walls that held multicolored imbued stones emanating pleasant, soft light. Everything around spoke of wealth and splendor, but the decorations lacked that blatant gaudiness many rich residences displayed.

At the center, at the end of the hall, was a stone dais with four statues. The likenesses of the Four were carved in Tivarashan blue marble, as famous as it was expensive, and unlike many other statues of demonic deities, they didn't conceal the true nature of the beings they depicted. No one in Tivarashan had a grain of doubt to whom they directed their prayers. Although Kamira loathed the notion of worshiping beings that might be more powerful than humans but sometimes equally petty and even more deceitful than them, she always gave the nod to the honesty of the Four. They've made a deal with her nation, simple and clear, and they didn't try to pass it as anything else.

"How may I help you, Child of the Four?" A priest stepped out from the side. Likely a low-ranking one, since he was awake, keeping guard in the main temple building.

Kamira removed the hood concealing her face. "Wake

up whomever you must, but let the Four know that First Archmage Kamira asks to receive their audience," she spoke carefully chosen words. She hoped that asking for an audience rather than demanding to speak with the Four would make them amicable and curious enough to agree. And as much as she cared little about her family back home, Kaighal's struggles weren't theirs, so she omitted her surname. It held no weight in Kaighal anyway, and it seemed best not to remind the Four and their servants that they could take out their anger on her relatives.

The priest nodded and rushed away.

Kamira strolled down the rows of pews. Even from the distance, the magic surrounding the statues teased her senses. This was their link to the human world and a place where they appeared before their worshipers. Back when she was young and she visited Tivarashan temples, the sight of ghastly figures appearing from thin air to not only speak to their flock but also to listen to them always left her in awe. Years later, with her arcanist training to aid her, she saw it as nothing but a trick of magic.

With her instincts screaming against such carelessness, she made it all the way to the dais and knelt in front of the statues, her head bent deep. In that position, one strike would end her life, unless she somehow sensed it coming, so her best bet was the hope that the Four would be curious enough to speak to her first. Or, seeing as she was of Tivarashan blood, they would suspect a trap and hesitate to act before knowing more.

Kamira waited, but no footsteps announced the arrival of another priest or priestess. She hoped it was the Four's test of her patience and perseverance rather than the negligence of the man she'd spoken to. Causing fuss and demanding to see someone in charge of the Temple could draw too much attention.

"Is that a sign of your surrender?" a deep feminine voice asked.

Kamira almost snickered, because the demoness must know that after the trouble Kamira had stirred, she'd not be the one to come crying and begging for forgiveness.

She lifted her head and looked the demoness in the eye. "A gesture of good faith," she replied. "We both were pulled into a fight we didn't intend to start."

Of course, the Four might be considering the expansion of their domain, but she doubted it. Not many people made pacts nowadays, but there were still enough around for demons to have their pick. However, if the Four decided to claim some more humans for their worship, thus taking away the meager choice their brethren had, they risked that their own kin would come after them. From what Fyertash had told Kamira, covenants among his kin were possible if the perceived threat outweighed personal risk of all involved.

The demoness's lips curled, caught somewhere between a smile and a grimace, as if she couldn't decide whether to be displeased at the reply or acknowledge the courage it took give it.

Kamira took her time to inspect the demoness's features, refreshing her rusty knowledge of the Four. The one speaking must be Zyreshi. She was beautiful, despite the elongated nose, which, truth to be told, wasn't as nearly as long and crooked as those of other demons. Gentle locks flowed around her face, stopping short of the chin and revealing a slender neck. Her hands were almost human, with her claws resembling overgrown nails rather than the weapons of a deadly predator, but it was the wings where the real threat hid. For an inattentive watcher, they were nothing special, and their span left much to be desired.

Kamira knew better. The wings' edges were as sharps as blades, and all the tales of Zyreshi's deeds made it clear that she knew how to use them in a fight. Her deceitfully filigree frame and those tiny claws must have misled many of her opponents who didn't take into account that, so small and light, she could move with great dexterity and speed.

"Why would the Four refuse to support actions of their faithful follower?" Zyreshi asked. "What can you give us to turn our heads away?"

Still on her knees, Kamira swallowed. "You know what I can do. You felt it." Even though there was no priest or worshiper in sight, she preferred not to mention the destruction spell. Undoubtedly, someone was listening in hopes of gleaning the archmage's secrets, even if Zyreshi forbade it. "I have a yalari obeying my command, mage killers by my side, and I could train others to do what I can do. If Tivarashan forces want to go south, we could go north to meet them."

Zyreshi regarded her with narrow eyes. "You aren't making a threat. I can appreciate that. But the hot-blooded child of the queen wishes for a war, and the Four cannot be seen as cowardly."

"She could have her war away from Kaighal," Kamira offered. "The Western Kingdom is about to make its move as well. Their scouts are already nearby, and their armies are likely to follow."

Gentle laughter filled the Temple as Zyreshi arched her head back in amusement. "Clever. Instead of dealing with two armies, you will have to deal with none."

"The yalari who crossed into our world are still coming for the city," Kamira said dryly.

The demoness looked at her sharply. "Indeed they are. It would be interesting to watch what you make of it, but now that I know your secret, I'd wager you'll find a way to win. Though I'd love to know why Veranesh and that scoundrel Fyertash are aiding you. If they left, they could give them a battle on their own terms or return to Yalarethe."

"Yalari's reasons are their own." Kamira shrugged.

Zyreshi leaned forward with a sly grin. "Clever," she said once more. "Trying to make me believe you're nothing but a pawn. Nevertheless, I won't waste time pulling secrets out of you. Instead, let's get back to our trade. Given what you can do and how it managed... to stir our boredom, I'll treat you as an equal this once. Speak of what you want."

"I desire for things to be as they were," Kamira replied. "For the city to be an independent port that welcomes people from all over the continent and also those who come from beyond it. I care not whether Tivarashan will conquer the Western Kingdom or any other land they wish to see as theirs. But the city of Kaighal will remain free."

The demoness gave a slow nod. "Anything else?"

"The priestess who fought me killed the child of the queen's blood," Kamira said. "As long as no finger points toward Kaighal, I'll let the Temple and the Four handle this matter however they see fit and confirm any story they wish to tell the queen."

"And what of our servant?" Zyreshi asked. "Have you taken her alive?"

Kamira shook her head, and the demoness grinned with satisfaction. Likely it was one less problem to deal with, and Bayena would not get to make accusations, spin lies, or reveal her accomplices. Undoubtedly, the Four would instruct their priests to handle the matter in a way that would yield the best outcome for the Temple.

"I like you, pactee," the demoness said with a hint of joviality. "You're courageous, but you also know that sometimes bending your head might get you what you want while threats or demonstrations of power won't."

Kamira stared back with an inscrutable face, knowing better than to react to the praise that was also a reminder of what her place was, no matter how much threat—if any— she could really pose to the Four.

"If you choose to accept, the Four will offer you a pact," Zyreshi continued. "We would all benefit from it, even if you stay in this city instead of joining the ranks of our servants."

Kamira's eyes widened. Zyreshi's offer wasn't some pact she wanted to make on the side that everyone would overlook. She spoke on behalf of the Four. Kamira must have impressed them enough if they wanted to make a pact without trying to convince her to join the priests, and she bent her head low. Such immense power and freedom from the Temple's rank would likely make her the most influential arcanist in her homeland, and perhaps even in the whole of Tyorane. And with no conditions given, she could hardly find a reason anyone would refuse.

Except for one.

"I'm honored to be worthy of the pact with the Four," Kamira said, "but I belong to Veranesh." In more ways than Zyreshi could even imagine. Not only did the stone scars bind her forever to his magic, but her time in the crystal had altered her. "Even if I was foolish enough to betray him, the Four are far too wise to draw his attention during the time when he's deciding who his enemies are."

She lifted her head, looking straight at the demoness. As much as the Four had little to fear from Veranesh, or any other demon, for that matter, in their cunning they must understand that a demon who had nothing to lose but had all the reasons to stir trouble and deal destruction could affect their demon and human domains more than they'd like, even if ultimately he'd lose against them. As far as she knew, the four demons who united their power and influence in more than some shaky covenant disliked anything that stirred their comfortable existence, and Kamira had no doubt that Veranesh could bring a lot of disturbance to it if he chose so.

Zyreshi regarded her in thought. "You're wiser than I thought you would be," she said calmly, as if refusal meant little to her pride. Her offer might have been genuine, but it seemed that it was also a test. "Therefore, I'll give you what you want, and even more. The Four will make a deal with you that will last past your lifetime. But yes, you will do something for us in return, and so will that scoundrel Fyertash." She lifted her finger before Kamira could protest. "If we can convince all of our human children to leave the city alone, I'm sure you can convince one yalari to do your bidding. Word is that this prideless hoyve already obeys your every command."

Kamira swallowed. Some things she wouldn't do, not even for Kaighal, but Zyreshi had already tested her, so the condition would be something that the Four wanted rather than an attempt to make Kamira miserable. There would be a price to pay, but perhaps it would be much less than she anticipated.

"Name the price," she said calmly, even though an invisible hand was still crushing her throat in anticipation.

Zyreshi's expression changed, and her smile was part sly and part amused. "Very well. We shall see if you truly love this city so much."

～

KOSHMARNYK CLIMBED the steps leading to the initiation rite chamber without rush. His wounds had healed enough for him to make the journey on his own, but he'd rather not risk straining his body too much. He'd already failed to help Kamira in her battle with the Tivarashan priestess, and he would not be confined to bed while she and Veelk faced demons.

Besides, all he'd been told was that an adept was requesting his presence, and the student who passed the message didn't convey any sense of urgency, so the matter could be trivial. If there was anything Gildya's bureaucrats excelled at, it was wasting other people's time. On the other hand—Koshmarnyk narrowed his eyes—this could have something to do with Mayetti. If that double-faced adept shared her ambush plan with anyone or had accomplices among her colleagues...

No. He shook his head. *They wouldn't try anything openly in the Towers.*

But they *could* accuse him of being involved in Mayetti's disappearance, and even if Koshmarnyk told the truth of the events, Gildya would disbelieve him on principle.

He shifted his focus elsewhere, since worrying was pointless. He'd deal with problems as they came.

The Towers had been emptier ever since Kamira brought down the former archmages, and even though enough students and teachers stayed to fill some of the corridors, dormitories, and classrooms, today was different. With the sighting of the demon army landing to the south, everyone who could abandon their duties headed for the city's walls. Undoubtedly, they also wanted to see what the first archmage would do, since early in the morning Kamira set out for the walls herself. If the onlookers expected a show of powerful magic, they were in for a disappointment, because she wasn't about to start a battle when the last piece of the city's defense still had to be put in place.

He walked into the initiation rite chamber, confident and at the same time slow enough to react to any threat, but the four people in the middle of the floor paid no attention to him. They were busy mounting pieces of a device on its metal supports.

Adept Davshil stood to the side, overlooking them, and, to Koshmarnyk's surprise, he offered an amiable wave.

"Koshmarnyk," he said.

Koshmarnyk had to arch an eyebrow at the adept using his preferred name. Such a courtesy came unexpected from a Gildya man. "Do you need my assistance?"

"We're almost done. The assembly was straightforward, thanks to your blueprints, but I thought you'd like to inspect everything personally."

Another surprise... Koshmarnyk couldn't help a suspicion that Davshil had hidden reasons for such amiable behavior, but he kept his face straight. "I appreciate it."

He stood by Davshil as his workers finished their work, fastening the last screws that held the device in place.

"I have to admit, this might be your brightest invention yet." Genuine respect rang in Davshil's voice. "A device emitting a solid magical barrier... I never thought it would be possible."

Koshmarnyk refrained from mentioning that Devanshari had an artifact that did exactly that... and so much more, if tales were to be believed. Sharing such knowledge could lead to inconvenient questions and make Gildya aware of involuntary ties between him and Queen Cahala. From what he knew, Devanshari had already crowned the queen's son as their king, but no one spoke openly about her death.

As the workers gave Davshil a nod, and he waved for them to leave, Koshmarnyk walked over to the device and inspected it. From what he could tell without tearing every piece apart, Gildya had stuck to his original design, offering no improvements or alterations.

"The adepts are mounting other devices along the battlements," Davshil said. "They will give instructions to the guards and switch them on at the signal."

"Gildya did well," Koshmarnyk offered. "To be honest, this wasn't something I expected with all the fussing from the council..."

Davshil let out a short laugh. "Oh, don't worry, everything else is as it was. I'm here because the council is still busy discussing what happened to Mayetti, and who's going to replace her in dealing with you."

Koshmarnyk made sure his face expressed nothing but a polite interest, concealing his own surprise. "And what happened?" He had to know how Gildya knew about it, or what, exactly, they did know. "If this isn't some inner politics you'd rather not discuss, of course."

Davshil shrugged. "Nobody really knows, and this is what has the council so riled up. She disappeared for a few days and came back badly wounded. From what I've heard, nobody could make sense of her ramblings."

Koshmarnyk froze on the spot. Mayetti had come back... It was impossible that she'd escaped the demon. He'd heard her scream echoing through the forest. That could mean only one thing: Myrkan had let her go. And a demon like him, finding delight in torture, wouldn't have had done so if he didn't have a reason.

"I can't say I'm surprised something like that happened," Koshmarnyk replied. "Mayetti always had a lot of underhanded dealings, and in the end, one had to go wrong.

Though I'm sure that once she gets better, she'll entertain the council with a tale that won't reveal anything she doesn't wish to be known."

A shadow passed over Davshil's face. "Mayetti didn't make it." His voice was quieter than moments ago. "She succumbed to her wounds. Though some say poison was involved... You can understand why the council worries."

"They don't suspect me, do they?" Koshmarnyk asked.

"I think they know you'd rather come openly." Davshil looked around as if checking if the workers had truly left. "I doubt they suspect the archmage, if that's what you're worried about. But it means that the council is even more concerned about an enemy they know nothing about."

"Or it might have been Mayetti's private dealings. She was from the Western Kingdom, and I wouldn't be surprised if someone out there was vexed enough to send killers after her," Koshmarnyk said. As much as he'd rather offer the truth, neither Davshil nor anyone else at Gildya was his friend, and giving his enemies openings for accusations or suspicions would only make the uneasy relationship between adepts and arcanists worse.

"Adept Ervan seems to think there's some bigger plot at play."

Koshmarnyk didn't hide his grimace. "Ervan."

"I know you hate him, but he has good reasons to suspect foul play," Davshil said, rushing to his fellow adept's defense. "A couple of weeks ago, thieves hit one of our storehouses... They almost made it away with a lot of our explosive devices." Davshil twitched and shut his mouth all of a sudden, as if he'd said too much.

Koshmarnyk wouldn't use the word "hate" to describe his feelings toward Ervan, but instead of wasting time on pointless explanations, he focused on the second part.

"Explosive devices? That's not something common thieves would know about."

"They might have not known what they were stealing." Davshil fidgeted, his discomfort clear.

"Or someone on the council was in on it," Koshmarnyk finished for him.

"Ervan suspected Mayetti might have had something to do with it and tried to get some answers, but she wasn't coherent enough to tell him anything before she died."

Koshmarnyk narrowed his eyes. "Sounds like the council indeed has reasons to worry."

Davshil sighed. "You didn't hear anything from me."

That much Koshmarnyk could promise him, so he nodded. "I appreciate you telling me."

The other man let out another sigh. "Consider it a peace offering. I still think you're wrong about putting those stones in your body, but the way the council treated you... Perhaps there was more politics to it than looking out for the good of Gildya and its future." He straightened invisible creases in his robe. "Now, back to what's important. Have you inspected the device? Is it to your satisfaction?"

"It is," Koshmarnyk replied. "Pass my regards to all the adepts involved, and I'll be sure to inform the archmage of Gildya's excellent work."

"I'll be on my way, then." Davshil offered a courteous nod. "Be well... Koshmarnyk."

"You too," Koshmarnyk replied. "And be careful. It seems that there's danger lurking within Gildya's walls, and even if you do not share my sentiment toward Ervan, watch out for him."

Davshil sent him a tired glance and a nod. As the man made his way toward the door, Koshmarnyk rubbed his chin. Ervan always acted like his work was his most important endeavor, and his many interesting devices and solutions for imbued stones had secured him a seat on the council, but Koshmarnyk couldn't shake the feeling the cunning adept had other, more secretive goals. Ervan had deceived Koshmarnyk in the past, spinning lies about Gildya's willingness to talk about the forbidden research while he prepared a trap for Koshmarnyk. Perhaps Mayetti was indeed incoherent, driven by pain and fear, but there was a chance that Ervan actually spoke with her and, by using poison, made sure no one learned about their conversation.

It was a reasonable suspicion, but proving it would be difficult. The council knew of the history between Koshmarnyk and Ervan, so they would discard any ungrounded accusation. He needed something to convince them.

A whoosh of wind made him look up. Fyertash was descending through the shattered dome.

"You look troubled." The demon inspected him with curiosity.

"Demons are coming. 'Troubled' seems appropriate," Koshmarnyk replied. "Is Kamira on her way back?"

Fyertash shook his head. "Still on the walls. But she's safe, you needn't worry. She's making sure that my brethren will be wary of getting too close to the city. They will send the asayalari, though, to test the defenses, and ultimately will work up the courage to take the risk themselves." He glanced at the device. "I hope these things will work as well as the archmage's plan."

Koshmarnyk offered the demon his half-smile. Even Gildya, as hateful as it was toward him, didn't question the quality of his designs.

He fished a small imbued stone out of his pocket. "The

barrier should be high enough to allow your flying in and out of this chamber, but you'll need this if you plan on venturing beyond the city."

Fyertash inspected the stone with narrowed eyes. "Such an item can be dangerous in the wrong hands."

"That's why I only made one, and no one but you, me, and Kamira knows about it." The demon had better understand the trust that he'd been granted.

Fyertash hid the stone in a nook of his leather outfit, which had a simple cut of a culture that valued efficiency over beauty. As demons used the power of their claws in a battle, it had no sheaths for weapons or other tools, and it bore no decorative markings or symbols of status.

"Very well. Anything else?" Fyertash asked.

"You can signal Kamira that the device is ready. We should raise the barrier before your brethren decide they don't fear you as much as they thought."

Fyertash flashed a grin, as if the suggestion amused him. His wings shot open, and, without any more words, he took off.

Koshmarnyk looked at the device. At least it was ready. If everything went well, it would provide Kaighal with protection that could rival that of the Devanshari kingdom. And with that out of the way, Koshmarnyk could focus on other dangers that threatened the city... on finding a proof of Ervan's underhanded dealings with Mayetti.

~

THE SUN WAS RISING over the sea as Kamira climbed Kaighal's battlements. After a trying battle, a late evening spent on sharing stories, and a night visit to the Temple of the Four, she welcomed the crisp air and a slight breeze, hoping they'd keep her sharp and awake.

Her new clothes, the formal outfit of an arcanist, irritated her skin and limited her movement. She'd rather wear her travel clothes, or at least something more comfortable that she usually put on when staying in the city, but this was the first time people in Kaighal were to see the first archmage, and she had to look the part at least this once.

The onlookers climbed the walls, and as more and more arrived, the city guards had a hard time keeping them away from the spots where Gildya's adepts worked on setting up their devices. At least the part of the battlements she was ascending remained empty. No one dared to disrespect the archmage's wish to be undisturbed.

To the south, beyond the thick stone protecting Kaighal, stretched a land covered with grass and rare shrubs—a familiar sight from her many travels. Over the centuries, desert had kept encroaching on it, its yellow sands glistening in the rising sun like piles of treasures.

Back in the past, Kamira had wondered why the archmages didn't try to reclaim some of that land with their magic. Even if the farming fields and meadows spread to the west and north of the city, providing enough space, there could always be fisheries set up, grazing lands to be chosen, and smaller settlements to be established. Kaighal could spread, and even if it would never match the grandeur of the Kingdom of Zemarion, it had a chance of creating its own great history.

But now she knew the archmages had reasons to keep the desert as it was. At least with the last of them gone, Kaighal could work on claiming those lands as its own.

If the city survives the invasion, she reminded herself as her eyes stopped on the dark silhouettes at the edge of the desert. From afar, the demonling army was less threatening than she'd expected, but as they got closer to the city, that illusion would fade. And if she read the magic disruptions around them right, the arcanists allied with demons were summoning more already. Still, the biggest threat lay in the three figures towering over the demonling masses. She had a hard time catching all the details, but the higher demons' shapes matched what Fyertash had told her about their adversaries.

As if responding to her thoughts, Fyertash descended from the air, landing softly beside her. "No more than three," he said. "That's good news. Perhaps the turmoil among the pactees prevented them from bringing anyone else."

"You'll have to tell me what exactly happened over there." Kamira squinted as if it could help her notice anything about the demons.

"When you have time to worry about it, archmage."

Kamira gave him a glare, but in the end, he was right. She was already pushing her previous night's conversation with Zyreshi aside, so that future problems didn't cloud her focus, and if no more demons showed up to aid their enemies, no matter what turmoil on Juamha had caused such an outcome, it was a concern for another time.

"Why did they bother taking all those demonlings?" she asked instead. "If they only took their arcanists, they could have crossed the sea faster."

"They wanted to ensure that the pactees were safe. We do not know how to summon asayalari, and without their protection, Arujhan's human servants are vulnerable." Fyertash looked toward the desert. "We learned that early on during our approach through the overseas kingdom. The humans opposing us set out ambushes, and even though many of them died in those skirmishes, they took our pactees along. Arujhan is not fool enough to repeat his past mistakes."

The answer suggested the demons were prepared for difficulties and would approach with caution rather than mounting a full-blown attack immediately. "How close do they have to be to bind you?" she asked.

Fyertash's face stretched in a wide, amused smile. "They won't try to bind me. Hardly any yalari bothers with it when they already have an advantage. It's faster to just go for the kill... or to maim the opponent if there's need for information or torture. Arujhan can overpower me easily, and I'm sure he's convinced he could best Veranesh as well."

Not exactly what Kamira would have liked to hear, but she appreciated the honesty. "But you would still try to bind them in such a confrontation?"

The demon shrugged. "Any yalari in these circumstances would try to run first, but yes, with no other choice, binding is their only chance." He grimaced. "A slim one, since the binding takes too long. If you have a yalari trying to rip you with his or her claws, there isn't enough time for it."

"Perfect." Kamira had come to the battlements with a plan in mind, and Fyertash's words had confirmed it could work. "I hope it's not beyond you to flee," she added with a cunning smile.

The demon narrowed his eyes, scratching his claw against his chin. At least he didn't seem offended by the idea of running. "If they think I'm fleeing, they'll go after me with little hesitation. That's the opposite of trying to keep them away from the city."

Kamira nodded. "But a good scare could force them to

back away for good. Like when they go after you and learn that you can bind them from a greater distance than they can reach you."

His expression changed as he put things together, and Kamira smiled. No matter how unnerving Fyertash's games were and how untrustworthy he seemed, his exceptional cunning allowed him to grasp ideas quickly.

Without delay, he lifted in the air, and... flew over the walls. Kamira half opened her mouth, because getting closer to their enemies was contrary to what she'd asked for, but she had to trust Fyertash knew his brethren better, so she said nothing. Besides, with so many onlookers, she'd rather not shake the people's confidence in her ability to fend off the invasion by showing she couldn't even control her supposed allies.

Within a few heartbeats, a single silhouette tore off from the demon horde, heading straight for Fyertash. He was the biggest of the three, so he had to be Arujhan.

The demon was closing the distance too fast for Kamira's liking, and Fyertash was hovering away from the walls. She glanced at the adepts setting up the devices, but even if they finished on time, the barrier wouldn't reach far enough to protect her demonic ally.

She took a deep breath, preparing for a possible battle. Defeating a higher demon with magic seemed like an impossible feat, but she couldn't stand idly if it came to the worst.

Down below, guards called out for someone to stay away, and Kamira turned her head at the sound of familiar voice. "Let them through," she ordered them.

As soon as the guards parted, Veelk started climbing the battlements, with Zelna and her companion following. Veelk's sister looked exactly like Kamira remembered, and her muscular body towered over the small man who accompanied her. According to what Veelk had told her the previous evening, his name was Mawi, and he was the tribe's chronicler, well versed in history and demons. That alone made Kamira eager to engage in conversation, but the time for introduction and sharing knowledge would come later.

"Did I miss anything?" Veelk asked as soon as he stood beside her. "How's your plan going?"

Zelna gave Kamira a short nod of recognition and then led the other tribesman to the side, keeping at a distance as if allowing her space for whatever she needed to do.

"About how one would expect from Fyertash," Kamira grumbled, focusing back on the demon.

Arujhan had to be within the range of a binding spell already, but the demon was still waiting.

"I'm not helping him if he takes on the bigger demon." The confidence in Veelk's voice made it clear he wasn't afraid of the challenge. He was simply disapproving of Fyertash not sticking to the plan.

As if Fyertash heard Veelk's words, he turned and dashed for the walls. A strong wind hit Kamira as he passed above them. "Now!" he said in passing, and headed for the Towers. At full speed, he seemed to be moving faster than Arujhan.

Without delay, Kamira started the incantation. Since the binding spell seemed a lot like high mages' art, she kept her voice quiet, enunciating words only enough to ensure the spell would work. The last thing she needed was people questioning why the new archmage trained in arcane arts was using high magic, especially as she had to keep the origin of the spell secret.

Arujhan stopped mid-flight as the tendrils of magic

reached him. Then he resumed his flight, and Kamira could swear there was urgency in his movement.

She kept chanting. Her plan relied on the panic that any demon would feel when they realized that their opponent could bind them from further away than he thought, so she had to go through the binding as quickly as possible, giving Arujhan no time to consider other possibilities or trace magic to the one channeling it.

The demon outside the walls stopped again. He was close enough for Kamira to be able to discern his features. His broad shoulders and even broader wingspan spoke of an imposing presence, but his rough, chiseled face lacked the deep thoughtfulness that always marked Veranesh's expression. Arujhan might have been smart enough to secure a position of power for himself, but something told Kamira that, given a chance, he'd still choose brute force over subtle manipulations. On the other hand, according to Fyertash, Arujhan was the one to create the plot aimed at Veranesh centuries ago, though the small demon claimed that this came from Arujhan's cowardice and avoidance of risky confrontations rather than from supreme cunning.

Arujhan hovered in place, looking around, and then he withdrew, as if lending truth to Fyertash's claims. Kamira didn't stop reciting the spell until Arujhan was out of its reach.

She exhaled. If she managed to convince Arujhan that Fyertash had abilities no other demon knew of, the higher demons should keep away from the city, at least for a while. Then, if Arujhan fell for Veranesh's trap, they'd only have Derazin and Myrkan to worry about. *If* Veranesh won his battle.

In the distance, murmurs rose. People were pointing at the retreating demon, their excitement mixed with the uncertainty as they glanced at Kamira. To them, it must have looked like she didn't do anything.

"An archmage whose very presence turns demons away," Veelk said in jest, though he was considerate enough to keep his voice down. "You'll go down in history."

"Or only 'go down' if the demons figure out our little deception," she couldn't help saying.

He offered her a wide grin. "As optimistic as always. I sure missed your cheerful demeanor."

Zelna and Mawi approached, both in their tribal outfits: loose shirts and pants gathered at the hem, so that the cloth would not tangle in battle, decorated with subtle embroidery that mimicked the patterns of their scars. They must have left their belongings at the inn from where Veelk picked them up, because they had no travel packs with them, only their weapons. Zelna carried a keshal strapped across her back, like her brother, and her companion had a short sword by his side.

"This was it? I expected at least some fighting," Zelna said.

Playfulness faded from Veelk's face. "There's going to be plenty of fighting."

Mawi approached Kamira. "Pleased to make your acquaintance. Veelk told us a lot about you, archmage, and we're grateful you took such a good care of him during his travels."

Both siblings arched an eyebrow, and Zelna even snorted. Mawi ignored them both, his genuine smile still directed at Kamira and his hand stretched. Kamira shook it.

"The pleasure is mine. Once time permits, I'd love to learn from you everything you're willing to share," she replied. Neither of them had any doubts that no secrets would be exchanged.

A shadow crossed over them, and Fyertash descended with slow beats of his wings. "This was a good plan, archmage. I doubt any of the kanyalari will risk getting close to the city again," he said. "I also spoke to the adept in the Towers, and he says the device is ready."

A sudden burden weighed on Kamira's shoulders. No matter how well her plan had worked so far, all would be in vain if the way to protect the city failed. Instinctively, she wanted to find an excuse for a delay, but the sooner they tested the barrier, the better.

"Very well," she said.

She walked over to the edge of the battlements, facing the city. With all Veranesh's power at her disposal, channeling enough energy was child's play, but to keep it condensed was another matter, and she put her focus into it. A ball of fire grew in front of her. The flames swirled, confined to the spherical shape she forced them into, and once she was done, she sent it up into the air. Then, with the flick of her fingers, she broke it apart. Fire spread across the sky, visible from everywhere across Kaighal, but she put it high enough that the flames and sparks died out before they reached the city.

People gathered on the battlements and by the walls pointed at it, their murmurs filled with excitement and curiosity, but as the last of the sparks vanished in the air, something else drew their attention.

One by one, Gildya's devices came to life. Barriers flickered in the air, but instead of taking up the dome shapes like all arcane protection, each formed only a slanted shield facing away from the city. Close enough to each other, the shields overlapped, and then, at the end, a domed cap appeared over the city, connecting with all other barriers.

Koshmarnyk must have activated the last device, the one meant for the Towers.

Kamira breathed out with relief. With the city having an irregular shape, she hadn't been sure it would work, but creating overlapping barriers instead of trying to shield Kaighal with one protective circle turned out to be a perfect solution. Even if their enemies breached a part of it, it should be easy enough to defend as long as the higher demons kept away. And as reluctant as Gildya might be in their cooperation, the council had reassured her that they had enough replacements ready.

A spark lightened her heart with hope. Many things could still go wrong, but at least Kaighal stood a chance against the invaders.

All around her, cheers rose, and people chanted, "Kaighal!" together. She smiled. As long as they didn't require her to deliver speeches, she would do her job as the first archmage and drive the demons away.

3

Atissa's old room reminded her of the life she no longer had. Even though it was pleasant to sleep in her own bed and experience the safety of familiar walls, she found little comfort in staying in her father's quarters. This was a place for an archmage, or at least a promising arcanist, and she was neither. At the same time, she had nowhere else to go.

She browsed through her belongings more to pass time than to decide what to do with them, as she still had to choose what kind of future she wanted for herself. Kamira's invitation seemed honest, but no matter what thoughts Atissa had recently had about her own father, it didn't change the fact that Kamira had killed him. Even if revenge wasn't Atissa's goal anymore, Kamira's presence—and her position of power—stirred many uneasy feelings.

A quiet knock interrupted her thoughts, and a young woman came in. She had the plain outfit of a high mage teacher, pleasant features, and warm brown skin surrounded by dark brown hair. A tray with a meal burdened her hands, but she wasn't a servant, and it took Atissa only a heartbeat to recognize her.

"Archmage Irtan had the need to check on me?" Atissa asked. She couldn't help hints of sarcasm and bitterness, as her conversation with the old man was still jarringly fresh in her mind. He acted loyal to Kamira and openly expressed his distrust toward Atissa, as if he wasn't one of the former archmages, and her father's colleague and rival. And now he'd sent his little protégée to gather information. "If he wants to spy on me, he should pick someone other than his own student."

Pelina shook her head. "I'm here at Kamira's request."

Atissa's curiosity spiked. The way Pelina used the archmage's name instead of the title and the tone of her voice suggested some familiarity between the two of them. "Did she change her mind and wants me to leave?"

"She thought you might prefer to eat alone," Pelina said. "And she asked me to talk to you."

"What about?" Atissa couldn't help her ire. She wanted to be left alone, to gather her thoughts and make decisions.

"About arcane arts." Pelina set the tray on the low table.

Atissa looked away from it and the two comfortable armchairs beside it. This was where her father used to meet his guests, engage in politics, or simply enjoy an evening with a book.

"You might have questions about the pacts and other things, and though I've never experienced the loss of magic like you, I am a high mage who became an arcanist." Pelina came closer, and her voice was soft, but she stopped a few steps away. "Arcane magic works a little different than high magic, but it's easy to grasp the basics. You could have your power back, and with all your previous schooling, you could quickly become skilled enough to—"

"No," Atissa interrupted before doubts took the better of her. "I will not make a pact."

Even as little as Pelina said had already woken up the craving for magic and power. It would be so easy to listen and give in, and to make a pact and learn the ways of arcane magic. Before she would know, Atissa would be once more involved in the Towers' politics, enduring jealous glares and trying to ignore vicious whispers. No matter how much Kamira's deeds might have changed things around, the Towers were still as they were before, and relying on magic meant that Atissa would choose the very path that she was trying to abandon. Perhaps it led to a different place, but she would rather not take the risk that it didn't.

"The city will need all the arcanists it can get," Pelina said. "You could help to save people and break your pact later."

"The city will need more than arcanists," Atissa replied. "Medics, messengers, helpers of all sorts. And the archmage will be better off without worrying where I direct my magic."

Instead of coming up with more arguments, Pelina nodded. "If you change your mind or have any questions, seek me out."

"Thank you," Atissa said just before the other woman left, closing the door behind her. Even if she didn't intend to stay in the Towers, making enemies was a bad idea.

She approached the table. The meal was simple but still warm, and Atissa's stomach rumbled in response to the aroma rising from the stew. She touched the armchair with hesitation. To sit in it meant going down memory lane. To eat in her room meant avoiding the harsh truth that she couldn't escape her past, at least not yet. Perhaps she should make a pact after all... But as she'd said herself, Kaighal needed more than arcanists, and if there was anything Atissa could do while she decided her future, it was finding a way to be useful.

She glanced at the door that used to lead to her father's bedchamber. He'd kept all his books and notes there, away from his guests' prying eyes. High magic was gone now, but it didn't mean she wouldn't be able to find something useful in his research. Her father had taken a keen interest in Gildya's work, keeping a close eye on their inventions, and once or twice she'd spotted items and books that looked old, perhaps even from before the Cataclysm. And the way he had trapped minor demons back in their family residence made it clear that he wasn't beyond straying toward the arcane ways if it served his needs.

Giving in to that thought, she rushed inside his old room. The familiar sight, marred by stillness and the absence of her father, twisted her heart, but she ignored her swelling emotions. She grabbed a pile of journals and loose notes and brought it back to the main room, as if lingering in her father's domain for too long would cast his shadow over her again.

With her mind already occupied with the first of the journals, Atissa stuffed the first spoonful of stew in her mouth. It didn't matter anymore that she was sitting in her father's armchair.

All she needed was to find a way to be of value.

ADEPT ERVAN CHECKED TWICE whether the door to his private quarters was locked. Once more, he pondered heading out into the city, and perhaps finding a room in an inn, but spies could as well follow him there. He was safer within the familiar walls of Gildya's main building, where strangers would stand out, and Ervan had to worry only about other adepts eavesdropping.

The thought, instead of comfort, brought a new wave of concerns, and Ervan wiped his sweaty hands against his expensive trousers. Even though the cold touch of the fabric did little to ease his anxiety, the adept exercised self-control. He was a member of Gildya's council, and he acted like a freshly admitted apprentice.

He looked around his quarters, seeking reassurance in the clean and orderly space. His drafting table, workshop in the corner, and desk were all arranged perfectly, with no single item or tool out of place. He kept all his notes and blueprints stored in locked drawers and cabinets, ensuring his plans and secrets were safe from other adepts, and this time would be no different. Even if he couldn't be certain no one eavesdropped at the other side of the door, he could at least ensure that they had a hard time hearing anything.

Without hesitation, he walked past his desk and entered his bedroom. It might not be the most prestigious place to conduct trade with a demon, but Ervan doubted the creature cared. He closed the door and fished a stone out of his pouch. Gray and shapeless, it looked so ordinary... Yet he knew better than to doubt what Mayetti had told him.

Until now, he hadn't dared test the stone, but he had to make the move if he wanted to stay ahead of the council and that blighted archmage. With every passing day, she gained more and more influence in the city. He'd already heard about her appearance on the city walls and gossip that she forced a demon to retreat with the mere power of her mind. Soon enough, people would forget that it was Gildya that provided the protective devices and attribute the barrier over Kaighal solely to her. The council was so inane that they'd allowed power to slip out of their hands, so Ervan had to do something himself.

He placed it on the nightstand. One more deep breath, and he moved one of his spare imbued stones closer to it. For a few drawn-out heartbeats, nothing happened. Then a shimmering mist surrounded the rock, and from it, a face formed. Translucent and small, it was barely big enough for details to be clear.

Ervan fought to keep his face straight at the sight of the creature's ugly appearance, with a lipless mouth and a nose that resembled a beak in its shape. But the eyes of the demon were the worst. Their gaze was intense, as if the hideous being could reach even Ervan's most secret thoughts, and their slanted shape brought both cunning and cruelty to mind.

So far, Ervan had had only to deal with a few demonlings. They all were vicious and aggressive, but also mindless. This demon had the same savagery about him, and, paired with his undeniable intelligence, it made him all the more dangerous.

Ervan swallowed, questioning his decisions, but then the creature smiled, and the adept's terror subsided.

"I see Mayetti found someone worthy of talking to me," the demon said. "Is she around?" His head turned as if he was looking around.

"Unfortunately, Mayetti didn't make it," Ervan replied as neutrally as he could. The last thing he needed was the creature to think he was making an accusation. "Before she died, she did tell me that you were seeking to speak with us."

The demon's smile widened, and he stared at the adept

as if he knew that it wasn't the wound that had killed her. "Are you of the council of adepts?"

"I'm Ervan. I'm of the council, but I do not speak for them all... not yet," he replied. "The council is weak, and they do not wish to make any bold moves."

"If you called upon me just to tell me so, you're wasting my time."

Ervan swallowed. "I'm sure there are still talks to be had and agreements to be made," he rushed a response before the demon decided to end the conversation. "Agreements that would make the council see reason. Especially that our goals align. We want the two demons gone as well."

The demon grimaced. "We have no need of agreements, human. We can destroy this city just like we crushed the kingdom overseas. If you wish to save it, you will find an offer that will be worthy of our time. Do not call upon me until you have something we can consider. Until then, we will proceed with our plans." Myrkan regarded him with smile. "We'll speak again when you find a way for us to reach... our common goals."

Before Ervan could reply, the ghastly apparition disappeared. Just to be certain, he moved the imbued stone away. The last thing he needed was the demon spying on him. Despicable creature! At the same time, he had to give a nod to how Myrkan established superiority and left Ervan no openings.

He sat down on the bed, sighing. Until now, he'd preferred caution and indirect manipulation to getting involved. Even the poison that caused Mayetti's death was administered by another's hand. It seemed that if he wanted to ensure not only his own but also Kaighal's survival, he would finally have to take matters into his own hands.

The very thought made his blood turn cold, but to his

surprise, a tinge of excitement warmed it. He'd spent his life in the shadows, and everyone around him thought he had little ambition and even less will to act. Perhaps it was time to show them his true brilliance. Like the new archmage rose to power, crushing all those who opposed her, so should he. If he found a way to meet Myrkan's expectations, he'd have a powerful ally to ensure that.

Ervan rubbed his chin, the sudden rush already fading as he pondered possibilities. The archmage was a cunning opponent, and he couldn't act brashly, hoping for the best.

He needed a plan, and a good one.

ONE OF THEIR pactees came to Myrkan dragging a man along. Myrkan cared little to remember her name. She was like all other of their pactees, scruffy and plain, and she had the same glint of insatiable greed in her eyes as everyone. That desire made them excellent tools in the yalari plans, but they were never to become anything more, so learning their names was pointless. If one died, two more would vie for a pact with a kanyalari.

The man she brought along was different. His outfit might be cheap, from what little Myrkan knew of human clothes, but he kept it in good condition, taking care to add a trinket or two. At the same time, his quick eyes and shrewd expression suggested that he wasn't anyone of importance, but a thug who chose his outfit to mislead those around him.

The pactee shoved him forward. "We caught him at the edges of the camp," she said. "He claims to be a messenger. Has a message for Arujhan."

Myrkan frowned. On one hand, a sight of a man

cowering in front of him was a pleasant change to a disastrous morning when Arujhan tried to go after Fyertash and had to withdraw. On the other, he had no doubt that the pactee only came to him because she feared approaching Arujhan himself, and the sting of being perceived as less threatening took away any satisfaction. Yet there was benefit in letting humans think they could come to him... Any information and any useful tidbit would first reach Myrkan's ears, and he would decide what to do with it before sharing anything with Derazin and Arujhan. That alone was worth suffering a jab to his pride, especially given that once all other yalari left the human realm, there would be no one to overshadow Myrkan.

"You did well coming to me," he said to the pactee. A little praise could ensure that the next time, she would come straight to him without even considering other yalari. He looked at the man. "Come with me."

Myrkan led the man through the camp, if a patchwork of crummy tents and campfires could be called that. The yalari had only a few dozen pactees at their service, and the rest of their army were asayalari. Derazin took it upon himself to ensure the mindless creatures stayed obedient and didn't go after the pactees. It must be straining on him to control such a horde, but it also gave him the sole power over asayalari. Even if asayalari were no match for any kanyalari, in such great numbers they'd provide enough distraction for Derazin to land the killing blow, or at least gain an upper hand if he decided to act against his allies. Myrkan almost sneered at the thought. The cowardly hoyve would more likely use that control to protect himself than to strike.

Arujhan was sitting on the beach, away from the camp. Cross-legged and with his interwoven claws providing support for his chin, he looked deep in thought, but he stirred at Myrkan's approach. If any uncertainty or fear stained his thoughts, he didn't show it.

"This human brought a message for you from the city," Myrkan said.

The man took a few shaky steps forward, his eyes wide as he took in Arujhan's massive body. "A message for demon Arujhan. Veranesh will be flying alone, southwest, through the desert, on the third day of your arrival to these lands."

Arujhan narrowed his eyes and waved the human off. Myrkan stopped him with a gesture. "Wait for me at the edge of the camp. I will have questions and work for you."

The human scum likely didn't know who'd sent the message through him, but there were other insights to be gained.

"It has to be a trap," Myrkan said once he was alone with Arujhan. "Unless it's Fyertash's doing..."

Arujhan snorted. "No. As much as I have no doubt that Fyertash is cunning enough for such a risky play, I think he truly sided with Veranesh." A grimace twisted his face when he spoke this name. "Besides, Veranesh is already gone from the city... This is why I haven't sensed him nearby." He stood up.

Myrkan looked at him in disbelief. "You aren't considering going, are you?"

"Veranesh might think he has the upper hand, but he's not the same yalari he was centuries ago," Arujhan said. "No matter what petty tricks he might have come up with, I'm stronger than him now, and it's a good opportunity to finally destroy him."

Myrkan hid his doubts. Veranesh, even in a losing position, was far too smart to become an easy victory for Arujhan. Whatever the trap was, it would become a challenge. "At least let me come with you." As much as his instincts rebelled at the mere thought of facing Veranesh, he had to ensure Veranesh fell.

The other yalari shook his head. "No, you have to stay here. You've already found potential servants in the city, and you'll be the one who will find a way to break its pitiful defenses. And then Fyertash's ability to bind us from afar won't matter anymore. You and Derazin will crush him." He spread his wings. "I'll let Derazin know of the plan and be on my way. The less time Veranesh has to prepare, the better for us."

Myrkan nodded, considering the question he was itching to ask. It could reveal too much of his desires and ambitions, but in the end, it had to be voiced. "Which of us are you choosing to lead in your stead?"

Arujhan regarded him for less than a moment. "Neither. I will not risk giving Derazin power to outweigh your say, for his cowardice might ruin our plans, and I will not insult him by giving such power to you." He stared at Myrkan coldly. "If you two can't find a way to an agreement and success, you deserve whatever petty schemes Fyertash might be weaving."

Not the reply Myrkan was foolishly hoping for, but still better than he had anticipated. He stood motionless, watching Arujhan's departure. Humans had all kinds of well-wishing: "good luck," "I hope you win," and many other phrases that conveyed the speaker's hope and trust. Yalari had no such thing, because, likely in the whole history of his kind, no yalari wished for another to succeed. Undoubtedly, Myrkan would prefer for Arujhan to dispose of Veranesh, but an outcome when both of them ended up dead was as good. And even if Arujhan fell... a weakened and wounded Veranesh could provide an opportunity for

Myrkan to rise above others with a victory he could otherwise only dream of.

Perhaps Veranesh, by setting a trap for Arujhan into which the foolish kanyalari was willingly walking, was doing Myrkan a favor.

That thought brought a smile to Myrkan's face.

4

The High Towers' library was never popular among prospective high mages. When they became students, they quickly learned that knowledge and mastery of high magic wasn't as necessary to climb the ranks as one would think. Of course, later down the path they would discover that to become an archmage, at least *some* skill in wielding magic was necessary, but most of the High Towers' students never bothered with such lofty ambitions. They wanted basic schooling, a few parlor tricks to amuse their families or to weave whatever schemes they were going to use to gain wealth.

After the high magic fell, the library became even emptier and quieter. The handful of teachers and students who decided to stay and make a pact had little need of now-obsolete high magic treatises and books of spells, though few still perused the library's shelves in search of anything that could be of use.

Atissa would consider them desperate if the same reason hadn't brought *her* to the library.

But contrary to everyone else, Atissa knew exactly where

she was going, and she had an idea what she was looking for. Without rush, she made her way to the far end of the library.

A woman, a few years younger than Atissa, stepped from behind the row of shelves.

"You shouldn't be here," she said with condescending confidence.

Atissa struggled to remember her name. *Grayda? Grida?* Yes, that must be it. Atissa's past life in the High Towers seemed like it happened decades ago already, and the woman in front of her was no more than another power-thirsty and manipulative student who would do anything to convince any of the archmages to take an interest in her.

"I have the same right to use the library as everyone else," she replied without even considering whether it was indeed true. Kamira had made no explicit provisions as to what Atissa could and could not do, and Irtan was more likely to send spies to keep an eye on her, hoping her actions would give him information, than to keep her confined.

"You're the lying archmage's daughter. You should bleed like they all did." Grida took a step forward. "Maybe now."

A faint aura surrounded her—something Atissa would have missed in the past, but her magic-less body craved even a speck of power. A small lumisphere formed on top of Grida's palm, and Atissa swallowed. Even if the visible strain on the other woman's face brought some satisfaction—Grida must be struggling with her basic arcanist training—the lumisphere could still cause serious burns, no matter how small it was.

"I'm sure the first archmage will be delighted to know that after she sacrificed so much to cleanse the High Towers of lies and corruption, her new students still insist on clinging to their high mages' ways," Atissa said.

The lumisphere wavered and vanished, testimony to Grida's poor control of the newly acquired magic. "Don't pretend that you're friends with her."

More than you, Atissa thought, even if her relationship with Kamira was nowhere near actual friendship. But at least the first archmage knew who Atissa was, no matter how tangled the feelings tying them together were, and the same couldn't be said about Grida.

"She'd have you cast out if she didn't have more pressing matters to take care," Grida added.

Atissa looked at her without concern. After risking her life to outwit a demon, standing her ground against the Western Kingdom's thugs, and killing a Tivarashan priestess, such petty threats meant little. "You could always go to Archmage Irtan instead," she offered in a friendly manner. "I'm sure he'll be delighted that one of the few arcanists left in the Towers wastes her time on a high mage has-been instead of practicing her new skills... which clearly could use some work."

Grida's face darkened. She pouted and turned away. Atissa wondered whether she'd risk it and go straight to Irtan, but in the end, it mattered little. Even if Irtan got suspicious and wanted to bar her entry to the library, Atissa would have all she needed before that happened.

No one seemed to have noticed their confrontation, or perhaps they chose not to notice—it might be another sign that things hadn't changed in the High Towers as much as Kamira might have hoped. But this was the archmage's problem, not Atissa's.

Undisturbed, she made it to the far end of the library, where, surrounded by walls of shelves, was a small reading nook with only one table. The chair had been missing for quite a while, and Atissa had no doubt that the archmages had had a hand in its absence, likely not wanting any students to linger there and make it harder to access the place that no student or even teacher should know about.

High magic might be gone, but not all the archmages' secrets relied on spells.

Atissa fished a small shard of an imbued stone out of her pocket. A spell of opening was something one would have to guard within a tight circle, and it was impossible to take away once someone learned it, while pieces of an imbued stone could serve as unique keys no one could copy. As far as she knew, only the first three archmages had one, and she'd learned about it only because her father had used her to fetch books for him in the past.

Come to think of it, with both Loktra and Kerl gone, and the future of their possessions uncertain, Atissa might be the last owner of such a magical key. *No.* She shook her head. *Irtan would have kept his key.* After all, nobody was foolish enough to entrust that lecherous drunkard Kerl with more knowledge than absolutely necessary, so he probably had never learned of the library.

Before she slid the shard into a well-hidden slot between the shelves, Atissa looked over her shoulder, but the nook's bookshelves protected her from prying eyes. As the imbued shard rested in its place, a quiet click announced that the mechanism was still working, and one of the shelves snapped out of its spot. Atissa retrieved the magic key and pushed the shelf enough to squeeze through, then let it snap back in its place.

The space inside was pitch-black, but having visited before, she knew her way around. She traced the wall to her right until her fingers found the oblique shape of another imbued stone. Rubbing it produced a faint glow, just enough to make it through the narrow corridor but too little for anyone to see light coming from behind the secret door.

There were more imbued-stone lamps in the small area at the end of the corridor, as the archmages didn't want to risk a lumisphere starting a fire among the precious and often centuries-old tomes.

As the light fell on the thickly packed rows of shelves, Atissa smiled. All the archmages' hidden knowledge was at her disposal, and with a little luck, she'd find exactly what she was looking for.

YALARI NEEDED no food nor sleep to survive, so once his preparations were ready, Veranesh found himself with plenty of time to be idle. After centuries in the crystal, motionlessness had become second nature, so he stood in his chosen spot, enjoying the touch of wind and sun on his skin and allowing his thoughts to drift. He kept his eyes closed. In the magic-less world, he'd sense his enemy's arrival from afar, so he could focus inward instead. There were plans to make and outcomes to consider, but everything depended on whether he would be able to dispose of Arujhan.

A slight grimace spoiled his calm face. Plans could fail if something happened to Kamira. At some point during his flight, he'd sensed she was in danger—her emotions were transmitted via the connection they shared through the pact —but she never called upon him, so no matter what kind of a threat she faced, she didn't need Veranesh's help. Perhaps Fyertash had finally stopped playing his games and was aiding Kamira instead of testing her patience and power.

Veranesh smiled. Once the two of his allies trusted each

other enough, he wouldn't have to concern himself with Kamira's safety anymore. Of course, Fyertash would solve problems as he saw fit, often in questionable ways, but it mattered little as long as he did what he'd agreed to.

Time passed slowly, days shifting into nights and then days again, the cycle marked by the change in temperature and brightness, and the longer Veranesh waited, the more he questioned his own judgment of Arujhan. If the other yalari turned out to be more of a coward, the trap could fail.

Veranesh tensed. He'd rather face all of his adversaries in an uneven battle if Arujhan brought them along than risk a full yalari force attacking Kaighal. No matter Veranesh's trust in Kamira's abilities, she simply was not ready to fight all of them.

Before doubt could set in, the familiar scent of magic arrived on the wind.

The wait was over.

Veranesh opened his eyes. On the horizon, against the backdrop of the sky too blue to remind him of his own world, a winged silhouette appeared. Even at that distance, Arujhan's posture emanated power and confidence. The yalari kept his flight steady, not rushing into confrontation, and Veranesh stretched his muscles one by one, waiting.

"I was beginning to wonder whether you would have the courage to face me alone," Veranesh said once his opponent landed nearby.

Arujhan looked around, caution in his movements, but with a smug smile on his lipless mouth. His bulky chest, strong arms with huge claws, and large wings told of a lifetime spent perfecting himself, likely with the help of the many pacts he must have made to stretch the limits of his own body. As much as Arujhan might look down on humans, their willpower helped many ambitious yalari gain advantages otherwise unattainable.

"And I thought you'd rather run than confront me," Arujhan replied. "You can't win against me. Not anymore."

Veranesh stared back at him, unwavering. No matter how true those words might be—a yalari without a domain and only a single pact standing against one with enormous power back in Yalarethe, and likely benefiting from the support of a dozen or more pactees, faced an uphill struggle at best—Veranesh would not show weakness. And his own confidence could undermine Arujhan's composure when the other yalari started to doubt his own strength or search for Veranesh's trap.

"Then what is stopping you? Fear of being destroyed?" Veranesh asked.

Arujhan smiled knowingly. Since neither of them would waste time trying to bind the other, he must be considering his towering body and sheer strength in predicting the outcome, and it came as no surprise when he lunged, his arm swiping wide. No matter what confidence he might have in his victory, he still aimed to finish the fight at the start.

Veranesh waited. Before the attack reached him, he focused. A barrier rose around him, barring the way. It flickered upon Arujhan's assault but ultimately held. "I've learned a few tricks in the last few centuries. You?"

Arujhan tested the obstacle with a swipe of his claw, then grinned. "You've brought her with you, haven't you?"

Veranesh let the yalari infer whatever he wanted. Deception gave him a good start in the battle, but now he had to use that advantage.

Without delay, he started the ripping part of the destruction spell.

Arujhan growled as magic rent his flesh, but showed no fear nor pain. He took off, scouring the nearby rocks and nooks, ignoring the constant lashes of energy at various parts of his body. As time trickled by, his search became more frantic. The gashes and splits in his flesh were small, like those inflicted by asayalari with notable claws, but they would clearly eat away any amount of flesh, given sufficient time.

Veranesh kept chanting. Soon enough, his opponent would figure out the truth.

"Where is she?" Arujhan roared, and turned toward the only visible opponent. Without waiting for an answer, he launched into the air and descended.

The barrier trembled around Veranesh with the impact of Arujhan's weight and claws. Arujhan pounded, raked at it, intending each strike to fell the magic protection, but it proved more resilient than expected. Though that didn't mean the barrier wasn't weakening; with each strike, each powerful slash of his claws, Arujhan was one moment closer to ripping his opponent apart.

Veranesh had no time to figure out how to strengthen it. Despite his gloating about learning new tricks, he hadn't studied whether yalari could use barriers as effectively as humans. So instead, he kept chanting. His instincts urged him to pick up the pace, but the faster he uttered the words, the greater the risk of mistake. After spending centuries in the crystal, practicing patience like no other yalari before, he had enough self-control to fend off his instinctual urges, and he kept the rhythm of the spell flowing.

Arujhan was coated in his own blood. Death by a thousand cuts had failed, but the gashes were still coming, and they were getting deeper. Many of them overlapped previous ones, steadily carving to the bone, and Arujhan paused. This must be the moment when he considered that losing was a possibility, but such realization wasn't to Veranesh's advantage.

And, sure enough, as two fingers on Arujhan's wing were severed cleanly, falling to hang by loose, bloody skin, Veranesh's opponent changed tactics.

The barrage of blows and strikes ceased, and Arujhan took several steps back. He vaulted into the air and landed heavily before Veranesh, driving his fist into the ground. The rock beneath their feet shattered, and the ground rippled. Fissures shot out, cutting through Veranesh's circle, and the barrier flickered. Without waiting for it to disperse, Arujhan tore through the wavering magic, leaving one of his wings behind.

Arujhan's imposing presence had waned slightly. The unending flow of blood, the bone-depth gashes, the visible tendons amongst the muscle tissue, and, lastly, the snap of his other wing at the shoulder betrayed Arujhan's waning superiority. And his steadily increasing rage foretold of certain desperation.

Veranesh took a step back within the barrier, raised his arms in defense, and braced for the coming assault. The first attacks were simple but powerful swipes. Veranesh deflected well with his wings, and began moving this way and that, spinning and twisting, throwing his wings out to impede Arujhan's advance, but when magic lopped one of Arujhan's claws from his hand, he expressed his rage with a resounding yell, lunged, and grabbed hold of Veranesh's wing to break each bone before yanking the chanting yalari closer.

Veranesh's wing hung limp from his back, and he was unable to free himself from his opponent's unbreakable grip. But this also provided him the satisfaction of a clear, up-close view when a large gash ripped up Arujhan's face straight through his eye, and any other time, he'd cherish his foe's suffering. Now, he only focused on his own survival, which was less likely with every passing moment.

Arujhan grabbed Veranesh's arm with both blood-covered hands and snapped it with moderate effort, ignoring that his ear fell to the ground. His expression revealed his ever-increasing desperation, the sort only found in battles to the death, and he grabbed Veranesh by his remaining good arm and his neck, planted his foot in his gut, and, after digging his claws in, kicked Veranesh to the ground, ripping flesh from his shoulder, arm, and abdomen. The force with which Veranesh was thrown to the ground cracked bones, and his guts fought to escape through the open wound.

Veranesh's chest was heaving from battle like Arujhan's did, and he knew both of them were approaching death at their own pace. Arujhan's only remaining wing, previously snapped, now showed bone and had little but tendons and muscle scraps holding it together, so when the random lash of the ripping spell popped the tendons, sliced through cartilage, and severed the ligaments, his wing dropped into the bloodstained sand to join with the many other body parts and chunks of rent flesh scattering the area. It halted his onslaught on Veranesh, but only for that moment.

Veranesh, still chanting, was struggling to regain his footing. Had his arms not been broken and rent to uselessness, he might have avoided Arujhan's pounce.

Arujhan slammed him back to the ground. Veranesh repeatedly struck him with his only good wing, but Arujhan ignored the weak thrusts, stomped on Veranesh's wing to pin it, and drove his clawed foot into Veranesh's stomach. He then settled his weight on Veranesh's chest to look his adversary in the eye with a sneer as he raised his arm and claws for the deathblow. He grabbed Veranesh's forehead and twisted his face to bare his neck.

Arujhan's eyes gleamed with excitement and dominance. Veranesh had no doubt that his opponent loved to indulge in his superiority, but Veranesh hadn't stopped chanting, and Arujhan gloated too long.

As his arm swiped powerfully at Veranesh's neck, his entire hand, claws and all, skidded across the sands, and blood splattered over Veranesh's neck and face.

The pain didn't interrupt either of the yalari, but Arujhan's pause, the slight easing of his grasp on Veranesh's head, was all Veranesh needed. He didn't have the power nor size to throw Arujhan about as he pleased, but he had enough to twist sharply with the help of his outstretched wing, and send Arujhan off into the sand.

Arujhan's balance wavered as he got back to his feet. He barely had a trace of skin remaining, instead now only covered with mutilated muscle tissue with bones exposed at his joints, but his focus on Veranesh was unbroken, and his determination was clearly growing even more. The cuts continued relentlessly to the rhythm of Veranesh's chant, and a grimace now spoiled his face. Nevertheless, he made his way toward Veranesh.

Veranesh gave up on trying to stand. The other yalari would overpower him again, and he'd suffer even more injuries from being tossed around and knocked to the ground.

"Such a pitiful end," Arujhan said. His labored breathing betrayed the strain as he made his way toward Veranesh. "You didn't even try to truly fight. I always knew that you were nothing but words."

Veranesh ignored the bait. Educating an opponent that

there were many ways to win a fight would bring no benefit, and he'd rather focus on the ripping spell. With the end of their confrontation in sight, every moment counted. If Arujhan wanted to waste his time on taunts, he was a fool.

Or, perhaps, he was not as strong as he wanted to appear.

With a desperate growl, Arujhan launched himself at Veranesh again, but he simply fell to the ground. Arujhan's legs had finally taken all they could and collapsed just as he tried to move. His left ankle had given way, and a moment later all the large tendons and ligaments in his right knee snapped.

Veranesh exhaled. Standing up required time and effort, but with his opponent immobile, there was no hurry. He could finally afford himself the pleasure of towering over the yalari who plotted his fall and imprisonment, and so he did.

With a quick stomp, he crushed Arujhan's remaining hand, grinding it into the stone. No scream tore the silence, but Veranesh didn't expect one. Unlike the pitiful Uganel, the truly powerful kanyalari neither showed pain nor begged for mercy.

"I promised Fyertash I'd mention his name before I'm done with you," Veranesh said.

"That little hoyve..." Arujhan spat. "I wouldn't be surprised if he is lurking at a distance, waiting to finish off the one who wins our confrontation." His subtle moves didn't escape Veranesh. Beaten and defenseless, Arujhan was still looking for a way to attack.

"That's not something *you* have to concern yourself with," Veranesh replied. "All you need to know is that he wanted you to pay for your betrayal."

Arujhan didn't ask which one, though there must have

been many during the long centuries of his life. "If not him, others will get you."

Veranesh looked down on him. "My pactee and her allies will take care of them."

Such a remark caused Arujhan to grimace, because no one in their right mind would speak of humans as a threat to yalari.

The conversation was growing tiresome, and Veranesh couldn't discard the possibility that his opponent had a plan or was stalling to give time for his own allies to arrive. As unlikely as both of those prospects were, one would be a fool to overly trust one's advantage. After centuries spent in the crystal, Veranesh had no desire to be fooled again.

Arujhan's entire physique had diminished under the ripping, and Veranesh knelt slowly on his neck, steadily applying more pressure until the satisfying crack and limpness of the body.

His own wounds stung, but pain was only a reminder that he'd won against all odds. It seemed that humans affected the world of yalari more than anyone realized. A few centuries earlier, he and Arujhan would clash in a violent battle, exchanging blows until one of them overpowered the other. Weaker kanyalari would keep their distance while trying to bind their opponent with a spell, so that they could finish them off without any risks. Instead, Veranesh relied on deception, choosing another way to conduct the battle. And even Arujhan himself, though this time relying on brute force, centuries earlier had prepared a trap that deprived Veranesh of his freedom for so long.

He turned north. Somewhere, beyond the horizon, Kamira was preparing the city defenses. But to come back in such a weakened state meant risking that Myrkan or Derazin, or any other kanyalari they were planning to bring to this world, would go after Veranesh before he reached Kaighal.

Besides—he couldn't resist a smile—Kamira already had all the means to succeed at her task if she used her allies and knowledge well, and Veranesh had his own goals to pursue while his enemies were focused on her and Fyertash.

He turned away from the northern horizon and barely glanced at the lifeless yalari at his feet.

With only one task left to do before his new pursuit, he started the last part of the destruction spell. Weaving Arujhan's name into it brought all the satisfaction from the win he needed.

KAMIRA COULD HEAR the screeches and howls of demonlings long before she reached the walls. They weren't deafening, but still loud enough to unsettle anyone who listened to them for too long.

Though the constant noise didn't reach the Towers, it spilled into the streets adjacent to the walls and affected not only the defenders but also people living or working nearby. Their tired faces surrounded Kamira as she made her way toward the strategy table. The grim atmosphere of concerns lined with fear hung in the air, and even though merchants and workers still went about their day, the city's mood had shifted. They weren't hopeless yet, and many called out to her or cheered as she passed by, so Kamira had to do her best to keep it this way.

Several Devanshari guards stood around King Allyv's table, and Kamira hoped for Ryell's face to appear among them. Even if relations between them were complicated, at least she could find comfort in knowing that he was doing what used to be his ambition.

Yet Ryell wasn't around, and she knew better than to foolishly believe he was helping at some other part of the walls. He'd left with Atissa and clearly chosen a path other than returning to the city and to his people. She could only hope that he'd found a new purpose, and perhaps one day, he'd let go of his demon hate.

Allyv noticed her from afar. "First Archmage Kamira."

His voice was respectful and courteous, making it clear he recognized her as a person of equal status.

"Your Highness." Kamira gave him a polite nod. With so many people watching them, she couldn't afford to break the rule that the first archmage of Kaighal bowed to no one, and it mattered not that the times might be changing. "How is the defense going?"

Above them, parts of the barrier fell and rose again in sequence as people turned off the protective devices to allow the defenders to loose arrows at the enemies. Kamira spotted a few arcanists hurling their magic in a crude but effective manner, and there were adepts tossing their explosive orbs.

"So far, it's easy. The demonlings can't breach the protection you created, and the higher demons keep their distance." King Allyv rubbed his chin. "Though one of them disappeared from sight, so they might be preparing something."

"Veranesh's plan was to lure him away," Kamira said. The trap had already been sprung, so she could discuss it freely without concerning herself with who learned about it. Even if the attacking demons had spies in the city, they wouldn't have easy means of sending a message to Arujhan, and if one of them set out across the desert to deliver the warning... Fyertash and Kamira would take the chance to dispose of the remaining demon.

A scowl passed over Allyv's face at the mention of a demon, but he regained control quickly. "It's going to get harder as the siege continues." His solemn voice contrasted with his youthful face. "Their demonologists will stay away from the city, protected by the hordes of demonlings, and they'll summon more and more. No matter how quickly we kill them, there will always be more, and over time, people will become tired, we will have wounded... Then the higher demons will strike."

"It seems that we have to tire the enemy out as well." Kamira indicated the stone stairs leading up to the battlements, and Allyv joined her in the climb. "The more demonlings we kill, the more they have to summon. And though there's always more creatures to be brought into this world, the arcanists who summon them are just humans. I've seen a higher demon push his pactee to the brink of exhaustion."

It would be much easier if they could deal with the enemy arcanists swiftly, but they were too far behind the lines of demonlings, and two higher demons protected them. With the constant threat from Derazin and Myrkan, any plan to take those arcanists out would be both risky and costly and could put her and her allies at a greater disadvantage. No matter how much the demonling hordes could strain the city defenses, it was the higher demons that posed the real danger to the city.

"They're cruel and merciless, aren't they?" Allyv said.

"Usually, no more than some humans," Kamira replied. "I understand the uneasiness your people experience in their presence, but not all demons aim to destroy us. At this very moment Veranesh is facing an enemy more powerful than himself to give this city a chance." It took some self-control to keep ire out of her voice. No matter how much the Devanshari had suffered at the hands of demons, allowing them to think all demons were alike meant creating a nation full of Ryells.

"I apologize." Allyv instinctively rubbed the side of his arm, and a faint trace of magic was released. This must be the spot where Koshmarnyk had blended a shard of an imbued stone into his skin. "When dark memories haunt every corner of our thoughts, it's so easy to forget that we have reasons for gratitude as well."

She let the topic die, especially since they were already at the top of the stairs. The battlements were full of people, divided into mixed groups of archers and guards. There weren't enough arcanists and adepts to be everywhere, but from what she could tell, Allyv had ensured they were stationed in somewhat even distances and could move around to aid other groups if needed.

A teenage girl was squatting by the nearest device, her expression determined rather than scared. Her tattered clothes suggested that she lived in the streets or in a poor district, so a demonling army, even one just outside the walls, was likely more of an abstract threat than hunger and thugs.

"Do you know how to work the device?" Kamira asked.

"Yes, archmage!" the girl replied with confidence. Her eyes moved quickly as she took in Kamira's outfit in an evaluating manner, as if she was deciding whether Kamira was worth respect. "One Gildya fella showed me. Says I gots a gift."

Kamira wasn't surprised the girl recognized an archmage in her. After all, most Tivarashan had left the city as soon as news of the upcoming siege broke, and those who stayed were more likely to tend to their property or business than visit the battlements.

"On my mark, you'll take the barrier down and won't put it back up until I tell you," Kamira said.

"Aye!" The girl's posture changed, indicating readiness.

Kamira came close to the edge of the battlements. Below her, demonlings screeched and clawed at the barrier, but their attacks were too organized for a chaotic horde like them.

Far in the distance, a demon stood motionless, and his bulging, maggot-like body towered over those he commanded. This had to be Derazin. No matter what little respect Fyertash had for the demon and his skill, the ability to control so many demonlings at the time meant Derazin could be a dangerous opponent. She played with the thought of binding him, but Derazin was likely as far away from the city as he could be while maintaining control over his horde, so he'd withdraw immediately if she tried. Instead, she gave the girl a signal.

The barrier fell. Demonlings stumbled forward, meeting no resistance, but their bewilderment wouldn't last long. As soon as they recovered, they'd scale the walls.

With everyone except for the creatures out of the way of her magic, Kamira unleashed her power.

Arcs of lightning materialized before her and sparked downward, into the mass of demonlings. Their screeches and howls changed when magic hit them charring skin, fur, and scales, and forcing their bodies to jerk and fly about.

Kamira kept channeling the energy, pushing it further into the horde. Behind her, King Allyv ordered the lowering of two more barriers so that nearby archers could provide protection for the archmage should any demonling escape the magic's reach and scale the walls. People cheered all around them, and many defense groups lowered their barriers to send more arrows toward the enemy.

If she kept going, she could possibly wipe out the whole horde... But as invigorating and enticing that thought was, Kamira stopped channeling. The enemy arcanists would replenish the demonling ranks sooner than she could regain her strength—no matter how much power Veranesh could offer her, and how much the time in the crystal had changed her, she was still a human. Even if her magic was limitless, the capabilities of her body weren't, and while the besieging demons had plenty of arcanists, she had close to none to take her place if she exhausted herself.

Allyv's eyes shone. "This was... impressive," he said. "I can understand now why you might succeed where we couldn't. If all the demonologists worked together, they could get rid of the demonlings."

The Devanshari king insisted on using the word "demonologist," but it wasn't the time for a lecture or request to use the arcanists' proper title. "We still have higher demons to concern ourselves about. It's too much of risk to exhaust everyone. Besides"—she had to be honest with him—"most of students don't have such power at their disposal, and they would be unable to wield it if they did. The art of arcane magic requires study and practice."

The excitement faded from his face, replaced by a solemn expression. "Then Kaighal is still in not much better position than our home was," he said. "Even if you can last longer against the demons, in the end they'll overwhelm us. Unless you have another plan, and you're waiting for something... Tivarashan aid? I've heard Queen Andalisha sent a royal envoy."

It was hard not to grimace at that name. A ruthless mother had sent her own son into a city that was facing a siege and possible defeat, giving him a mission to win the archmage's favor and gain control over Kaighal, while his sister plotted the assassination of that very archmage. Back when she lived at her family home, Kamira heard countless stories of the games the royal family played, with two sisters competing for the crown already at their young age, and the queen herself encouraging fierce rivalry—a tradition spanning generations at that point. Prince Jalyn got caught in their plots, and he'd paid for it with his life.

Kamira's expression hardened. "The Tivarashan nation has been asked to not interfere with the matters of the Free City of Kaighal," she said loud enough for anyone around them to hear. Even if some were looking forward to such aid and would lose hope for Kaighal's victory, at least she could stifle any harmful gossip about her planning to surrender the city to Tivarashan rule.

Allyv looked like he was about to bring up arguments, but then he nodded. "I trust your judgment, archmage."

His voice was stiff and controlled enough to reassure Kamira that the young king was having doubts whether staying in Kaighal and supporting her was the right choice for him and his people. She couldn't blame him, but she couldn't offer any reassurances, either. Kaighal might have a better chance than his homeland, but it could fall because of a single traitor, just like the capital of Devanshari did.

Having no words of comfort or reassurance, Kamira turned away from the battlefield. It was time she returned to the Towers.

Gasps and shouts made her look over her shoulder. Defenders were crowding at the battlements, pointing to the southwest, so she followed their gazes.

Far off in the desert, a ball of energy rose. From a distance, it looked almost like a lumisphere expanding over the sands, but Kamira knew better. She'd seen an explosion like that up close.

Her heart skipped a beat as soon as her memories of battle with Uganel resurfaced, but she kept the emotions from showing on her face. That fight had long ago ended, and the fear and pain she'd experienced had no place in public, where people looked up to her for reassurance and hope.

While everyone's attention was on the explosion, she reached for her magic. Her pact was still there, reassuring her that she could still channel it at will. It seemed that Veranesh had succeeded against Arujhan. If she could, she'd wake up the nightfly to speak to him, but it had to wait until she was alone. Not only because the last time she called upon him, Veranesh asked to not be disturbed—she also had to consider that spies could be lurking, and to let the enemy demons know she had a way of communicating with Veranesh meant giving up an advantage.

The explosion was still bright and spreading, and people around her were stirring. Even centuries after the Cataclysm, the tales of it still lingered in Kaighal, and she was certain more than a few people remembered that Veranesh was the one who had caused it.

"Archmage Kamira?" Allyv asked, concern clear in his voice. "Do you know what this is?"

"This is what I've been waiting for, Your Highness," Kamira replied with more confidence than she felt.

Veranesh had said nothing of his plans to destroy Arujhan, and even though such a move made sense, she had never considered it before.

She looked around, at the people who now watched her expectantly. "The light you see on the horizon is the sign of Veranesh's victory. Many of you saw him leave or heard of his departure. Some may have thought he was running. Now, when his trap has sprung, I can reveal the truth. He took the risk to defeat the most powerful of our enemies. Demon Arujhan is dead."

People looked at her and at each other, their whispers rising with a mix of uncertainty and relief.

"How do you know it's not Veranesh who is dead?" someone called from among the crowd.

Without hesitation, she summoned a lumisphere. Its shape and glow should be familiar to the people living in the shadow of the Towers, but some still backed away, as if it was about to produce an explosion similar to the one they just witnessed in the desert.

"I still have my magic. If Veranesh was dead, my pact would be gone," Kamira replied with confidence. She didn't bother explaining the differences between being alive, dead, and destroyed. Common people had no need for in-depth knowledge of demons, and the simpler she put it, the fewer doubts they would have.

Everyone looked up at the sound of beating wings. Fyertash descended in a slow, non-threatening manner, his cunning eyes fixed on Kamira.

"Archmage," he said with respect she didn't expect. "A word with you, back in the Towers."

His behavior was perfect, yet Kamira couldn't help her growing suspicions, as if Fyertash's inherent slyness lined his words whether he wanted it or not. It also couldn't be a coincidence that he requested a conversation right after the explosion.

A cold shiver ran down her spine. Fyertash was the one who'd lured Arujhan into a trap. Veranesh had trusted him, but it didn't mean the sly demon wasn't weaving his own plots.

She gave him a nod. "I'll be there shortly." It seemed she'd know soon enough.

Fyertash was already flying toward the Towers, so she turned to Allyv and gave him an apologetic smile. "I apologize, Your Highness, but this will require my attention."

"I understand, archmage. Be assured that these fine men and women will hold the monsters away for as long as you need."

Before departing, Kamira looked around, acknowledging all the defenders who had recognized their own lack of experience in war and entrusted their strategy to a foreign man. They looked up to her for guidance and defense, but without them, the barrier would be threatened and the future less certain. They made her own task of defending the city easier.

"Thank you for your hard work," she said with gratitude. "Kaighal can be proud of its sons and daughters and everyone else who chose it as their home."

As she descended the stone stairs to disappear into the streets, their cheers followed her. She wanted to find comfort in their reaction, but inciting hope was easier than proving she was actually worth the trust they were putting in her, so she walked back into the city streets with grim thoughts still hanging over her.

5

When Kamira entered the initiation rite chamber, Fyertash was sitting cross-legged in the middle, casual and relaxed. She risked turning her back to him to close the door—he likely would have asked her to do so anyway, and their discussion was to be one of those better not witnessed.

He watched her intently as she made her way toward him. One time, his eyes shot toward the spot where he knew her invisible circle was. Undoubtedly, he wondered whether she would choose to hide within its safety before starting the conversation.

Kamira stopped halfway through the chamber. Her instincts tugged at her composure, demanding she seek protection of magic in the confrontation she was sensing to come, but no matter whether Fyertash was playing with her or testing her, showing weakness would put her at disadvantage. Besides, she still had a few tricks up her sleeve, and the demon knew only of one circle in the chamber. Should it come to a battle, he'd bar her way to it, which meant she'd have more time to reach another one.

"It was quite a speech you gave," Fyertash said. "A short one, but seemed to work better than I thought. One flicker of simple magic, and nobody even questioned whether it was Veranesh who was defeated." He gave her a sly smile. "You've already tried speaking to him, haven't you?"

Kamira kept her face neutral. It couldn't have been hard to guess that once she was safe from onlookers' prying eyes in the Towers, she'd tried to reach Veranesh. The nightflies had risen, obedient to her will, but the demon's presence didn't manifest through them.

"It's happened once before. Veranesh didn't wish to be bothered, and he didn't respond to my calls until he chose to," she replied, a half-truth. Back in the cave, when she was searching for a way to free him from his prison, he didn't speak to her for days, but it was because of the magic surge when she shattered their test crystal.

"Or he can't respond because he's gone."

She gave him a stern stare. "I still have my pact."

The demon shifted, cocking his head to the side. "Do you really believe so? Maybe your magic now comes from the stones you put in your body. Maybe you don't need a pact anymore."

Her eyes widened before she could control her reaction. Only two other people and one demon knew of the powdered stones in her skin, and Fyertash didn't count among them. She doubted Veranesh had shared this secret with him.

With her face having already betrayed the truth, she could ask, "How did you know?"

Fyertash arched his eyebrow as if he'd expected lies and denial. "The energy around you is too strong to be that of a mere pact. Your lover is a man who openly puts stones in his own body. And your clothing covers most of your body. It was a mere guess, but if I figured it out, so could others. You aren't a lone pactee in a city of high mages who are blind to any subtle energy changes anymore. There are more pactees around, and other yalari nearby."

"I'll deal with it when the time comes," Kamira replied.

So far, their conversation had followed its usual course, with Fyertash lazily testing the boundaries of her patience and cunning but not risking an open confrontation. Yet there was something different about Fyertash's behavior, and she'd rather learn sooner than later what scheme he'd prepared.

"Are you done with your games, whatever they might be, or is there something else?"

Fyertash became serious. "Veranesh is not coming back. I believe he was successful in destroying Arujhan, but by doing so, he also ensured his own death. He will be reborn, of course, but in the yalari realm, and I doubt he has any plans to return to this world, even if he had the means to do so."

Kamira drew a slow breath. The demon was about to reveal his intentions, and she wouldn't put it past him to turn on a former ally now that Veranesh was out of reach and no consequences would follow. Part of her wondered whether Veranesh had considered such an outcome in his plan, and whether he truly cared about her and the city's survival. As much as she wanted to trust her pact demon—and in the past, he'd done nothing to raise doubts—he was a higher demon. All his truthfulness and support might have been just a means to ensure he wouldn't be disturbed while he destroyed his greatest rival and departed from this world.

"If he left us, it means he trusts that you and I will succeed in bringing down the other two yalari on our own,"

Fyertash continued, then gave her a sly grin all of a sudden. "But since he's not here, we will do things the way I choose." Still in his cross-legged position, he leaned forward. "Would you like to learn the things he kept from you?"

She narrowed her eyes, but nothing in his offer gave her a clue about the trap he must be setting. "Why are you so eager to give away his secrets?"

Everything within her screamed to run for the safety of the circle. The longer the conversation lasted, the more her composure was stretched, and she wasn't fool enough to believe that just because she'd won against Fyertash once, she'd be able to do so again.

"Veranesh and I have... our differences," Fyertash said with a hint of amusement, as if he was talking about a friendly discussion over a bottle of wine. "He wanted to keep secrets from you, so you don't get distracted, and you stay focused on defending the city you care about so much. I, on the other hand, think that your lack of knowledge might become your downfall." He spread his hands to the sides in a very human gesture showing goodwill and honesty. "So the question is whether you're strong-willed enough to learn what I have to show you and keep your focus where it needs to be."

Kamira swallowed. How could she possibly answer such a question? She wanted to trust Veranesh, but he wasn't around anymore, and even though it seemed that Fyertash didn't intend to turn on her, he could change his mind if she proved too unyielding. She couldn't fight other demons if she had to look over her shoulder all the time.

"Very well, let's have it your way."

Odd satisfaction showed on Fyertash's face. He nodded but didn't move. Instead, he stared at her intently and started whispering. Instinctively, she took a step forward, straining to hear his words, but with the distance between them, it was impossible. Fyertash didn't invite her to come closer to share in whatever secrets he knew, and she opened her mouth to demand explanation.

Then she caught the rhythm of his words. *The binding!* She searched for a hint of another demon's presence or any other reason to recite the spell.

Fyertash kept looking at her, and he said one word louder than the others: "Kamira."

Understanding dawned on her at the same moment strings of energy reached toward her. Fyertash was about to bind *her*.

She stumbled backward, feeling the touch of magic on her skin while her mind repeated one word. *How?!* The high mages might have imprisoned her in a crystal using a perverted version of the binding spell along with a circle of their corrupted magic, but what Fyertash was using sounded exactly like the spell that Veranesh had taught her. It was supposed to only work on demons.

Instinctively, Kamira brought up a barrier, but the strings of energy sank through it, reaching for her. She tore away, but the magic followed. Demons could bind each other from quite a distance, so even if she made it to the door, Fyertash might still succeed.

She grimaced. The last thing she needed was anyone learning what had transpired if she became bound somewhere in the stairs, so she fought against the urge to flee.

Magic condensed around her and restricted her moves more and more, making it clear that whatever decision she was about to make, she better make it fast.

Without hesitation, she ran for her circle, the one further away from Fyertash.

Since the barrier didn't protect her, she doubted that circle would enforce her protection enough to prevent Fyertash from binding her, but within it, she should be safe enough to find a solution. Unless...

The blood in her veins froze.

Unless Fyertash went straight for the ripping.

She made it into the circle. The barrier rose around her. Any other time, the shimmering wall of magic would offer her the feeling of safety, but now it only highlighted her helplessness.

Without rush, Fyertash finished the binding.

Magic held Kamira tight, but if she used enough strength, she had limited movement. Not enough to free herself but enough to do something—if only she had an idea what! The memory of Uganel fighting against his bind resurfaced. There had to be some irony in her ending up the way he had...

"Another circle. I didn't expect it." Fyertash approached. "How many more do you have here?"

"In here? Four. Not counting the one you know of and the one that is a trap," she replied honestly. With Fyertash having control over her life, it seemed pointless to conceal the truth. If he wished her dead, she'd never live long enough to use any of them.

"I'm impressed," he said without sarcasm. "But you would be dead nonetheless, should I choose so."

"You get your payback, I suppose," she said, referring to when she was the one to bind him. "What now?"

The demon was willing to talk, so he wasn't about to kill her, and unless he was about to savor her defeat and make her suffer the uncertainty, there had to be another purpose for this demonstration.

Fyertash squatted in front of her. "You will have to find a

way to free yourself of the binding. We use our sheer strength to tear through it, but you have none of it. No claws or wings, either. So take your time." He gestured invitingly with his claw. "Figure it out. If someone comes in, I'll release you."

With a sigh, she shifted in her binds. The magic held her tight, making it clear that Fyertash was right about her inability to tear through them like demons did. Even with their impressive strength they needed time to do it, so she had to think of something that would work faster.

The barrier also wasn't an answer, and she hadn't expected it to be. If she could bind a demon from behind its protection, it meant a demon could do the same to her. *Except...*

She looked at Fyertash. "How did you manage to bind me? I thought the spell worked only on demons."

"I had only guesses... But you survived being imprisoned in the crystal, and Veranesh doesn't do anything without a purpose."

At first, Kamira wanted to remind Fyertash that she had been the key to Veranesh's freedom, but if the demon wanted only that, he wouldn't have to bother himself making sure she stayed alive. "And do you know that purpose?"

"I think that you are an experiment." Fyertash looked at her inquisitively, searching for a reaction. "A few exceptions aside, yalari have no families, no children, no friends, and no allies. Most times, we don't care, but there are circumstances when having an ally would be of great benefit. When carefully chosen and properly groomed, humans make good allies, but they are of no use if they die."

"I can still die," she remarked. The whole explanation made little sense to her.

"So do we," Fyertash replied, and the sly smile foretold a cunning remark to come. "The question is... can you die more than once now? And where would you be reborn?" His claw stroked her barrier in a teasing way. "I'd be tempted to find out, if I hadn't made a deal with Veranesh."

Kamira's heart beat in an erratic manner as Fyertash's words sank in. She mustered self-control, as the demon was still watching her. "That's something I can worry about later." No matter how much the thoughts of what she'd become would haunt her, nothing that Veranesh did affected her immediately. And if she died, she either wouldn't have to worry about it anymore or would have all the reasons to solve any problems that came with her supposed rebirth.

"Except for the binding." He became serious. "I doubt many yalari understand such notions, but someone might start wondering why Veranesh cares so much for one pactee... It's better for both of us that he's gone. You and I make much more believable allies."

She couldn't help arching her eyebrow. "I'd love to learn how you came to such a conclusion. Neither of us trusts the other much."

"It's simple," Fyertash replied, amused. "You're a desperate human who would take any help offered to defend her worthless city. I'm a weak and pitiful yalari who has to stoop to finding help among humans. And trust is not something that yalari require for an alliance. Quite the contrary; it often becomes a burden when the purpose of the alliance is fulfilled."

It was true for human alliances as well, but she was sure Fyertash knew it. He was studious, and he'd spent enough time around humans to have learned it already.

"Now, has our conversation given you any ideas on how to deal with the binding?"

Fyertash's question brought her back to reality. Wrapped up in his revelations, she had of course let herself forget what brought about the situation in the first place. She moved in her binds, but they held as firm as before.

"No," she replied. Perhaps if she had more time and could study the binding closer, there would be a way, but with the siege already started, she couldn't afford such distractions. "If it comes to that, I'll have to rely on killing my opponent first."

Fyertash must have learned enough from their previous confrontation, because he didn't burst out laughing. Instead, he regarded her with narrowed eyes. "Trying to bind them before they can bind you is risky. Even if you're faster, they can get to you before you finish."

"The barrier should hold them off long enough," Kamira replied. "But I wouldn't be binding them. I would go for the kill instead, just like they would."

She channeled energy and indicated for Fyertash to look up. His eyes widened at the collection of massive ice spikes hanging over him. And then they fell.

Fyertash ducked instinctively. With so much ice, he had no time to leap away.

Before the spikes reached him, Kamira raised a barrier over him, letting the shards shatter against it.

Fyertash straightened his back and gave her a nod of approval. "You might just live through an encounter with a yalari, should one come," he said without a trace of mockery. "But do not hesitate. We do not have to bind to do the ripping."

She didn't try to hide the slow breath she drew. Fyertash knew that Veranesh had taught her the ripping and that she'd witnessed Uganel's destruction. The cruel demon's screams still echoed within her memories. Now, with the newly revealed truth, it became clear that such pain could become hers as well.

Could a human even survive it?

She looked at Fyertash hesitantly.

"No," Fyertash said before she even mustered the courage to ask. "I will not submit you to it."

The strength he spoke with surprised her. She would have expected that he would give in to both his curiosity and a chance to show Kamira her place.

His expression softened. "I will not risk your life should the pain turn out to be too much for your body to bear," he explained. "Not for the sake of your or my curiosity. And I will not risk that the pain you'd experience will haunt you and paralyze you in that moment when the speed of your actions will matter most. You can count on both Myrkan and Derazin simply trying to kill you. Use that time well and see to their deaths before they feel threatened." He looked at the shards melting around them. "Ice is good. Most energies won't harm us, but this... this could be as good as claws."

Fyertash made no gesture, but the binds holding Kamira in place fell. She lowered the barrier.

"I don't suppose you'll tell me why you're still here?" she asked. "Veranesh is gone; you said it yourself. Why not leave as well?"

He hesitated, his face inscrutable. "I made a deal with him. He has already seen to his part of it by disposing of Arujhan for me. Derazin will meet a similar end once we send him back to Yalarethe. I'm not fool enough to turn on him now."

Kamira couldn't help the feeling that there was something more to Fyertash's motives than simply keeping his part of the deal, whatever it was... that he was actually being *loyal* to Veranesh. Undoubtedly, Fyertash wouldn't appreciate it if she voiced her guesses out loud, so she simply nodded.

"By the way." A sly expression returned to Fyertash's face. "It could be a good idea to check if the binding works on your two companions. They might have not spent the time in a crystal, but I wouldn't be surprised if Suzhaul went down the same path Veranesh did, and the mage killer has quite an amount of his power within. More than he had before. And the adept... He's also using Suzhaul's gift to alter himself, isn't he?"

Kamira glared at him. "You just can't help yourself, can you?"

To her surprise, the demon shook his head. "I was thinking that you should be the one to try. Neither of them will play as nice as you do."

Kamira almost smiled. Fyertash was right: both Veelk and Koshmarnyk would go for the kill, and she wouldn't bet on the demon surviving such a confrontation. As eager to play his games as he was, Fyertash was not one to fall for their allure when they could bring him no benefit.

"I'll consider it," she replied. Even though she'd share the secret with both of her friends, and upon their agreement, she'd test the binding spell against them, she would not oblige herself to share any of her findings with Fyertash.

"I'm sure you will." He looked at the door. "But I took too much of your time already. Seek me out when you're in need of my aid, knowledge, or you came up with a plan for how to deal with the two remaining yalari."

He spread his wings and took off, heading for his favorite spot at the edge of the broken dome. From there, he likely had a good view not only into the chamber itself, but also across the whole city and beyond it. The watching place of someone who liked to know all there was to know, patiently waiting rather than charging in headfirst. No wonder his brethren underestimated him, disregarding his power, taking his patience for weakness and cautiousness for cowardice.

She took a few steps into the chamber, so that he could hear her. "You don't really think either Myrkan or Derazin will figure out that secret, do you?"

"No. But I thought *you* should know, and Veranesh is not here to disagree with me," Fyertash replied.

"Perhaps next time you could simply tell me instead of playing games? Make me believe we are, indeed, allies?"

The only reply was Fyertash's laughter, and she hadn't expected anything else. But in the end, if the price for his help and knowledge was a few games she had to play, she'd suffer through it.

THE WESTERNERS, or the Baxayalans as they called themselves, turned out to be reasonable and friendly people, and Ryell enjoyed their company. They didn't hide their hopes of conquering Kaighal, but there wasn't any hatred when they spoke of the city. Their homeland, the Kingdom of Baxayal, was a union of merchant principalities that sought to expand their reach and bring prosperity through trade. Making Kaighal a part of the kingdom would allow them to reach cities and states in Juamha. Slaughter and destruction wasn't their goal, so even though Ryell still fidgeted when they discussed their hopes, he couldn't help giving a cautious nod to their reasoning, and he could even see how Kaighal would benefit from their protection against the power-thirsty Tivarashan that went about imposing their demon worship on everyone.

The Baxayalans also wanted to learn more about Ryell and the Devanshari, and their curiosity seemed genuine. They asked questions about Devanshari culture and history, expressed their outrage at the kingdom's fall, and talked much about how once they gained control over Kaighal, they could help the refugees regain their lands.

"Demons might still be roaming the Devanshari," Ryell replied to one of the scouts' excited plans to build many ships that would go across the sea.

"I'm sure our army can handle one or two, and once we bring the news back, our inventors will be quick to find ways to fight them most efficiently," Captain Seraine said, joining the conversation.

From what Ryell had gathered, Seraine was of noble descent, but the way she behaved around her men was nothing like the Devanshari nobles. Although she gave orders and kept control over her scouts, she didn't bark her demands, and she listened to their ideas and suggestions. Her relationship with them reminded Ryell of the times he'd spent with the border guard. Far from the palace and the capital, those men and women cared little about etiquette or status, and they created bonds stronger than any order could impose.

He forced a smile at Seraine's reassurance, despite the bitter taste in his mouth that his memories had brought. In the past, when he was already a royal guard, he'd cherished the moments spent with the border guards, and returned to them often when the palace's intrigues and politics became too much.

But now... Now those images of joy haunted him with

what came later. The border guards were the first ones to encounter demons, and though some survived and pulled back deeper into the kingdom, they were still sent back into guerilla battles against the foe's overwhelming numbers. And then the port's defense, when they all perished in a lost battle.

Ryell tensed. By the queen's order, he was supposed to die there too.

"Is something wrong?" Seraine inspected him with concern.

"Just memories," he replied with honesty, hoping that the captain wouldn't dig deeper. No matter how fond he was growing of his accidental companions, some things weren't for them. Cahala qi'Devanshari's betrayal and her death would remain a secret forever.

A cold wave rushed through his veins at a sudden thought. Kamira knew of it all. But then, she was an archmage now, and to reveal his involvement in the events that had occurred in a certain forest clearing would also mean revealing her own role in them. Even if Ryell couldn't trust her anymore, she wouldn't let the secret out in fear of how it would affect her new status.

"I apologize on behalf of me and my people," Seraine said. "It wasn't our intention to bring back those difficult moments. We will be stopping for the night soon, and although we can't erase those dreadful moments from your memory, let us ease them with bright stories of our homeland, if you'd like to hear them."

She must know that such memories could only fade with time, and their shadow would always haunt Ryell's thoughts, but her offer was that of hope: that despite all his past experiences, he could find happiness, and that—perhaps—it was waiting for him in the Kingdom of Baxayal.

"I'd love to."

~

THEY WERE ALONE in the initiation rite chamber, and Kamira did her best to hide her tiredness from Irtan. Even though her body took the prolonged work and lack of good sleep surprisingly well, the mental strain was wearing on her more and more. Back when high magic was still prominent, archmages had plenty of assistants, teachers made their own decisions, and the first archmage didn't have to bother herself with anything she didn't want to. But with most of the students' and teachers' departure, there were too few people left to perform too many tasks that seemed to multiply because of the upcoming siege.

"Since there wasn't enough time to train everyone properly," Irtan continued his report on the progress of preparations, "I divided students into groups, ensuring each had at least one person skilled enough to hold a steady barrier. Others were schooled into channeling energies, and if they aim for the enemy, they shouldn't do too much harm to their allies."

"How many are there to hold a barrier if needed?" No matter how much she feared the answer, the question had to be asked.

"Enough," Irtan replied with confidence. "Unless the whole net falls in the assault, isolated breaches should be easy enough to defend, provided that the adepts will do their part and fix or replace the broken devices without delay."

Kamira rubbed her temples. Too many things hinged on everyone doing their part, and making them happen wasn't as easy as when she'd only had Veelk—one reliable companion—to concern herself with. Yet she couldn't do anything more. There weren't that many arcanists in Tyorane to begin with, and at the news of the High Towers' fall and demons coming, the cunning ones were more likely to flee toward the Western Kingdom than aid the city that had been a seat of high mages for centuries.

Irtan watched her with interest lined with hints of amusement, and she threw him a nasty glare, ignoring any proper behavior one could expect from the first archmage. No matter how helpful the old man might be, and no matter how much his surprising mastery of the arcane arts lent credibility to his claims of secretly acting against the other archmages, Irtan was still too engrossed in deception and games, ready to exploit any weakness of a rival. And Kamira had no doubt she was his rival.

A quiet sigh escaped her mouth at the memory of Master Tijhran, who, despite being her teacher, had always been friendly and supportive. "Do what you think is best. They'll get proper schooling once everything is over. Perhaps you could decide on some incentive for those who put the most effort?"

Irtan shrugged in a noncommittal manner that didn't reveal whether he disagreed with her idea or simply didn't know how to put it in motion.

A quiet knock barely carried through the length of the chamber. Irtan tensed in an instant, but Kamira didn't bother with caution. Assassins weren't in the habit of politely announcing their arrival.

"Enter!" she called out.

Atissa poked her head in, scanning the surroundings before she came inside. Her eyes glazed past Irtan, but the slight grimace didn't escape Kamira. The old man must have noticed it too, but he made no offer to leave, and he didn't relax.

Kamira gestured Atissa to come closer. The young woman hesitated, then rushed over to the table as if making up her mind on a matter known only to her. She carried a bunch of papers with her and laid them out on the table before Kamira and Irtan.

"I found something that might be of help with the siege," Atissa said directly to Kamira, ignoring Irtan. "Old demonologist diagrams for healing."

Kamira's eyes widened. Circles of healing had been long lost, and no arcanist she knew had any idea how to draw them. Even in Juamha, where the arts had survived in better shape, such a skill was unheard of.

"Where did you get these?" Kamira asked. One glance at the papers was enough to tell her that these were indeed arcane circles, but it would take time to study them properly and determine whether they could help in channeling magic into healing.

"The archmages' secret library." Atissa glared at Irtan.

The old man smiled gently. "I've been told you were poking around the library, but I didn't expect that your father told you about something that was meant only for the first three archmages." He sent Kamira an apologetic smile. "I thought this was something that could wait until after the siege."

Of course he would have thought that! *I wonder how many other secrets he's kept for himself.*

Irtan and Atissa were exchanging accusatory stares, and it wasn't the best time to question either of them. Besides, as much as Kamira would love to solve the problem of their loyalty and truthfulness here and now, it wouldn't go quickly or easily, and the city's future was more important that her own feelings of safety and comfort. As long as they both were willing to lend a hand, she would allow them whatever plots they might be weaving, at least for the time being.

She looked at the circles once more, the longing of an explorer awaking. If she could spare some time and look through them properly, they had the potential to save many lives in Kaighal... or they could be useless. Time was too precious to risk learning that, despite Atissa's possible good intentions, the circles had too little information for the arcanists to heal with them. Even if Irtan said he could spare some time to look them over, she'd rather have him focus on the defense and other pressing matters. Besides, this presented an opportunity to learn how much Atissa had truly changed, and what she was willing to do to prove herself.

Atissa must have sensed Kamira's eyes on her, because she shifted with unease, avoiding meeting Kamira's stare directly. There was no hate in her expression, just unease. No wonder—she was offering aid to a woman who had killed her father and ruined her bright future, all in one day.

"This is of no use for us as it is," Kamira said without malice. "And neither I nor Irtan have time to spend on such research. You, on the other hand, have all the time to learn and discover." She looked Atissa in the eye as soon as the young woman raised her head. "You will make a pact, learn to wield your new magic, and study these circles to discover if they can truly be of help. If you have questions about the arcane arts, ask Pelina. She'll find time."

Defiance flashed on Atissa's face. "Why wouldn't you want to take them for yourself?" She was clearly about to say something more, but she glanced at Irtan and shut her mouth.

Kamira had an eerie suspicion that Atissa meant to say, "Irtan would." No wonder—no archmage in the High Towers would pass on an opportunity to further their power and knowledge.

Kamira sighed. No matter how uncomfortable it was to share personal thoughts with Atissa, who perhaps wouldn't even understand them, she had to say something. According to Pelina, Atissa was adamant in her refusal to make a pact, and the longer she stayed idle in the Towers, with no prospects or a clear path, the more likely she'd grow bitter and dangerous.

"I don't need any more recognition that I already have," Kamira said, her voice calm and quiet. "No matter what I do, I'll always be remembered as the one who caused the high mages to fall and who brought demons to Kaighal. Even if I fight the invasion off, everyone will see it as simply cleaning up my own mess. Besides, when the demons storm the city, I'll be standing on battlements, fending them off. There will be no time for healing others."

Atissa nodded hesitantly, as if she followed the logic but remained unconvinced.

"You cared enough to bring these to me," Kamira continued, "and since you were helping in King Allyv's asylum, you might have what it takes to become a healer. I'm entrusting these notes to you, because you told me you wanted a chance, and this is how you can make something of yourself. How you can be remembered not as Yoreus's daughter but as the first-in-centuries arcane healer in Tyorane."

Atissa swallowed. "I understand." She gathered the papers from the table. "I'll come back later, when I have something you can use, archmage."

"Focus on the ones that can deal with battle wounds or

help sustain life. Anything more complex will have to wait till after the siege," Kamira said.

"I will." Without even acknowledging Irtan, Atissa rushed out of the chamber.

The silence that accompanied her departure didn't last long.

"I didn't know you were so trusting," Irtan remarked with enough snideness to grate on Kamira's nerves.

"*You're* still around, aren't you?" she fired back. "And so is your demon."

"I keep wondering whether my demon is still mine." As if out of habit, he glanced up at the edges of the shattered dome, but Fyertash wasn't within sight.

She didn't fall for the fishing. "I think it's better to give her a worthy goal that will absorb her. Less time to ponder the turn her life has taken and its consequences, and that means fewer chances she'll start plotting."

Irtan regarded her with unconcealed doubt. "And what if she decides that with her newfound power and recognition, all she needs is the title of the archmage, along with a little revenge to sweeten her ascension?"

Kamira grinned. "She can only kill one of us before the other one gets her, and I'm not quite sure she'd be going after me first."

It was a shot in the dark, but from the moment Atissa entered, she'd made her dislike for Irtan clear. Kamira couldn't tell whether it was a disdain for the opportunist who'd turned on his allies to retain his influences and power or if Atissa's feelings ran deeper, but either way, it was a good argument.

"And if I'm wrong, I'm sure you won't be too broken up about becoming the first archmage again."

Irtan spread his arms, offering a jovial smile. "I'm

starting to enjoy my place as the second archmage. It's amusing to see someone else make mistakes I wouldn't be able to afford were I in their position."

"You spoke the same way to Archmage Yoreus?" She couldn't resist, though she could guess the answer already.

"Age does come with benefits, my dear." He stirred, and the amusement left his face, replaced by seriousness. "Now, if you'll excuse me… We both have more important things to do than question each other's motives and decisions."

Kamira held off her sigh until after he'd left the chamber. There was much in Irtan that reminded her of her teacher. He had wisdom, composure, and just enough sense of humor to make him someone more than yet another power-thirsty mage. Perhaps, in other circumstances, they could become friends…

She discarded that thought, recognizing her own longing for Master Tijhran's company and advice. Irtan might be an arcanist, but he'd spent decades in the Towers as a high mage and as an archmage, climbing his way to the top, and that alone had corrupted him enough to change him into a man her teacher never was, nor strove to be.

6

Derazin was sitting at the seashore, away from humans, but none would dare to approach anyway. After the bright explosion far in the desert, they were all too fear-stricken to act.

Pitiful creatures, Myrkan thought. If he didn't need their servitude, he'd indulge in spilling their worthless blood. But to show such rage would sow discord among the already unsettled pactees. He had to resist his instincts and appear as strong and confident as Arujhan would.

With that in mind, he approached the other yalari.

"We're done here," Derazin said grimly.

"We haven't lost yet," Myrkan replied.

The other yalari looked at him in disgust. "Arujhan did. And even if the destruction killed Veranesh, he will be reborn in Yalarethe soon enough. With Arujhan's domain unclaimed, there's going to be a lot of turmoil. We would be fools to miss such an opportunity and give Veranesh time to prepare."

Myrkan swallowed. He couldn't deny Derazin's logic. When half of their pactees had lost their pact, Arujhan's demise became indisputable. And Myrkan had no doubt that Veranesh would rather die himself than risk confronting two enemies weakened by his previous battle. To Derazin, Fyertash alone wasn't worth delays, and he would not agree to continue the siege.

"We would be fools to go back now," Myrkan said. He had one chance at convincing the other yalari to stay. "If Veranesh bested Arujhan, he would dispose of us even easier."

"That's why we have to go now. Prepare. Find new allies." Derazin lifted his claw before Myrkan could protest. "Veranesh already destroyed two of our kind. Others *will* feel threatened, and if we get back in time, we might convince them to join us against him."

Myrkan cursed under his breath. Out of all time, the coward Derazin had decided to exercise reason and levelheadedness this very moment, possibly ruining all of Myrkan's plans.

"Or they will decide that meddling isn't worth risking their own lives," Myrkan said. "They might just allow Veranesh to exact his revenge, hoping that things will get back to normal after his thirst for blood has been sated."

Derazin grimaced. "Staying here is worse than an exile."

"I agree," Myrkan lied smoothly. "Yet we could use our time here to get an upper hand. We now have but a handful of pactees, and the power of their wills isn't enough for either of us to grow in power much during our rebirth. But there..." Myrkan paused and pointed at the city. "There are countless humans who would worship us in exchange for keeping their worthless lives going." He leaned forward with a greedy smile. "Think of it. We might not become a match to the Four, but Veranesh... He'd stand no chance."

Only a slight shift on Derazin's face betrayed his

wavering resolve. Myrkan waited. Greed could work even on most cowardly of the yalari, and Derazin had to have *some* courage if he'd managed to keep his place among the kanyalari. The prospect of power gained easily and without much risk must have its appeal, too.

Yet, instead of agreeing, Derazin narrowed his eyes. "Why tell me all of that? Why share the power with me?"

"Because I can't take the city on my own with Fyertash around," Myrkan forced himself to say. No matter how humiliating such a confession was, it would play right into Derazin's feeling of superiority. "The two of us can corner him, and he can only try to bind one of us."

Derazin looked at him with doubt. "It can't be that easy."

"It will take time, but it can be done. I already have willing tools within the city's walls." Myrkan didn't mention that those tools would be close to useless if he didn't sway the adept to do his part. "They'll cause enough commotion to keep Veranesh's pactee and Fyertash occupied while I make sure everything's ready. All you have to do is keep our pactees obedient and send as many asayalari onto the walls as possible."

"They will never break through the barrier."

"Leave the barrier to me." Myrkan would say anything to make Derazin stay, but a plan was already forming in his head. If he used his mediocre tools well, perhaps he could pressure the tool he needed to finally make a step. Ervan was a cautious man—one who would rather pass on the opportunity than act too abruptly, but Myrkan knew that the right circumstances could push even a man like him to make brash decisions. With enough power behind the asayalari attacks, Myrkan could convince Ervan that the siege was about to end, and if the adept didn't do his part, he would not taste the fruits of the yalari's victory.

A smile stretched Derazin's plump features. "Very well. We'll stay long enough to ensure the city is ours."

Derazin hobbled away, and his posture indicated enough confidence for humans to believe that recent events had brought no concerns to him.

Myrkan had no doubt that the cowardly kanyalari was already picturing himself as the ruler of the city, with terrified humans bowing their heads and raising their prayers to him, perhaps even *only* to him. In his blind pride, Derazin would never see the blow to the back coming. With Fyertash dead as well, Myrkan would be the only yalari left in the human world, safe from all others and free to do as he willed. Veranesh would exact his revenge on the unsuspecting Derazin and turn toward securing his new domain, likely one built on the ruins of Arujhan's holds, never looking toward the human world again, so as long as Myrkan stayed here, he was safe from Veranesh's wrath.

In the distance, Derazin was already ordering the pactees around, and the asayalari stirred in anticipation of an attack. Blinded by the dreams of grandeur and besting Veranesh, the foolish coward would do exactly what Myrkan wanted him to. Now it was time to ensure that his human tools did the same.

With his ultimate reward within grasp, Myrkan would neither hesitate nor fail.

As Veelk joined his sister on top of the battlements, she turned to him, discontent clear on her face. Below them, hordes of demonlings clawed at the barrier. Their screeches and howls carried with the wind. Groups of defenders launched well-executed counterattacks, lowering their parts of the barriers only long enough to send arrows or magic down to the attacking creatures.

"We should be down there, killing as many of them as possible," Zelna said. "Instead, she keeps us idle."

Veelk nodded, but even though he shared her desire to spill blood, he understood Kamira's plans. He pointed at the horizon, where the two demons lurked. "Our quarry is there. It would be foolish to pass on the biggest battle in the history just because one of us got wounded by some clawed abomination."

Zelna grimaced, but at least she didn't argue. She watched the creatures below them. "I hope she comes up with a plan soon enough. The longer we wait, the more likely something will go wrong." She glanced at one of the devices Gildya had prepared, her dubious expression revealing her thoughts.

Veelk kept his mouth shut. If only coming up with a plan was that easy! They had to find a way to dispose of the demonlings and arcanists, so that there would be no interference in the battle with the demons. Four people and one untrustworthy demon seemed like hardly enough to take down two powerful enemies, and Veelk almost shuddered at the memory of his confrontation with Uganel. They'd won back then, but it was a slim and pricey victory. At least this time they wouldn't be destroying those wretched creatures. Sending them back to their own world would be enough.

"So, how did it go with Lefna?" Zelna changed the subject.

"She wasn't there." Veelk mustered a shrug. "When the news of the demons' coming spread in the city, her father sent her west, to some distant relatives." She was still looking at him, so he added, "Opyr wasn't unfriendly, but I think he'd rather not see me around. He probably realized that Kamira and I put our friends and companions in danger."

Zelna looked at him with a glimmer of compassion but said nothing, and Veelk didn't expect any words. He had to go to the Jagged Swordsman, because it would be discourteous to return to Kaighal and avoid Lefna, but he had little hope for a teary reunion. Lefna knew what kind of a man he was, and she didn't strike him as in love, just infatuated enough to enjoy their time together while it lasted. And the grueling experience the bastard Phuran had put her through must have wiped out any affections she could have been growing. It might be for the better that Opyr had sent her away before Veelk returned. At least they avoided the awkward silence of a reunion.

A short scream drew their attention. One of the devices farther down the wall crumbled in a flash of magic. That portion of the barrier faded in an instant, and assigned people rushed to the edge of the battlements, loosing arrows. An arcanist released her magic chaotically, as far as Veelk could tell, but finesse wasn't necessary in battle.

The demonlings' screeches and the clattering and scratching of their claws grew louder as the creatures scaled the unprotected wall. Those assigned to nearby devices abandoned their posts, rushing to aid the defenders.

"Looks like they got this," Veelk said with disappointment. He'd much rather join the citizens of Kaighal and taste the rush of battle than stand idly by, but their help wasn't needed.

Zelna murmured something that sounded like reluctant acknowledgment. She turned her head toward the horizon, longing clear in her eyes, and then gave Veelk a broad smile that said: "Soon." Soon their blood lust would be satisfied.

More shouts rose around them. Veelk couldn't make out the words, but caught the alarm and urgency. As he looked for the cause, more devices flashed with magic and fell apart, and barriers faded at several defense points.

Veelk and Zelna exchanged glances and unstrapped their keshals. As much as they wanted to respect Kamira's request to restrain themselves, they had to ensure demonlings didn't make it into the city. They split up, running in opposite directions.

Veelk reached a broken, abandoned device as the first demonlings made it onto the battlements. His first swipe clipped through two heads, and one's guts poured forth as the two collapsed and the next wave clawed their way to Veelk's blade. Several waves steadily fell, and blood stained the walls as if merely offering Veelk a training regimen.

Most had no idea what awaited them on the battlements, which left them easy prey clamoring over their dead. One had the time and awareness to screech at Veelk and launch itself at him, claws flailing. Veelk bent back and snatched the creature from the air by its ankle, and the screaming nuisance became a short-lived flail. Veelk slammed his newfound weapon into its brethren until its skull shattered to mush. It fared well in knocking demonlings back off the wall, better than his keshal, even, but it lost its effectiveness quickly. Veelk threw it at another, and both sailed clear of the wall back to the horde below. Several had squeezed next to each other to scan the battlements for prey, only to be shouldered right back to whence they came.

It was hardly a worthy battle, and Veelk itched to leap over the wall and descend through the climbing demonlings, bloodletting along the way. But it wasn't what

Kamira and Kaighal needed from him, so he pushed the urge from his mind.

The bodies mounted quickly, and blood gathered underfoot until a larger, winged demonling appeared with arrow-ridden, leathery wings and an elongated, birdlike face. In a way, the creature's visage mocked those of higher demons, but Veelk had no time to ponder it. The demonling ascended before shooting down with outstretched claws.

Veelk sidestepped and swung his keshal. The wide blade bit deep into the creature's ribs but didn't cut through. The creature tried to escape up and away. Veelk yanked down on the keshal enough to get his other hand on the shaft, and then sent the demonling flying. It smashed into the battlement wall, then struck several other demonlings. Bones cracked, demonlings screeched as they were sent writhing from the battlements, and despite its wounds, after the large demonling skidded to a stop, it clumsily tried to regain its footing, but Veelk jammed his keshal's thin blade straight through its eye and out the back of its skull.

A woman in Gildya's robes accompanied by several armed citizens was running along the battlements toward Veelk. She was carrying one of the devices, so Veelk dispatched the most recent demonling arrivals and moved to allow her to pass. As she worked on setting it up, her armed accompaniment took to defending the wall.

"Make sure she's safe," he said as more demonlings appeared. In the limited space, they would only get in each other's way.

They fell back, forming a protective semicircle around the adept, and Veelk focused on their opponents.

He managed only two swipes before the woman called out, "Coming up now!"

The device hummed and the barrier rose in an instant,

slicing some of the demonlings in half and barring the way for the others. Their claws sought grip on the smooth surface of magic and failed, sending the creatures down to their deaths with howls and screeching.

"Well done," Veelk said in passing, already searching for the next battle.

Farther away, a lone arcanist stood, focus and sweat on his face as he held a barrier up. It wavered but was enough to keep the demonlings out. Another group consisting of an adept and several guards was already making its way to him. In the other direction, Zelna stood among the bodies of demonlings, both her keshal and clothes stained with their dark blood. She sent Veelk a grin.

Several other battles were already dying out, with replacement devices already set, and only several stray demonlings caught within the protection. There were a few wounded, but the unexpected breaches didn't turn into slaughter, proving that people of Kaighal were as brave and ready to defend their city as their ancestors.

In the distance, the Devanshari king was calling out commands, sending aid to the affected groups. Veelk caught concern flash on his face as he spoke to several adepts.

"They don't know what happened, do they?" Zelna joined Veelk, her keshal already clean and strapped to her back, but she hadn't bothered to wipe the dark blood smeared on her face. "All those trinkets are useless in the end."

"Or we have traitors in our midst." Veelk scanned the groups of defenders and the onlookers, but with so many of them, it was impossible to pick out one suspicious face. Besides, more devices failed at the same time, which suggested there were at least several people in Kaighal who'd chosen to side with the wrong demons.

"I'll leave the traitor hunt to Kamira. As long as all of the devices don't fail at the same time, we can keep those wretched creatures out of the city. Go." She waved at him. "Let her know. I'll stay around, just in case."

The wide grin on her face made it clear enough that Zelna would welcome another breach of the barrier, but Veelk would rather see her return to the inn bored. Even if she wasn't foolhardy, a fortunate strike or the sheer number of demonlings could leave her wounded.

Zelna waved him off again as if she knew exactly what he was thinking. The grin still lingered on her lips, but her eyes remained focused, inspecting both the demonlings below the walls and the humans around her. It might not be the battle lust that made her want to stick around, and Veelk gave her a nod before departing. He'd return later, to allow her some rest, and they could take turns ensuring that broken—or sabotaged—devices didn't cause the city's fall until Kamira found a way to deal with the higher demons.

Veelk walked away from the walls, heading straight for the Towers. Kamira had to learn about the subterfuge sooner or later, so he might as well tell her himself.

HER NEW MAGIC itched like a rough garment. It assaulted her with new sensations, distracting her with all the various flows around the Towers that Atissa had never noticed before. Pelina had promised her that the feeling of uneasiness would pass, but until then, Atissa was stuck with an itch she couldn't scratch and damaged focus that affected her progress. She'd grasped enough of her new art's basics to summon a lumisphere, determined not to do worse than petty Grida, but left on her own, she'd hardly had an idea what to do after that.

The old books she'd brought over from the library offered her lengthy explanations but no insights on how this kind of magic felt in practice. They came from the times where arcane magic was the only magic and everyone already knew how to perform it.

Atissa pressed her lips together. She would have to figure it out by trial and error, until she understood how it worked. The floor was already messy from the circle she'd drawn to make a pact, so it could serve her once more. The privacy of her father's... no, of *her* chambers ensured that no one would see her on her knees, wiping the chalk marks with a piece of cloth as if she was a lowly servant.

She paused. In a way, she was worse off than a servant—a daughter of a defeated and disgraced archmage whom everyone suspected of malicious intent.

Not everyone, she reminded herself. Veelk had saved her life and didn't turn on her even when he learned who she was. Kamira was willing to give her a chance too—even if only to ensure her own safety. Even Pelina, though not friendly, seemed to have some compassion and understanding. And no matter how conflicted Atissa felt about Kamira, the new archmage was right: if Atissa proved herself, there could be more people willing to forget about her past.

With a renewed resolve, she worked on removing the chalk marks and then copying one of the simple circles from the book. This would have to do for a start.

Once everything was ready, Atissa sat down in the middle of the circle with a thin dagger in her hand. Before its blade got close to her skin, she paused. She'd had minor cuts before, and it was nothing unbearable, but at the same time, the memory of Myrkan ripping stones out of Koshmarnyk's body and the adept's screams paralyzed her. To willingly cause harm to herself...

She shook her head, chasing those thoughts away.

"Don't be silly," she said out loud, as if she could scold her own fearful mind. "It's nothing."

The blade skimmed the skin on her forearm, splitting it. The cut stung, but her instincts calmed at the little harm done. She didn't have to cut deeper for the first try, and if she succeeded, she could always find people in need of help to practice her healing.

Unsettled by both anticipation and fear, Atissa took a deep breath. Even though she tried to maintain focus, the voice at the back of her head reminded her that no one had performed healing with magic for centuries, and while part of Atissa clung to Kamira's suggestion of making a name for herself, the other doubted whether such healing was even possible. If it was, some arcanist would have figured it out by now, even if archmages did their best to limit the access to knowledge.

That thought, so familiar, eased her nerves. It was so like the archmages to take away something they couldn't do themselves. According to her father's notes, with high magic relying on spells rather than channeling the energy, it was impossible to create a spell that would bring forth the exact amount of magic in healing form to ensure proper mending. Too little could result in death, while too much could have other unpleasant consequences. Her father had made some attempts early in his years as the seventh archmage, but in the end the work turned out too uncertain to pursue. After all, one didn't gain better status or advance in ranks by wasting time on work that could never bear fruit.

It seemed somewhat ironic that his own daughter would follow the same path, but as an arcanist.

Channeling magic was nothing like reciting a spell, and Atissa shifted with uneasiness. Whenever she started, she could swear that the demon she had a pact with stirred in the other world, but nothing else followed. It seemed that the creature was satisfied enough with making a pact alone, as it—*he*, she corrected herself—made no demands and listed no expectations. According to Pelina, for a demon like him, any pact would be good. In the future, a pact with stronger demon could be possible, but Atissa wasn't sure she wanted to tie herself with a powerful demon. Maybe not all of them were cruel and violent like Myrkan, but even the one that lurked around Kamira, Fyertash, had something sly about him. If she could heal with her mediocre pact, she didn't need more magic.

All of this thinking is pointless if I can't figure out how to heal. And, as hard as it was to admit, it was an excuse to allow herself to succumb to her own fears, to find a reason to not to try.

She steeled herself and began channeling.

The circle around her lit up with a delicate glow of magic. It pulsated to the rhythm of her heart, and Atissa fought to keep her eyes on the wound. Little by little, the cut on her skin began to mend. As it healed, her skin began to itch, and Atissa huffed at herself for allowing such a minor thing to distract her. In response to her reaction, the flow of the magic changed. Like a wave breaking through a dam, energy escaped her control. The wound on her arm split and grew. Blood burst out of it, flowing down her forearm and staining her clothes.

Panicked, Atissa stopped channeling. The magic around her died out.

She scrambled back onto her feet. If she remembered correctly, there were some ointments and bandages in her room from when she was taking care of Ryell. She rushed in there, painfully aware of leaving a trail of blood. She'd worry about it later.

The bandages were still where she'd left them, but she'd have a hard time dressing the wound with one hand. She hesitated only for a heartbeat. The blood flow might not be heavy, but if she dawdled long enough, she could faint before she stopped it. She grabbed a piece of an old shirt, pressed it to her wound, and rushed out of her room.

The part of the Towers where the archmages lived had not been frequented much even before the fall of high magic, as the men and women in power cherished their privacy, and now the corridors leading to their old chambers were empty most of the times, with only Kamira and Irtan around.

At first, Atissa considered running to either of them, but it was unlikely they were in their chambers. She turned the other way and ran for the stairs leading to the lower levels instead. Teachers and other students might not like her, but if she made enough ruckus, someone would help her, if only to make sure they looked good in the eyes of others.

In her rush, she took a turn too fast and smashed into a wall... that wasn't supposed to be there. Then the wall moved.

Atissa looked up, straight at Veelk's familiar grin.

"That's quite a rush you're in," he said, but his expression shifted into seriousness as his eyes skimmed past her arm. "And quite a wound."

"An accident," she muttered. "I was going to get some help. I can't dress it myself."

"Do you have bandages?"

She nodded, indicating behind her, at the still-open door to her chambers.

"Let's go, then."

"I don't want to take your time. You were going to see the archmage, weren't you?" It felt safer to call Kamira by her title, as if the emotions weren't stirred that way.

"Kamira can wait. She's likely busy annoying another demon, and she's well capable of doing it all by herself," Veelk said. "You, on the other hand, look like you could use some help."

Protests would only waste her time, so she led Veelk back to her chamber and into her room. In passing, he glanced at the chalk circle, the dagger, and the marks of blood, but no comment accompanied his brief inspection.

In her room, Atissa pointed at the bandages and sat on the bed, still pressing the crumpled cloth to her wound. Veelk pulled up an armchair for himself with such ease it could have been a tiny stool. When he sat down, she half expected the seat to break under his weight, but the furniture turned out sturdy enough.

With the skill of someone who had performed the task dozens of times, Veelk cleaned and dressed her wound.

"So, what happened?" he asked.

She had no doubt that there was more than pure curiosity to his question. No matter how much Atissa might have helped them with the priestess, she was still the daughter of Kamira's enemy, and anything she did could turn out to be a deadly plot.

"The archmage... She entrusted me with figuring out the healing circles," Atissa said honestly. "But I'm barely an arcanist, and I can't wield that magic well. I think I lost focus, and something went wrong."

"And you thought experimenting on yourself was the

best idea?" he asked with an arched eyebrow and enough playfulness to make it clear he wasn't about to give her a lecture.

"You know who I am." She looked away. "Do you think anyone would be willing to help me, especially with all the risks involved? And if I gave someone a wound like that, there would be no end to the accusations."

Veelk grinned. "Have you thought of getting an animal for the test instead?"

She stared at him, dumbfounded. Having lived all her life in the Towers, such an idea had never crossed her mind, even though, in hindsight, it made sense.

Her shoulders slumped at her own lack of thought. Before jumping into making circles and using magic, she should have stopped and considered all possibilities.

"But first, you should learn to control your magic," Veelk said. "I know little of how it's done, but I saw Kamira practice. She summons light or water and focuses on its flow. Don't do fire or lightning, because it gets quite messy."

Practice, practice, always practice. Even high magic required it for perfect spell recitation, and she shouldn't have expected that arcane magic would be easier. "The siege won't wait until I get it right," she said with a sigh. The appeal of being the first healer faded with the thought that before she could become one, many people would die.

"Then you better learn quickly," Veelk said. "What does healing magic require you to do?"

The only answer she had was a shrug, because the books didn't explain the process in detail. Back before the Cataclysm, understanding must have been a part of basic schooling.

Veelk was still looking at her expectantly, so she said, "All I know is that you need the right circle for the right kind of healing, and then you're just supposed to... channel the magic?"

He gave an absent-minded nod. "Perhaps you won't have to practice long." Without warning, he held her healthy arm and pulled her hand to his chest. "Go on, channel."

Horror overwhelming her thoughts, she tore away. Without the healing circle, she couldn't hope to do anything good with her unsteady magic. She closed her fist, tense. She would not risk the life of the one man who seemed to care little about her past.

"You aren't going to hurt me," he reassured her with all seriousness.

Hesitantly, Atissa reached her hand out. Veelk didn't strike her as a fool who'd take chances, and after all, he'd been around Kamira, so he likely knew more about arcane magic than Atissa did. She leaned forward and put her hand close to his chest. Her demon stirred as she channeled magic, enough for a spark.

Veelk's skin lit up with intricate lines of scars. Their gentle golden glow made Atissa lean closer, but they faded before she got a better look. His scent enveloped her, and she inhaled it slowly. Veelk smelled like confidence and protection, a mixture she'd never experienced before. Atissa almost closed her eyes, as every gentle breath she took in had a calming effect longer. If she could, she'd stay close to him until all her fears faded.

"Good." Veelk's voice pulled her back to reality. "Now channel more."

He didn't seem bothered by her face almost in his chest, and Atissa blushed as the memory of what her father had learned about the mage killer resurfaced. According to his spies, Veelk enjoyed the company of women and had many lovers. Yet nothing in his behavior struck her as seductive.

Don't be silly, she told herself for the second time this afternoon. Instead of letting her mind wander in the wrong direction, she should be grateful for his help.

With less hesitation, she channeled magic again. It sank into his body in a steady flow, and his scars once more glowed golden.

Fascinated by the sight, Atissa kept channeling. With enough focus, the magic was obedient to her will and didn't fluctuate like the first time, and that alone gave her hope. Perhaps she didn't need much training for simple healing tasks.

The magic waned all of a sudden. Atissa sighed. "That's all I have." Pelina had warned her that unlike high magic, which provided unlimited amounts of power, pacts had their limitations, especially when made with minor demons.

"You did well," Veelk said. "Once you have your magic back, practice more. Then you should be able to heal without any danger." He rubbed his chin. "But if you're serious about it, you will need a better pact soon. I'll let Kamira know."

Her mood soured. "Why would she allow it?" Atissa could understand being entrusted with research for healing, because it kept her busy and focused on things other than revenge, but Kamira would have to know better than to let someone she couldn't trust rise in power.

Veelk looked at her with all seriousness in his eyes, and she knew that he wouldn't give her empty reassurances. He wouldn't tell her that he believed she was good and she would never do it.

"With the demons at the gate, we need all the help and allies we can get," he replied. "A healer without her magic will be of no help. Besides"—he looked her straight in the eye—"do you think she has any reason to worry? Do you think I'd let anything happen to her?"

The message was clear: if Atissa ever became a threat to Kamira, he'd stand in her way without a second thought. The memory of how he'd rushed to Kamira's side without hesitation and without even asking who her attacker was brought a wave of jealousy. To have a friend like that, to have someone that loyal...

Atissa exercised discipline before any emotions showed on her face. "Thank you for your help." She pointed at the bandage. "And for a lesson in magic," she added with genuine gratitude.

He rose from his seat and flashed his grin, all seriousness gone. "My pleasure. But perhaps next time don't go about it by wounding yourself. Asking for help doesn't hurt, unless they try to kill you for it."

She couldn't keep the chuckle in, and Veelk's departure left her in a lighter mood. The wounded arm was sore and it could affect her focus, but with her demon's magic gone, she wouldn't be able to practice for a while anyway. At least she could still pore over the books, in search of clues and answers. She had to know how big the circle had to be, if she could use the same one for more than one person, and how she was supposed to know when to stop channeling magic.

As she stepped out of the room, the smeared chalk on the floor and droplets of blood reminded her how the encounter had started, but instead of weighing on her shoulders with the burden of failure, they spoke of the progress she'd made.

A smile came to her face. She'd get some food, clean up the mess, and do more research. And later—her heart sped up at the sudden excitement—she'd practice her new magic again.

7

E veryone in Gildya seemed in a rush, and hardly anyone paid attention to Koshmarnyk making his way through its halls. Even with evening already upon the city, nothing indicated a time of rest for the guild of inventors. Adepts carried blueprints and device pieces, while apprentices heaved heavier crates, likely containing all the parts their tutors needed for the construction of many useful contraptions. With the city's safety challenged, Koshmarnyk hoped that most were focusing on the replacement devices for the ones lost to the saboteurs and demonlings that had made it inside the walls when parts of the barrier fell.

The eyes of Gildya's guards followed his passing with focus and caution. The council must have told them who Koshmarnyk was, but it seemed, that aside, he was allowed unrestricted entry. This meant he wouldn't have to stop to explain the reason for his visits or have a guard breathing down his neck all the way through the building.

Nonetheless, he made his way through the halls in a quick manner that made him look like yet another adept rushing off to work on an urgent project, but slowed to assure those watching him that he had no ulterior motives for his briskness, and he reached his destination undisturbed, save for the guards' watchful scrutiny and an occasional curious glance from a younger adept or apprentice.

This time he wore long sleeves, unwilling to display the half-healed wounds caused by Myrkan's claws, especially since the ripped stones had started regrowing, much like Veranesh had said. The disturbing sight aside, Koshmarnyk would rather not let adepts know the stones, once blended, would remain part of the body forever, even when torn out of it... The less they knew about the blending, the fewer arguments they could conjure against such a practice.

The adepts' quarters were in the west wing of the building complex. In comparison to the entrance halls, with their stone floors covered in geometric patterns, pillars, and sculpted wooden doors, the living quarters lacked exuberance and sophistication. Plain wooden floors, clean, but showing the wear that came with time, plain white walls —at least freshly painted, from what Koshmarnyk could tell —and unassuming doors with no decorations except for the plaques in the middle announcing the resident adepts' names.

According to one of Koshmarnyk's teachers, such plainness was intentional, as Gildya's founders had aimed to reiterate that all adepts contributing to the organization's progress and wealth were equal. Perhaps it was meant this way—maybe it even *was* so back when the first adepts joined their efforts for the common good—but then there was the council that elevated some adepts above the others, nowadays rarely doing so with merit and value in mind. Politics penetrated most aspects of Gildya's activity, causing the west wing's lack of splendor to be a sad reminder of past ideals. Adepts could have decorated the bare corridors, but perhaps they wanted to keep the illusion of their founders' dream still being alive—with the minimal effort of keeping one wing of the building plain.

Several flights of stairs and identical corridors later, Koshmarnyk knocked on Davshil's door, and soon enough the adept's tired face appeared in its crack.

"To what do I owe such a late visit?" Davshil asked, letting Koshmarnyk in.

"You haven't heard about the walls?"

The room was much like Koshmarnyk remembered from his previous visit to Davshil's quarters, even if this time he was viewing it from the doorway instead of a window ledge.

"The council was on it the whole afternoon," Davshil said. "We can't figure out what's wrong with them. We followed your blueprints closely... unless someone decided to add 'improvements' to their assigned batch."

Koshmarnyk appreciated that Davshil refrained from a more direct insinuation that there must have been an error in the blueprints. "We believe that there might be sabotage involved," he replied. "I've been to the walls and checked several faulty devices myself. The damage is too random to be caused by a design flaw."

"But... saboteurs?" Davshil shook his head. "No one would be stupid enough to want demonlings ravaging the city."

"There are those stupid enough to take coin for a task without asking important questions," Koshmarnyk said. "Others might see it as a chance to change things in the city, disregarding the severity of the demon threat. There are

Tivarashans and Westerners as well, and they would care little about Kaighal's destruction if they can claim its ruins."

He knew better than to mention Mayetti's involvement with the Western Kingdom, since the deceptive adept was already dead, and Koshmarnyk had no proof other than his own word. Gildya would sooner choose to discard an inner threat than believe him.

"I prepared some adjustments to the device that might make it harder to sabotage it," Koshmarnyk continued as Davshil remained silent, "but I'm open to Gildya's suggestions as well. By now, I'm sure some adepts might have ideas of their own." He took a bunch of folded pages from the bag slung across his body.

Davshil accepted them. "How certain you are it's sabotage?"

"I have no proof, if that's what you're asking," Koshmarnyk replied. "But I'd be surprised if anyone finds a construction flaw in the device." He hesitated, before adding, "Besides, this happened in Devanshari as well—our demonic ally said so." No need to mention Kamira had her own source as well. "They couldn't breach the barrier the Devanshari artifact created, so they resorted to subterfuge. And as diverse and often divided as Kaighal is, the demons wouldn't have a hard time finding willing helpers in the city."

"At least you aren't throwing accusations at Gildya," Davshil remarked bitterly.

"Gildya is pulling its weight in the defense effort," Koshmarnyk offered in a noncommittal manner. Had he any evidence of Mayetti's involvement with the Westerners and Myrkan, he would not be so diplomatic. "If any saboteurs get caught, we will find out the truth. Until then, we have enough enemies without making more with empty accusations."

Davshil nodded. "I'll let the council know about the new threat and pass your blueprints to the adepts responsible for constructing the devices. Last time I checked, the council was still having a meeting behind closed doors, so it might not be until morning before they hear about it and make any decisions."

"I understand," Koshmarnyk said. "I'll be on my way, then, and await a message from you if any is necessary. Be well."

"You too."

Koshmarnyk left without delay as Davshil's passing remark made him think of the other reason he'd gone to Gildya in person—the evidence he needed to expose any and all traitors.

If Davshil was right, and the council was still discussing things—and likely making little progress—it meant that Ervan would be occupied for a little longer... and Koshmarnyk would bet he still lived in the same quarters, not far from Davshil's room.

There weren't many guards in the west wing—most kept watch at the few entrances to the living quarters—so there was little risk someone would spot him. He made his way down the corridor and stopped by the door that bore Ervan's name on the plaque.

Without hesitation, Koshmarnyk knocked. If the council had already finished its meeting and Ervan was back in his quarters, Koshmarnyk could use the news of saboteurs as an excuse for visiting.

No one opened the door, and from what he could tell, no one moved about the room either. He knocked again. No answer. Ervan could already be asleep, but Koshmarnyk had to take that risk.

From what he remembered, most locks in the living quarters weren't sophisticated. The adepts trusted their guards, and back when he was still part of Gildya, at least several times he'd caught apprentices picking locks to his teachers' quarters, sometimes to set up a prank, and sometimes to simply prove they could.

But the lock on Ervan's door looked complex and new. The adept must have something to protect... or hide. Trying to pick it would take time, and Koshmarnyk had to ensure nobody saw him snooping around Ervan's quarters. Brute force would leave marks, raising the adept's suspicion, but it was a faster and surer way to get in.

Without more delay, he closed his hand around the handle. His strength, speed, and other abilities had never disappeared, despite what Myrkan did to him, but his body was still that of a human, and the freshly healed wounds put more strain on it than he'd hoped for. But, in the end, the handle lost the battle, and the door creaked open. Koshmarnyk slipped in, holding it closed.

Even dressed in a falling darkness, Ervan's room was exactly how Koshmarnyk remembered: clean and tidy, with everything of importance hidden from incidental guests. With the amount of cabinets by the walls and the drawers in Ervan's massive desk, it would take Koshmarnyk a long time to find anything worthwhile, but he had little choice.

He took a chair and put it against the broken door, forcing it to stay closed. If any passersby didn't pay too much attention going through the corridor, they would likely miss the damage to the handle, and if someone tried to open the door, the noise of the pushed chair would give Koshmarnyk enough time to act.

With that in mind, he cracked one of the windows open.

Like most adepts' quarters, Ervan's rooms overlooked a small side street, and so late in the day, there weren't many people walking by. With the darkness falling and only a few lamps, Koshmarnyk should be able to make his way out unnoticed. Of course, in a rush, the three-story climb down could prove challenging and noisier than he'd like, but if it turned out too much of a problem, he could always climb *up* and make his way across Gildya's roof before finding a more suitable place to descend.

With his escape route plotted, Koshmarnyk rushed to the desk, betting that Ervan would keep the most important things close. He hesitated when he looked at the desk lamp. It wasn't dark enough to affect his movements, but he'd have to strain to read any document, and without knowing what exactly he was looking for, he had to be able to get through any writing quickly. It seemed that light was yet another risk he had to take.

Koshmarnyk turned the knob on the lamp, allowing the magic from the imbued stone flow just enough to result in a faint glow. With the lamps outside, in the corridor, shining bright, hopefully no one would notice it, or they'd think it was Ervan who lit it.

Koshmarnyk went for the drawers first. Their locks were no match for his strength, but their content disappointed. Several blueprints proved that Ervan hadn't entirely forgotten an adept's trade, and Koshmarnyk gave a nod to the complex designs he would gladly inspect thoroughly, had he time for it, but they gave no indication of Ervan's shady dealings. Several cryptic notes with coin amounts listed in neat handwriting were more promising...

After a closer look, Koshmarnyk discarded them as well, because without any revealing details, these could be anything from expenses for a mistress Ervan wanted to keep secret from Gildya to paying off a thug to sabotage a fellow adept's work. Undoubtedly, the documents pointed to something Ervan would rather not reveal, but they *proved* nothing.

The drawers that weren't locked held even less exciting content. Blank pages for future notes or blueprints, some private correspondence that Koshmarnyk skimmed in the vain hope of finding a clue, and carefully logged requests to Gildya's quartermasters, all inconspicuous enough to suggest Ervan had nothing to hide when it came to his work as an adept.

With little hope, Koshmarnyk glanced at the cabinets. If the desk held no answers, it was unlikely they would give him any either. His risky escapade was turning out disappointing, and he hesitated. Reason demanded he leave before someone discovered him, but something still tugged at his instincts. Koshmarnyk couldn't quite describe the feeling that demanded he stay, but he knew he wasn't done with Ervan's quarters yet. Perhaps the sly adept didn't keep his secrets where he knew a thief would look. If they were so dangerous that they could reveal his dealings with the demons outside the city, they would be in another place, not a desk or cabinets.

Koshmarnyk checked the desk's exterior, searching for any indication of hidden compartments or mechanisms, then he repeated the process along the room's walls. Unless Ervan was a craftier adept than Koshmarnyk thought, there was no secret stash within the room. That left the bedroom.

As soon as Koshmarnyk approached the door, the nagging feeling intensified. Magic! He entered the dark space with caution, already knowing it had something familiar in it, but contrary to his expectations, no trap sprang at him. Instead, an intense wave of magic hit him, and he finally placed its origin.

The bedroom was full of Myrkan's energy.

Koshmarnyk might not have the sensitivity to magic that an arcanist boasted, but one of the imbued stones in his body helped to compensate for it. He could sense magic around, be it a circle or a device powered by the stones, but it was the time he'd spent close to Myrkan that made him recognize the origin of the energy in Ervan's room.

There wasn't much furniture to search, and, using the faint light coming from the other room, Koshmarnyk rummaged through it in a rush, eager to discover proof of Ervan's part in a conspiracy. The magical trace of Myrkan's presence might be proof enough for Koshmarnyk, but Gildya's council would need something tangible. Otherwise, they'd likely be more willing to believe Ervan's lies than Koshmarnyk's accusations.

Nothing in the room gave him what he wanted. Even the nightstand, where the energy seemed the strongest, contained neither clue nor proof.

Before Koshmarnyk could search for hidden compartments, the sound of the door being kicked in, along with the rumble of the falling chair that blocked it, announced that his break-in had been discovered.

WALKING to the city walls and back took more time than she had, but Kamira insisted on daily appearances among the defenders. She talked to King Allyv, she asked men and women on the battlements for their insights, and she made a spectacle of magic, wiping out waves of attacking demonlings. It could hardly break the siege with so many more creatures coming, but the people of Kaighal had to see her doing her part... doing *something*. If she never peeked out of the Towers, she would be a ruler, not a leader.

At the same time, every stroll reminded her that she couldn't enjoy anonymity anymore. Even though she wore her plain clothes, the people around recognized her and stepped to the side, fear or respect on their faces. Perhaps if she stayed on the wall longer than for an inspection, and shared the defenders' sweat and blood, some of them would come to see her as a comrade instead of the first archmage, but she knew better than to indulge in such fantasies. Kaighal had many able men and women willing to guard its walls, and the city needed a leader who not only would make decisions, but also come up with a plan to save them all.

"Archmage, I have to speak with you!" a woman behind her called out with urgency.

Kamira stopped and turned. The woman wore flashy clothes of mediocre quality. It was the type of outfit worn by commoners who were trying to elevate their status in the eyes of others. Perhaps she was an impoverished merchant still trying to keep up appearances.

"What is it about?" Kamira asked. The way the woman looked and moved tugged at her instincts, but with everyone else watching, she couldn't walk away. They needed to see that the archmage had time to listen to them.

The woman approached, no hesitation in her steps. "The demons are going to—"

Kamira almost fell for her act, but a glint in the woman's eye warned her. No blade she could see came at her, but she still called her magic forth into a barrier. The sounds of someone striking her barrier and a cry of pain drew her attention, and when she turned, a man staggered backward in the street, cradling his arm to his chest. On the ground just outside the barrier lay the dagger undoubtedly meant for her.

People in the area scattered to a safe distance, far enough to retreat but close enough to keep watching. None were warriors who would instinctively react with aid, only townspeople, and they likely trusted that a powerful arcanist would have no problem handling the threat, but in the distance, someone was calling for guards.

Then two more assailants stepped out of the crowd and circled her with anticipation while the wounded man backed away.

Their movements told Kamira it wasn't their first assassination, but they weren't even half the threat of a Darethal's Thorn. After enough encounters with Kaighal's thugs and ne'er-do-wells, Kamira was confident that she could make this a demonstration, as opposed to staying safe behind her barrier. Many local thugs would think twice before taking the job if they heard the archmage single-handedly took down four opponents.

She ignored the small voice in her head whispering that Veelk had been by her side for most previous encounters. After all, Veelk, though protective and eager to fight, had never doubted her capabilities, and she'd never hear the end of it if she cowered behind her barrier instead of disposing of her opponents.

The man further away fished a small orb from his outfit. Kamira couldn't tell whether it was poison like the Thorns used or a fiery one like Veelk had come across, but it didn't matter. She'd rather not make it common knowledge that she could withstand poison, and a fire explosion could injure people in the street.

Kamira's barrier dropped as a thin spike of ice

manifested near her outstretched hand, then vanished, leaving just enough of a trail of frosty air to follow its path. The man's head snapped back, and both he and the orb dropped to the ground. The orb rolled across the cobblestone until finding its final resting place in a divot, still closed.

The swipe of a thin blade cut close to Kamira's arm as she turned and stepped back from the lunging woman, but only far enough to then swat the advancing attacker with pure, condensed magic bound around the same arm the woman had come so close to rending. The attacker shot down the street, rolling to a stop as tendrils of electricity arced around her, and then the bolt struck.

The stench of charred flesh rose as people jumped away and shielded themselves from the clap of thunder that accompanied the bolt.

In other circumstances, Kamira would have ensured the woman's unconsciousness or death before turning her attention away, but there was no Veelk to watch her back. As she spun, she expected to be dealing with a blade in her face, but the man had abandoned his assault for the orb.

Kamira cursed under her breath.

Long ice shards shot forth again. The man dove away from her toward the orb just before the shards whipped over him to shatter against the cobblestones.

It would be better if instead of hurling easy-to-avoid projectiles she used fire or electricity, but she wasn't sure how the orb would react. The last thing she needed was her own magic activating it.

With few options, Kamira called upon Veranesh's energy, and drenched the whole street in a sudden downpour. Drops as big as Kamira's fists pounded everything, and onlookers fled, seeking shelter wherever available. Stalls wavered, canopies gave way, and everything was instantly soaked, but the thug maintained his footing. He grinned at Kamira, holding out the orb as if it was a trophy.

Kamira grinned back. She wasn't done yet.

She dropped her arms from reaching toward the sky to point directly at him, and by then it was too late. The magic had already changed, and a bewildered expression was etched onto the man's face as his entire body snapped rigid in a sheath of ice. Kamira didn't express too much of her satisfaction as the frozen statue fell.

With the threat gone, Kamira turned back to the woman, confident that she had either escaped or was dead, since no knives were whipping about.

When she turned, it became obvious the woman was quite dead, as Veelk was retrieving the thinner blade of his spear from her body. His arched eyebrow suggested he had a remark ready about Kamira's carelessness, and she had to appreciate that he kept it to himself instead of dishing it out with so many of Kaighal's citizens around.

Behind Veelk, two city guards were approaching, and Kamira immediately addressed them. "These three people attacked me." She almost said four, but the last member of the group was nowhere to be seen. "The fourth ran away. His hand is wounded. I trust you can handle whatever investigation is necessary?" She'd love to collect information herself, but those thugs likely knew little beyond the face of a middleman, likely another hired thug, because she doubted that whoever had hired them would have done so in person. She'd waste time chasing clues that were unlikely to lead to the real threat.

"Yes, archmage!" one of the guards replied immediately.

It didn't escape Kamira that they both eyed Veelk with a mix of suspicion and concern.

"He's with me," she said. The playful side of her nature demanded she tease the broad-shouldered warrior with remarks of what a lousy protector he was arriving so late, but the circumstances demanded she act like an archmage. *By the pact!* She hadn't realized how much she'd missed Veelk's company.

"And be careful with the orb in the frozen hand. It might be a device that spits out poison or fire. Perhaps someone from Gildya could assist you." She hoped the adepts would appreciate being put in charge, even if it was a minor matter. "If there's anything else you need, send word to the Towers," she added as she walked away.

Neither of the guards tried to stop her, and she sent Veelk a quick smile. Being the first archmage of Kaighal *did* have some advantages.

"I thought you solved the problem of assassins," Veelk said once they put some distance between them and the site of the attack.

"I solved the problem with the Thorns," Kamira replied. "That doesn't mean some lowlifes won't take a contract from a disgruntled Gildya member or a former high mage."

Veelk gave her one of his grins, and that alone brought relief to her tiredness and frustration. "Maybe I should follow you around everywhere? No one will try anything with a big warrior always by your side."

If only he could! Kamira bit her tongue before agreeing to the idea. They both knew she didn't need protection, and Veelk's skills were of use elsewhere. "I need you on the walls." She didn't hide her regret as she said it.

To her disappointment, Veelk didn't tease her by questioning her fighting prowess. Instead, he gave her a solemn nod.

· · ·

HE'S CHANGED.

She didn't catch the bitter thought in time, and it soured her mood even more. Even if he still acted like the Veelk she'd traveled with for so long, the subtle shift in his behavior told her he considered the mess they were in as much his responsibility as hers.

There was also the matter of Lefna, the powdered imbued stones being now more than just a small part of him, and perhaps even the last brush with death, one that would see him die alone in the desert. Until recent events, they'd always faced dangers together and could find comfort in either dying together or hoping the other would survive.

"Just when I thought you couldn't get any grumpier, you make all the effort to prove me wrong," Veelk said, his voice almost as playful as in the past.

She had no good reply to that, at least not one that didn't venture into topics Veelk likely wouldn't want to discuss, so she rolled her eyes. "I think you just forgot how grumpy I truly am."

The broad smile she received in response filled her with hope that maybe there was enough of the old Veelk left, unmarred by all the grueling experiences, and he wasn't putting on a show just for her benefit.

"You know," he said, that comfortingly familiar smile never leaving his face, "there are other cities like Kaighal out there. No need to stick to this one after the siege."

Her eyes widened as the meaning of the words dawned on her. Kaighal was their home, but it was also a home they'd chosen. When all this mess was cleaned up, and when the city didn't need them anymore, they could set out again... find another home.

"What if I decide I like being the first archmage?" she couldn't help teasing.

"You can be the first archmage somewhere else," Veelk replied in an instant, making it clear he'd never really considered her actually liking the position of power. "If it makes you better, I can even call you archmage when I'm in a good mood."

Kamira chuckled, not bothered that passersby threw her curious glances. "Were you on your way to the Towers?" she changed the topic. No matter how much she wanted to indulge more in their usual banter, she had duties as the first archmage, and Veelk had taken it upon himself to help the city as well.

"To the walls. Zelna and Mawi kept watch there through the night, so they deserve some rest," Veelk replied, serious expression back on his face. "I was headed there when I heard someone calling for guards, and arrived right in time to see that you still haven't learned a thing about fighting."

"Why learn fighting when I have magic?" She arched her eyebrow.

"To not leave opponents behind your back alive?"

Kamira grinned. "Is that the only fault you found?"

He shook his head. "I don't remember you fishing for compliments so crudely. But you'll deserve one when you figure out how to get rid of the demons."

She became serious too. "We might just have to fight them," she said quietly. "The longer we wait, the more they might wear us down, or find someone skilled enough to kill one or all of us."

"We took one demon down, only the two of us," Veelk said. "Now we also have Koshmarnyk, Zelna, Mawi, and the whole city to help us."

"And our own demon," she added when he didn't mention Fyertash.

Veelk's expression was skeptical. "If we don't have to kill him next."

The hill and the Towers came into view, and Kamira didn't bother with reassurances about Fyertash's loyalty. Veelk trusted the demon enough for now, and his vigilance could prove useful if Fyertash decided to turn on them later.

"Don't get yourself killed on the walls," she said as a farewell. "It would be a waste if I took all the glory for single-handedly defeating both demons."

The wide grin he gave her made it clear that, even gravely wounded, Veelk still wouldn't pass on a chance to take on such powerful foes. As he walked back down the street, she turned toward the Towers with her resolve strengthened and spirit lifted.

Tiredness only aggravated Ervan's frustration as he made his way through Gildya's halls. The council was weak and fearful, and it seemed that no one else would back him when he spoke of negotiating with the attacking demons. Even the sabotage of the protective devices Ervan had so carefully organized didn't push other adepts into action, choosing a solution that he presented as best. Instead, they talked about how to improve the devices' design to make them more resilient, pondered whether the Towers would blame Gildya for some construction failure, and discussed at length all the possible candidates to take the free seat in the council. The seat that Ervan made free...

That made him think of Mayetti, and for this once, he regretted having her killed. Not only would her survival have taken one topic off the council's agenda, but the cunning adept would also back his demands for negotiations with the demon. After all, she was the one who had enabled him to communicate with Myrkan.

No, she was better dead. As much as Ervan's tiredness and frustration made him long for a capable ally, Mayetti was too dangerous to leave breathing. Not only could she expose Ervan's subtle attempts to get rid of Koshmarnyk, but she also had ties to the Western Kingdom. Even if Ervan wasn't sure of her involvement's nature, he knew enough of such bonds to avoid getting tangled in them.

Besides, Mayetti was simply too smart. She weaved her own plots, into which he had few insights, and he couldn't discard the possibility that when he outlived his usefulness to her, she'd have disposed of him just like he did to her.

Self-reassurances could only help so much, though, when Ervan was losing his footing and the battle against the council's stubbornness. Myrkan was growing impatient, and the demonling attacks at the city had become fiercer and fiercer. Come to think of it, Ervan's very actions might have been making it easier for the demons to claim the city without any need for negotiations.

A wave of cold fear passed through his body. If he didn't hurry, he'd be left without any gains, having handed the demons their victory.

These thoughts haunted him all the way back to his quarters, but apart from ruining his mood, they offered no solution. Ervan brushed the stone in his pocket. Myrkan would grow even more impatient, or worse, the demon would stop talking to him.

The pressure of finding a way to turn that near-defeat into a victory weighed heavy on him as he approached his quarters. Perhaps a full night of rest would bring him fresh ideas.

Before he reached for the handle, Ervan froze. Anyone

not paying attention would have missed it, but the door was ever so slightly ajar.

An intruder!

Adrenaline pumped through Ervan's veins as he considered his choices. The best would be to enter immediately, exposing the thief and preventing him or her from running away, but a one-on-one confrontation could end up in the thief's favor. Ervan was no fighter, so it would be easy to knock him down and dash out the door. And if the intruder had a knife or other weapon...

Even the adrenaline couldn't counter the fear that overcame Ervan's limbs. Approaching his own quarters, Ervan had hardly paid attention to being quiet, and the thief might have already heard his footsteps. A vision of a dark figure moving inside, taking the best spot to remain unseen and deliver a deadly strike, overtook his mind, and without any more doubts, he turned and walked away, trying to keep his pace similar to the one he had before.

Only when he'd made it far enough down the corridor did he allow himself to rush. If he wanted a chance of catching the thief, he had to be decisive.

Two guards stood at the entrance to the west wing. They looked bored, and Ervan hesitated. It would be better to get someone with a less lax attitude to their duties, but more delay could allow the thief to get away.

"Adept," one of the guards said when he noticed Ervan wasn't just passing by. They both straightened their backs.

"You two, with me. There's a thief in my quarters." He didn't wait for their questions, already turning and heading back into the west wing.

With the guards' heavy steps behind him, it would be impossible to approach quietly, so Ervan rushed through the corridor until he reached his door. It was exactly how he'd left it, and the faint glow of light was still coming from the inside. His heart picked up its pace in anticipation: the thief hadn't left yet!

At his signal, one of the guards kicked the door open, and they both rushed in. Safe behind their backs, Ervan followed inside. The lamp on the desk provided barely enough light to see, but the chair lying on the floor and the open drawers of his desks confirmed that someone had been combing through his documents. But whoever it was, he or she must have made their exit already.

The open window suggested an escape route, and even though one of the guards checked Ervan's bedroom, the adept had little hope of learning anything. The anticipation faded, replaced by concern. He had been careful to conceal his various unscrupulous activities, leaving as little trace as possible, but he could have overlooked something. The last thing he needed was scrutiny from the council if a rival brought some of his secrets to light.

"Did you leave the windows open, sir?" The other guard returned. "The one in the bedroom is open as well."

It seemed the thief was more than prepared: first the intruder opened the window in the office, in case sneaking out through the door was impossible, and then did likewise in the bedroom.

Ervan's fingers closed over the stone in his pocket and relief washed over him. Had he left it in his nightstand, trusting the lock on his door, not only could he have lost the means to communicate with Myrkan, but also made it clear that he'd committed a crime far more serious than some underhanded dealings with the local thugs and smugglers. Even the thought that most thieves would overlook a plain-looking stone couldn't comfort his shattered composure.

"Leave," he ordered the guards before they could see him lose his calm, "and find someone to repair my door."

If they took offense to this menial task, they didn't show it.

As soon as they left, Ervan inspected the door, but as he suspected, the mechanism had been forcefully broken. Had the thief picked the lock instead, the door could be closed again, instead of revealing an intrusion. That didn't seem like a work of an experienced thief—

Alluvendran! It struck him unexpectedly, but the longer he thought about it, the more sense it made. With all the stones in Alluvendran's body, breaking forcefully through the door would be child's play for him, and the council had given him access to Gildya's buildings. It was enough for him to make an excuse of visiting an adept, even Ervan himself, to gain access to the west wing if anyone questioned him.

Ervan rubbed his suddenly sweaty hands against his robe. If Alluvendran was poking around, he must suspect something. Perhaps Mayetti had revealed information on Ervan's involvement when they were both Myrkan's prisoners for some time. Or, for all Ervan knew, Alluvendran might have been searching blindly, driven by the need for revenge after Ervan saw him chained and imprisoned a decade earlier.

He looked around the room in search of anything that would confirm the thief's identity. Without proof, he wouldn't be able to convince the council to act. They were more likely to doubt his words than find the courage to take any steps.

That thought gave him pause. He was becoming like them—too scared and too cautious to act. If he had barged into the room instead of seeking the guards' assistance, he would have caught the thief red-handed, and the council would have to believe his word. Now, with the guards already involved, he couldn't even lie that he indeed saw Alluvendran leaving through the window.

Resigned, Ervan closed both windows. Even if Alluvendran couldn't find any proof, he likely had enough suspicions now to watch Ervan closely. That meant watching his words in public and keeping an eye on spies lurking in the shadows, and it would make the game Ervan was playing even more dangerous.

And as much as he shuddered at the thought, if he wanted to ensure his win, he would have to act fast and decisively, taking little time for preparations and considerations.

8

As Kamira finished the binding spell, she inspected Veelk, who was sitting relaxed in a chair in her chamber. Nearby, Koshmarnyk watched them with curiosity, having been subjected to the same spell earlier on. She might have been vague when talking to Fyertash, but the truth was that she had to know if the spell affected her friends.

"Are you sure you felt nothing?" she asked when Veelk showed no reaction, just like Koshmarnyk moments before. "No magic strings reaching out for you? No energy binding your moves?"

Veelk stretched lazily. "I told you the demon had played you. You shouldn't trust anything that scoundrel says." There was no reprimand in his voice, only playfulness, as if he was challenging her to abandon her concerns.

She nodded, not ready to give in to the lighter mood just yet. At least she could stop worrying that her best friend and her lover could be as vulnerable as she was when dealing with demons. Out of the three of them, she was the only one who could be bound by the demonic spell.

Veelk hissed with disappointment and looked at Koshmarnyk. "I thought you were supposed to make her happier, not grumpier."

The adept shrugged, making it clear he wouldn't be dragged into any squabble. When he looked at Kamira, his expression was serious. "At least you don't have to worry about us."

"I still have the whole city to worry about," she muttered out of habit, and as a reward, she received Veelk's snort. That brought a small smile to her face, because in the past, he always complained that she complained too much.

"And the plan...?" Koshmarnyk asked.

At first, she wanted to tell them that she was working out the details and soon she'd have answers, but before she spoke, she looked in their faces. They weren't simple citizens of Kaighal, eager to hear that she had everything under control and the siege would end soon. They didn't need hope. She could give them the truth.

"I can't think of anything solid," she said. "Any idea I come up with requires either too much risk or both demons to fall for it."

"And Myrkan's not stupid," Koshmarnyk summed up. "No matter what you do, he'll suspect deception."

"Then we use no deception," Veelk said. "You said it yourself back in the street—we might just have to fight them."

"Without a plan? Without a solid advantage? Without knowing if we even have a chance?" Her barrage of questions rang with every bit of desperation she felt. Their plan didn't have to be perfect, but they needed one. Otherwise she could be making a decision to send them all to their deaths.

"Wouldn't be the first time and the first demon," Veelk replied casually.

"If we wait longer, Ervan might do something that will make any plan impossible," Koshmarnyk added.

Kamira grimaced. The revelations of Gildya's council secretly dealing with Myrkan, which Koshmarnyk had shared with them earlier, only added to the feeling of urgency. Even if Ervan was acting without the council's knowledge, sooner or later he would enact whatever scheme he was concocting. With the barriers failing, any bigger sabotage could mean the city's fall.

She took a deep breath. "Give me one more day. Maybe I'll figure it out."

"I'll let Zelna know to preserve her strength, so that she's ready." Veelk rose from his seat. "You two should get some rest," he added without conviction, as if he knew neither would listen. Before he left, Veelk gave her a quick hug. "Don't worry... too much."

"He's right, you know," Koshmarnyk said when they were alone. "If Fyertash helps, we aren't at a disadvantage. Both you and he can do the binding, and Veelk, Zelna, and I can keep them off you."

"And who's going to deal with the demonlings and their masters?" she couldn't help asking.

"You forgot we have the whole city full of people ready to fight for their home."

She nodded slowly. Weeks in the first archmage position still hadn't removed her instincts to rely only on herself and a few chosen allies.

Koshmarnyk closed her in his embrace, and his presence was enough of a reassurance. She couldn't help noticing the magic within him becoming stronger, as if the regrowing stones had regained their power.

"Do you want me to talk to the council about Ervan?" she asked quietly, reluctant to ruin the intimate moment.

Koshmarnyk shook his head. "Without proof, they'll see it only as hatred between us. Ervan was one of the adepts who made my imprisonment possible, so if I speak against him, they'll think I'm simply seeking revenge. Or that you're using my need for revenge to sow discord in Gildya."

"But if we do nothing, he might convince the council to side with Myrkan and Derazin."

A playful smile was a rare occurrence on his face, so she cherished it as he said, "Then we should make sure they have no one to side with, right?"

Wise enough to not ruin the mood with her grim thoughts, she leaned on him, enjoying the embrace. The feeling of peacefulness was unfamiliar, and Kamira couldn't help wondering whether she could truly settle somewhere, but she didn't let the thought linger. Even if the battle for Kaighal was won, there would be other matters she had to take care of and her part of the deal with Zyreshi to fulfill. Any hope for something stable would only get in the way, enhancing her ever-present concerns over her friends' lives.

"Do you think you could take Veelk's advice and get some rest?" Koshmarnyk whispered into her ear. "Or do you plan on worrying all night long?"

She nestled in his arms as if she intended to fall asleep there. "Only if you keep holding me like that."

Tomorrow... Tomorrow she'd be the archmage again, unyielding and confident, and ready to take on the demon army. But tonight, she'd indulge in moments of selfishness and perhaps a dream of an unexpectedly tranquil future.

Without a word, Koshmarnyk lifted her, his strong grip proving his wounds had already healed, and carried her to the bedroom.

~

BAXAYALANS MIGHT NOT BE ACCUSTOMED to vast forests, but they moved through the woods with such stealth and confidence that Ryell could hardly believe their homeland was mostly plains and rolling hills. This scouting unit had to have been chosen for their specific skills, and even though the forest around them posed no threat, they still kept to their rules. They traveled in a loose formation, and Captain Seraine sent out forward scouts to ensure their passage would be unnoticed.

"This forest is on the Tivarashan border," she explained when Ryell asked about those precautions. "And though we're still on lands considered part of Kaighal, there are no border stones to mark where one country starts and the other begins, so it's likely that we'll come across a Tivarashan patrol that decided to venture south further than usual."

Ryell shook his head. The idea that neighboring lands would not decide on firm borders seemed strange to him. On the other hand, if both sides were in agreement on which settlements belonged to which country, it still created a border, if a blurry one.

He immediately thought of home. The borders of the kingdom of Devanshari were firmly set to the distance that Hajihali's power reached, but even then, some people chose to expand the kingdom's lands, dealing with the magic deprivation either by regularly visiting regions closer to Hajihali, or by taking the essence, the distilled power of the artifact. Little did they know that after the kingdom's fall, everybody would become reliant on it.

He held off a sigh. Hajihali's protection was also the first line of defense when the demons came... Until the general at the palace realized that the ancient artifact, no matter how much people believed in its infinite power, couldn't hold a barrier of that size for long. With each week, they moved it closer and closer to the capital, leaving hardly any time for people to flee. So many were forced to abandon their livelihoods to seek shelter within the protective barrier.

The unpleasant memories crept in the corners in his mind, and Ryell forced his focus outward instead of inward, but his surroundings didn't help. The forest on the Tivarashan border reminded him of home even more.

He glanced at Captain Seraine, desperate for any question he could ask.

Before he grasped for any topic that would steer his thoughts away from Devanshari, two scouts emerged from the bushes, and their concerned expressions got everyone's attention.

"We've found a Tivarashan scout," said a scrawny, short woman with her light brown hair in a tight ponytail. "There's a camp ahead, and it's empty but not abandoned. And a big one, too."

Captain Seraine became serious. "How big?"

"Enough for a whole army," the other scout chimed in. If Ryell remembered correctly, this wiry and agile man's name was Fyrwol.

"Maneuvers?" Ryell asked.

"That would be unusual for Tivarashan forces. They usually keep deeper into their lands. And if they wanted to claim Kaighal, they wouldn't be that far west," the captain replied. "We need to know more." She looked around at her people. "We'll go through the camp until we find the commander's tent. Quietly, so dispose of anyone who could raise the alarm. Groups of two... no, three." She turned to

Ryell. "I can't ask you to join in our fight and kill people who did you no wrong."

Sudden fear clenched Ryell's heart. He'd just found worthy companions, and he wasn't ready to part ways. The Light had guided him to them, and perhaps it was also forcing him to make a choice. He could leave and continue down the path of uncertainty and indecisiveness, or he could finally take a step to truly abandon his old life. Otherwise he'd just be clinging to the scraps of it, to the uncomfortable memories and grim thoughts.

"You're right that the Tivarashan did me no wrong," he said, though the mere thought of Kamira made him wonder whether it was indeed true. "But you welcomed me in your company, offered food, safety, and information. I can't travel with you and at the same time refuse to aid you when you need it." He straightened his back in a soldier-like posture and looked her in the eye. "Captain, if you would have me, my sword and skills are at your service. I've spent a good portion of my life in the woods, so I'm sure I can be of help, and if being your companion means spilling Tivarashan blood, so be it."

The captain's expression suggested that she liked what he'd said, and several of her people gave him nods of approval as well.

"Very well," Seraine said. "You'll be with me and Zimfe. The rest of you, split into groups and start making your way through the camp. Collect any information that could be of value and kill anyone in the way if they are alone. Keep an eye out for more lookouts, too. If you find the command post, let me know. We'll use our usual signals."

The squad divided into groups in an instant with an efficiency that made Ryell long to be a true part of it. He was already standing by the captain, and the man called Zimfe joined them soon enough. He was taller and with broader shoulders than most of the Baxayalans around, and though the man wore a scout's outfit, Ryell had no doubt that Zimfe was a skilled swordsman as well. One who could protect the captain if needed and stand his ground against a seasoned warrior.

Everyone took off, spreading out, and Captain Seraine followed at a distance, with Zimfe and Ryell at her sides. With his hand on the hilt of the sword and his steps light on the soft forest floor, Ryell enjoyed the anticipation that invigorated his body. He hadn't experienced such a rush for a long time, even before the demons attacked, because his last years in Devanshari had been dedicated solely to palace duty. To be in the forest again, with a clear goal and dedicated companions, meant washing all the bad memories away.

As the camp scattered among the trees came into view, Ryell didn't hesitate. He chose the right path.

FYERTASH SAT PERCHED at the edge of the broken dome. The spot not only allowed him a discreet peek into what was going in the chamber below—now empty, thus giving him some privacy—but also provided a good view of the city, including its surroundings. The distance was too great for Fyertash to see his adversaries, but he knew they were to the south, hiding behind the hordes of asayalari and their faithful pactees.

He shifted with unease. His little trick with binding had worked well and bought them time, but the confrontation was coming, and so far, Kamira seemed no closer to coming up with a plan than she was when the other kanyalari arrived.

If it wasn't his own life at stake, he'd find some satisfaction in her struggle, but on the other hand, he was no better than her. He had no cunning plan of his own to offer. And the longer they waited, the more likely Myrkan would find enough human lackeys to do his bidding, and put his own plan into motion.

Fyertash grimaced at the memory of the siege on the other side of the waters humans called "sea." At first, it was enough to keep pushing forward to weaken the barrier surrounding the human lands, but as the protected area shrank, the power of the barrier grew, and no amount of force seemed to break it. Yet, with Myrkan's schemes, one day the protection became weaker, and then even weaker...

Even though Kamira claimed that his spy was dead, the city had plenty of willing fools who would carry out Myrkan's orders.

Fyertash clutched the dome's edge, his claws grating against stone, at the very thought that there might be no plan to be had, and the only solution was to go to battle before their enemies chose their time and place. This prospect tugged at his instincts, bringing a slight tremble to his hands and a grimace to his face.

For centuries, he'd worked hard to never experience fear again, and now it was creeping up on him again. If he was to make a guess, Kamira battled similar feelings, though he would bet that her concerns centered around her allies rather her own wellbeing. To free Veranesh, she had put her own life at stake, so he wouldn't be surprised if she did so again for the city she cared for and for her friends. And if she did, Fyertash would have to do everything in his power to protect her... even die.

As long as Derazin fell before Fyertash did, it was an acceptable price, but the thought of being taken down by a petty kanyalari like Myrkan grated on his pride.

There had to be another way... Perhaps, in the end, Kamira would come up with a cunning plan. So far, she hadn't disappointed Veranesh's expectations, and she might yet surprise Fyertash.

The door to the chamber opened, and Fyertash immediately ensured his face expressed nothing and his muscles relaxed. He would not give any human the satisfaction of seeing him distraught or concerned, even if there were justified reasons for such emotions.

To his disappointment, it wasn't Kamira who walked in. Her presence would have gifted him a game or a duel of words, allowing him to put aside the grim prospects for the future, but instead, the visitor was his own pactee.

Irtan walked through the chamber casually and with a jovial smile, but the appearance of a content old man was a mask to fool everyone. Though Fyertash wasn't quick to admit it, Irtan's cunning could be on par with his own. Any other time, he would indulge in the satisfaction of having chosen such a fitting and capable pactee for himself, but now it only meant more frustration.

Irtan stopped in the middle of the chamber and looked up. "Care to spare time for your pactee?" he asked with a friendly smile. "I'm in need of your wisdom."

That, of course, meant fishing for knowledge that Fyertash wasn't necessarily willing to share. Yet his pactee had never disappointed him, and he owed the old man at least *some* answers.

He spread his wings and descended into the chamber.

Irtan waited for him to land then asked, "Veranesh isn't coming back, is he?"

"No." Fyertash had no reason to conceal the truth. With what had happened to Uganel not so long ago, the old man had to know yalari could not survive such an explosion of energy.

Irtan narrowed his eyes, cunning shining in them. "But Kamira still has her magic. If she made a pact with you, she wouldn't be that powerful anymore, so it has to be someone else... Had she sought the aid of the Four?"

"No," Fyertash said again, painfully aware that the word alone would not suffice. "She still has a pact with Veranesh. He isn't dead. He simply returned to Yalarethe." Even if his answer wasn't entirely accurate, it was close enough to the truth.

"How?"

"Not asking why?"

Irtan shrugged. "A yalari like him must have been itching to reclaim what he'd lost, none of which is here, in our world. So the only question left is *how*, but I have a feeling you will not be forthcoming about it."

If only he could be *less* forthcoming! Fyertash sighed. The more answers he gave, the more likely Irtan would be satisfied for the time being. Of course, he'd still look for more information, but any delay would be of benefit.

"When we die, we are reborn. It takes a while, but we return. If I die, you will not lose your pact."

"I see." Irtan still watched Fyertash intently as if searching for any sign of deception. "So there is no way to truly kill a yalari?"

The way he asked the question reassured Fyertash that the old man already had his guesses, and avoiding an answer would do more harm than good. Irtan was still his pactee, and a worthy one, all things considered, so Fyertash preferred to remain amicable. "I'm sure you already know there is, but I'd be a fool if I shared it with any human, including you."

Irtan arched his eyebrow. "Even Kamira?"

"Especially her." The grimace on Fyertash's face was genuine—he recalled how she'd outsmarted and bound him. And he hadn't even lied; had Kamira not known about the destruction spell already, he'd be in no rush to tell her. "Is that all the questions you have? As much as I am fond of you as my pactee, there are secrets yalari aren't willing to share with humans."

"Then maybe I should change the topic of the conversation," Irtan replied in a lighthearted manner that carried hints of both sarcasm and reprimand. "Though I suspect that you will be as unwilling to share information about Kamira as you were of other secrets."

"You are my pactee, and she is Veranesh's." Fyertash let ire ring in his voice. "By asking for her secrets, you're asking me to go against him, and I will not do that. Not even for you."

"Cunning." Irtan gave him a nod, joviality gone from his posture and tone. "Blame Veranesh for your unwillingness and flatter me by implying that had she made a pact with any other demon, you'd be more helpful. So, with flattery out of the way, what will be next—threats?"

Fyertash shook his head. "I've warned you once already."

"Indeed."

They stared each other down in silence for a few long heartbeats. In moments like that, Fyertash envied Myrkan's unstable and explosive nature, which allowed him to act on his emotions and deal with the consequences later. A pact severed and a swipe of Fyertash's claw would be enough to deal with the problem Irtan was becoming. Yet it would also mean depriving himself of the power advantage that came from their pact and disposing of one of the two truly skilled arcanists the city had, so Fyertash had to refuse himself the indulgence of a swift kill. And by coming to the chamber and asking questions so bluntly and openly, Irtan must have assumed the same: he was too valuable to be done away with, and if he lost his pact, he'd simply make another one. Many kanyalari would vie for someone like Irtan.

"I don't suppose you could settle for the position of the second most powerful man this once?" Fyertash asked.

Irtan smiled gently. "Have I ever?" He lifted his finger before Fyertash could speak. "But I can promise you that I'll wait till the city is safe. Perhaps, by then, the problem will have solved itself. Knowing Kamira, I wouldn't be surprised if she did something foolishly heroic and life-ending to save the city. I only have my guesses, of course, but somehow I think those two outside the walls aren't the first demons she's faced."

Fyertash narrowed his eyes, thinking back to his own confrontation with Kamira, but then it dawned on him: Uganel. Irtan suspected she'd had a hand in the events that led to his destruction.

"Very well," Fyertash replied. "We will speak again after the city is safe."

To his surprise, Irtan shook his head. "I'm not a fool either, and I remember your warning," he replied without his usual joviality. "When I decide to play my game, you'll be the last one to know."

With that, Irtan turned and walked out of the chamber.

9

Kamira might have kept up appearances, but with each passing day she felt the burden of taking on too much. When the high mages were in power, the Towers had nine archmages to divide duties among themselves, and the first archmage led and made decisions, not personally supervised almost every single task and solve every problem. Not to mention—the thought crooked her lip in a bitter smile—that the high mages didn't have to deal with a demon invasion.

Yet she hardly had anyone to share those burdens with. Archmages Irtan and Varessa took some duties upon themselves, but Kamira still couldn't bring herself to trust the old fox. Defending the city might be in Irtan's best interest, but that aside, he was not an ally, and if she allowed him closer, he'd be keener on learning her secrets than supporting her efforts.

And Varessa... Kamira had to admit that part of her reluctance stemmed from Varessa being a former high mage, but at the same time, Varessa showed little interest in anything beyond teaching. Even her duties as the Towers administrator centered on students and their welfare. If she could, she'd likely oppose sending those unschooled arcanists to the city walls, as if the siege could wait until everyone in the Towers mastered their new arts to a satisfactory level.

At least Fyertash was leaving Kamira be, as if he sensed she wasn't in the mood for his games.

She glanced up at the broken dome. The demon sat higher than his usual perch, at a spot from which he undoubtedly could see the city walls and the threat stretching beyond them. His hand, resting at the edge of the dome, moved every now and then, claws grating against the stone. Slow and not strong enough to leave scratch marks, those motions still revealed Fyertash's unease. He must be anxious, trapped in a city with no way out while two more powerful demons sought a way to get to him. As he'd said himself, any demon in his situation would rather flee than seek a confrontation he could not win.

Kamira sighed. Another task on her shoulders: find a way to deal with the threat before their enemies breached the city's defenses. If only she knew how to separate Myrkan and Derazin... With the help of the arcanists and guards, Veelk, Koshmarnyk, and Zelna could likely keep one of them occupied while she helped Fyertash deal with the other. Then, with only one left, they could have a slight advantage. Unless, of course, something went wrong.

She smiled. Without a plan to push the two demons apart, she could well ignore all the possible outcomes of the confrontation.

The door opened, making her instincts respond with the urge to take a battle stance. Local thugs might have learned their lesson if word of her brush with assassins in the street had spread, and Zyreshi and others from the Four might be willing to honor the agreement Kamira had made with them, but it didn't mean no one else in the Temple wouldn't be tempted seek an easy way to power or glory. After all, ambitious Tivarashans preferred to seek forgiveness rather than to ask permission, and some were desperate enough to make risky moves. She also couldn't put it past the Four to let Queen Andalisha know that Prince Jalyn had died in Kaighal, conveniently forgetting to mention the Temple's involvement. A grief-stricken queen who sought revenge would be easily brushed off as something beyond the Four's control... if Kamira survived to argue that the demons hadn't kept their part of the deal to begin with.

Once more she considered posting guards in front of her chamber, but it felt like giving someone else control over who was allowed to see her and when. It was enough that Irtan liked to decide for her, making visitors wait or turning them away... She couldn't entirely blame him for stopping Veelk when he arrived for the first time, since she had asked to not be disturbed, but if her friend hadn't made it up to the chamber on his own, Kamira's battle with the priestess might have gone in a more dire direction.

No, she decided. *No guards.* She could handle assassins well enough, and at least she would ensure that she didn't miss any important information or lose an ally because someone else refused to grant a visitor an entry.

A boy slipped inside her chamber. No more than twelve, he wore the tattered clothes of a street urchin, and his face bore marks of a rushed, hardly thorough cleaning. He stopped a few steps from the door, with his back straight and hands pulling down on his tunic as if he could make it look more presentable.

She gave him an encouraging nod, making sure her expression wasn't too stern. No matter how much respect and distance the first archmage's position dictated, she wasn't about to start scaring children.

"A message fur m'lady archmage." The boy reached for his pouch. "Fur yur eyes alone." He held out a small package.

Her suspicions surfaced again. The Four would send a priest, and the Gildya would choose an adept or at least an apprentice. Even the city council would pay someone respectable to deliver a message. A street urchin suggested some underhanded dealings... Unless it was Veelk who found it amusing to send word this way.

"Leave it on the table," she replied. "Have you been paid?"

"Yes, m'lady archmage." The boy made his way to the table in the middle of the chamber. "Been told no reply needed." As soon as his hands were free of the package, he backed away. "G'day to you, m'lady archmage."

He was out of the chamber before she had a chance to ask any questions.

Kamira stood undecided. The package was small, but that didn't mean harmless. After all, the destructive orb Priestess Bayena had brought with her fit in the palm of her hand, and from what Koshmarnyk and Veelk had said, it seemed Gildya could make deadly devices of similar size.

The package emanated enough magic to have an imbued stone or two inside, and that alone spoke of unknown dangers.

A whoosh of wind announced Fyertash's descent. He picked up the package. "It's Myrkan's doing."

She took a step closer, but a gesture of his claw made it clear she should stay away as he carefully unwrapped the package. She kept to herself the question whether it was care for her wellbeing or distrust that dictated Fyertash's request.

From what she could see from afar, the package contained an emblem of a foreign make. Fyertash lifted it close to his face and inspected it with narrowed eyes. "There's writing inside the paper," he said without looking at her.

Kamira considered it an invitation and made her way to the table. The note was simple. "'Archmage, it's time we spoke,'" she read out loud. "'A drop of your magic is enough to summon me.'"

"So that's how he reaches his spies..." Fyertash said with a hint of approval. "This item... it's likely similar to your crystal creatures, though it lacks Veranesh's thoughtfulness and sophistication. I doubt Myrkan is able to do anything through it." He put it on the table. "Go on, speak with him. Perhaps you will learn something of use or find a way to lure him away from Derazin."

Fyertash took off, and from the spot she was in, she couldn't tell whether he'd truly left or lurked just outside the shattered dome. Knowing the demon's cunning and manipulative nature, she bet he stayed to eavesdrop on her.

The emblem turned out to be a brooch, with little gemstones arranged in the pattern of a leaf. The faceted greens shimmered when Kamira picked it up, and the intricate work left no doubt that the item used to belong to a human—likely a Devanshari noblewoman. She doubted Myrkan had picked it for its beauty or craftsmanship, but perhaps he wanted to make her believe that he respected her enough to send an item of value... or hoped she wouldn't destroy something she would perceive as precious.

She allowed herself a snicker. After so many years of collecting trinkets in forgotten ruins, Kamira's approach to jewelry was the same as Veelk's: it only mattered how many coins those pieces would fetch at the market.

Up close, it emanated a faint magic energy, and Kamira inspected it with interest. The letter was unsigned, but Fyertash had no doubt it was from Myrkan. The demons must have a way to recognize each other's magical aura, perhaps in a similar way that animals caught scents.

Once more she glanced at the short letter. The only instruction mentioned was a drop of her magic, so the brooch had to be activated in a similar way to her nightflies. Kamira channeled a tiny bit of energy, focusing it on the tip of her fingers, then sent it toward the piece of jewelry.

A ghastly shape formed over the table. Even without her recent encounter with the Four, Kamira would have recognized the immaterial manifestation of a demon, so she stood calm and composed. The shape swirled and wavered, but soon enough solidified into a face.

Myrkan, if that was truly him, seemed similar to Fyertash—the same elongated nose crooked like a beak, and a narrow face in which the shining, cunning eyes stood out all the more. But where Fyertash's expression carried some amusement and joviality, as if the demon was aware of his own shortcomings even if he would not admit to them out loud, Myrkan's face bore the marks of cruelty and savagery, and in this, the ghastly demon apparition reminded her of Uganel. She could only hope that Myrkan shared even more with the demon she'd vanquished back in the desert, and he would succumb to anger as easily, forgetting his cunning.

"Archmage," Myrkan said. "I'm glad we're able to finally meet." His head turned from side to side. "You're alone. Wise."

Kamira took note of his ability to see around him, but otherwise kept her expression neutral. "You wanted to talk."

"I've learned enough of you to believe you're reasonable," he said. "And with Veranesh gone, there's nothing stopping you from making your own decisions. Ones that would benefit the city and us both."

"Don't waste my time on flattery," she replied.

Part of her wanted to mention how not so long ago he was pondering sending Koshmarnyk back to her in pieces, but it seemed unwise to give the demon information he might not be aware of. Even with spies in the city, he might have missed that Koshmarnyk had made it back, or he could have assumed that the adept was too wounded to speak.

"You have an offer, so share it."

If her cold demeanor annoyed Myrkan, he didn't show it. "You're from the Four's lands and you are a pactee, so I assume you know what yalari get from making pacts with humans, yes?" He waited for her to nod. "Then you should be able to understand why I'd rather keep this city as it is instead of slaughtering every single human within it."

From what little she understood about the demon world, it made sense. Myrkan must desire power, more than he could gain on his own with more powerful demons ready to bring him down if he tried to step out of the line. "So, I raise you a temple in the city, and you leave?" she asked.

The corner of his lips crooked, sloping downward at her mockery. "You will give me Fyertash *and* raise me many temples," he replied. "And I'll leave the city untouched, with you ruling it."

She had no doubt that her "rule" would be under Myrkan's direction and focused solely on making sure all citizens of Kaighal prayed to him.

"You can keep your pact with Veranesh," Myrkan continued. "He has more power, and you'll need it to make sure others stay obedient. But if that double-faced yalari ever severs it, I will make one with you. I might be less powerful than he is, but the more eagerly you find me worshipers, the more my power will grow."

Kamira arched an eyebrow. She hadn't expected Myrkan to admit so openly he was no match for Veranesh, and she'd thought he'd demand her pact be severed, but in the end, making such a concession made him look like someone who was willing to negotiate rather than order her around. In his eyes, with Veranesh gone from this world, it mattered little whose pact she had, while giving up Fyertash meant depriving herself of the only demonic ally she had here.

"Very well," she replied without hesitation, and watched the demon's face stretch in a smile of satisfaction. "You will have your city full of worshipers, and I'll help you kill Fyertash... when I see Derazin fall. As soon as you kill him, I'll order Fyertash to attack you and aid you from behind."

This time, Myrkan grimaced. "Making demands, archmage? When all I have to do is crush your pathetic protection and destroy the city you rule?"

"Do you take me for a fool?" she replied. "I give you Fyertash, and you'll forget about your promises quicker than he changes sides. Give me Derazin as a sign you truly intend to leave the city be, and you'll have all that you want."

"The traitor first."

She hadn't expected him to agree, but the hatred with which he spoke the words told her how much of a blow Fyertash's betrayal must have been to Myrkan.

At the same time, the conversation was likely to lead nowhere. With not enough knowledge and her unwillingness to give Myrkan any openings, Kamira had no way of fishing for information that could prove useful.

Part of her itched to see if she could bind Myrkan

through the brooch. She could reach the Four through their pactee, but would an item be enough?

She discarded that thought. Back with the Tivarashan demons, she only needed them to back away, so succeeding at the binding mattered little. With Myrkan, she couldn't risk failure. If he severed the connection before she was done with the binding and ripping, he'd become aware that she knew the destruction spell, and she'd lose her advantage.

"Why would I swap one demon who obeys me for two that don't?" she asked. "Perhaps instead of talking to you, my time would be better spent building a temple for Fyertash instead." If she couldn't outsmart Myrkan, she might as well make him lose his wits in rage.

The twitches on Myrkan's face suggested her words had hit the mark. "He will turn on you like he turned on us and Veranesh."

She ignored the remark. Myrkan was clearly grasping at anything that would cause a rift between her and Fyertash. If that was all he had, he was wasting her time.

She leaned forward. "Kill Derazin, and then we will talk."

"Or, perhaps, I'll kill you instead. I'm sure the former high mages will be more willing to make bargains with us. After all, they already had one in the past."

Kamira bit her tongue before remarking that Uganel had seen no help from the high mages when he fell. Even so close to succumbing to rage, Myrkan could be cunning enough to figure out how she was involved in Uganel's demise.

She stared back at the demon in silence.

"I'll be seeing you soon, archmage."

The ghastly image wavered and disappeared.

Silence fell in the chamber, and Kamira looked up, expecting a shadow to pass over the shattered dome, but Fyertash didn't descend. She was certain he'd stay close to eavesdrop on her. No matter what deal he might have made with Veranesh, Fyertash didn't seem like someone who would allow her to bargain with his enemy unsupervised.

With a sigh, she wrapped the brooch in the packaging paper. There was hardly a safe place to store an artifact like that. On one hand, it made sense if she kept it close, but on the other, she hated the idea of possibly allowing Myrkan into her conversations.

"I like the idea of a temple," Fyertash said behind her.

She spun on the spot, not even trying to hide her startled expression. The demon was descending through the dome so slowly that only a slight gust of wind betrayed his presence.

"But not the part where I offer your life to Myrkan?" she asked.

The demon shrugged. "I think it was reasonable, since you demanded Derazin's death in return. Had Myrkan agreed, you'd have rid yourself of all three yalari..." He sent her a knowing grin. "Because I'm sure you'd finish off the last one standing."

She chuckled. "If you bested Myrkan, I'd let you live." Then she became serious. "It's time to get ready."

Fyertash's grin faded. "You taunted him on purpose. I take it that there's no clever plan to ensure our success?"

"None of us has come up with one so far, and the longer we wait, the more they wear us down." She looked him in the eye. "No matter what deception we might come up with, Myrkan will likely be too suspicious to fall for it."

"And Derazin is too much of a coward. Taunting Myrkan means that he won't use his wits against us." Fyertash nodded. "I'll keep him occupied while you and your allies deal with Derazin."

"Alone?" Such an offer was unusual for a cunning and cautious demon.

"I can hold him off for a while, and after that... I doubt he'd want me dead quickly. I hope that the aid I've given you so far will incline you to finish off your own quarry quickly enough to get to us before Myrkan's done." He dipped his head. "Archmage, I'll see you at the walls."

He took off in a rush, as if he didn't want Kamira to question his decision any further. It didn't escape her that his face expressed equal parts determination and concern.

Ervan's hands were sweating. He brushed them against his tunic, but the feeling of stickiness remained. Even if the demon missed the gesture, Ervan's nervousness was likely showing.

Way to negotiate, he scolded himself. He couldn't help feeling like an apprentice adept who'd failed a simple task, and the demon's ethereal yet threatening presence only added to the discomfort.

"You have to understand that I need more time," Ervan said. "Your constant attacks on the city make the council suspicious of any peace offerings. How can I convince them you don't wish to see the city fall if all they see is the demonlings attacking?"

The demon grimaced. There was something different about him this time, as if he was losing the rest of his patience.

"I gave you enough time." Myrkan's voice rang with more frustration than usual, but Ervan couldn't tell whether the ire came from their conversation once more leading nowhere or if something else affected the demon's mood. "If the humans you're dealing with refuse to see reason, dispose of them and seek others. We are ready to take the city now, and while your discreet help with the barrier around the city is appreciated, it will have gained you only your own life. Once the city falls, I'll allow you and your few chosen allies to leave it unharmed."

Ervan swallowed hard, his eyes widening. To leave Kaighal meant to abandon all the power and wealth he'd amassed over the years. Even if he survived the city's fall and Myrkan kept his word and let him go, it would be Ervan's utter defeat.

"What would you have me do?" he asked. His voice came out weak, like a declaration of surrender.

The demon's face shifted in slight satisfaction. "You know what I want."

Cold sweat covered Ervan's skin. Yes, he knew what Myrkan wanted him to do, but to even think of such a deed paralyzed him. After his having led a life of cautiousness and manipulation, any open action seemed like a risk not worth taking.

"Speak to me again only if you're willing to do what's necessary," Myrkan added.

The demon's ghastly image flickered and disappeared. Ervan exhaled, but the tension in his body didn't leave. His thoughts were still running. He knew what the demon wanted, and he knew how to go about it, but the prospect of failure kept him in place.

If he succeeded, his reward would be great, but defeat would see him humiliated. Ervan could easily picture the council's condemnation and disgust as they judged him for all his transgressions, true or false. They would all be so eager to show their superiority and righteousness...

He shook his head, chasing those images away.

If he did nothing, he'd suffer an even worse defeat, and he couldn't shake the feeling that the longer he hesitated, the smaller his chances for success became. Just like when he wasn't ready to take the risk when a thief broke into his quarters, and he missed the chance of possibly catching Alluvendran snooping around. Had he acted, the rogue adept who had been his rival for so long would have been dealt with, and even the archmage herself would do nothing to save his stone-adorned skin.

Ervan stood up, securing the magicked stone in his robes. The time for subtlety had passed, and if he wanted to see his desires fulfilled, he had to become a man of action. He'd see his plan through, no matter the cost.

With newfound resolve, he headed for the door, not willing to admit that his rushing stemmed from the fear he'd change his mind and allow his lifelong habits to paralyze him again.

As he touched the door handle, a new thought struck him. He was already going to put everything at stake, so he could as well teach the council a lesson.

The device he had in mind rested secure at the back of one of his cabinets—an inconspicuous cube. It wouldn't fit into any of his pockets, but perhaps it didn't have to. He could bring it in as his new invention, one that would turn the tide of the siege. And turn the tide it would, though not in the way the council would envision.

To his surprise, the new prospect brought a rush of blood through his veins, so different to the cold flow of paralyzing fear. He explored and cherished the feeling, but didn't dawdle long. Myrkan had mentioned the final attack on the city was coming, so time was short. Besides, the daily council meeting was coming soon, and it would be a perfect time to see all the members without having to gather them himself.

Despite the excitement, he kept a steady pace as he made his way through Gildya's corridors and halls. He had to appear casual enough to not draw attention, and at the same time walk so briskly as to make it clear he had no time for conversation, long or short.

Several adepts and apprentices passed him by close enough to exchange greetings, and Ervan caught a few curious glances at the device he carried. Once more, doubt washed over him. After all was done, those people would remember he had it, and learn the truth.

He forced himself to focus on his goals. When he succeeded, he'd make sure no one questioned his actions as a savior of Kaighal. And if he failed... adding one more transgression to the grand betrayal he was about to commit would matter little.

Once he climbed the last flight of stairs leading to the meeting chamber, he slowed down. All the members of the council should have already gathered, but he had to put together a plan in case some were running late. He couldn't reveal too much about the device until everyone arrived.

Perhaps he didn't have to. It should be understandable that he wanted to wait for all the members to be present before he proceeded with any explanations.

Two guards stood by the door to the chamber, and Ervan stopped before entering. "Have all the council members arrived yet?" It didn't hurt to ask, giving himself a moment to prepare for what waited inside.

"Yes, adept," one of them replied.

He gave him a short nod, enough to express gratitude.

Keeping everyone amicable always brought benefits, and perhaps in the future he'd be in need of the guard's services or support. He never was too friendly with anyone, but if his spies were right, most adepts and apprentices considered him a reasonable and thoughtful man who didn't let pride dictate his words and offered time and support when others needed it. That served Ervan well. With other council members often exercising less restraint in their behavior, it was easy to become the man everyone wanted as a leader. It would also be easier to convince Gildya members later that he simply did what had to be done.

That thought offered him reassurance, and Ervan stepped into the chamber with confidence. The guards closed the door behind him.

The council members stood in small groups, but so few men and women couldn't fill the empty space. He'd never understood why the council resisted the idea of bringing in chairs and tables for the convenience of the adepts engaged in matters of importance that would affect not only Gildya, but often the whole of Kaighal. He found it foolish that adepts argued having comfortable seats created the impression that the council considered itself above others. The council *was* above others. The council was the one to make decisions, pass judgments when necessary, and represent all the adepts when it came to dealing with the Towers, city council, or any other groups.

Yzean stepped forward, his slow movements betraying his advanced age more than his gray hair. "Adept Ervan, I'm glad you were able to join us." Not a single note of reprimand rang in his voice, and that alone grated on Ervan's nerves. "We've been having some informal discussions, and so far, everyone seems to agree that Adept Davshil would make an excellent addition to the council.

He's a hardworking member of Gildya, and though his inventions can't always be considered ingenious, he might be just the man this council needs. Someone that all the lower-ranking adepts can relate to, and someone they will feel is their voice in here."

Ervan allowed himself a small grimace. There used to be a time when one only received an invitation to the council after consistently presenting useful and creative inventions. On the other hand, this would have gained Alluvendran a place on the council in the past, so perhaps it was better the way Gildya operated now.

At least Davshil's candidacy was nothing to be concerned with. The adept seemed uninterested in politics, and if he accepted the position, he'd be more likely to abstain from any voting than propose changes.

Like it's going to matter, Ervan realized. After Myrkan had the city in his hold, Ervan would be its sole leader, and he would pick members of his own council to execute his decisions and oversee mundane tasks.

"I understand that this is rather unconventional choice," Yzean added, likely in response to Ervan's reaction, "but I think we're all tired of endless discussions on the topic. The city needs us, and here we are, still unable to come to such a trivial decision as replacing a missing member on the council."

"Very well." Ervan pretended the old man had convinced him. "I'm sure that, when given a chance, Adept Davshil will offer valuable insights."

At the old man's sign, Adept Hybal headed for the door. "Find someone to pass a message to Adept Davshil. The council summons him." His voice carried through the chamber.

"Is there anything else the council members wish to

discuss while we wait for Adept Davshil's arrival?" Yzean asked while Hybal returned to his spot beside two other council members, Zaveshan and Yinka.

"Yes," Ervan said. "I've been working on a device that I believe might be helpful in the siege and finally give Gildya the success we've all been hoping for."

The last remark got everyone's interest, and Ervan cherished their reaction. The council was so afraid of the archmage that it wasn't willing to make any bold moves, but their eager response made it obvious they were desperate for anything that would give them the upper hand or any bargaining power. For a heartbeat, he savored the attention. Adept Ervan, the savior of Gildya... He would be, but what the council didn't understand was that saving Gildya required changes and decisive actions. And to think that he used to be like them, fearful and defensive!

"Let me demonstrate. It'll be easier than trying to explain." He took several steps back, toward the door. "The demonstration will require a bit of space."

As expected, everyone stepped away, widening the distance between Ervan and the rest of the council. *Perfect.* He fumbled with the device, pressing the buttons in the right order. A design he'd thought would ensure the device didn't accidentally activate on its own turned out quite a hindrance. His fellow adepts would wait patiently enough, but if an aggressive enemy was in their place...

Ervan almost shuddered at the thought of Alluvendran standing there, ready to lunge. In the future, when he had enough time, he'd have to make improvements.

The buttons finally clicked, and Ervan threw the device onto the floor, into the empty space between him and the council. The cube landed heavily, with a slight slide, and stopped. *It didn't go far enough!* Ervan froze mid-move when he realized that he'd never make it to the device on time to correct his throw. Now he understood why everyone, including Tivarashan Thorns, insisted on using round shapes for designs. A ball-shaped device could roll in an unexpected direction or go too far, but at least it had a better chance of reaching the target.

"Adept Ervan?" Yzean must have caught the panic in Ervan's expression.

Ervan didn't bother coming up with any explanations, instead using the precious time to back-pedal toward the door. He'd only taken two steps back when the device spat out smoke. Its color was nothing like the vibrant green of Tivarashan poison, but Ervan had tested the mixture long enough to know it would work as splendidly.

"Ervan!" someone from the council called out.

He didn't bother to respond. Violent coughs sounded across the room. Several adepts headed toward the windows, sleeves pressed to their faces. Zaveshan managed to open one of them, but the gust of air didn't help him, and he collapsed. Then the device spat out more smoke, the fumes coming out more violently this time.

The satisfaction faded from Ervan's face when his nostrils caught the acrid scent of his own creation. Poison immediately irritated his nose and throat. Like everyone else, he instinctively pressed his sleeve to his face, even though he knew it wouldn't help. At least he had a way out. He turned and rushed toward the door, trying to fight the coughing fit rising in his lungs. Instead of bringing relief, it would make him breathe in even more poison.

He stumbled outside, startling the two guards. They stood over him, unsure how to act.

"Betrayal..." Ervan said, the first word that came to mind, but then a lie formed in his head. "Alluvendran has poisoned the council!" It was so easy to put the blame on the rogue adept, even if such deception wouldn't last long. "Find someone to deal with the poison cloud inside and get medics to help other council members. Alluvendran has escaped through the window," he added, remembering how it had happened in his own quarters.

As Ervan leaned against the wall, greedily taking gulps of air, the guards rushed away. At some point, there might be an adept who asked why Alluvendran had used poison, given his martial skills. Perhaps someone would even remember Ervan himself walking through Gildya with the deadly device in his hand.

But all those doubts and questions would come too late. When someone finally caught up with Ervan's plot, he would already be celebrating his many successes: the defeat of the council, the fall of the first archmage, the saving of Kaighal... maybe even Alluvendran's death.

That thought brought him back to reality. The hardest task was still ahead of him, and that sneaky rogue adept could ruin everything. Ervan straightened his back, exhaling deeply to ensure most of the inhaled poison left his body. There was comfort in his past failures to mirror the green smoke's properties in his own poison. Had he succeeded, he'd be lying back in the chamber, dead like the rest of the council. So many things could have gone wrong, and some of them hadn't turned out exactly like planned, but he had succeeded.

A smile suddenly stretched his lips when he made his way down the corridor. It seemed that luck was on his side.

10

Koshmarnyk, Irtan, and Varessa answered Kamira's summons quicker than she'd expected. She hardly had time to lodge Myrkan's brooch under the dwindling pile of crystal pieces that used to be her prison. It made for a poor hiding place, but with all the energy surrounding the shards, it was the best spot to hide any demonic magic emanating from the piece of jewelry. If she was lucky, Irtan wouldn't notice anything, because the last thing she needed was a lengthy explanation of Myrkan's attempt to sway her.

Koshmarnyk and Irtan walked shoulder to shoulder, and from what Kamira could gather from the tone of their conversation carried within the chamber, they were engaged in an amicable exchange. Varessa followed, and her frown made it clear she didn't appreciate being dragged away from whatever duties she'd assigned herself. No wonder this woman hadn't been quick to ascend in the Towers' old power structures.

"I have a reason to believe that our enemies will mount a powerful attack soon," Kamira said. "We will need all the forces we can muster at the walls. As soon as we're done here, we'll send word to Gildya, and to the city council as well."

"I've already sent anyone I could to defend the city." Varessa didn't hide her displeasure. "The ones that are left don't have enough of a grasp on the arts to be of use as arcanists."

"But they can still be of help," Kamira replied. "Defenders will need all kind of assistance. Our students can aid the medics, carry messages, or even bring water and food." She looked Varessa in the eye. "I know you care about them, but I've seen girls and boys much younger than them doing their part at the walls, and I won't have anyone say that, in the time of greatest need, arcanists hid in the Towers."

Varessa curled her lips in a grimace, but in the end, she nodded. "I'll lead them myself and ensure they are assigned to posts befitting their skills."

Undoubtedly, the stubborn archmage would do everything to keep her students out of harm's way, but Kamira couldn't oversee everything anyway. As long as arcanists were seen at the walls, as long as there were no grounds to claim that they didn't do everything in their power, she would let Varessa have her way. At least those who were trained and picked by Irtan were already at the walls, and from what Kamira had seen, they were doing better than anyone would have expected them to, given they'd only received a few weeks of schooling.

Irtan looked up toward the dome. "Fyertash?"

"Already headed to the walls," Kamira replied. "I'll need you to stay here."

The old man shook his head. "I hope you aren't concerned with my age, my dear," he said jovially, though his expression made it clear he would not concede. "This was my city long before it became yours, and you would be a fool to leave the second most skilled arcanist behind. Besides, I wouldn't let you take all the glory for yourself," he added jokingly.

It was polite of him to consider her more skilled in the arts, but she would not allow any flattery to sway her. "I need someone to protect this chamber and the device," Kamira replied, glancing at Koshmarnyk. "We have reason to believe there are traitors among Gildya's council." She didn't have to remind him that even though each device created its own piece of the barrier shielding the city, they all relied on each other to make the protection complete, and the device in the Towers was the crucial one.

"Pelina can stay behind," Irtan replied. "With the regular guards at her disposal, she should be enough."

Kamira pressed her lips together. She'd rather order Irtan to stay, but the old man had a point. He was skilled, and he had the pact with Fyertash, which meant he could hold off hordes of the demonlings threatening the city while she and others dealt with the higher demons. "Very well. I'll trust your judgment. Let her know that anyone from Gildya might be a threat. Especially anyone claiming they're coming from Adept Ervan."

"Is that all?" Varessa asked.

"Once we get to the walls, I and the chosen few will try to get to the higher demons," Kamira said. "Don't come to aid us, no matter what you see. You have to make sure the city doesn't fall."

Both archmages nodded and left the chamber in a hurry. As the door closed behind them, Kamira caught the echo of Varessa already ordering servants to gather students and teachers.

"I hope you aren't going to ask me to stay as well,"

Koshmarnyk said, and though a hint of playfulness lingered in his words, his expression made it clear he would not take such a request well. "I'm healed enough."

She shook her head. "I wasn't going to, no matter how much I'd rather see you out of harm's way until you're healed more than just enough. I have a few allies I can trust, and I need you, but you might not like what I'm going to ask you to do." She looked him in the eye. "Myrkan sent a message in a way that confirms your suspicions about Ervan. You're the only one among us who knows the adept well enough to spot anything out of ordinary. If we're busy fighting demons, the last thing I need is Gildya's betrayal."

Koshmarnyk shifted uneasily, and she had no trouble at guessing the battle within, but instead of trying to convince him, she waited patiently. He had no obligations to her except for those born of their intimacy, and she had no right to ask him to put the city's safety over his need to protect her.

"I'd rather be by your side," he said with the openness she'd expected, and a half-smile eased his stern face. "Or even better, I'd rather see you safe at the walls. But you aren't going to be alone, and you are capable of seeing this through without me protecting you. You need me to do it, so I will. Besides, if there's a chance I can prove Ervan's involvement, I'd be a fool to not take it."

Kamira looked at him with gratitude and relief, wondering if enough of those feelings showed on her face. Some cunning Tivarashan woman would have made a proper display, with exalted words of gratitude, even throwing herself at his neck, but it wasn't Kamira's way.

"I appreciate it." She wanted to say something more, something to reassure him; she really did... but the right words weren't coming, and the more she thought about them, the more she feared she'd end up making promises for a future she didn't know yet. Perhaps all that mattered for now was that Koshmarnyk had agreed, and the time to talk was later. They had feelings for each other, that much was true, and the rest simply had to wait.

"I'll get ready, then," Koshmarnyk said. "I'll send word to Zelna and Mawi, and get someone to inform Gildya as well. If the final attack is coming, we will likely need the adepts' help, even if some might turn out to be traitors."

He leaned closer and placed a kiss on her cheek. Before he could move away, she closed him in a tight embrace.

"Don't get yourself killed. I'd hate to have to go after Gildya just because one of their lousy adepts bested you," she whispered playfully.

"Hard chance, archmage," he replied as he returned her hug. "But same goes for you fighting demons. I'm hopeful for a future in which the city doesn't mourn your death."

The choice of his words didn't escape Kamira. "You couldn't have been vaguer."

A full smile was a rarity on his face. "A future when both of us are alive is a future when we can make all the plans, isn't it? We both have things to do until it comes, but at least I can be hopeful."

"I like the idea of making plans," she replied. There was a promise in his words, but one that didn't demand obligations. As if he knew that what each of them wanted from life might differ. Making plans meant discussions and finding the best way instead of giving painful ultimatums.

"Well then, my dear, go and get rid of those demons, so it's only humans we have to worry about," he said cheerfully as he headed for the door.

Kamira stood alone in the chamber, its silence offering an opportunity to cling to a dream of the future for a little longer. Then, with a longing sigh, she rushed out of the chamber as well. She had less to prepare than others, but people at the walls would likely expect a speech, so she had to come up with something reassuring—and if she was to face two demons, she might as well wear something more battle-appropriate.

～

THE TOWERS WERE much quieter than in the times of the high mages, and Atissa couldn't help a mix of discomfort and relief as she rushed through the familiar corridors. Their stillness reminded her of all that had transpired, but at the same time, it allowed her to move through the Towers without feeling the many judging gazes of students and teachers.

Atissa couldn't help the bitter thought that no one would dare stare like that at Irtan, even though the old weasel was a part of the secret that had kept high mages in power. But none of it mattered when he announced that he was an arcanist and his pact demon would help defend the city alongside Veranesh.

Despite being alone, Atissa hid her grimace. She was so used to others watching her that she had a hard time letting go of old habits, of hiding her feelings.

Bitter thoughts swarmed her head. Irtan enjoyed respect and almost the same power he'd had before, while she, who was much less at fault for anything that had happened, became a scapegoat. It seemed that she would forever be "Yoreus's daughter" to everyone in the Towers.

At least now she had a chance to make a name for herself, and perhaps one day hardly anybody would remember who her father was. The voice of reason whispered that Yoreus's name would forever be tied with hers, but perhaps over time that bond would fade from people's memory enough for her do be just Atissa... the healer.

A meager smile stretched her lips as a daydream took her. She'd help those in need of treatment, and they would welcome her presence instead of throwing judging glares and whispering behind her back. All she needed was a little more time in the Towers, a little more practice, and she could go anywhere else. She wouldn't have to be tangled in the games Irtan and Kamira played.

The thought of the new archmage and her father's killer brought another wave of uneasiness. Kamira seemed to recognize the complexity of the relations between them, but that understanding and calmness of hers grated on Atissa's composure. After all, Kamira was a Tivarashan woman, and to act the way any situation required would be a child's play. On the other hand, a man like Veelk not only followed Kamira but also considered himself her friend and defender, and Veelk didn't strike Atissa as someone easy to deceive.

She allowed herself to linger on the memories of their short journey and the short encounter when he'd helped her with her wound. Strong but gentle, confident but caring... What was a man like that doing by Kamira's side?

Atissa abandoned those thoughts before jealousy got the better of her. She had to focus on her new magic. The sooner she mastered healing, the sooner she could leave, and leave the past—and the present—behind.

Reaching Pelina's quarters brought relief, even if asking for help meant another possible humiliation. But Veelk was right, and if she wanted to succeed, she had to swallow her pride.

She knocked on the door decisively and waited.

No answer came.

Atissa looked around, but as she expected, the corridor was empty. This part of the Towers used to be where teachers resided, but with so many of them gone, knocking on the rows of doors in the hope someone would open seemed like a waste of time. Besides, whoever answered might not know where Pelina was anyway.

Resigned, Atissa headed toward the initiation rite chamber. No matter the time of day or night, Kamira seemed to be there. If Atissa was lucky, maybe Irtan wouldn't be present, though the prospect of meeting with the Tivarashan archmage alone was hardly an appealing one.

Atissa steeled herself, finding comfort in the vision of a future full of healing and people welcoming her.

Then she rushed to the topmost tower.

Even with the little attention she paid to her surroundings, it didn't take her long to notice that the Towers were even quieter than usual. Many teachers and students had departed, but the stairway to the initiation rite chamber always had at least a few people traveling up or down. With the archmage meeting everyone up top, they had to climb the only stairway and leave the same way, but as Atissa made her own ascent, there was no one around.

Another battle? Her heartbeat sped up. She'd had enough of fighting and danger, and the memory of killing the priestess made her shiver. As always, she chased it away before she could ponder it any longer. With all that was happening and her own desperate attempts to carve a path that would be her own, Atissa didn't need the additional burden of the deed. There would be time for it later.

The chamber's door was within sight, and she slowed

down. Barging into a middle of a battle could get her killed, and she didn't owe Kamira any help. At the same time, as unnerving as she was, Kamira was still better than Irtan or someone who would hand the city to the demons.

The image of Myrkan's cruel face was enough to freeze Atissa in her steps, and she struggled to keep control over her rebelling limbs. If Myrkan took Kaighal, there would be no place Atissa could hide, and she'd seen up close what he did to Koshmarnyk.

She swallowed and forced herself to keep climbing the stairs. A quick peek should suffice to figure out what was going on, and, if needed, she could always run for help.

At the top of the stairway, Atissa quietly made her way to the door. With her ear to the wood carved in decorative patterns, she listened for any signs of battle, but the chamber seemed eerily quiet. Not even a faint echo of a conversation carried through the door.

With no other choice, slowly and cautiously, Atissa cracked the door open. Still, no sound, and no one in sight. It seemed that she'd have to poke her head in, but at least with the eerie silence, perhaps there wasn't much risk.

The door swung open with force, and Atissa fell into the chamber, tumbling to the floor. She scrambled back onto her feet, ready to get scolded for eavesdropping.

Instead, she faced Pelina. The young woman was standing a few steps away, her expression tense and body in what could be an arcanist battle position. Energies seemed to flicker all around her, ready to be called upon, demonstrating the perfect control Pelina had over her magic.

"You..." Pelina said, surprised. "What are you doing here?"

"I was looking for you," Atissa replied as she looked around. "Where is everybody?"

Pelina's expression became grimmer, and she didn't relax. "The archmage suspects a forceful attack is coming. Everyone got sent to the walls to help as much as they're capable."

Atissa nodded and swallowed to get rid of the bitter taste in her mouth. Everyone but her... It would be like Irtan to conveniently forget her, and no one else had likely even *thought* about her. On the other hand, she should have done a better job keeping up with what was going on in the Towers.

"And you?" Atissa asked.

Pelina hesitated, then indicated the device in the middle of the chamber. "Someone needs to protect it. I'm skilled enough for the task, but not powerful enough for my presence to be missed at the walls."

Though Atissa tried, she couldn't catch a single note of bitterness or hurt pride in Pelina's voice, as if the young woman was happy with her task and wasn't bothered that her power didn't match that of Kamira or Irtan.

"You said you were looking for me?" Pelina said when the silence between them lingered.

Atissa waved her hand in a dismissive gesture. "I was, but it's not that urgent. You have an important task, and I don't want to distract you."

"You could stay here, if you want," Pelina offered. "I can always use help if trouble comes."

It sounded almost friendly, as if Pelina didn't care that she was speaking to the daughter of the man who had been her teacher's rival. Perhaps, in a way, they had something in common—both were used by archmages in their games. Pelina found her own footing and didn't mind staying in the shadow of the more powerful arcanists, but she also wasn't the daughter of their enemy.

Atissa shook her head. "I better go. If the archmage is right, they'll need all the help at the walls they can get." She turned and headed outside.

"Good luck!" Pelina called after her.

Hesitation lasted only for a moment, and Atissa looked over her shoulder, bringing a gentle, friendly smile to her face. "Good luck to you too."

After she closed the door to the chamber, Atissa rushed down the stairs. Even though she hadn't found the help she was hoping for, it didn't matter anymore. With the final attack coming, there would be enough gravely wounded to volunteer. No matter how risky and untested healing magic was, she couldn't imagine anyone dying would refuse a chance at life.

THE TIVARASHAN CAMP seemed to be spread all over the forest, with the groups of tents scattered between the trees. Ryell couldn't understand how they could efficiently defend it or pass information quickly. On the other hand, if Tivarashan land was mostly woods, it made sense they adapted to their surroundings. Perhaps there were even advantages to such a setup, but he chose not to ponder them.

Captain Seraine's people moved through the camp with efficiency, checking tents for anyone who could raise an alarm and dealing swift death to any enemy they came across. But Ryell couldn't shake the feeling of something not being right. For a camp that size, there were too few people around, and even though it made the Baxayalans' task easier, it also screamed of a trap or unforeseen dangers.

Of course, the Tivarashan couldn't have known of a small scouting parting traveling back west, so there had to be something else at play. *Demons?*

A drop of sweat ran down Ryell's spine. Those creatures had wings that could carry them as far as they wished to go, and he'd heard one nearby Atissa's mansion, which made it clear those wretched creatures didn't intend to stay close to Kaighal.

A thought of Atissa brought about guilt. No matter how selfish and childish she'd turned out to be, his exit was hardly that of a mature man. In anger, without a word of goodbye... He hadn't even cared enough to ask the Baxayalans to stop by her mansion and let her know that a demon lurked nearby.

He shrugged off his doubts. Atissa was consumed by her need for vengeance, and there was no point in warnings or persuasion. She'd made it clear during their last conversation.

Despite his self-reassurances, guilt still nibbled at his thoughts, and Ryell flexed his fist, itching to place his hand on the hilt of his sword. Yet there were no enemies nearby, as other members of the group had cleared the way for Seraine and her companions. He could take off on his own and search for an adversary to take his mind off the past, but if he wanted to convince the Baxayalans he could become a valued member of their party, he had to show that he could follow orders.

The sounds of a scuffle drew his attention. Two of Seraine's scouts were trying to overpower a large Tivarashan man who'd emerged from one of the tents. His outfit suggested a smith or a worker rather than a warrior, but his broad shoulders, bare and gray, made it clear he wasn't an easy target. One of the scouts was struggling to keep the man from shouting out, while the other was trying to stick the blade of her knife past the frantic flurrying of muscled arms.

Ryell's hand moved to his side, but before he could draw his sword, an arrow cut through the air with a quiet whistle. It buried in the Tivarashan's eye, and the man stopped struggling. The two scouts laid his body on the ground, pulling it into the tent.

No matter how quiet the scouts tried to be, Ryell expected others in the camp to hear something, but no one emerged to alert everyone to the intruders.

Once the nearby tents were cleared, Captain Seraine gave him a signal, and he followed with a feeling of uneasiness tugging at him. It wasn't only the unfamiliar setup of a forest camp or the foreign symbols on the tents and flags, many of which bore unfamiliar crests. If only he could figure it out...

By the time they reached the tent that had to be the center of command, Ryell hadn't pulled his sword out once, and the feeling of uneasiness only intensified. Once or twice, Seraine threw him a curious glance, but she never asked a question. After all, being in the middle of scouting an enemy camp wasn't the time to inquire about something that might have no consequences for the task at hand.

The command tent was empty as well. Seraine entered and headed for the strategy table, while her companions sifted through other documents, packing away anything they deemed important.

Ryell kept back, near the entrance. He had no clue what would be of value to the Baxayalans, so he could keep an eye out. Even if part of the squad was still scouring the nearby tents in search for enemies, with the camp so spread out, it would be easy for a Tivarashan man or woman to slip past the few groups scattered around.

Trying to ignore the uneasy feeling, he sought comfort in the sounds of the forest. Its near silence, with the whispering of the wind, animal sounds, and the gentle whooshing of branches always had a soothing effect on him. Perhaps he could find solace here, despite being so far from home.

He dared not close his eyes and let his guard down, but he strained to hear the familiar melody of the woods. Instead, his ears caught a different tune.

"There's a battle nearby," he whispered as soon as he recognized the sounds.

All the scouts' attention turned to him, but he had nothing to add.

Seraine walked toward the tent's exit. "We have to know what's going on. Lyezi, Fyrwol, you stay here and see if you can find anything of worth. The rest of you—with me."

This time, they made their way through the camp quickly, relying on other party members to take care of any enemies. To the southwest, the trees were getting scarcer, foretelling a clearing or even the end of the woods, and the sounds of the battle grew stronger. Yet before they made it to the edge of the trees, Captain Seraine stopped them with a gesture.

At the edge of a forest stood a group of the well-dressed Tivarashans, looking away from the camp, likely down at the battlefield. They had heavily armored guards with them, spread out in a semicircle as if to protect the group from any enemy intrusion.

Ryell narrowed his eyes, because there had to be

somebody protecting their backs as well, but perhaps they felt safe with the campgrounds behind them.

Then he spotted several of Seraine's scouts dragging away two sentries that must have been patrolling the edge of the camp.

"Captain, look." One of the scouts pointed toward the Tivarashan group.

Ryell struggled to see what exactly the man was pointing at. They were all nobles, some wearing expensive clothing adorned with unfamiliar crests, some having chosen more battle-appropriate attire that still announced their status. There were also a few that wore ceremonial outfits, and Ryell's skin crawled. Even from this distance, he sensed faint magic around them.

Demon worshipers! They likely were there to provide protection for the group. Any intrusion, magical or not, would come to a swift end.

Only then did he finally spot the person that the scout was pointing at. The woman had gray skin and black hair, and her armor was of the finest make. The sword by her side had a faceted gem at its hilt, and there was a golden circlet on her head with a similar stone.

"Princess Mefina," someone whispered.

Ryell held his breath. Tivarashan royalty stood so close to them, unaware of the danger lurking behind her back. It seemed like a perfect moment to strike and throw the enemy forces in disarray.

Yet Seraine didn't give the order. Instead, everyone around Ryell stood silent, listening to the battle. Ryell could hardly make the battle cries out, and the different signals told him nothing of what was going on, but the scouts seemed to have an idea.

"They're fighting our army." Seraine must have caught

his confusion. "Our forces were supposed to head east, toward Kaighal, and meet us halfway there. But it doesn't explain what the Tivarashan are doing here. One would think they'd be more interested in taking the city."

"Someone must have told them. Perhaps your spy in the city got caught," Ryell replied. It seemed pointless to conceal what he had already picked up from scraps of their conversations: that they had people in Kaighal bringing them information, and maybe even working on sabotaging Kaighal's defenses.

Seraine shrugged at that. With the battle already ongoing, it likely mattered little to her what had caused the two armies to meet.

"What do we do, captain?" one of the scouts asked.

They all seemed ready and eager to leave, and Ryell didn't blame them. With their compatriots so close, there was no reason to linger... except for one.

"We could take out their command," Ryell said, "and perhaps turn the tide of battle." If Tivarashans were using their demonologists, the odds might not be in the Baxayalans' favor.

Captain Seraine looked back and forth at him and her companions, making no call.

"A group of scouts is not going to be of much help in a large battle like that," Ryell argued. "But we can do a lot of good here. If we take out at least a few from their leaders, the rest of their army might fall into disarray."

"You've done it before, haven't you?" Seraine looked at him with a mix of curiosity and caution.

"Yes," Ryell replied. Back in Devanshari, he and his companions had been attacking demonologists in the hopes the demonlings they commanded would succumb to their instincts and turn against each other, but the principle remained: if Tivarashans saw their leaders fall, their discipline would turn into chaos, and their morale would plummet.

"Do you have a plan in mind?" Seraine asked.

For a heartbeat, he stared at her dumbfounded. It was her decision and her people, and yet she was clearly asking him to advise. He gave her a nod as he realized that her group of scouts had likely never engaged in an open battle or prepared an assault like that. In their eyes, Ryell must be the one with the most experience, considering his past in the royal guard and time spent defending the Devanshari lands.

"An arrow from a distance would be the safest way to deal with the princess alone, but a missed shot will make us lose the advantage of surprise, and she might not be the one giving orders. I'd say have your best archer take one, but prepare to go in. After the shot at the princess, we will have to take down as many guards as possible before the skirmish starts," he said. "I'd have archers climb into the trees. Then all that is left is to fight our way through, killing as many of them as possible before we have to fall back." He looked back at the camp. "Perhaps one or two people could cause a distraction to cover our escape as well."

Relief flashed on her face, as if she had feared that he'd suggest an all-out attack that would see most of her people dead. He'd already seen her care for them, but perhaps her soft heart was also the reason she chose to lead scouts instead of a warrior unit. Unseen and swift, scouts had a better chance of survival than the men and women who were told to charge at the enemy headfirst.

"Very well, let's do it," she whispered, and looked at one of her companions. "Get everyone here. The sooner we're ready to strike, the less likely someone's going to interrupt us. Zimfe and I will lead the attack."

She gave Ryell a serious nod, leaving no doubt that she was aware of the risks. The attack, even if successful, would see some of her companions dead, and leading the charge, she could well become one of the bodies left behind. He found no fear in her expression, nor the desperate bravado of those resigned to their fate, and that alone made Captain Seraine a leader worth following.

Ryell lifted his chin. He would not let those men and women bear the consequences of his plan while he stayed safely behind. "And I'll be in the first line with you."

No protest came, and the scouts' silence was the strongest sign of their approval Ryell could have asked for.

11

When Kamira got to the battlements, hardly anyone paid attention to her, let alone expected her to deliver a speech. People moved around and completed tasks with an air of urgency around them, but she found no desperation or panic in their actions. Kaighal was ready for the battle that was coming, and Kamira could only hope that she would live up to her own obligations.

It was easy to spot Veelk and Zelna's towering figures among the defenders, and Koshmarnyk stood beside them. All three of them looked battle-ready, and it brought a smile to her face.

Mawi was nearby, talking to King Allyv, and down by the walls, Irtan instructed a group of students and teachers. There were fewer of them than Kamira had hoped for, making it clear that Varessa kept most of them under her protection. A foolish choice, if someone asked Kamira, because if the defense failed, they would die just like anyone else, while their presence on the walls could make a difference. Yet she kept a frown off her face. Her disapproval wasn't what people needed right now.

"Archmage," Koshmarnyk said while she made her way up to them. A glimmer in his eye suggested the display of respect was a hidden tease.

Veelk and Zelna gave her polite nods, suitable for two fearsome warriors from a far-off land.

Before she could exchange more personal greetings with them, King Allyv approached. Even in his armor, finely made leathers reinforced with metal plates, he still looked like the young man he was. His grim and tired expression couldn't sharpen his still boyish and innocent features, but he walked and spoke like Kamira thought a king should. She couldn't help remembering the spoiled Tivarashan prince who'd sought the crown solely to fulfill his desires. How much Prince Jalyn could have learned from the Devanshari king if he'd had more time.

"Archmage," Allyv greeted her politely, but she caught tension in his voice. "I've been told we're to expect a battle."

She appreciated he didn't question how she knew it. He likely assumed that Fyertash had some insights into his brethren's choices, and she'd leave it at that.

"I can't be certain, but I'd rather see everyone ready than taken by surprise," she replied.

"There is some commotion among the demonlings, but they haven't attacked yet," Allyv said. "It might be nothing but an attempt to wear us down."

He glanced up, distrust clear on his face, and Kamira followed his gaze to find Fyertash hovering over the city and watching the lands beyond the walls.

"If they don't come at us soon, we can allow some defenders to rest nearby," she replied. "I'll leave it to you to decide, Your Highness. You've been organizing this defense so far, and I won't question your judgment now."

"Very well," Allyv replied. He looked up again when a

shadow fell over them both. "If that's all, I'll leave you to your duties now, archmage." He rushed away before Kamira could find any courtesies to say as Fyertash descended.

"I don't see Myrkan anywhere," the demon said with clear concern. "He wouldn't have fled, not after... what transpired earlier. If he's not here, it means he's up to something."

"We'll stick to the plan," Kamira replied. "Keep an eye out for him and don't go after Derazin unless there's no other choice." With so many people around, she'd rather not say "unless we're losing."

The corner of Fyertash's lip curled upward ever so slightly, as if he'd caught the true meaning of her words. "As you wish, archmage."

His wings moved slightly, suggesting he was about to return to hovering over the city, searching for Myrkan, and Kamira turned away from him.

A shout of alarm, along with feral screeches, drew her attention. One of the devices further down the wall had failed, and the first demonlings were already leaping onto the battlements. Acting on instinct, she drew magic, even though the breach was too far for her to reach without hitting any defenders, but as the group assigned to that part of the walls handled the oncoming demonlings with ease, she relaxed. Before long, a man in Gildya's robes was at the device, and the barrier flickered back to life.

"They're doing well," Veelk said with approval, and it sounded as if he wasn't only praising this particular group of defenders. Spending most of his days at the walls, he must have gotten used to breaches in the barrier.

Such words coming from Veelk were of the highest praise, and Kamira smiled. She opened her mouth, but before a reply left it, more shouts rose around them. All along the walls, the devices were failing, and in many places the barrier had already faded. The demonlings screeched louder, and Kamira could swear there was excitement in their inhuman voices.

"Ervan..." Koshmarnyk closed his fist, and as his body tensed, the magic within his regrowing stones intensified. "I should have dealt with him instead of being concerned about the council."

"Myrkan might have other spies as well," she replied.

Veelk and Zelna exchanged nods. "We'll help the defenders," Veelk said, and looked at Koshmarnyk. "Stay with her." His eyes shifted to Kamira. "You know best what to do."

She swallowed but nodded. If she had a chance to deal with Derazin, she'd take it. At least Koshmarnyk would watch her back.

Veelk and Zelna took off, and Mawi promptly followed the latter, leaving Kamira and Koshmarnyk alone. She rushed over to the closest device. "On my mark, take the barrier down."

A boy in his late teens flashed a confident grin at her, as if he alone could hold their defenses together. "On your mark, archmage."

Beside her, Koshmarnyk readied his knives, and she called upon her magic. Their goal was to kill Derazin, but first, she had to ensure the city survived.

She gave the signal, and the barrier in front of her fell in an instant, proving the boy knew his task and paid attention.

Below, the horde of demonlings scratched at the walls, already climbing to reach her, and their twisted, monstrous faces grew bigger as they go closer. Kamira could almost feel the magic tingling at her fingertips, ready to obey her command.

Without hesitation, she unleashed fire onto the monsters.

~

As a rule, Ervan didn't visit the High Towers if he could help it. To make an appearance in the high mages' domain meant to put himself in an inferior position, become a supplicant, and give Gildya's rivals even more power. No, Ervan had messengers if he needed anything from the Towers, and he let Gildya's council handle communications with the archmages... which they also avoided doing in person, unless absolutely necessary, and even then, they often picked neutral grounds to speak to a chosen archmage rather than visiting the Towers. It was all about appearances and power plays.

Yet sometimes necessity dictated taking things into one's own hands, and thus Ervan found himself climbing the winding road leading to the High Towers, though he doubted the new archmage would keep the name much longer. He'd already heard from his informants that arcanists referred to their seat simply as "the Towers," and he wouldn't be surprised if the name changed soon, along with some clerical alterations to how the school was run to give the impression of deep and profound changes.

Up close, the building looked even more imposing, with its mismatched multitude of thin and thick towers reaching far into the sky. Gildya might have its grand hall and many buildings scattered across the city—workshops, storages, and adept quarters—but it never dared to build up, to distinguish itself from the somewhat even lines of Kaighal's rooftops reaching no higher than four or five stories. It never dared to rise above the other citizens, to show the archmages that adepts were equal to them, to throw the challenge of a building as tall and marvelous and imposing as the High Towers were. No wonder that, despite the supposed balance of power between the council and the archmages, the commoners always said it was the archmages who ruled the city.

Two guards, a man and a woman, stood at the entrance, and they barred his way as he approached.

"By the order of the first archmage, no one is allowed to enter," said the man.

The other guard looked at her companion hesitantly, and Ervan hid a smile. He knew this woman's face, and he knew the amount of coin she'd received from him.

"I'm here by the order of the first archmage herself," Ervan replied with confidence. "The protective devices are being sabotaged, and she wishes for Gildya to find a solution. Do you want the barrier protecting the city to fall?"

The man hesitated, and that was when the woman chimed in, "It's going to take too long to send word to the walls, and if it's as dire there as it seems from a distance, the messenger might not be able to get to the archmage."

Ervan kept his face neutral, though the hidden suggestion that the archmage was leading the battle herself was unnerving. The Tivarashan woman had certainly made sure others *saw* her as the savior of the city, but he doubted she actually did anything that would endanger herself.

At least she wasn't in the Towers, which would make his task easier... to a point. If all was to be done properly, she had to die as well. He'd have to find a way to lure her back here.

"Look," the woman continued. "It's better to risk it and then be praised for making the right decision than do nothing and be blamed for the city's fall. Because I'm sure that if something happens up there"—she waved upward—"the archmage will blame us for not letting him in instead of admitting that it was her order that kept the adept away."

This was an argument that spoke to anyone who had dealt with people of power. In the eyes of commoners, leaders never admitted to their mistakes, and nothing the archmage said or did would change that perspective.

Ervan took a mental note to send more coin the woman's way later. Lackeys like her, cunning enough to manipulate others instead of just carrying out simple orders, were worth the extra payment.

"Fine. You can come in," the male guard said. "Just don't dawdle. Do you know the way?"

"I've been here before," Ervan replied. It'd been years since he last visited, but it was better to get lost than to have the guard accompany him. "Thank you. I'll be as quick as possible, but feel free to send a messenger to the archmage. She needs to stay informed of all happenings, of course."

He hoped that would suffice in drawing the archmage back to the Towers. Alluvendran must have warned her, so if all went well, she'd return to stop whatever threat she perceived and arrive just in time to meet her doom. On the other hand, everything could get more complicated if Alluvendran or anyone else accompanied her.

It doesn't matter, Ervan thought. There were things he could plan and control, and possibilities he could only best prepare for, hoping they'd turn favorable. For now, he'd focus on the first part of his task, and then he'd worry about the rest.

As he walked into the Towers, the female guard didn't even so much as glance at him, as if they were strangers. Perhaps she should have acknowledged him—after all, she'd argued in his favor—but it didn't matter much, since he'd been granted entry anyway.

The inside of the Towers was how Ervan remembered, speaking volumes about how high mages preferred to preserve tradition than carve new paths. And yet something was different about the building full of narrow corridors and steep stairways.

Ervan made his way through the reception area, stepping deeper into the building, and it took him a moment to pinpoint the change: the silence. The Towers seemed eerily quiet, almost tranquil, as if all its inhabitants had abandoned the place. Of course, he'd heard that after the turmoil, many teachers and students *had* left, not interested in the arcane arts that replaced the high magic, but according to Ervan's informants, enough of them had stayed to fill at least some of the halls and dormitories.

He remembered the stairway, wider than the others, that should lead him close to the topmost tower and the initiation chamber, which, according to Adept Davshil, housed Gildya's device. He rushed up the stairs and made his way through even more stairways and corridors. The haunting atmosphere of the Towers weighed heavily on him, and the lack of anyone's presence didn't provide any distractions from his own thoughts... from what he'd done.

Of course, on the spur of the adrenaline-filled moment, it was easy to deal with the council, and even now he saw the wisdom of his decision. Other adepts had always held him back, being so similar to high mages in their attempts to preserve power and influence. Under his command, Gildya would finally thrive, and with the archmage out of the way, there would be no one to challenge his position. No one except for Myrkan...

Ervan shivered but pushed the thought of the demon

away before fear could trap him in its clutches. Besides, once he fulfilled Myrkan's request, the demon would be much more appeased, and the threat looming over the city would fade.

And I would be Kaighal's savior.

He clung to that vision, allowing it to bring him strength and resolve.

There were no guards at the topmost level, and Ervan looked around. Dealing with so much mental strain already, and with his memories of the Towers' many stairways and hallways rather blurry, he wouldn't put it past himself to have taken the wrong turn and ended up in the wrong tower, but the large door in front of him suggested he'd found the right place.

He straightened his back and walked inside like a confident adept would.

The round chamber was empty and devastated. Signs of fires marked many columns, and several tall windows had broken panes. The huge dome, in the past visible from many points of Kaighal and shining in the sun like a true magical jewel, was now a gaping hole that let the elements in. To the side of the chamber lay a pile of crystal, and though Ervan couldn't be certain, it seemed to emanate the same eerie energy that always unnerved him when he worked with imbued stones for too long.

But if the crystals were filled with magic, it was odd that the archmage would keep them in an untidy heap like that instead of having them sorted and stored. Unless it was a part of some elaborate plan of hers. Maybe she wanted to show her power by indicating how little such stones were of worth to her.

He pulled his eyes away from the crystals and his

thoughts away from idle considerations. Deeper in the chamber stood the familiar device and his goal.

"Who are you?" A woman stepped from the side.

With the shadow of the column cast over her, Ervan took her for the archmage, but as she approached—cautious and slow—the shade of her skin turned more brown than gray. At a closer look, she was also way too young to be the archmage. She wore the outfit of a high mage, which meant she was likely one of those teachers who'd decided to stay in the Towers.

"There is a flaw in the devices that allows saboteurs to damage them," he replied with confidence. "I've been sent to install additional protection that will ensure the devices' undisturbed workings."

"I know nothing about it," she replied.

Ervan hesitated. Any lie could be his last, and he had to be prepared to act. Fear once more took control of him. He simply didn't know enough. The woman, though a former high mage, could be trained enough to wield the new magic, and she could pose a threat. On the other hand, if he did nothing, he'd fail at his task.

"I have a writ from Gildya's council, and the message to the archmage has been sent," he replied, pretending to shuffle through his pocket. "I'm a council member myself. My name is Ervan..."

Though the expression on the woman's face remained unchanged, Ervan caught her eyes widening at the sound of his name.

She knows!

Without hesitation, he lunged, his heart racing as he gripped the hidden knife. The blade felt awfully small in his hand, even though a bigger one would have made no difference in a situation like this.

The woman took a frantic step back, losing her balance as she lifted her arms in an instinctive defense. Magic aura surrounded her hands. Ervan was faster. He crashed onto her, pushing her to the ground and striking at her as they both fell.

She let out a yell of pain, though it carried more anger than fear. Ervan struck once more, but before he could do anything else, a gust of strong wind pushed him away.

As he scrambled to his feet, so did the woman, despite the patch of blood growing on her clothes, and he was at a disadvantage now. Instead of trying to attack again, he dashed back, putting the device between him and the mage. She would not throw magic at it, so all he had to do was wait till she bled out.

His mood soured. Until it happened, he couldn't damage his only protection, and the more time passed, the more likely something would go wrong, but he couldn't risk a direct attack. Too bad he hadn't thought of bringing more poisonous devices with him, but back then it seemed better to not draw too much attention. A member of Gildya's council hefting a bag on his own would raise too much suspicion, and he couldn't have risked taking any apprentices with him.

The woman's gaze became unfocused, and the way she stood suggested that despite her attempts to stop the bleeding, she'd pass out soon. Slowly, she backed toward the door, never taking her eyes off him.

Ervan hesitated. If she got out, she could get help, but with her wound, she likely wouldn't make it far... or fast. Before anyone learned of what happened, he would be already done with his task.

By the door, she almost collapsed, but pulled herself up

along the wall and stumbled outside. Ervan kept his eyes on the door, in case she decided to turn back, but then his attention shifted toward the device. He'd spent enough time on the blueprints to know every piece of it, but it looked different now... Alluvendran must have made alterations after Gildya delivered it into the Towers.

His frustration faded as quickly as it appeared. In the end, it didn't matter what improvements that wretched rogue adept might have made. No device would work without magic, and its source was clear enough.

With confidence, Ervan pulled the imbued stone out. It looked much like the crystals in the nearby pile. The device whirred and its hum became irregular, but it kept working. An additional power source! When he thought about it, it made sense that Alluvendran would make the device work on two stones instead of one. This would ensure that whenever one needed replacement, the other would keep the barrier up.

It didn't take Ervan long to locate the other stone, and he pulled it out. The device went silent, and the barrier above the broken dome flickered. The deed was done, and now all that he had left to do was ensure the demon knew who'd helped him. He pulled Myrkan's stone out of his pocket and moved it close to the crystals he'd removed from the device.

It took a moment, but the demon's ghastly face appeared before him.

"I've done what you've asked for," Ervan said before Myrkan could take control of the conversation. "Soon, the barrier over the Towers is going to vanish, and you'll be free to enter the city. I'm sure the archmage will arrive here shortly to see what happened. I made sure word reached her."

Myrkan smiled. "You did well. I will keep my word and spare the city if it surrenders."

Ervan swallowed, because it would be up to him to convince the citizens of Kaighal that yielding was a better choice. "I'll return to Gildya, then, and wait for your word." No matter what the demon was planning to do, Ervan preferred to be as far away as possible. With the archmage and possibly even the other demon involved, the Towers might not survive whatever confrontation was coming. "As soon as you make your offer of a peaceful surrender, I'll make sure everyone accepts it."

"And your council? Will they still object?"

He allowed himself a confident smile as he looked the demon straight in the eye. "I made sure they won't."

Myrkan grinned with satisfaction. "Well done. Go now if you value your life."

The ghastly apparition disappeared, and Ervan once more stood alone in the chamber. For a heartbeat, he cherished the feeling of triumph that washed over him, but Myrkan's last words reminded him that he still had to survive to see the conclusion of his bold choices.

Over him, the barrier kept flickering, unstable, and that meant the archmage had to be on the way here, and with her, her demon and Alluvendran would likely arrive too. As much as he wanted to see the rogue adept put in his place, this could wait. Even if Alluvendran didn't come or survived the encounter, Ervan could deal with him later, using the convenient accusations regarding the council's demise, and there would be no one to protect Alluvendran anymore.

Outside the chamber, a steady trail of blood told him that the woman had made it further away, but even if she survived despite the significant blood loss, it didn't matter.

Any alarm she could raise would rally people back to the chamber, where they would witness destruction and nothing else.

Ervan would be long gone by then.

12

Atissa did her best to ignore the sounds of battle waged up on the walls and—it seemed—all around her. There was only the circle, and the wounded lined up beside it that two older men, perhaps unfit for fighting duty, kept carrying in and out.

Mindful of the advice she'd received about the limits of pacts, she did as little as possible to keep the wounded men and women alive. The disappointment on their faces when they realized they still would be in pain and recovering for weeks to come haunted her, but after her second wounded guard and with her pact magic already stretched thin, she considered it a better choice than completely healing one person and letting dozens of others die.

A screech way too close for comfort pulled her back to reality. Her first instinct was to raise a barrier protecting herself and the injured woman in front of her, but it wasn't as easy as reciting a well-rehearsed spell anymore. She needed focus and magic to sustain it, and that meant no healing.

Shuffling and more screeches behind her tugged at her

instincts, especially with the frightened expressions of her two helpers clear in sight, and she fought to not look over her shoulder. Seeing the battle taking place so close to her was going to destroy any focus she might have left.

Atissa took a deep breath and closed her eyes for a moment. Then, without delay, she channeled magic into the woman. When the wound closed enough, Atissa motioned for the helpers to take her away. Medics would have to take care of her from now on.

The screeches behind her back faded, and Atissa breathed out with relief as the men carried her patient away, but when she looked up at the walls, it seemed that the battle was still as fierce as when she'd arrived.

Shouts of surprise and pain drew her attention, and as she turned her head to find their source, one of the barriers flickered and died. Within heartbeats, a swarm of demonlings flooded over the battlements, swiping the few humans standing in their way and spreading along the walls to search for more targets. One paused and stared down.

Atissa froze under the gaze of the beady, bloodshot eyes. The creature had almost human arms, but its hands resembled animal paws, with long claws caressing the stone it stood on. One more moment, and it would leap.

A huge figure smashed into the wall, scattering the demonlings, including the one that was about to attack Atissa. A demon swiped through the running creatures, the movement of his claws controlled and efficient. There was no rage on his face, and Atissa found no malice either, as if the killing brought him no pleasure. With his face calm and focused, he was so different from Myrkan, but Atissa couldn't help her instinctual fear. It took her all willpower to turn away and focus on the next wounded being laid down in her circle. At least with the demon fighting the demonlings, she didn't have to worry about her own safety.

The man in the circle was unconscious. His body was a mangled mess of blood, flesh, and torn clothes, as if a demonling had not only attacked him, but stomped into the man's chest repeatedly, digging its claws deeper and deeper. Atissa hesitated, but in the end, she knew little of actual wound dressing and what steps were necessary to ensure proper healing. What she knew, though, was that without her help, the man would die anyway, so she had to try. She channeled magic once more.

The magic flowed... and stopped.

Panicked, Atissa reached for her magic again. At first, she thought her demon had broken the pact, but the connection was still there—there was just no magic to draw from.

Then it dawned on her. Weaker demons had only so much to offer, and Pelina had warned her that magic was likely to run out, unless Atissa made a pact with a higher demon.

"What's going on? Why aren't you helping him?" a woman standing nearby asked.

"I don't have any more magic," Atissa replied through her clenched throat.

The woman muttered something under her breath, and Atissa could have sworn it was "useless," but she didn't linger to deliver complaints or lectures. Instead, she motioned at Atissa's helpers. "Bring him to the medics' post immediately, where he can get some actual help." Her disapproving expression made it clear what she thought of Atissa's attempts.

They left quickly, leaving Atissa alone. She sighed, her

shoulders slumping and eyes filling with tears. How foolish of her to think she could really make a difference!

At least I know that the healing circle is working, she thought to seek some comfort. No matter how much her personal defeat stung, she still could prove herself later. With a better pact, perhaps, and more knowledge on how to improve the circle and make it more useful than simply closing the wounds, she could become a true healer.

"How badly do you want more magic?" a deep male voice asked behind her.

Atissa flinched. She knew that inhuman tone, and even if the demon behind her wasn't Myrkan, she couldn't shake the memories easily. These creatures were vile and vicious, and even if this one was aiding the city's defense, it didn't mean its true nature wouldn't come out at some point.

Yet to ignore him could cause even more harm than risking a conversation.

Atissa turned to face the demon.

The nearest breach of the walls had already been contained with a new device creating its part of the barrier, and most of the defenders moved to other breaches, except for the few that were finishing off wounded demonlings and pushing them off the walls. The demon didn't seem interested in joining another fray. Instead, he landed nearby. If she recalled correctly, his name was Fyertash, the smaller of the two Kamira had brought into Kaighal. He was looking at her with eyes narrowed, calculating and cunning. Even if she caught no maliciousness in his expression, it could mean he was simply better at hiding it than Myrkan.

"Without magic, I can't help," Atissa said.

"I could offer you a pact."

She regarded him with suspicion. "You're Irtan's demon."

He burst out laughing. "Now that's an amusing way to put it, but you should already know that a pact is not a matter of one belonging to the other. A yalari can have many pacts, and he or she can care as little or as much about them as he or she chooses."

Atissa grimaced. He couldn't have been oblivious to what she really wanted to know, yet he chose to deflect her question. "What's in it for you?" she asked bluntly. A demon who had a pact with Irtan and who seemed to willingly serve Kamira couldn't be seeking new pacts for no reason, and if he did, there were plenty of more promising arcanists.

He looked her up and down. "If you succeed in your pursuits with the aid of my magic, my name will be remembered along with yours. But there's more." He gave her a playful smile. "I get to see what the first archmage thinks of it. I wonder whether she'd approve or disapprove."

Suddenly, his first question made sense: how *badly* did she want more magic? Only someone desperate would make a pact and get herself tangled in the games that the demon, Irtan, and Kamira were likely playing.

Atissa pressed her lips together. No matter what she did, no matter how hard she tried to keep a path different from the one her father had chosen for her, someone always pushed her back onto it. Escaping seemed impossible, so she might as well ensure that she had enough power to have a say instead of remaining a pawn.

"Very well. Do you want me to draw a summoning circle?"

Fyertash smirked as if amused that she knew *something* of the arcane arts. "I'm here already. Just say the words."

Atissa hid her relief. Remembering the summoning spell was easy for a former high mage used to memorizing countless spells and chants, but if he decided to test her knowledge of the circles, she would fail miserably. When she first made a pact, she'd copied the circle from the sketch Pelina gave her, never paying attention to the details or understand its working—after all, she would only need it once. Since then, she'd paid more attention to the healing circles but never had time to draw any general knowledge from them.

Without delay, she spoke the words of the summoning spell, finishing it with Fyertash's name. Magic condensed in the air, creating a spectacle of flickering lights missed by all but the few that were close enough.

"I accept the pact," Fyertash said, his voice devoid of any sarcasm or playfulness.

A single silvery beam of magic traveled from him to her, and once it struck, Atissa gasped. The demon's magic seemed endless. If Atissa wanted, she could hold a barrier all day long or heal dozens of people with ease.

With a gesture, Fyertash stopped two people carrying a wounded man. "Bring him here." He pointed at the circle, and they obeyed. Then he looked at Atissa. "Make a good use of my offering, pactee."

He took off in the air, but Atissa paid no more attention. With a wounded person already within her healing circle, she had a job to do. The energy flowed smoothly as Atissa channeled it, but she resisted healing more than necessary. The memory of magic running out still stung, and she wouldn't risk depleting Fyertash's gift before all the injured people had been seen to.

At the back of her head, a small voice whispered about consequences to come: Kamira's anger or suspicions, Irtan's manipulations, and Fyertash's true intentions—but she'd deal with them as they came. For now, she would simply enjoy the feeling of working with magic and helping those who were looking death in the eyes.

~

Allyv wiped his forehead with the sleeve of his shirt. The battle raged on, and it was as fierce as Archmage Kamira had predicted. The protective devices kept failing, and some people blamed Gildya for not pulling their weight, but from what he'd seen, poor adepts were tirelessly running along the walls, providing new devices and fixing the broken ones, so sabotage was more likely. The memory of the demon speaking of a traitor among the Devanshari still stung, but at least the archmage wasn't casting any accusations at Allyv's people.

He chased those thoughts away. Overseeing the battle was his main concern for now, especially since Kamira was right, and Kaighal's officials had little knowledge of strategy and logistics. At least they were eager enough to give Allyv freedom to make decisions, and they didn't mind when he consulted the few Devanshari commanders who'd made it to Tyorane with the rest of the refugees. Unfortunately, it didn't stop them from arguing among themselves.

"What good are those devices if they keep failing? We should ask the mages... the demonologists to protect our people with magic," one of them said. He was a thin man whose frantic moves spoke of a volatile temper.

"It's Gildya's fault, so they should send more adepts to remedy the problem," argued a middle-aged woman with sharp eyes and a pointy nose. Her outfit and behavior made her look like a noblewoman, if Kaighal cared for such titles.

Allyv sighed, only half listening to their bickering. From

what he understood, both Gildya and the Towers had given as much as they could, and there simply wasn't more to ask for. At the same time, if no one came up with a solution, the defenders would tire quickly under the constant attacks of the creatures who could scale the city walls with ease, and there were always more coming.

He looked down at the map of the city. So far, the demons had kept to the south, with groups of demonlings spreading westward, but they hadn't attempted to surround Kaighal, pressuring it from all sides like they did back in Devanshari. If needed, people could still flee through the northern gate and to Tivarashan...

A sudden realization struck him.

"Call back as many forces from the northern walls as you can," he said. "Leave enough to defend and keep eyes on the devices, but you should be able to bring about half of the defenders here."

Both the man and woman looked at him in disbelief, and even his own comrades, though more restrained in expressing their thoughts, were glancing at him doubtfully.

"We can't leave part of the walls vulnerable," argued the thin man.

"They might be waiting for us to weaken the northern side," the woman added, glaring at the man as if she was unhappy to be on the same side.

"The demons won't go north," Allyv said with more confidence than he felt. People around him needed decisiveness, not an opening for more arguments. "They won't go near the lands that belong to other demons. And we need more forces to relieve defenders here, otherwise it won't matter whether the northern walls are protected or not."

Neither the man nor the woman could argue with that.

Someone waved at the messenger girl and stepped to the side to give her instructions. Allyv focused on the map again.

He was about to ask for any new reports from the defenses when a shout on the walls drew his attention. A protective device exploded in a small ball of fire, driving nearby defenders away, some already licked by the flames. They scrambled back, but with other groups already engaged in battle, they were on their own.

It took a single long breath for chaos to break loose. An adept was already running up the stairs with another device, and the people assigned to this part of the wall readied their weapons, but this was all they managed before a horde of demonlings leaped over the battlements. A few engaged their nearest opponents, but others poured onto the stairs. The adept who was in their way died before he even realized he was facing monsters, and the creatures rushed toward the strategy table.

The woman beside Allyv screamed and back-pedaled, and the thin man stared motionless. Without hesitation, Allyv drew his sword. It was a short blade, suitable for a young man who never had to defend himself, but in close quarters it would serve him better than a larger, more unwieldy weapon.

"Protect the king!" one of his commanders shouted.

Allyv tensed. Back in the Devanshari, he had never lifted his blade, at all times protected by devoted royal guards. Obeying his mother's orders, they'd shielded him all the way from the palace to the port. But this wasn't Devanshari, and the queen wasn't around to coddle him.

As the creatures drew closer, Allyv took a slow breath, hoping to steady his racing heart. He sought no glory nor adventure, but at the same time, he wouldn't allow his people to see him cowering behind others. They needed a strong king, and he had to prove he was one.

The first demonling charged at him wildly as Allyv exhaled, preparing to receive his attacker. It lunged ferociously, but fought like an animal, easy to predict, and thus easy to counter. Its tiny, sharp claws thrust for his throat, and Allyv turned sideways and stepped into the attack, shouldering the creature to the ground, and then jammed the short blade through its chest.

Another followed, and Allyv dispatched it easily enough.

His combat trainers had told him that in the chaos of a real battle, survival mattered more than stance, form, or other formalities, and on occasion they arranged chaotic bouts and brawls for him to partake in. Despite the wooden swords, bruises and scratches were unavoidable, and Cahala qi'Devanshari had many times expressed her disapproval of such teaching.

Now, slashing through swarming demonlings, Allyv appreciated every single one of those brutish lessons.

A few Devanshari joined him, and together they stemmed the stream of creatures, but more were still jumping over the battlements. With the adept dead, and no others nearby, Allyv couldn't help wondering how long they'd hold out. If only they could get up the walls and try to bottleneck the creatures at the battlements...

A man to Allyv's right fell to the ground, gurgling from his ripped throat, and the demonling that landed on him glared at Allyv. The eyes of the monster were vicious, full of fury, but unlike with true beasts, there was a glimmer of intelligence in them, warning Allyv to not make an abrupt decision. If he attacked thoughtlessly, the creature would take advantage of him.

The demonling leaped at Allyv, spreading its large claws, and he sidestepped, parrying the wide swipe with his blade. The creature landed on the back of an unsuspecting defender, and a short scream was all the woman managed before collapsing to the ground.

"Protect the king!" someone shouted again, but Allyv paid no attention.

To his surprise, the demonling didn't turn back to him. It stood on the dead woman's body, looking to the sides—a perfect opening. Allyv lifted his sword to strike, but his instincts once more warned him of the creature's intelligence and something else... He trusted it, spinning in place and striking as another demonling leaped at him. His sword cleaved the ugly head. Before Allyv could pull it out, the first demonling was already darting at him.

Oh, Light...

His heartbeat deafening in his ears, Allyv struggled to free his blade before the creature cut the distance between them. Its screech sounded triumphant.

A shadow was cast over him, and the demonling flew into the air, squealing and wriggling in Fyertash's grip. The demon landed nearby, stomping another creature, and he threw the one he was holding at the demonlings scrambling through the battlements.

Then, with a focused expression, he took a step forward. A quiet growl was all that left his throat, but the demonling yelped and whined, backing away. Some retreated over the wall, while others huddled together like terrified rabbits. Then, in a rapid shift, they lunged at their own brethren with furious shrieks.

"Get someone up there," Fyertash said. "My will won't last long over Derazin's power."

"Do as he says," Allyv told one of his commanders, and

he looked at the demon. "Thank you for your aid," he forced himself to say. Fyertash was one of the demons who'd destroyed Devanshari and slaughtered his people, and that couldn't be forgiven, but his help had to be recognized.

The demon looked at him strangely, curiosity mixed with amusement, as if he knew what Allyv was thinking about. Though, truth be told, it wasn't difficult to guess, since throughout the siege so far, Allyv had made a point to avoid the demon and any conversation with him.

"There's a pactee healer nearby." Fyertash pointed south. "If you have any gravely wounded, she might be able to keep them alive."

The demon took off without waiting for a reply and headed to what looked like another serious breach.

Allyv sighed. A pactee healer must mean magic, and he tensed. Subjecting his companions to demonology made his stomach churn, but he steeled himself. If demon magic could keep his people alive, it was all that mattered.

At the walls, the defenders had already killed the remaining demonlings, and a newly arrived adept was setting up the protective device. Allyv cleaned his sword before sheathing it, and headed for the toppled strategy table. The map was already gone, carried away by the wind or drowned in someone's blood, but he still set the table back in place.

"Someone get me a new map," he said loud enough to be heard over the sounds of the ongoing battle. "And if you have any gravely wounded, send them south. There's a skilled healer there."

With so many Devanshari around, he'd rather not divulge that the skill was magical. They could lodge their complaints later, when they all survived.

KAMIRA HAD no doubt that they were losing the battle. To others it might seem like Kaighal was holding its own, pushing away the hordes of demonlings and replacing sabotaged devices with new ones to ensure the continued protection of the walls, but she knew their defeat was only a matter of time. Soon enough, the defenders would become exhausted, with others too wounded to keep fighting, and Gildya would run out of the devices... The arcanists serving Myrkan and Derazin would tire at some point too, but there were enough of them to take turns in summoning the demonlings, sending wave after wave at the city.

At least things had calmed for the time being, with most devices working and the barrier restored, so the defenders got a moment of rest, but she had to use this opportunity to search for a solution. For the city to survive, she needed one fast.

Even if she could hold her part of the walls for longer, in the end, she would succumb to tiredness like all others, and so would Koshmarnyk.

A shadow of smile passed her lips when she thought of Veelk, who would likely outlast them all: the defenders, the demonlings, and even the demons. Sadly, he was the only one, because Kamira doubted even Zelna matched both his thirst for battle and endurance.

"First archmage, a message!" a girl called from behind.

Kamira turned, wary of possible assassins using a child as a decoy, and by her side, Koshmarnyk corrected the grip on his knives.

The girl couldn't be more than thirteen, but she carried herself like an adult, likely having done messenger work for weeks, if not months. "A word from the Towers. An adept arrived to fix the barrier device. Says Gildya found the weak spot that causes them to fail. Will there be a message back?"

Kamira exchanged glances with Koshmarnyk, and his tense expression was enough of a tell. "No. Thank you for your work," she replied without even looking at the girl, regretting she had no time to offer her more attention and appreciation.

"It must be Ervan." Koshmarnyk looked toward the Towers, tense and anxious.

"Go," Kamira said softly, trying to lessen his doubt. "This *is* what I asked you to do."

He nodded, but the pain of a difficult choice still marred his face. "I'll be back as soon as I can."

She had no doubt that he worried about her and the looming battle with demons, but his lack of fussing about her safety made it clear his worries stemmed from the relationship they had, not from thinking she wasn't capable of doing what she had to do... Just like she worried about him. Even if Ervan was not a warrior, and definitely not a match for Koshmarnyk, he likely had a nasty trick or two prepared.

"Nyk," she said while he cleaned blood off his blades. "Do what you have to... I'd rather apologize to Gildya for his death than risk whole Kaighal's wellbeing just to play by the council's rules."

"That makes two of us," he replied, and took off.

Kamira turned away as soon as he made it down the walls. If it was up to her, she'd watch his departure until he disappeared deeper in the street, but the archmage had obligations, and demonlings wouldn't wait until she fulfilled her personal desires.

She glanced over the walls. The creatures were keeping their distance. They snarled and growled, and their red eyes were full of hate and eagerness, yet they didn't attack. Perhaps arcanists were keeping them away until they could summon more of those despicable creatures.

Fyertash descended, hovering above her. "Still no sign of him."

She acknowledged him with a nod. They both knew there was a trap coming, but to discuss it without any new insights was pointless.

Veelk and Zelna made their way to her from their respective parts of the walls. Both bore marks of battle, sweat mixing with blood on their skin and outfits, but she spied no wounds, and that brought relief.

"I sent Koshmarnyk after the adept," she said when they were within earshot. With so many people around, she could only do so much to ensure no one eavesdropped on their conversation, so vague remarks would have to do.

A grimace passed over Zelna's face, but she didn't criticize her openly, and Kamira appreciated the courtesy. "It might be a part of something bigger."

Fyertash nodded, which brought another grimace to the tribal warrioress's face. "Myrkan hasn't shown up yet. It would be a crude plan, but they might be trying to draw us out. If we take our chance with Derazin, Myrkan will attack."

Kamira narrowed her eyes, looking beyond the hordes of demonlings. "There has to be more than that. We already know there's two of them."

A powerful, challenging roar tore through the air, and Kamira could swear Fyertash tensed. "Derazin's feigning courage," he whispered. "Be prepared. They'll attack again."

As if confirming his words, the demonlings stirred and responded to the higher demon's roar with their own screeches. Even from this distance, the noise was near deafening, and Kamira fought the urge to take a step back. Beside her, Veelk and Zelna corrected the grips on their keshals.

The barrier all along the walls flickered.

Even if Myrkan had dozens of spies, it would be impossible to make all the devices fail at the same time...

Her eyes widened in sudden understanding, and she looked over her shoulder. The barrier over the Towers that provided the cap over the city, stabilizing all other barriers, was wavering.

Fyertash followed her gaze. "Myrkan's finally showing his hand. Can you provide protection until your adept fixes the device?"

"I'd never get there on time." For this one time, her neglect of extensive physical activity was going to be of deadly consequence, and not only for herself but for the whole city.

Veelk snorted as if his thoughts followed a similar path. "He'll carry you there," he said in the way that suggested personal experience.

Fyertash flew down to the street, scaring off several defenders who were sorting out arrows and other supplies. He paid no attention to them, focusing on an abandoned stall instead. He ripped off the fabric stretched over it. "This will do." He made it back to her, holding the fabric like a makeshift swing right in front of her. "Archmage?" he said with a hint of challenge.

Veelk gave her an encouraging nudge. "It's not that bad," he muttered.

She'd love to offer him a witty remark or two, but they had no time. "Be careful. We still don't know what Myrkan's planning. I'll be back with Nyk soon."

The only reply was Veelk's confident grin, and she

couldn't decide whether she should find comfort in it or worry that it meant her friend was planning to take on two demons all by himself. Not that he would ever tell her if he intended the latter.

Without any more delays, she climbed into the fabric pouch and sank in. Instinctively, she clutched it, trying not to think how little protection it really offered. If Fyertash dropped her or the fabric ripped...

The slight swinging motion suggested the demon had taken off, and Kamira focused her eyes and thoughts on the Towers. The flight was so different than the one she'd experienced through her crystal nightfly on a few occasions —not as smooth and a lot more breathtaking. Her heart raced, and no reassurances could alter her body's reaction.

The Towers were getting closer at a speed that promised her ordeal would be over soon enough. The barrier still flickered, giving her hope of making it to the chamber on time. She dared not look down, at the winding path leading to the Towers, to see if Koshmarnyk had already made it there.

Fyertash lifted her higher in the air, and her stomach showed signs of rebellion. She fixed her eyes on the broken dome coming into view and focused on taking steady breaths.

The barrier above them flickered for the last time and disappeared. Kamira cursed under her breath. In flight it would be impossible to conjure any stable protection for the city.

Her fabric cradle swung dangerously as Fyertash sped up, and the stone base of the shattered dome was coming close fast. In a smooth move, he lifted high enough to make it over the edge, and Kamira peeked down, into the initiation chamber.

An angry roar tore across the sky, but before she had a chance to look up, her cradle swung in a violent manner, sending her against the dome's edge. The motion wasn't enough to break anything, but slamming into the stone sent waves of pain across her body.

Then the fabric around her went limp.

13

Once the archers were in position, Seraine, Zimfe, and Ryell got as close as they could without risking being spotted. The attention of the Tivarashan group was on the battlefield, but one turn of a head could be all it took to notice the three intruders hidden in the bushes at the edge of the forest.

Ryell couldn't help glancing beyond the gathering, at the battlefield itself. Two masses of people were clashing in chaos with little respect for tactics. He had no doubt that the generals and other commanders were doing their best to keep the armies in line, issuing order after order, but he had enough experience to know that once blade met blade and blood stained the ground, primal instincts often took over.

In the rain of arrows and with natural and magical fires blazing all over the battlefield, it was harder to hold the line, and soldiers from both sides merged into a single mass, exchanging blows and—Ryell was certain—desperately trying to survive.

He might have never partaken in a battle that big, but even small skirmishes with the demonologists and their monsters had taught him enough ugly truths about war. What felt worse was that in this battle, people fell on both sides, and there were no monsters to drive away, only fellow humans. On the other hand, just like the demonologists back in Devanshari served demons, Tivarashans worshiped them, so perhaps they deserved all the death coming their way.

Ryell forced his eyes away from the battle before the memories of the war with demons dimmed his reason. He had a task at hand, and if he wanted to succeed, he needed his head on his shoulders, not sunken in the mire of past tragedies.

Beside him, Captain Seraine lay motionless, with her attention on the gathering before them. As a scout, she had to be accustomed to prolonged waits like this one, and he couldn't help wondering in which direction her thoughts traveled. After all, this was a risky plan, fit for a group of trained assassins rather than a handful of scouts who'd happened upon the opportunity to change the tides of a battle.

Even though he still struggled to shed the memories, Ryell didn't miss the quiet whoosh of an arrow. He immediately sprang into action, not waiting for it to hit.

The projectile reached the end of its journey, but as the princess turned that very moment—perhaps warned by the same whoosh that told Ryell when to move—its tip grazed her decorative metal shoulder pad and fell off without doing any harm.

Three more arrows were loosed immediately, hitting two of their marks, and two demonologists fell to the ground. The third one, perhaps quicker in his reactions than the others, swung magic in a desperate wave of his arms, pushing the projectile away.

Having fought demonologists before, Ryell went straight for him.

The demonologist was still facing the trees, likely looking for the archer. As Ryell got close, the Tivarashan turned, panic clear on his face, and waved his hands once more, taking instinctive steps backward. Ryell sneered, lunging. Demonologists were formidable opponents at a distance, with the demons protecting them and time to unleash a plethora of destructive magic. But up close, when they weren't prepared, the odds were drastically against them. Ryell had killed enough demonologists in Devanshari to know that a blade could be faster than any channeling, and his opponents often hesitated, trying to make a choice between raising a barrier and throwing magic at him.

The Tivarashan demonologist was no different, and his lack of decisiveness cost him his life. Ryell thrust his blade quickly through his opponent's throat, severing the spine in one decisive motion.

Nearby, Captain Seraine had dispatched two noblemen before they were even aware of her, and those that noticed the situation grasped at weapons too slowly to defend themselves.

Before Ryell focused his assault on the demonologist, he saw Zimfe going straight for the armored guards with all the thundering confidence of a charging bear. It looked like the warrior would crush his enemies with the sheer strength and speed of his charging, but the guards were well trained, and Ryell wasn't surprised to see Zimfe still fighting. His sword clashed with theirs in quick exchanges. His defensive style of sword fighting, once engaged, left his opponents still standing, but so was he, and at least he kept them occupied, so Ryell sought another.

More guards were approaching. Some headed straight

for Zimfe, likely seeing him as the biggest threat. Others stumbled as the arrows of the scouts still hidden up in the trees reached them. Two made it to Ryell, and he dodged their crude attacks with ease. If they had the fencing training he'd expect of royal guards, they chose not to show it. Or perhaps they didn't consider commoners like Baxayalans worthy of such swordsmanship.

Ryell assumed an extravagant fighting stance, unfit for real skirmishes. The guards exchanged confused glances for the moment Ryell needed. Contrary to his initial stance, his attack was simple and effective. In a situation like this, speed and precision mattered more than sophistication. After all, he had to take one of them down before they caught on.

Ryell's low, quick strike to the leg bent the guard down onto one knee. As the guard's head dropped, and Ryell's blade reached to the sky, an arrow thudded into the man's eye, and his body fell. Without delay, Ryell turned to his other opponent to see a blade bursting forth from his sternum. Seraine flashed him a smile and moved on to the next target as the guard's body crumpled to the ground.

Moments later, Ryell pulled his sword from a Tivarashan captain and looked around to maintain his bearings amongst the chaos known as battle. Most of the guards were still on Zimfe, and the large warrior looked wounded, but other Tivarashans were fleeing, calling for help, or searching for the enemy, weapons drawn. Every now and then, arrows cut through the air, hitting limbs, torsos, and occasionally the ground.

The assault was going well, but sooner or later, the Tivarashans would realize that there were only three assailants among them and a few archers in the trees. A rally and reinforcements were likely soon to come. Perhaps it was time to withdraw...

Then he saw her.

The Tivarashan princess stood unmoved by the chaos of blood and battle around her, confident and calm, with her hand on the hilt of her sword in that casual manner of someone prepared for a fight but not concerned about it. The two guards that died must have been her defenders, but she displayed no reaction to their demise.

Ryell gritted his teeth. When their eyes met, the princess curled her lips in a mix of disapproval and contempt, and in that moment, she reminded Ryell all too much of Kamira. It seemed that all Tivarashan women were the same, proud and deceitful, looking down on everyone else.

Without hesitation, Ryell broke into a run.

The grimace she had for him changed into a wicked smile, and she drew her sword. Their blades met, and to Ryell's surprise, she didn't lose her footing, even as she received the full charge of his body weight behind his blade. And it became apparent that she had more strength and skill than he'd expect from a noblewoman. Back in Devanshari, a princess would do some light fencing, but nothing too straining, and he doubted the queen herself, Cahala qi'Devanshari, could even hold a sword properly.

He didn't linger on the thought, as the Tivarashan woman kept pressing on, her technique flawless and strikes precise. Having had so few opportunities to practice in the last months, Ryell found himself at a clear disadvantage.

He clenched his teeth again. He refused to lose to a manipulative gaharra from a demon-worshiping land. She might have superior skills, but this wasn't a courtly duel. This was a skirmish, and a dirty one at that. Ryell had seen his fair share of underhanded fights back in Devanshari to know that rules did not apply, and he'd bet that this was the first real fight for the princess.

After finding a good, solid clump of moss and an arrow in the ground near it, he offered the princess a tell and a swing. She reacted in proper form with a parry and powerful strike, just as he'd predicted and wanted. He feigned a stumble and fall, and as he touched the ground and rolled, he grabbed the moss, then the arrow in the same hand. As he returned to his feet, the princess pressed forward, only to stop as she was forced to evade the clumsily lobbed arrow, but as she resumed her advance with a triumphant glint in her eyes, he followed with the moss.

She lifted her arms defensively to the unexpected projectile, and Ryell struck with precision. His sword tip touched one of the armored plates just beneath her breastplate, and he thrust upward, allowing him to guide the blade under and behind the breastplate. The blade met flesh, but as she moved and then stumbled backward, crying out in pain, he couldn't be sure of the depth of the wound. But she at least fell to her knees, abandoning her sword to grasp at the wound, and red blood trickled between her fingers.

"Princess Mefina is wounded!" someone shouted.

Everything around them shifted. The remaining guards abandoned Zimfe and rushed to their princess, and even some nobles mustered courage. One of them came at Ryell, slashing fiercely as if trying to sever every single limb from his body.

Ryell back-stepped in desperate defense while he fended off the crazed flurry of disorganized sword swings. The Tivarashan woman never saw Zimfe coming as she rained attacks on Ryell, and the Baxayalan warrior smashed into her at full speed. The ground she covered in flight was fitting, considering Zimfe's size, but it was nevertheless impressive.

"Time to go!" Captain Seraine yelled from just behind Ryell.

They rushed toward the trees. The archers covered their escape with several well-placed arrows, but hardly anyone gave chase. All of the survivors were surrounding the princess, and as Ryell looked back over his shoulder, he saw a few men were carrying the Tivarashan royalty away, with the guards and others providing protection. It didn't escape him that the princess lay motionless in their arms, and the bloodstain had covered the entirety of her torso and upper legs.

Captain Seraine grinned at him. "If she somehow survives, she'll forever remember your blade."

The remark brought Ryell satisfaction he hadn't felt in a long time.

As he was nearing the bottom of the Towers, Ervan slowed down. It would raise the entrance guard's suspicion if he was rushing out. At the same time, if they noticed the barrier becoming unstable, running would look more natural. An adept like him would be hurrying back to the council after his attempt to fix the device failed...

His pride made him hesitate. To appear as an incompetent adept, even if for mere moments, would be humiliating, and he could pretend to be unaware of the barrier's wavering... He'd stroll out with confidence, and if they pointed out problems, he'd insist on reporting it to Gildya rather than going back. If he calculated the device's capabilities correctly, he'd be halfway down the hill before the barrier fell.

With the decision made, he was ready to step outside, but a voice held him in place.

"I've been told an adept arrived in the Towers. Has he left yet?"

Ervan froze. Alluvendran! The archmage had sent him instead of coming herself!

Cautious to not make any sounds, he took several steps back, withdrawing into a side niche and listening in.

"No, he's still inside," the male guard replied.

"Very well. If he comes down, you are to stop him from leaving," Alluvendran said. "If you fail, you will be executed for treason."

Ervan narrowed his eyes. Alluvendran, he knew, had never lacked confidence, but he rarely exercised power over others or issued threats. That cold, almost cruel voice could just as well belong to another man. Or, perhaps, unbound by Gildya's rules and protected by the archmage, Alluvendran was finally showing his true colors.

Ervan pressed himself to the wall as steps echoed nearby, but the other adept was already rushing by, not bothering to check all the nooks. He must have assumed that Ervan was still up in the top chamber, sabotaging the device. *Good.* It gave him time to solve the problem of the guards.

He shifted uneasily. Maybe he should find a better hiding spot instead. Alluvendran would likely encounter Myrkan upstairs, sealing his own fate, and all Ervan had to do was wait the battle out.

No, he scolded himself. Staying in the Towers not only meant the risk of losing his life, but he could also run into the archmage. He had to get back to Gildya, taking control while everyone was shocked by the council's demise, and prepare to enter negotiations with Myrkan as the city's sole representative. Hiding like a coward would simply not do.

He considered his options. The guardswoman had helped him get into the Towers, as there was little consequence to it, but he hadn't paid her enough to ensure her loyalty when Alluvendran threw death threats. But if he attacked the other guard, she could come to his aid... A small injury would then suffice in convincing everyone that she'd tried to stop Ervan.

He grimaced. The thought of attacking a skilled man without knowing whether he'd have aid sounded like a fool's errand.

Perhaps he should search nearby chambers and corridors for a window low enough to climb through. It wouldn't be the most dignified departure from the Towers, but it was unlikely anyone would witness it.

He shifted but didn't move. A search meant risking being heard or seen, and the last thing he wanted was to confront Alluvendran while he was at a disadvantage. Out of the two options, fighting with a guard would be a better choice than fighting Alluvendran. Maybe he should try bribing them instead... If they refused—though Ervan was certain the woman wouldn't if she was alone—he could tell them both that before Alluvendran could make good on his threats, the archmage would be gone, and Gildya would be the one making decisions. If it failed, there was always the blade...

He reached for the knife that had already served him well, but he couldn't get rid of his doubts. Offering a bribe first would strip him of the advantage of a sneak attack, and a knife was nothing against an armed man.

A rumble sounded within the Towers, and Ervan could swear a tremble traveled along the walls. Myrkan must have entered the city and started the destruction already—a clear sign that Ervan should make his escape instead of pondering all the possibilities. Decisiveness! Why did he always lack it when the time was short and the situation difficult?

"Something's wrong," the guard outside said. "Is the protection over the city gone?"

"Maybe the mages are trying to fight back," the woman replied without confidence. To Ervan, it sounded like she was rethinking her association with him. A few weeks earlier, when he'd made a deal with her, he should have paid her more, but how he could have known that beforehand?

Another rumble, this time louder, sounded in the distance.

"Look out!" the male guard shouted.

The walls and floor trembled even more, and the loud crashes outside suggested the Towers' pieces had fallen off. Adrenaline rushed through Ervan's veins. Time was running even shorter.

"Deshi?" The sounds of small rocks being thrown around came from the outside. "Deshi?! Demons take it…"

Ervan stepped out from his hiding spot and moved slowly around the chamber, to get a better view of what was going on. The male guard was kneeling by the pile of crushed wall pieces, removing the smaller parts in rushed desperation. Soon, he'd realize the woman couldn't have survived it, but until then, it was Ervan's best chance.

Taking advantage of the noise the rubble was making, he didn't bother with stealth and rushed to the door. The guard must have caught a sound or noticed movement in the corner of his eye, because he turned his head… All too late. He was kneeling, and his hands were on the rubble, not on his weapon. Ervan lunged at him, striking repeatedly at the man's head and neck. The blade slid off several times, but it also dug deeper into flesh on occasion.

The guard grunted, but he pushed himself up as if the weight of Ervan on him meant little. He threw Ervan to the ground.

"You." His eyes searched for Ervan's weapon, and he ignored the red blood trickling from his head and neck.

He took a step and collapsed.

Ervan breathed out with relief. His body ached from the violent throw, but it didn't matter. He'd succeeded. Once he made it back to Gildya, he'd assume leadership and ensure no other adept questioned it.

Another rumble shaking the Towers reminded him that the danger was still there, with the piece of the wall on the dead guardswoman a warning of what could happen if he dawdled any longer. Ignoring the aches in his limbs and back, Ervan stood up and walked down the hill. He'd rather run, but his body protested against the strain, as if the recent rush of blood and confrontation with the guard had drained him of all strength. Besides, even battered, he was making good pace, and Kaighal's buildings grew closer and closer with each step.

"Ervan!"

He froze at the sound of the familiar voice. So close! If only he'd made it down the hill, he could have disappeared into the many alleys and made it back to Gildya. He could still try to get to safety, make one last desperate attempt to reach the city that would offer him concealment, but deep inside he knew he wouldn't be able to outrun the man behind him.

With no other choice, he turned and faced Alluvendran.

14

His sprint through the city was a blur. Koshmarnyk used all the strength and endurance he had to make it to the Towers as quickly as possible. All he would remember from this run was the magic emanating from the stones in his body, pumping power into his muscles, and the startled faces of a few Kaighalans as he passed them at a speed no human should go. Thankfully, most people were either at the walls or sheltering, so there weren't too many witnesses for his enhanced abilities.

When he reached the Towers, the barrier was already wavering. Ervan had had enough time to figure out the alteration Koshmarnyk made to the device, and arriving too late was what he had expected. That was why when the guards told him that Ervan hadn't left yet, he allowed himself a glimmer of hope. He'd catch the scheming adept red-handed, and even the council wouldn't be able to brush it off.

He made his way up the many stairs at the same speed he'd run through the city, aware that he'd likely have to pay the price. The stones in his skin might have already regrown, but his human body needed more time to recover after Myrkan's torture. Magic helped him move about as if he was healthy already, but it could only do so much when he decided to exert himself in such a way.

A small smile creased the corner of his cheek. After the battle concluded, he'd either have enough time to rest or it wouldn't matter.

Up ahead, a trail of blood on the stairs made him stop. It led up to the topmost chamber, or down from it, and turned where the stairs connected to a side corridor leading to another tower and another stairway. Slight movement in its shade put him on alert, but the motion was sluggish, non-threatening.

A closer look revealed a woman slumped against the wall. They'd only seen each other a few brief times since they were both imprisoned in Cahala's secret mansion, but he recognized her.

In a few quick steps, he was beside her.

"Ervan?" he asked, examining the wound in her chest. Her clothes were drenched in blood, and it was a feat to have made it all the way here from the initiation chamber.

Pelina gave him a weak nod. "I wasn't quick enough to stop him. He's gone now. He was in such a rush, he didn't see me here."

Koshmarnyk looked over his shoulder. If Ervan had already left, they should have seen each other along the way. Unless the scheming adept veered off the way somewhere within Towers, smart enough not to use the main entrance anymore. There were a few other exits, for workers and suppliers, and though all had been barred before the arcanists set out, a bottle of acid or an exploding orb could open the way easy enough.

Pelina clutched his arm. "Please, I need..." She looked deeper into the corridor.

Koshmarnyk hesitated, but with Ervan likely already gone, he could spare a moment. This poor woman had suffered enough in her life. "I'll find some bandages," he said, though the amount of blood she must have lost made him wonder whether any effort would save her.

"No... If you could carry me, it's not far."

She had something in mind, so arguing would only waste what little time she had left. Koshmarnyk lifted her with ease and carried her down the corridor. She gave him directions until they stopped in front of unassuming door. Her quarters? They were, after all, in the part of the Towers where the archmages and teachers lived.

The door was locked, and with Pelina on the brink of losing consciousness, Koshmarnyk didn't bother asking her for a key. Magic pulsated within him as he used it to enhance his strength and force the door open.

The chamber inside looked like the archmage quarters he'd seen, including the ones Kamira chose for them, with a spacious main room and two doors leading out of it, likely to bedrooms. What was different about this chamber was the large circle drawn on the floor. Chalk aside, the floor was also marked with dark spots... spilled wine, perhaps.

"In the circle," Pelina requested.

He put her down in the middle, careful to not smear any of the lines.

"Thank you." She looked at him with genuine gratitude. "That's all I need."

Koshmarnyk hesitated. To leave her alone in the moments that might be preceding her death seemed cruel, but perhaps she wanted solitude. A circle suggested an arcane ritual, and maybe she wanted to speak to her demon in private.

"I'll come and check on you later," he promised. If nothing else, he'd ensure her dead body was treated with the respect she deserved.

"I hope you'll make that adept pay," she said in a lighthearted manner that contrasted with her fading life.

He gave a nod and left. If he couldn't help or comfort her, he could at least put his efforts into catching the man responsible.

The strain of the previous run was already taking its toll as Koshmarnyk made it back to the main stairway slower. Either Ervan was still in the Towers, or he was long gone, so speed didn't matter.

The Towers shook in violent trembles, one after another. He looked up. He had expected the device to have failed already and Myrkan to have made his way into the city, but why would he waste time destroying an empty chamber? Fyertash must have spotted the other demon and gone after him. This meant Kamira and Veelk were likely preparing to take on Derazin.

Koshmarnyk's heartbeat picked up its pace. He had to get back to them! With the damage to the city's protection already done, Ervan would have to wait.

With another strenuous run ahead of him, he took a deep breath. He could get back to the walls quick but likely be useless in a battle with a higher demon, or take his time to let his body regain its energy and risk arriving too late. Or...

He looked up the stairway. He could go and help Fyertash instead. As much as he wanted to aid Kamira, she was all the way across the city, while the demons seemed to be fighting in the Towers. His knives meant little against any demon, Derazin or Myrkan, but at least he could provide some distraction.

He made it to the topmost level of the Towers in no time, but when he pushed on the door to open it, it didn't yield. Two deep voices came through the thick wood, confirming the demons were inside and fighting, but the way in was barred. Koshmarnyk put most of his strength into prying the door open, but with no results, he gave up.

So much for this plan... Frustration tensed his muscles. There was likely a piece of rubble blocking the entrance, and he'd waste time trying to get in.

Resigned, he descended the stairway again. He never should have left Kamira's side... He should have been the one to guard the device in the Towers... He should...

Koshmarnyk shook his head. Hindsight always provided missed opportunities, better decisions. But Kamira had asked him to go after Ervan, neither of them aware of what would happen, and he did without second-guessing her decision.

The Towers trembled, but their structure had to be solid enough, because no cracks or other signs of collapse appeared, so he likely had a little time. Part of him wanted to get out of the Towers and further down the hill, in hopes of finding out what was going on upstairs, but it would make no difference if he couldn't get in, and Kamira had likely already seen it from the walls. With nothing else to try and no new information, he could check the Towers for the treacherous adept's presence. Ervan would regret it if he was still around.

Koshmarnyk reached the bottom floor of the Towers. He'd speak with the guards and see if they'd seen or heard anything, then start a meticulous search. If there were no open windows or unlocked door anywhere, it would mean that Ervan was still hiding somewhere. Likely not far from exits, since the Towers' shaking structure would fuel his cowardice.

The reception area looked normal, but as soon as Koshmarnyk approached the door, a motionless body on the ground outside came into view. Instincts urged him to rush to the unconscious or dead guard, but experience demanded caution.

Before he made it outside, he moved around the entrance door, getting a better idea of what waited for him. It seemed no one was lurking nearby, though an assailant could be hiding further away or behind the rubble Koshmarnyk spied during his quick inspection, but he doubted it. The guards had mentioned nothing of Ervan having any companions, and the adept himself was too cowardly for an attack, even a sneaky one.

With due precaution taken, Koshmarnyk walked outside. He knelt by the guard, confirming he was dead and still aware of his surroundings, but then his eyes followed the path down the hill, revealing a lone figure. Ervan was headed for the city unhurriedly, as if nothing could threaten him. A closer look revealed stiffness in the adept's movement, suggesting an injury, likely from a scuffle with the guard. Koshmarnyk glanced at the dead man's wound to confirm it was an unskilled assailant's work.

Then he ran down the hill. The treacherous adept would finally pay for everything, his schemes old and new, and for putting the whole city in danger.

"Ervan!" he called out as he got closer.

~

RETREAT WAS something Ryell knew all too well. Too many times he and his companions had frantically dashed through the woods, hoping that demonlings would lose their scent. Back in Devanshari, most of their ambushes demanded a price in blood be paid, and each time they set out to take down a demonologist or wipe out a small group of demonlings, they were aware that not everyone would make it back.

This time it felt similar: a run among the trees, the scents of forest—pine and moss—familiar in Ryell's nostrils, but instead of drowning in unpleasant memories, he noticed the differences. It wasn't even about his companions being from another country, or the fact that he wasn't in charge, like when he was leading the border guards. It was the mood that was different. They might be running, trying to lose the warriors chasing them, but morale remained high, and once or twice Ryell caught wide grins on his companions' faces. Their retreat was a strategic one instead of a desperate one, and the air of success surrounded them.

They kept the good pace of a trained team that knew to preserve its strength. Accustomed to speed and with their armor light, the scouts could easily outrun and outlast any heavily armored pursuers, so if they kept a steady pace, they should put enough distance between them...

Hopefully soon. They needed a rest stop, because both Seraine and Zimfe had wounds that needed attention, and Ryell himself wouldn't mind a moment to catch his breath. His armor weighed more than the scouts' equipment, and months spent idle in Kaighal had affected his endurance and strength more than he was willing to admit. At the same time, he would not ask them to stop and put everyone in danger just because he was at his limits.

Captain Seraine glanced over her shoulder and sent him

a smile. Then, unexpectedly, she lifted her hand, and everyone slowed down.

"We're going to rest here," she said. "Don't unpack anything and be ready to run again. Lyezi, Banrih, you're on lookout. Anything moves behind us, and we're taking off again. I also need some bandages for Zimfe and myself." She looked at Ryell. "Are you wounded?"

He shook his head as the two scouts were taking their positions as lookouts. "I was lucky."

"It was more than just lucky," Fyrwol said. "I saw you, and your skill outmatches even the Tivarashan nobility. If not for you, our assault would have failed. It was your sword that felled the Tivarashan royalty."

Several men and women around him nodded.

"Ryell the Queenkiller!" someone exclaimed, though in a muffled voice, as if taking care for the sound to not carry far.

Ryell lifted his hand in protest. The woman he'd fought was just a princess, and not even a confirmed heir to the throne, from what he understood, and he hadn't landed a killing blow. If Tivarashans had good medics—and undoubtedly only the best would take care of their royalty —the woman could still pull through. The title wasn't his to be had...

He froze. Or was it? After all, what Baxayalans didn't know, was that he indeed had a queen's blood on his hands. A righteous deed done in the dark of night and with secrecy would never receive its due recognition, so why not take the title for defeating the princess instead?

Others had already picked up the moniker, chanting it in hushed voices, their faces full of smiles and excitement, and he smiled back at them. Ryell the Queenkiller. Their hero.

"Your plan was daring, but it got us a huge victory,"

Captain Seraine said. She was sitting down nearby, her wounds already being taken care of by another scout. "Even if it didn't turn the battle in our favor, we've caused Tivarashan a lot of trouble, that's for certain. If you choose to travel with us a little longer, I'll make sure our commanders know of your deeds." She paused and looked him up and down. Even seated, she emanated confidence and authority, and Ryell hid his unease at her sudden scrutiny. "And you know, we could use a skilled swordsman among our ranks. I'd be happy to see you among our scouts, but if it's too much running and not enough fighting, I'll whisper a word or two to other captains."

Ryell didn't respond immediately. This wasn't what he'd had in mind when he left Atissa's home. To join the Baxayalan military meant to side with them in whatever conflicts could come, and he had no strong attachments to Kaighal, should the Westerners' eyes turn to conquering the city, but his compatriots had still chosen it as their place of refuge. He wouldn't be able to cross swords with them.

But such thoughts also meant clinging to the past and to obligations that perhaps were already gone, along with the kingdom of Devanshari. If he was determined to make a new life for himself, he had to make decisions that best served him, not the painful memories of his past.

He looked around, at the scouts he'd spent the past days with. They waited for his reply, some hopeful, some friendly... none ill-wishing, as far as he could tell. Their lives were simple and so different from the intrigue-filled palace of Devanshari, where being a royal guard meant being more of a schemer than a warrior. They reminded Ryell of his time spent with the border guards, at first when he was young and ambitious, and later, when he was assigned to lead them into uneven battles against the demonling hordes. Pain pierced him at that memory, but he didn't let it linger. His former companions were long gone, and nothing would bring them back, but he had a chance at forming new bonds and finding new friends.

Come to think of it, it'd been a long time since he'd felt such a sense of purpose and companionship. It'd been a long time since he'd felt... at peace. All the struggles of the past months, all the doubts, trying to find the answers and purpose—all of it was gone in the instant he found people that were willing to welcome him among themselves and trust him. The Light itself, still existing even if gone from the artifact in his capital, must have led him to the Baxayalans.

"I'd be honored to travel with you longer," he replied, "and if your commanders find my sword and my skills of worth, I'd be happy to lend them both to Baxayal."

His response seemed to satisfy Seraine, and a round of cheers traveled among her scouts.

"All right, enough of this," Seraine said, all her wounds already dressed. "Have a last sip of water or bite of rations, and we're setting out. There will be time for celebrations later, when we're safe behind our lines."

If the Tivarashan warriors hadn't caught up with them by now, Ryell doubted they were continuing their pursuit, but he kept the thought to himself. He could understand that after long weeks spent in foreign lands, Seraine was eager to bring her people back home, or at least back to safety.

Before they set out, Ryell's hand brushed a medallion tucked safely in his pocket. Back when Cahala qi'Devanshari met her end, he'd promised himself that he'd deliver it to her son, the rightful heir, but with all the commotion in Kaighal and Kamira's schemes, he hadn't had the time to do so without revealing his involvement in the queen's death. One day, perhaps, he'd revisit the promise and be able to pass the medallion to its rightful owner.

One day, far, far into the future, because for now, his new life awaited him, and he wouldn't let the past mar his happiness ever again.

15

Veelk couldn't help a smirk as Fyertash carried Kamira away in his makeshift sling. Once all was done, he'd likely hear all the complaints about the means of travel, because he doubted Kamira would enjoy the experience of being out of control and vulnerable. He had to admit he shared that perspective, but at the same time, Fyertash's ingenious solution was what had saved his life. Otherwise he'd never have made it back home in time for the elders to treat his wounds.

He narrowed his eyes, watching the demon's flight.

Nearby, one of the devices failed, and a small wave of demonlings attacked. Zelna tensed, but Veelk held his arm out. "We wait." Something was coming, and he'd rather be prepared for it when it happened than be distracted by something the defenders could probably handle on their own. "Until all of them start failing, we don't move."

Zelna nodded without a word of protest, and he appreciated the trust she put in him.

He turned to face the plains beyond the walls. So far, except for the small group of demonlings that had gone for the unexpected breach, none of them had moved. All the creatures kept away, barely within arrows' reach and not close enough for arcanists' magic.

Their obedience and seeming calmness unnerved Veelk. They were ferocious and aggressive monsters that attacked on sight and rarely had enough wits to even circle their victim in search of a weak spot.

His mind traveled back to their first meeting with Uganel. According to Kamira, the demon had controlled the creatures too, but since they were meant to attack anyway, it seemed like minimal direction was necessary. All it took was ensuring that the demonlings didn't scatter and stayed their aggressive course. In this case...

He looked further away at the figure towering in the distance. To have such control over so many demonlings, Derazin must be truly powerful.

Veelk corrected the grip on his keshal. This wouldn't be an easy battle.

An angry roar sounded over the city, way too powerful to be from any demonlings and way too close to be Derazin's. Veelk's blood rushed as he turned around just in time to witness Myrkan's fierce attack on Fyertash. He froze as the demon, while defending himself from the assault, tried to get Kamira to safety. Myrkan must have realized Fyertash's intent, because he only halfheartedly swiped at Fyertash to force defense, and instead focused his real attack on the fabric, tearing it from Fyertash's grip.

In the same moment, the demonlings behind the walls surged forward. Their shrieks drowned out the defenders' calls, but Veelk didn't have to hear them to know that at least some of the devices had failed again. All of that didn't matter. The two demons over the Towers kept fighting, and

Veelk kept watching, hoping for a glimpse of Kamira or Fyertash's sign that she was fine.

Zelna put a hand on his shoulder. "She's either already dead, or she won't need your help. She and the demon can handle the other one, and this is our chance as well."

Any other time, Veelk would have agreed with her. Kamira had been well capable of taking care of herself even long before she made a pact with Veranesh, and after the demon granted her almost infinite power and a pair of crystal nightflies, hardly anyone could match her. But he saw her fall into the Towers, and the initiation rite chamber was tall enough to make it a painful if not deadly experience.

The thought of her lying on the floor, alive but broken and unable to defend herself, made him want to rush to the Towers, but Zelna was right: Kamira was either dead already, or she'd find a way to survive. Besides, Koshmarnyk had set out to the Towers, so he could help with Myrkan.

Veelk looked back at the attacking demonlings. The devices nearby hadn't failed yet, but he suspected it was only a matter of time. Myrkan must have found quite a few willing lackeys in the city to make it happen, or perhaps Gildya had traitors who damaged the contraptions before they even left the adepts' workshops.

"It's not going to be easy to get through them." Zelna pointed at the swarming demonlings.

He nodded. Neither of them shied away from a fray like this one, but their goal was beyond the hordes, and the less strength they used to get to Derazin, the greater the chance of taking the demon down.

"I've got an idea," Veelk said.

He took off, and Zelna followed. They ran along the walls, ignoring the many small skirmishes and swiping their weapons only when they had to clear their own way. Some of those people would die without their help, but Veelk couldn't trade a few lives for the whole city. If he did, he'd never hear the end of it from Kamira.

Archmage Irtan had his post further down the walls, but Veelk and Zelna made good time. The old man stood alone at the battlements, an inactive device by his side, and treated climbing demonlings with fire and lightning. The confidence in his moves made it clear the old fox had truly been practicing arcane arts for years rather than converting shortly before the fall of high magic.

As Veelk and Zelna arrived, he gave them only a glance, focused as he was on the creatures beyond the walls.

"Can you clear the way for us?" Veelk didn't waste time. "As far as your magic can reach."

Irtan hesitated, and Veelk didn't blame him. He had no doubt that the old archmage had enough power to make that happen, but he had a pact with Fyertash, so his magic had its limits, and he was risking that it would run out too soon. On the other hand, he must know that if they didn't deal with Derazin, it didn't matter how long his magic lasted.

"I can do it," the archmage said. "But only one time, so once you're out there, you're on your own, no matter what goes wrong."

Zelna looked around and then took off at a sprint toward one of the scattered caches of supplies along the walls, and as she returned, she threw a heavy load of rope at Veelk.

The archmage summoned a barrier to keep the demonlings out while Veelk secured the rope.

"It might not be long enough," Irtan said.

Zelna gave him a grin. "With all those bodies down there, landing will be soft enough."

"We're ready," Veelk said.

The archmage gave a quick nod and looked beyond the walls. The barrier he held dispersed, bursting into flames that roared across the plains, consuming the demonlings in their wake. The creatures screeched and tried to flee the fiery storm, but the conflagration caught most of them. The flames were still advancing to the sides when Irtan threw his hands up, bringing icy spikes up from the ground below, forming a narrow corridor as deep into the enemy's lines as he could summon.

"Hurry," the archmage said. "It won't last long."

They leaped over the battlements without delay, Veelk first, Zelna right after. With their youth spent in the mountains, descending the wall was an easy task, and thanks to Irtan's icy corridor, no demonling waited at the bottom.

Veelk caught the archmage calling for a device to be brought over. He'd likely drained himself performing such a feat, and even if Fyertash had more magic to offer, there was only so much a human body could endure—Veelk had seen Kamira bring herself to the brink of exhaustion before, and Irtan was much older and more fragile than his companion.

Veelk didn't let the thought linger. The old man was safe for now, so it hardly mattered. Instead, he focused on their goal. He and Zelna kept running along the icy corridor, their feet squashing many demonling corpses, but as the archmage had said, their protection wasn't going to last. In several places the ice was already cracking. No demonling had made it through yet, but the sounds echoing around them made it clear that their time was running out.

"There's no fighting Derazin if we have to fend them off," Zelna said from behind.

Veelk kept running, and with the end of the icy corridor

in sight, he had to make a decision fast. "Go after the arcanists," he yelled before he made it out of the ice and into a horde of monsters.

If they wanted to survive, someone had to ensure no more demonlings were summoned, but that also meant the other one would be facing Derazin alone, and Veelk would sooner die than see his sister do that. She could aid him later, but first he had to ensure that the demon didn't go after her if he noticed his servants were in danger.

The demonlings obviously lacked understanding of what was happening when the ice spires jutted from the ground, but as soon as Veelk and Zelna appeared from the narrow path between, they rushed in from all sides.

Veelk focused on advancing and was barely aware that Zelna tore away from him in another direction. Little skill or finesse was needed to deal with the demonlings, and Veelk quickly and steadily moved toward the towering demon with wide swipes of his keshal in a bloody harvest of heads and limbs. The demonlings jumped, lunged, and launched themselves at him with abandon, only to fall helplessly onto the tip of his weapon, be cleaved in two, or be raked across the ground and mutilated.

Magic in his skin pulsated, providing him with what seemed like endless energy, but Veelk knew better than to lose himself in battle. Even small wounds would take their toll sooner or later, and any one of them could fell the mightiest warrior when a strike reached the right ligament or artery. Besides, the demonlings were not his goal, and he could tell he was nearing the end of them, as his attackers grew sparser.

The fewer there were, the more Veelk turned his attention to advancing on the demon. Wide swipes of the keshal sent most of the remaining demonlings away, and

Veelk turned to ducking and dodging those that leaped at him. He knew the whole pack would not give chase, so he headed for an open area to kill the few tenacious enough to pursue him.

A skirmish that lasted all of four deep breaths left Veelk standing amongst scattered body parts, looking at the reason he was there.

Up close, Derazin was massive—not only taller than Uganel but also bulkier. At least he moved in a sluggish manner that suggested he wasn't one for speed... Unless controlling all those demonlings prevented him from moving any faster.

Veelk didn't ponder it long. He'd know soon enough. Back when he had inspected the etchings Fyertash made on the Towers' wall, Derazin seemed like a shapeless maggot, and up close, the impression remained. The bulk of his body rested on the ground, with the small limbs that supported it at the sides, making Veelk wonder if their only purpose was to stop the demon from falling over. His wings looked too small to support flight, and Veelk doubted the demon could jump or leap, so their fight would take place on the ground.

And as far as Veelk was concerned, that meant an even battle.

Derazin turned his bulbous head toward him. Out of all the demons Veelk had seen so far, Derazin's features resembled a bird's the least, but his nose still had that elongated, beaklike shape.

"One human?" the demon rumbled with some amusement. "All Fyertash sent against me is Suzhaul's dog?"

More demonlings rushed from behind, but at Derazin's growl, they backed away, and Veelk smiled. If there was an advantage to coming alone, it had to be the demon's conviction he wouldn't be a threat.

"It's the archmage of Kaighal who sent me," he replied. Not that it mattered, but he preferred his name be kept away from Fyertash's.

"She sent you to die, then."

The way he said it was almost casual, but Veelk didn't miss the cues, and when the attack came, he was prepared. Still, the swiping twist of Derazin's lower body seemed lousy even for a demon who likely avoided open confrontations, and Veelk realized that his evasion of Derazin's slow attack primed him for the incoming attack from behind.

Three demonlings jumped him, one from behind and two from his side. Veelk opted for the two, cleaving straight through them more easily than expected, but the third struck his back and dug its claws in deep, trying to cling to its prey. With Veelk's twisting motion toward the other two, and the demonling's own weight, it failed, but left deep gashes across Veelk's back before the keshal split its head against the ground.

The attack was no more than a distraction. There would be no one-on-one confrontation with Derazin, and though Veelk somewhat hoped for it, he had never been under the illusion that it would be so. Demonlings continued to gather... and Veelk grinned.

This time a small swarm of demonlings surged at him, but just as Veelk turned to handle them, he saw the shadow and leaped to the side as Derazin thrashed the ground and the demonlings from above—another distraction.

Veelk had narrowly escaped, and the dodge put him right next to Derazin's blubbery body. He took the chance, and the keshal's thin blade cut deep into thick skin and fatty flesh, making it clear that even if Veelk thrust the whole of his weapon into the demon's body, he would still likely fail at reaching any vital organs. A thick, gooey substance spat and oozed from the wound over the crushed demonlings. Their skin sizzled as the vile mucus melted away muscle and bone.

Veelk took a step back as the giant slug of a demon slowly twisted his body to right himself, and with a quick glance, he made sure the caustic fat hadn't fallen on him or the wooden shaft of his spear. The blades themselves would be fine with Suzhaul's powerful magic enhancing them, but the shaft was vulnerable.

Demonlings continued to gather. Veelk flipped his weapon to favor the broad blade and cut across Derazin's body again. The fatty substance blossomed from the wound, and he scraped a slather of it on the flat of his blade before the demon could move away.

The creatures attacked again. They were likely meant to distract him so that Derazin could reposition, but Veelk had adapted to the demon's tactics. The sweep of his keshal was precise and quick, and the fatty sludge sprayed forward in a graceful arc over the advancing demonlings. He jumped amidst the creatures and dispatched several with the second swipe of the blade. But he could feel Derazin behind his back, and he knew better than to let the demon have total control over the battlefield, so he turned again and sprinted to the far side of Derazin, ensuring all his enemies were on one side.

The demon attacked again, rolling over the ground before Veelk could get opposite the demonlings, but Veelk leaped at the oncoming blubbery mass as if to run up the side of the demon, and then launched himself over by jamming the thin blade of the spear into Derazin's fat and vaulting with the aid of his keshal.

Derazin let out a short growl and recoiled as he uprighted and moved away.

Veelk grinned. The time had come for offense.

He lunged with wide, powerful swipes of his keshal, forcing the demon to withdraw. The blade didn't connect, but Derazin's panicked dodge, a cumbersome and thundering roll, sent a wave of demonlings flying, and he crushed many others with his enormous body.

Ignoring the small creatures, Veelk kept pressing the attack and let the demon wipe out his own allies with every roll.

Derazin must have realized that, because instead of dodging the next powerful swipe, he pushed his great mass up and toward the mage killer. Veelk dove to the side to avoid being crushed, and ducked the swipe of the demon's claws that followed. Derazin must not be accustomed to being put on the defensive, and reacted with all-out offense.

The demon attempted to roll sideways again, and Veelk avoided him. His prowess had peaked, as it did in any life-threatening battle, but even with magic in his re-created skin providing him with what seemed like endless energy and the rush of lethal combat, he needed to finish the fight soon. Back in the city, Kamira might need his help.

He used his spear again to support a vault, lunging into the air up and over his opponent. Derazin was straightening up from his last attempt to crush him, and Veelk jammed a dagger into the thick skin on the demon's back to hold on while Derazin spun in place, trying to shake him. The defensive whipping of Derazin's body would provide the momentum Veelk needed to release the dagger and fly toward Derazin's head, and though he found himself falling short of a decisive blow, he drew his keshal in an arc to thrust the wide blade at the demon's neck. It buried deep, and dark blood erupted from the wound. It drowned the shaft of his keshal instantly, and the wood broke off.

Derazin roared in pain and curled backward violently as Veelk fell from his side. Despite the piece of metal wedged deep in his neck and blood still spurting out, he kept thrashing in a frantic rage. His attacks were powerful, if for no other reason than his sheer size, but too chaotic to be a threat. Yet, as Veelk landed and gathered himself, a small group of demonlings found their way to him, circling wide around the flailing demon. With only half of his spear and no dagger, he couldn't dodge Derazin's attacks and fight the creatures at the same time.

Magic and adrenaline coursed through his veins, enhancing the anticipation. If this was to be his last battle, he would at least ensure his task was complete.

The demonlings were upon him, and Veelk had to grapple those that he couldn't cut down with half of his keshal. His weapon still did most of the work, but those that Veelk had to kick, crush, or punch—or even grab hold of to twist their bones to breaking—suffered far worse. Staying away from Derazin to quickly handle the demonlings seemed easier than he'd expected, making it clear that the demon was focused on keeping Veelk at a distance more than attacking. The coward had to be dreading another painful wound, and Veelk had put an end to the tactics of distraction.

Correcting his grip on the broken spear, Veelk eyed his opponent. Other demonlings were already slowly gathering, but they wouldn't swarm until there were at least four or more, so he paid no attention to them.

Derazin backed away, waving his short arms in desperation. From behind him, two demonlings emerged, likely Derazin's personal guards, if demons had such things.

Two large creatures with a glint of intelligence in their eyes advanced toward Veelk with low growls.

One was taller and slenderer than the other, with longer serrated claws. The shorter, more muscular one seemed the calmer, more intelligent of the two. Not that it mattered, as the slenderer one burst forward, and that served Veelk well. If he could fell the first attacker quickly enough, it would be two consecutive one-on-one battles, as opposed to a single, two-front battle.

But his hope evaporated when the beast drew only close enough for tentative, defensive swipes. It moved around him, lunging in and out, but Veelk caught on quickly. It seemed the same tactic Derazin was addicted to: one always a distraction, while another was always the real threat. If the two swapped roles well, they could drag out the fight longer than Veelk had time for... but only if he too fought defensively.

He allowed the first, faster demonling to hold most of his attention, but not so much that he would lose track of the other's whereabouts. When the thundering, four-footed approach of the other grew close, he turned, gripping his spear tightly.

The beast had leaped at him, but instead of evading or defending, he advanced. The beast's claws raked down Veelk's left shoulder and ribs, tearing flesh and cracking bones, as Veelk's spear split the demon's sternum and heart. Its other clawed hand swung at Veelk's head but missed as the body fell heavily. As soon as his broken keshal struck home, Veelk yanked on the haft, leaving it retrievable, and when the body came to rest, he snatched the spear from the beast's chest and turned.

The other lunged, but Veelk stepped into its advance, throwing his body weight at the creature, and it responded as Veelk expected. It abandoned its attack in favor of avoiding his, and Veelk's eyes turned to Derazin.

"Suzhaul gives, and we accept," he muttered.

The demon patron of his tribe had always been generous, allowing mage killers to transcend the capabilities of a human body and be ready to face any rogue arcanists or mages, but Suzhaul had given him much more than anyone would expect. Without the demon's gifts, Veelk wouldn't have survived his wounds, and it was time to make use of them and prove himself worthy of the gifts he'd received.

Magic pulsated through his body in an odd, intense way as he leaned forward, and he couldn't help wondering whether it was similar to what Kamira felt calling upon her magic. Yet, unlike her, he didn't have to control the energy coursing through his body.

He charged full speed and could feel the energy building, pushing him forward, as he clenched the smooth wooden shaft of his weapon.

The remaining demonling gave chase and was gaining slowly. Other creatures rushed from the sides, but only one was unfortunate enough to throw itself in range of Veelk's reach. The rest fell in behind, unable to keep up.

Magic swelled in his legs, and the scars began to glow like magma pushing its way through the cracks in his skin.

Derazin was twisting to strike with his tail, but a look of terror overtook his expression when Veelk launched into the air much higher and further than previously. The demon turned to whip his sluggish hind parts at Veelk, but he was too slow.

Veelk readied his throw, magic coursing through the scars on his arm, and when he realized how slow Derazin's response was, he compensated for the sluggish movements. Then he loosed his keshal.

Derazin's tail connected, but so too did Veelk's weapon, burying itself deep into the demon's skull.

Veelk had known he would likely take a solid strike, and was prepared for it. Magic rushed into body, compressing the muscles around the bones as Derazin's tail struck. Veelk was shot across the battlefield at the ground, and he tensed into a ball just before he hit rock. Bones broke, but so did the rock, and Veelk rolled several times then up onto his feet.

Derazin clumsily swatted at invisible attackers, and Veelk could see the broken haft of the keshal jutting from the top of his head. It was a risk leaving himself weaponless, but it didn't matter anymore when Derazin fell to his side, still twitching, his head thudding on the ground erratically.

The demonlings had changed course and were, at first, amassing into a wave headed for Veelk, but as soon as Derazin rested motionless, they slowed. Suddenly confused, they were sniffing the air and snarling at one another, and a moment later—all-out bloodshed as they turned on each other.

Veelk watched their fierce battle as he made his way toward Derazin's body. The demonlings were more interested in tearing each other to pieces than in his presence, and he didn't waste the opportunity to retrieve both ends of his keshal.

It seemed their intelligence only went so far, and without Derazin's domineering will, they reverted to their lowest instincts and fought for superiority.

First Veelk climbed the giant slug's body to fetch the broad blade. It took some effort to carefully remove it while avoiding the caustic substance that oozed from the wound, but few demonlings could see him, and of those, none showed him interest. As he slid to the ground, making his way to Derazin's head, he saw up close how bestial the demonlings were.

He minded the closer ones as he yanked the spear tip from Derazin's skull, but their chaotic battle to establish dominance was short-lived, and though they wouldn't likely use intelligent tactics as a group, they were demonlings, and demonlings would attack him as soon as they had no other target.

His heart called for him to return to the city as soon as possible, because the thought of Kamira facing unknown dangers on her own twisted his stomach with fear and rage, but if he wanted to make it through the hordes of demonlings in haste and—more importantly—alive, he needed Zelna's aid.

He corrected the grip on his two blades and pushed the pain of broken bones and torn muscles out of his head. If his sister had turned out foolish enough to get herself killed by a bunch of half-baked arcanists, he'd make sure none of them made it out of the battle alive.

KAMIRA WAS HANGING over the initiation rite chamber, her body supported only by the strength of her arms as she clung to the edge of the shattered dome. Outside, judging by the roars and grunts, Fyertash was still fighting. Once, she caught a glimpse of him as he tried to make it to her, but Myrkan pulled him away before the demon could help her.

She was on her own, and that meant dying if she didn't think of something before her muscles gave out. With not enough strength, she could only dream of pulling herself up, and the curved underside of the dome offered no foothold. She refrained from glancing down, her eyes fixed on what was above.

If only she had a way to get up to the ledge... There might be nowhere to go from there, but at least she'd be safe enough to wait for aid.

As a rumble shook the building, and a nearby part of the wall collapsed, she reconsidered the likelihood of her survival.

The pain in her muscles made it clear she didn't have long, so she chanced the first idea that came to mind: *the nightflies!* The crystal creatures weren't large enough to lift her up, but she had used them in the past to support her weight.

She woke them up and sent them down. As the nightflies coiled around her ankles, Kamira almost breathed out with relief with the strain in her arms and hands easing. With the nightflies helping, she slowly pulled herself up until she could throw her elbow on the roof. A little further and she could fall forward onto the rooftop, but she froze at the sight of two demons tightly clutched in a grapple as they shot toward her from the sky. There was no evasion, no magic defense, no jumping to safety; they either struck her, or they didn't.

Another rumble shook the tower. Kamira's heart pounded as she struggled desperately for only a moment before the large demon masses smashed through the roof, and the portion Kamira clung to fell free.

She was still processing the demons' faces, twisted in hatred and anger, when the world spun sharply. She expected to fall, but instead swung to and fro a few times and then stopped upside down, the floor still rushing toward her, but slower than a free fall, as the nightflies did everything they could to support her weight. And though the descent was slower than falling, it wasn't slow enough.

In desperation, she called upon her magic, channeling it all into wind and pushing it toward the floor. *Not enough!* As the floor approached, she drew more energy. The returning gust hit her face, taking her breath away but slowing her descent, and then she hit the floor... hard.

She rolled to avoid breaking anything. When she finally gathered herself, her ankle and shoulder rebelled with piercing pain more so than the many other aches fighting for attention, but she made it to her feet and recalled the nightflies to her wrists. As she glanced up, searching for any sight of the fighting demons, a cold realization dawned on her. With the long drop she'd survived, whatever slight fractures, bruises, sprains, or strains she might be suffering were minor in comparison to what she'd almost suffered. The mere fact that she was standing without aid was more than remarkable.

The door to the chamber lay buried under a pile of stone from a collapsed wall, so she couldn't count on any allies coming to her aid.

Nearby, Myrkan was on top of Fyertash, ripping at the bloodied arms guarding his face.

Kamira hesitated. If they were to have any chance, she had to help Fyertash, but to do so without the protection of a circle would likely mean her death. He would have to wait until she ensured her own survival.

Every movement was hampered by pain. Some she could push through, force her body to do as she commanded, others hindered her with reflexive pauses, but one of her concealed circles wasn't far, and her stubborn hobble brought her closer with each step.

A roar warned her. As she looked back, Myrkan's wings

were spread, blood-covered arms out to his sides, left leg forward to support his forward leaning, aggressive posture, maw gaping open with spittle and blood mixing with the yell of anger and supremacy, though it lasted but a moment before he was darting toward her with open, poised claws.

They connected with her barrier. The energy wavered at the strength of the demon's attack, and Kamira guessed it would last but a few hits more.

Myrkan looked her in the eye, and a cruel smile bloomed on his ugly face, suggesting that he knew it as well. He lifted his arm once more, but Fyertash slammed into him from behind before he could strike. Both collided with the barrier and tumbled off the side of it.

Kamira caught a glimpse of Fyertash's rent and bloodied forearms as she dove onto the circle and poured her magic into it. The barrier grew around her once more, this time stronger, more stable.

Those few heartbeats that Fyertash had bought her were paid for in flesh and blood, as Myrkan took his rage out on him. Myrkan came out on top and tried to bury his claws into Fyertash's ribs over and over again with frenzied swipes and thrusts, but Fyertash only fueled Myrkan's anger by defending, again sacrificing his arms, until he finally got his wing dislodged from under his opponent's back. With Fyertash's quick swat to Myrkan's face, they rolled across the floor, each trying to pin the other. Neither succeeded, and both were on their feet again.

Fyertash was again forced to suffer one of Myrkan's powerful blows, this time sacrificing his wing to deflect it as best he could, but it bought him the opening he needed to drive Myrkan back with an unexpected kick. Fyertash's wing broke and ripped, but Myrkan's stomach suffered similarly.

Kamira took the opportunity and threw ice spikes in

Myrkan's direction, not bothering to ensure they hit. It was only misdirection to make the demon believe this was the way she intended to fight him. At the same time, under her breath and keeping her head down to conceal her lips moving, she was already muttering the ripping spell.

Myrkan swatted at the ice shards, breaking them into the pieces. "Pitiful. Not that I expected much from a human." Then his expression shifted. "No..." He looked around in disbelief as cuts tore across his skin.

Fyertash took the opportunity to catch a few breaths and then strike. His claws caught his opponent's wing, but Myrkan paid no attention as he leaped into the air before Fyertash could grab hold.

"Where is he?" Myrkan roared. "Where is that coward?"

Kamira smirked when it became clear that Fyertash wasn't going to let the distraction go to waste. With a quick leap, he grabbed Myrkan's ankle in a firm grip and brought the demon down, smashing him against the floor. The marble slabs shattered, and stone exploded in all directions. The towers' already collapsing walls shook dangerously, and more debris fell loose. Kamira eyed it warily, but most was falling outside the Tower rather into the chamber.

Myrkan beat his wings once against the floor to lift himself to his feet, and then began swiping at Fyertash in a mad flurry. His attacks missed as often as they hit, as if the demon cared little about the result. The gashes in Myrkan's flesh were beginning to overlap and deepen, and his hint of desperation meant he felt it.

"*Where is he?!*" The last words became a half howl, and the bones of Myrkan's wings, being the thinnest and most fragile, began splitting in various places.

"Close enough," Fyertash replied with a sinister grin.

"But I won't let you find him until he's done." He didn't attack, instead circling his opponent.

Kamira saw the wisdom in his restraint. He must be preserving his strength and would attack only when Myrkan tried to flee.

Understanding dawned on Myrkan's face. "No, he's not. Otherwise he'd be the one doing the fighting, while you'd be cowering somewhere to enact the ripping spell." His eyes fixed on Kamira. "You've taught a human."

Fyertash smirked. "I'm certainly not the first one to share secrets that weren't meant for them."

With their deception revealed, Kamira picked up the pace of the spell as she watched Myrkan's moves. She didn't bother engaging in the conversation. Fyertash would play for time, so she better use it wisely.

Again Myrkan roared, spreading his wings, arms, and claws, and leaning forward on his left leg before darting toward Kamira, but Fyertash once again slammed into his enemy, jamming his claws into open wounds from the ripping. Myrkan grabbed Fyertash by the base of his wing and slammed him to the floor. Stone slabs again shattered under the assault, and Kamira swallowed hard at the sight of her ally beaten once more.

Even the loss of Myrkan's blood didn't slow him down. To her relief, he didn't scream as much as Uganel did, only a few stifled groans every now and then, but his lack of reaction to the ripping left little for Kamira to gauge its effects.

Myrkan grabbed Fyertash by the legs and heaved him at Kamira's barrier. Fyertash tried to soften the impact, but the magic protection wavered at the force of the attack, and he grunted in pain as he hit the floor. She half expected a remark of how she should hurry, but instead, he pushed himself back onto his feet... just in time for Myrkan to slam him into the barrier again.

Fyertash pushed off the magical protection, forcing Myrkan back. His moves were becoming slower, betraying his weariness.

"She will do the same to you once she's done with me." Myrkan's face twisted in pain, but otherwise he showed no reaction to the ripping. He threw another broad swipe of his claws. "She's too smart to risk you turning on her just like you turned on us."

Fyertash's laughter was the only response. Preceded by another angry roar and spread, aggressive posture, Myrkan lunged at Fyertash, burying his claws deep to grab hold, and lifted him before smashing him onto the floor again.

The battered floor was starting to give way, and at the sight of cracks spreading from the point of impact, Kamira almost lost her rhythm. To her relief, the floor didn't collapse, but the fissures reached all the way to her circle. The energy around her shifted. The barrier still stood, but with the cracks having broken the circle, her magic couldn't anchor in its lines.

Myrkan pressed Fyertash's chest to the floor with a foot on his back, and seized hold of Fyertash's wing. A moment later, the splitting of bones echoed throughout the chamber, but Fyertash only growled at the pain and tried to throw the weight off his back, to no effect.

Kamira dropped her barrier and channeled energy. Five ice spikes grew and danced in the air, and then launched at the towering demon. Three missed, but two buried themselves between his ribs. Myrkan groaned and looked at her with hate, then grabbed hold of Fyertash's other wing and dragged him to the edge of the Tower and threw him out.

He turned to Kamira. "Your turn, little human. You'll regret meddling in yalari affairs."

The memory of Koshmarnyk's many wounds told her that it mattered little to Myrkan whether she had meddled or not. She stopped reciting the spell. Without Fyertash's aid to keep the demon away, she'd have little chance to finish it. Ice didn't seem to work as well as she'd hoped, so she needed another plan. Yet summoning more couldn't hurt while she thought—anything to keep the demon busy.

"Pay attention," she said, hoping that the words would make him miss that she'd lowered her barrier.

He stared at her, confused, and she used that time to channel as much energy as she could. Countless ice spikes rained down on Myrkan, and he only spotted them at the last moment, but he didn't dodge to the side or leap backward as she'd hoped. Instead, he lunged forward, right at her.

Kamira twisted in desperate evasion as she tried to throw up her magic in defense, but as she fell to the side just before her barrier appeared, the tips of Myrkan's claws found her back, ripping through her clothes and scoring the skin. The wounds stung, but her spine was untouched. The barrier wouldn't last if she kept moving, but perhaps it would buy her a few steps, some distance between them. With the chamber thoroughly demolished, she couldn't count on any of her other circles to be intact, and that meant she couldn't hold her own in a typical duel, arcanist versus demon. She needed something to even the odds.

Myrkan stayed right on top of her, clawing at the barrier. She sent a ball of fire toward him. He paused his assault long enough to offer a mocking expression that told her flames wouldn't bother him, but she didn't expect them to. The demon charged straight through the fire, and so she changed the nature of her magic. Such manipulation would have been impossible from afar, but his aggressive approach made it possible. She closed her eyes for the moment that her flames burst into an orb of light.

The strobe stopped him in his tracks, and Kamira had bought herself an opening before his blindness subsided and he realized the attack was but a lumisphere. She woke up the nightflies and directed them straight at Myrkan's face. Their spiky bodies buried themselves into his eyes, but as the demon reared back, roaring in pain and anger, it became clear that the attack had failed to end him. At least now, blinded, he would have a harder time tracking her.

She called the creatures back to her forearms. As useful as they were, they couldn't kill him, and she'd rather not risk the demon catching and destroying them.

Despite his wounds, Myrkan still stepped forward with broad, sweeping swipes. Kamira backed away, throwing ice at him, but her spikes hardly penetrated the demon's flesh. The wounds wouldn't be enough to kill him, and she doubted she had enough time to wait for him to bleed to death.

She raised another barrier. It would give her time to think while Myrkan tore through it.

Not fire, lightning, nor wind could injure him, and ice didn't seem enough. To bury it deeper into his body, she needed something better. Magic itself was not an issue, but bigger spikes meant a harder time keeping them up in the air... There was a reason arcanists didn't go about flinging rocks and other objects.

Kamira rolled to the side, keeping low, as Myrkan shattered her barrier. In his rage, he made it to the chamber's edge, slamming into one of the remaining portions of the wall, but to her disappointment, he didn't lose balance.

The demon stood straight and turned, his head moving to the sides as if he was listening for her footsteps. "There's nowhere for you to run, and your magic can't hurt me." He lifted his claw to his face. "And I can smell your blood easily enough."

Kamira didn't reply, focused on finding a solution. She needed something to drive the ice deep into his body. Conjuring it high up could provide enough force, but before it struck, the demon could move, and she needed her barrier down to do so. If he lunged at the same time... She pushed away the image of his claws reaching her. Fear was only going to be a distraction.

Myrkan started in her direction and smashed into her barrier. She extended it, pushing him back. A growl rose in his throat. He lunged with a force she didn't expect, almost tearing through her magic in one motion. She strengthened it, resisting the urge to back away as an idea came to mind.

Perhaps she didn't need more power—just more cunning.

She summoned another barrier.

"Out of words, are we?" Myrkan mocked. "Regretting you didn't take my offer?"

"Why speak to you when I'm about to kill you?" she replied. If her plan was to work, she needed him enraged again.

Myrkan laughed. "All you can do is hide behind your protection, but I'll tear through each of them."

With the force of her will, she extended the barrier, pushing on the demon. "You're pitiful. A magic-less woman and a half-dead adept outsmarted you not so long ago, and you talk about taking *me* on?" A tiny voice at the back of her mind whispered that if she failed, she'd pay dearly for such bravado.

The demon reacted as she expected, smashing onto her barrier. It held through two assaults, then flickered, and Kamira let it fall, summoning another one. Even though the demon was powerful, much stronger than Uganel, she kept her barriers weak. He had to believe she couldn't do better.

"When I'm done with you," she continued, "I'll have your dead body nailed to this very tower for everyone to see that one human was more than enough to bring you down."

Myrkan postured and roared then tore through her barrier so fast that she barely had enough time to summon the next one. He slammed into it, and it wavered.

"Empty words," Myrkan replied, rage echoing within. "I'll get to you before you manage to finish the ripping."

Kamira couldn't help smiling. He'd just given her what she needed: the last piece of deception.

"I have enough magic to keep you away for however long I need," she said, so overconfidently, so arrogantly, so perfectly as to conceal concern and fear.

Myrkan wasn't a fool; he'd catch it and conclude that she wasn't as confident as she wanted him to believe she was. If he was convinced she would try to finish the ripping part of the destruction spell, he wouldn't expect any other attack.

Without delay, she started reciting the ripping spell. She could have picked up where she left off, but it didn't matter, so long as Myrkan believed using it was her plan.

More gashes split his flesh, and he grunted. "I'll rip your tongue out!"

He smashed through her barrier, and promptly did away with the next one she raised. With each one, he got closer and closer, and Kamira played her voice like an instrument, a tune that conveyed steadily growing fear as she kept reciting the spell.

The ripping cuts were beginning to reach Myrkan's bones, but it hardly seemed to affect him, save the look on his face of ever-increasing rage.

Finally, when he was only a few steps away, she extended her barrier again, pushing him back and hoping it looked like a last desperate attempt to keep him away.

He took several steps back, postured, and roared.

Kamira had partaken in enough battles to know this one was coming to an end. Despite Myrkan's confidence, he had to stop her before she damaged him with the spell enough to immobilize him.

She took a deep breath, steeling herself and gathering magic, but she didn't send it to her barrier. She needed it weak.

The demon lunged. Her protection vanished as he smashed through it with force and rage, headed straight at her.

Kamira's hands trembled. Her instincts demanded she use her power as soon as possible or use it to protect herself, but she ignored them. She only had one chance, and to succeed, she had to take the risk.

As Myrkan leaped, his claws stretched high, ready to strike, she unleashed her magic.

Energy, obedient to her will, rushed from behind her like a huge gust of wind, wrapping around her as it shot toward the demon—and ice followed in its path, forming a cocoon around her from behind and ending in huge ice spikes jutting forward. The ice crackled, and the air hissed as it froze just before the demon impaled himself.

Blood sprayed, dark and thick. Myrkan grunted and

froze, his face showing shock. "You..." He coughed, sighed, and fell limp.

Kamira stood in her icy cage, cradled from the outside by the demon's body. Part of her expected Myrkan to spring to action again, to take her life... But he was silent and motionless.

Hesitantly, she pushed between his leg and the ice and got out. The wound on her back still stung, promising her a new set of scars, and her whole body ached from the fall, but that would be a small price to pay for getting rid of a demon who'd threatened the city.

She looked around. The initiation rite chamber was destroyed, with only few sections of the wall still standing. Rubble covered the floor, which also bore the marks of the demons' battle, with holes, cracks, and claw scrapes.

The sight brought Fyertash to mind, and Kamira made her way to the edge. She hadn't heard him fall, so perhaps... Careful not to cut herself on sharp edges of crystal, she peeked through a destroyed window.

A few stories down, Fyertash clung to the tower, and the trail of blood and crushed stones on the wall below him suggested he'd been making his way up for a while. His determined expression softened when he saw her.

"You killed him," he said with a hint of praise.

She could swear he picked up his pace, as if curiosity drove him, but it still took him a while to make it back to the top. Finally, he crawled onto the floor, his eyes instantly on Myrkan.

He inspected the dead body in silence, suggesting he was making guesses about how the battle had gone. Then he moved to the remaining part of the wall and carefully seated himself against it, watching Kamira. His arms were almost shredded to pieces, his face bore claw marks, and his wings were torn.

"What now?" he asked.

Kamira knew he wasn't asking about Derazin or how the fight at Kaighal's walls went. Neither of them could make it there, let alone take part in another battle, so she had to hope others would deal with the other demon without her.

She couldn't help remembering what he'd said about alliances and how trust got in the way once the common goal was achieved.

"Once you've regained some of your strength, I'd ask you to clear the exit," she replied with caution.

Fyertash arched his eyebrow. "And then?" His amused voice suggested he'd caught on to her avoidance. "An ice spike to my back?"

Kamira grimaced. He should know her better by now. "I assume you'd rather return to your world on your terms."

"And what if I wanted to stay?" No smug smile or playful tone accompanied the words, as if it wasn't one of his games.

"Why would you?" she asked, half curious and half demanding.

"Yalarethe is going to be a tumultuous place in the near future," Fyertash replied, "and I'd rather not draw attention to myself. Some might go after me if they learn I aided Veranesh. And he himself..." He shrugged. "He would have reasons to go after me as well if I returned. If I remain here, I'm still watching over you, as I agreed."

She appreciated his honesty and straightforward answer, but to let a demon stay in the human world was asking for trouble. Not to mention that she'd be much safer without Fyertash breathing down her neck and drawing attention to her.

"I also have information that could make it worth keeping me around," he added with a cunning smile. "I'm sure you'll be interested in what happened on the other continent. Not to mention that even though no other yalari joined the three who arrived here, it doesn't mean they don't roam distant lands."

Kamira smiled back at him, making her decision. With the battle for Kaighal hopefully coming to an end, she could stop playing ruthless archmage and go back to the way she used to be.

"You don't have to bargain, though I do hope you'll share with me what you know." Letting Fyertash stay in the human world would likely have consequences, but she couldn't demand he leave after he'd aided her in the fight against Myrkan... and Bayena, because if he hadn't held off the Four's priestess long enough or hadn't disposed of her body, along with the explosive device, Kamira could be long dead.

Surprise flashed on his face, and then he inspected her with curiosity and—dared she say?—respect. "We should both see to our wounds and rest before we talk. Though, I suppose, you'll want to check on your other allies first."

With visible strain, he lifted himself and made it across the chamber, to the rubble blocking the exit. Kamira stepped away, giving him space to remove the collapsed columns and rooftop. The wording he chose hadn't escaped her, suggesting he counted himself among her allies, but she knew better than to press for a clear answer.

"I do hope you have enough wits to not charge into any other battle," he remarked when the door was cleared.

For all she knew, another battle waited for her whether she wanted it or not. "Thank you for your aid today," she said instead.

"You did well." The serious, appreciative tone of his voice was so different than his usual teasing and games.

He moved back to his chosen spot and slumped against the wall, his face turned toward the dead Myrkan. The ice was already melting, causing the body slide onto the floor, but Fyertash didn't seem to care. Under the coat of tiredness, his face expressed satisfaction.

"Leave Derazin for another day. The coward might decide to return to our realm anyway, since he never wanted to stay here for long to begin with," he added.

Kamira couldn't help the thought that, as beaten and wounded as the demon looked, he was taking his last breaths that very moment. Perhaps all that talk of staying in the human world was nothing but a way to divert her attention from his pitiful state.

She gave him one last look and left the destroyed chamber. No matter how unnerving he was at times, he deserved some peace and quiet, whether he wanted to die alone or simply rest.

She, on the other hand, would have neither until she ensured that Derazin was dead and all of her friends were either alive or avenged.

16

Koshmarnyk slowed down as Ervan turned around. If he wasn't running, he could be preparing for a confrontation. The treacherous adept might have dealt with the guard in a direct and violent way, but Koshmarnyk doubted he would choose the same approach dealing with him. Deception was more likely, as was poison and other sneaky means of disposing of an opponent.

"You came too late," Ervan said. "It's all done. Myrkan is in the city. You and your demonologist gaharra have lost."

"Do you think this will stop me from making you pay?" Koshmarnyk asked.

Ervan paled and swallowed, looking around desperately as if in search for anyone that would come to his aid. "If I die, the demon won't spare anyone here," he replied in a high-pitched tone.

"Not if we kill him first. Maybe we already did." Koshmarnyk indicated the building behind him. The battle on the topmost tower must have ended already, because there wasn't any sound coming from above, but without one demon emerging victorious, it was hard to tell who'd won.

The other adept huffed. "You only have your guesses."

Koshmarnyk said nothing and corrected the grip on his knife instead. It didn't matter how the battle between the demons went. Ervan would pay for his betrayal.

"Adept Koshmarnyk!" a male voice called out from behind Ervan.

A group of men and women in Gildya's attire made their way uphill, led by Davshil. It didn't escape Koshmarnyk that most were armored and armed.

Ervan's expression turned smug. "It seems that you're finally going to be held accountable for all your transgressions. This time I'll ensure your prison is one you won't escape from."

Koshmarnyk didn't reply. He wasn't looking forward to shedding the blood of other adepts—even if he despised a lot of what Gildya stood for—but he wouldn't let Ervan get away with treachery and killing at least two people.

"Adepts, seize that man," Ervan said as the others approached.

Davshil shook his head. "We're here for you, Adept Ervan." At his sign, the guards surrounded Ervan. "Adept Koshmarnyk, I apologize. This is Gildya's matter."

Koshmarnyk took a step forward. "What's this about?" It could be Ervan's ruse to hide under the council's protection, and Koshmarnyk would sooner fight than let the traitor escape.

"Adept Ervan is accused of murdering the council. A deed he was ready to blame you for." Davshil's tone left no doubt that he considered Ervan guilty.

"You can add two more murders and letting a demon into the city to the count." Koshmarnyk stepped aside, allowing the others to see the Towers guard's body in the distance.

Davshil stared wide-eyed while Ervan reddened in anger.

"He's lying!" Ervan pointed at Koshmarnyk. "Alluvendran's hate for me and for Gildya is well known! He concocted this plot to get his revenge."

"Yes, in the past, Adept Koshmarnyk expressed his thoughts on Gildya clearly," Davshil said, "with the same straightforwardness and honesty that marks all his words and deeds, so if he wished to act upon those feelings, he wouldn't have used a poisoning device. Much like the one some adepts and apprentices saw you carrying into the council meeting." As he spoke, a guard tied Ervan's hands behind his back. "Adept Koshmarnyk, I assure you that Ervan will be punished for what he did."

Koshmarnyk closed his fists. Gildya's justice was hardly what he'd consider just, but to dispense punishment here and now meant wasting time and energy on a fight. Besides, no matter what light judgment they passed, at least they would ensure that Ervan didn't do more harm while Koshmarnyk went to find Kamira and Veelk. They were likely already aware of the battle between the demons and had set out to fight the other one, but not knowing was gnawing on his thoughts.

Besides, with Ervan out of the way, he could offer his meager aid in the fight.

"Very well, I'll entrust him to your hands." He looked at Davshil coldly. "But should Gildya fail to recognize the gravity of his deeds, I'll hold you responsible."

Davshil nodded solemnly. "I hope you'll allow us some time, since with the council's demise, Gildya is... in a bit of disarray. But once proper justice can be ensured, I'll personally bring news to you and the archmage." His companions were already leading Ervan away, but he hesitated. "You are, of course, welcome to come over if you choose so."

"To be judged as well?" Koshmarnyk couldn't help a challenge.

To his surprise, Davshil's grim expression softened with a smile. "No. I and many others might frown at what you did to your own flesh, but you have proven more trustworthy than one of our own. And as much as I hate the idea, with the new threats looming over the world, including the demonic ones, perhaps such research, no matter how dangerous it could be, is needed. If Gildya doesn't do it now, we won't be ready when others do."

Such a confession came unexpected to Koshmarnyk. "Once the siege is broken, I'll come by Gildya. I might be the sole witness to what Ervan did here."

Davshil looked up the Towers, likely taking in the extent of the destruction for the first time. "The demon that entered the city... Is he dead?"

"I'm about to find out," Koshmarnyk replied. "I'll send word to Gildya and to the walls as soon as I know."

"I'll be on my way, then. We'll speak again once all the mess has been sorted. Be well."

Davshil rushed away, and Koshmarnyk couldn't help wondering whether the other adept was dreading the prospect of being invited to accompany him. As entertaining as the thought was, when Koshmarnyk turned toward the Towers, his amusement faded. If Fyertash had lost, Myrkan could be regaining his strength with every passing moment.

The prospect of facing the demon on his own was a grim one, but he had to know what happened before he sought Kamira and Veelk, even if he had to tear the closed door to pieces to get in.

THE FIRST THING that came into view when Kamira exited the chamber was a trail of blood. Her heart skipped a beat even though she didn't know who'd bled, and when. She hadn't seen Pelina back in the chamber, which was a relief, but since the barrier device protecting the Towers had stopped working, Kamira had to assume that the young arcanist had confronted Ervan, or...

She pushed away the idea that it was her lover who got wounded.

With her throat tight and mouth dry, she followed the red trail. To her surprise, it didn't lead to the bottom of the Towers, instead taking a turn into the corridor leading to another part of the building—the archmages' quarters. By the wall, blood pooled, telling her that the wounded had rested there. There were footprints there as well, and from what Kamira could tell, they belonged to a man.

Then the trail continued, and Kamira finally stopped by what she knew to be Yoreus's chambers. She narrowed her eyes. Last time she'd caught a glimpse of Atissa, the young woman was at the walls...

Knocking meant announcing her presence to a possible assassin, so Kamira pressed on the handle instead. The door wasn't locked, and it yielded to her cautious touch. She barely cracked it open, then took three steps back—as many as the corridor allowed. Tension building in her body aggravated the pain in her back, and she used her magic to summon a gust of wind strong enough to push the door open.

The chamber inside was in a pitiful state. Blood both old and fresh marked the floor, which also bore marks of chalk —a complex circle, now smudged and barely visible.

In the middle of it lay a woman in bloodstained clothes.

"Pelina!"

The woman didn't react.

Torn between the need to help and caution, Kamira chose the former but summoned a barrier as she passed through the door. The magic wouldn't last, but it could slow down any attack, should one be coming. Reasonably, she knew that it would be unlikely for any assassin to set up his or her trap this way, away from the initiation rite chamber, but she knew better than to be carefree. After all, Ervan could have chosen this room as his hiding place, knowing that anyone would first go to Pelina's aid—and the footprints she saw in the corridor suggested someone might have come here with the wounded woman.

The doors leading to other rooms were closed. Kamira knelt beside Pelina, making sure all entrances were still within her view.

The woman was unconscious but alive. Her blood-drenched clothes suggested a wound, but all Kamira found was a cut that didn't look serious.

Kamira smiled when all the pieces fell into place. *Atissa must have figured it out!* With renewed interest, she inspected the circle, but a lot of the markings were smudged and illegible. It still teased her with the temptation of using it and closing the wounds on her own back, but Master Tijhran would rise from his grave if she was foolish and careless enough to try. Without knowing how the circle worked exactly, she'd risk bringing unwanted effects. Perhaps this was what had happened to Pelina.

Kamira once more checked if the woman was going to be fine, then rose to her feet. She couldn't indulge in taking care of one person when the whole city still relied on her. With a heavy heart, she left the chamber.

As she made it back to the main stairway, a blurry figure passed in front of her, going down. At first, Kamira called upon her magic, but whoever it was, he or she didn't seem a threat. She stepped out.

"Nyk?!"

She couldn't be sure it was him, but he stopped and turned. His expression was wary, but he moved smoothly, and she spotted no blood.

"Kam…" He was by her side in a few heartbeats, looking her up and down, likely searching for her wounds as she'd searched for his a moment ago. "I spoke to Fyertash. He said you were fine, but…" He shook his head. "It didn't look like an easy battle."

"I was lucky. Mostly bruises and scratches," she said, even though she wasn't sure if the deep gashes on her back could be considered scratches. "Fyertash suffered much more."

Koshmarnyk nodded. "It doesn't look like he'll be flying anytime soon. But one demon is dead."

"And one to go." All she wanted was to fall in his embrace and stay in it forever, or at least long enough for the day to end, but that dream could only come true if they dealt with Derazin. "Come, you can tell me everything on the way back to the walls."

She hissed as he touched her back, and in an instant, Koshmarnyk was inspecting her once again. "This is more than bruises and scratches."

"It'll heal," she replied grumpily. Part of her acknowledged that she refused Koshmarnyk the same fussing over her wellbeing that she had over his not so long ago, but she couldn't indulge in being cared for, not yet. "We have no time."

The look he gave her left no doubt that he'd rather see her in bed until she recovered, or at least take time to dress and clean her wounds, but he nodded.

"What about Ervan?" she asked as their made their way down the stairs.

Her back ached, and she couldn't go as fast as she'd like. They had to get back to Veelk and figure out what to do with Derazin. If the cowardly demon learned of Myrkan's demise, he could flee. As much as it would give them the victory they needed, she hated the thought of Derazin lurking somewhere and waiting for an opportunity to strike.

"Gildya took him," Koshmarnyk replied. "Adept Davshil said he's accused of killing the whole council."

"Do you believe him?" Such a claim seemed almost absurd when she considered what she'd already learned from him about Ervan. On the other hand, he did attack Pelina, so perhaps there was a grain of truth in Gildya's claims.

Koshmarnyk shrugged. "At least he's not our problem for a while, and that's what we need."

She nodded. Ervan had already done the crucial damage to the city's defenses, and she and Fyertash had almost paid with their lives for his deeds—and if he was behind the sabotage of the devices, many defenders had died because of him too. Whatever scheme he could come up with to save his skin would be child's play in comparison, even if he had truly found enough determination to murder the council.

And if the accusation was but a ruse, and Gildya wasn't about to provide justice for Ervan's other crimes, it would learn firsthand what the first archmage was willing to do to put them in their place. But that all had to wait until the city was safe.

"Let's hurry. If we don't, Veelk might get the foolish idea of taking on a demon and his whole army on his own," she said in the lighthearted manner.

For a heartbeat, Koshmarnyk looked like he was about to argue, but then, without a word, he started down the stairs. After all, he also knew Veelk well.

17

Archmage Irtan was too experienced to waste time on watching the battle between Fyertash and Myrkan. It was enough to see the initial attack and Kamira's fall—now he had to focus on his own battle. He'd have no influence on what would happen in the Towers, and most outcomes would be in his favor anyway. Fyertash and Myrkan could end up killing each other, and since his pact demon had already revealed that death was not something demons were concerned about, Irtan wasn't either. He'd still have his magic even if Fyertash fell, and that was all that mattered.

If Fyertash won, and Kamira didn't survive the fall, there would be no man or a woman left to challenge Irtan's ascension back to power. If Kamira survived but Fyertash didn't...

Irtan smiled. His pact demon wouldn't be able to interfere in his plans.

He gazed into the distance, where two figures were making their way through the corridor of ice he'd prepared for them. Such a complex channeling had turned out to be quite a challenge and drained him more than he'd expected, but the effort was worth it. The two mage killers could succeed at slaying the other demon. If everything aligned, all his enemies, rivals, and threats would kill each other in battles, leaving Irtan to collect the rewards.

"Any news?" he called out without even turning his head, still pouring magic onto the demonling hordes below. He had to be careful with his magic now, but still had enough to show that the oldest archmage in the Towers was more than a frail man.

"No, Archmage Irtan," a girl replied in a high-pitched voice. Too young to participate in the defense efforts in any meaningful way, she was his lookout. Smart and observant enough, she could be groomed later to become a skilled arcanist. "The demons fell into the highest tower, knocking some of it down, but none came out yet. No sign of the archmage, either."

The archmage. Irtan couldn't help a smile. That rebellious former student of the Towers had ensured that her name would always be the one to remember. No matter what he did, even if he became leader again, he'd be just one of the long line of first archmages that came before him and would likely come after as well: yet another name in the annals, maybe more significant than some others, but eventually forgotten as well.

But Kamira... Kamira was to forever be *the* archmage, the one and only. Her name could vanish from memories, but not who she was and what she did.

His smile didn't fade. She'd played it well, though he doubted she had any intention of making herself known like that, and he'd let her have the glory. Only a fool wasted his time and efforts on fighting what was inevitable.

She was the archmage, but he would be the first archmage again, one way or another.

"Very well. Let me know if any of the demons emerges or you see any sign of magic," he replied. If he knew whether Kamira had survived, he could plan accordingly.

The screeches of demonlings beyond the wall changed, and Irtan forced himself to focus on the battle. Yet the creatures weren't testing the barriers, including the one he summoned, and very few made it to the breaches that were still occurring along the defense line, despite Gildya's efforts... or perhaps due to them, if Kamira was right about the traitor adept or adepts.

With caution, Irtan stepped closer to the edge of the battlement. Demonlings below were engaged in a fierce battle with one another, clawing and biting with such ferocity that they ignored the attacks still coming from Kaighal's defenders. Many died from arrows and magic fires, yet they paid no attention to humans, still trying to reach their opponents with their dying breaths. No wonder the higher demons were such cruel and distrusting beings if they'd evolved from creatures as vicious and aggressive as demonlings.

He looked further into the battlefield. Derazin's body still towered in the distance, but the demon remained motionless, and the odd twist of his bulging torso and head suggested that he would never move again.

Between him and the walls, cutting their way through the hordes of demonlings, were two familiar figures. They were both covered in blood, and the way they carefully carved their way forward suggested wounds, but they kept on pressing, clearly determined to reach the city walls.

Irtan shook his head in disbelief. Kamira's allies had shown more power than he'd expected. It would be fortunate if they perished among the demonlings, but since they'd managed to defeat the demon, likely also killing the arcanists that served him, they would make it back to Kaighal.

Irtan pressed his lips together. A confrontation with Kamira while the mage killers were by her side would be a difficult one, but with so many witnesses around, it'd be hard to pretend he didn't see them. If he didn't offer aid, the mage killers would come after him, and even if they didn't make it, Kamira would make him pay for leaving her friend to die.

There were too many "ifs" for Irtan's liking, and he hated making decisions without enough information. He allowed himself a sigh. He'd do what was expected from the man everyone thought he was, and he'd deal with the outcome when he knew more.

Channeling energy now came with more strain. His body almost gave up when he called forth a storm of lightning, reaching far into the battlefield, but the sight of demonlings twitching and jerking in response to his magic brought satisfaction. Since the creatures were focused on slaying their own kin, they were less likely to pay attention to the two humans making their way through the patch of dead demonlings.

"Bring some rope!" he called out. "The higher demon is dead, and his slayers are returning!"

His words stirred the defenders. Their tired faces brightened, and their moves became more vigorous, as if the news of Derazin's death wiped away their tiredness. Irtan would love to relieve at least half of them, now that the biggest threat was gone, but he had still no news of Myrkan, and if the devices kept failing, the city would be unprotected should some demonlings decide to venture into it.

But he smiled. There was one thing he had to give Kamira and her allies: they didn't seem interested in amassing power and influence for their own sakes, but used it to do what they thought would benefit the city. Before, Irtan wasn't certain that Kamira antagonizing Gildya's council and turning down Tivarashan aid were the right choices, but it seemed that she'd had a plan all along. He'd made a good choice in reminding her that by winning against Yoreus, she'd become the first archmage—otherwise she might have left the Towers, and perhaps Kaighal altogether, leaving Irtan in a much drearier situation. Though it also meant he'd have a harder time making her leave now, when she was the one to set the rules.

With most of the demonlings in their path already dead, the two mage killers made their way to the walls much quicker. As they climbed the rope—the woman first, the man second—Irtan stood nearby, ready to protect them from any stray creatures. Until he knew all the pieces, it seemed better to stay on their good side.

The man, Veelk, still eyed him with distrust as he climbed over the battlements to the cheers of the city's defenders, but he did give Irtan a courteous nod.

"Any news from Kamira?" he asked immediately, seemingly paying no attention to the deep gashes on his shoulder and chest, and as he moved, no grimace betrayed any pain. Mage killers were truly fearsome if they could shrug off such injuries.

"I'm afraid not." Irtan didn't try to put any concern in his voice, as the man before him didn't seem one to fall for false caring. "None of the demons emerged either."

The mage killers exchanged glances.

"We'll head to the Towers, then," Veelk said. "The demonlings outside are busy infighting, so they shouldn't pose too much threat, but we still need someone here to watch over things in case some stray arcanist survived and tries to take control over them."

Irtan had no doubt that Veelk wanted to keep him away until he knew whether Kamira was fine. Wounded or unconscious, she'd make an easy target for assassins... or rivals, including Irtan himself.

"If Myrkan's alive, you'll need all the help you can get." The thought of facing a demon wasn't an enticing one, and his body was already aching in response to all the magic he had used so far, but for the city to survive, they had to ensure the other demon had been dealt with. "I'll go with you."

"That won't be necessary," Veelk replied, looking down the walls.

At first, Irtan was about to scold the stubborn mage killer about expressing distrust when they all needed to work together, but the shouts rising from the street below them made him follow Veelk's gaze.

Kamira was walking toward the walls, accompanied by Adept Koshmarnyk. People stepped to the side to make way for her and excitedly carried the words she said.

"The demon is dead!"

She held her head high, but the bloodstains and her stiff moves didn't escape Irtan. Surviving the fall he'd witnessed was an impossible feat already, and her other injuries suggested that she'd still faced Myrkan after that.

For the first time in decades, Irtan shifted uneasily under a sudden wave of doubt. Her skills, cunning, and allies had already made Kamira into the most dangerous opponent Irtan could imagine, but it was her courage and determination that gave him pause. It was one thing to engage in games with petty men and women like Yoreus or

Loktra, and another to stand against someone who didn't crave power like many lesser people did.

He was certain that if he wanted to, he'd find a way to gain the upper hand. After all, her strength could also be her weakness when exploited in a skillful way, but instead of satisfaction, such a victory would bring him self-loathing. Perhaps it was time to truly step aside and recognize her as worthy of rule over Kaighal.

Or perhaps—the old man smiled as he watched Kamira reuniting with Veelk—there were other ways to achieve his goal... Ways that would see Irtan and Kamira as something other than rivals. He had to admit that for a man like him who had spent decades plotting and playing games against other archmages, first carving his path to the top, then fighting hard to maintain his power, this was a startling thought. But with all the changes that Kaighal had endured in the past weeks, it was also an enticing possibility, so Irtan let it linger.

ATISSA HAD NEVER BEEN SO exhausted. Even her father's various punishments, what back then she'd considered hard labor, paled in comparison to channeling magic all day. Fyertash's power allowed her to heal continuously, but it also meant she didn't think of having any rest. With the barriers failing constantly and the defenders doing their best to keep the demonlings from getting into the city, there was no shortage of wounded, and even though medics took care of those with minor injuries, everyone who was less lucky ended up in Atissa's circle.

She looked around confused as people on the walls started to cheer.

"What happened?" she asked a defender passing by.

"The tribal warriors defeated the large demon!" he replied, excited.

Tribal warriors? Atissa furrowed her brow. The man was already halfway up the stone stairway leading to the battlements, likely to have a look himself, leaving her to ponder what he meant. Kaighal had no tribal warriors, and there were no tribes in the neighboring lands.

Except... Except for Veelk and his companions. Her eyes widened at the thought that they alone had gone against a demon. She'd only seen the creature for a glimpse a few days earlier when curiosity drew her to the walls, but even from a distance, towering over the hordes of demonlings, it looked like a formidable opponent. On the other hand, Veelk seemed exactly like the man who could take on a demon and emerge successful.

As if summoned by her thoughts, he and his sister emerged from behind the walls. They both looked tired and wounded, and Veelk's odd weapon was in two pieces. Atissa hushed the urge to run over them to offer her help. Irtan, that slimy old man, was already there, and he'd likely do all in his power to keep her away. Especially that she was no one now, just an apprentice arcanist.

Perhaps later she'd find an opportunity to talk to Veelk.

A group of people carried another wounded into her circle, so Atissa focused her attention on the middle-aged woman. Thankfully, her injuries weren't extensive. The thought of channeling any more magic made her want to collapse, but she healed the woman anyway, trying to find comfort in how wielding arcane magic felt. Compared to dryly reciting spells, arcane magic was more like a skill or even art, more personal and visceral. But no matter how exciting it was, it did leave her exhausted.

Another round of cheers made her lift her head.

Kamira entered the street running along the walls. Adept Koshmarnyk accompanied her, but she didn't seem to need help despite the bruises and wounds Atissa spotted. People were shouting about the other demon being dead as well, and Atissa allowed herself a small smile. It looked like the worst of the siege was over.

Veelk and his sister made it down the walls, and the four engaged in lively conversation.

Atissa sighed, finishing her healing and waving the woman away. At least with all the attention on Kamira, she could hope for a moment of respite. It'd been a while since she could rest, and she was so busy with the wounded, she hadn't even found a chance to find a sip of water. Once or twice she'd seen other arcanists passing by, too young or too unskilled to partake in the defense, but none bothered to offer any help to the daughter of a dead archmage.

"We have more wounded!" someone called out behind her.

Atissa hid her desperation and turned to greet a group of people approaching her circle. Most of them could walk on their own, with only few needing support to move, and all were conscious. Her shoulders slumped. They would likely recover on their own, but to refuse could mean stirring their anger. She had neither the position nor the friends to allow herself the risk of turning people against her.

Resigned, she indicated the circle.

"Enough!"

Kamira's voice sounded much closer than Atissa expected.

She glanced over her shoulder. Kamira was approaching with confidence and a stern expression on her face.

"All of those people are well enough to wait," she said. "I

won't allow Kaighal's only arcane healer to collapse of exhaustion just because some of you can't suffer a few cuts and bruises."

Atissa gasped as Kamira walked past her. On her back there were three long gashes, looking a lot like claw marks. Until now, Atissa had pictured Kamira using her magic or Fyertash in the battle, but it seemed that Veelk wasn't the only one who had gone hand to hand with a demon.

Then Kamira turned to Atissa, allowing all the gathered wounded to have a peek at those very marks, and Atissa couldn't help thinking that Kamira did it to let people see that she was injured too, and yet she didn't demand healing. A clever play, and one that got Atissa out of either refusing or exerting herself, so she gave Kamira a grateful nod.

"Your circle in the Towers saved Pelina," Kamira said softly. "And you should return with us. Your chambers are a bit of a mess, but there's plenty of space in the Towers where you can rest undisturbed. Can you walk on your own?"

"I think so," Atissa replied carefully, unsure how much strength her body truly had left.

Kamira waved for her to follow, but then stopped abruptly, inspecting her with narrowed eyes. "A new pact?"

There seemed to be more curiosity than suspicion in her question, but Atissa tensed nevertheless. She'd rather not discuss it in public... if at all. "Fyertash," she replied with resignation. "But it's not like I refused."

Kamira huffed. "I imagine he found it amusing. Nevertheless, you've used it well." She waved at her again, walking away. "Come, let's get out of here before someone else remembers they need something. Irtan can handle dealing with the remaining demonlings on his own."

Atissa smiled at that. The old archmage would likely

welcome being the only man in charge. If she and Kamira had something in common, it was the distrust toward Irtan —not enough to bring them closer, but better than remembering that they also had one death in common...

She pushed the thought of her father away.

Kamira was already back with Veelk and others, and Mawi joined them as well. She was looking back, clearly waiting for Atissa to join them. Others were smiling at her, even Zelna, and Mawi waved.

It might be a bad idea to go back to the Towers following the woman who, in a way, had taken everything from her, but Atissa gathered her meager belongings and rushed to them. They'd likely never be friends, Kamira and her, but it seemed that Kamira wasn't interested in being enemies, inviting Atissa to do the same.

"I heard you did well as a healer," Veelk said as soon as she joined them. "You must have done well with your channeling practice."

Atissa blushed. How come the praise that came from Kamira's friends and even Kamira herself sounded so much more genuine than when her father, or anyone else for that matter, noted her achievements? "Your advice helped a lot."

"You managed to heal with magic?" Mawi was by her side in an instant. "I'd much like to hear about it."

Hiding her disappointment, Atissa matched her pace with Mawi's to oblige him with answers while Veelk caught up with Kamira, and they were deep in exchanging stories in an instant. Clearly, she wasn't meant to have a conversation with that broad-shouldered warrior, but at least it seemed that he didn't mind her being around and was impressed by her mastering the healing magic to whatever meager level she'd managed.

Walking toward the Towers and drawing shapes in the air to explain the concept of circles—those bits of knowledge she had—to Mawi, Atissa allowed herself a glimmer of hope for a brighter future.

18

Kamira was lying on the bed, on her stomach. Before he left to meet with Davshil at Gildya's halls, Koshmarnyk had taken care of her wounds, but turning on her back didn't seem like a good idea. The claw marks were deep enough to cause discomfort, and she had no doubt they would be an impressive addition to her ever-growing collection of scars.

The Towers were quiet, though she knew Irtan had already returned with most of the arcanists and students, leaving only a few at the walls. The old man hadn't visited himself, sending a messenger instead. A quick note suggested that Kamira should have a well-deserved rest while he ensured all the mundane matters were seen to. That alone made her want to get out of the bed and track him down, but reason demanded she take his offer, no matter what hidden motives lined it. She needed that time to figure out what came next.

For a moment, she entertained the thought of life as the archmage. But nothing she could do would put Irtan in place for long enough, and she despised the thought of having him killed—no matter how much she distrusted him, his leadership skills and wisdom were unquestionable. If he challenged her openly, she wouldn't hesitate, but the old man was too cunning for an open confrontation. Staying in the Towers would mean constantly looking over her shoulder.

Besides—her mood soured—there was also the matter of her deal with Zyreshi. The demoness had allowed Kamira to think about it "until after the siege," but with war parties sent out from Kaighal to slay the remaining demonlings, that time was nearly up.

The door to her bedroom opened, and Koshmarnyk walked in. As he had no visible signs of battle, she had to assume the adepts were amicable enough.

"Gildya's truly in disarray," he said, as if guessing what she was thinking about. "Ervan did assassinate the council, and Adept Davshil is scrambling for any kind of leadership. There are hardly enough worthy adepts to form a new council, and with no one to choose from among them, there's going to be even more turmoil. Davshil was desperate enough to offer *me* a seat."

She held her breath as she sat up to talk to him. During the time they'd spent together, Koshmarnyk had never expressed any ambitions toward leadership, but it didn't mean he wasn't looking forward to finally having a real life and a respectable position in Gildya. It didn't escape her how devoted he was to creating the blueprints for the protective devices she could only vaguely imagine. Inventions were both his passion and his calling, and only chance had put Kamira in his path.

"I told him I'd think about it," he said with a half-smile, "otherwise I think he'd crumble under the responsibility that suddenly fell on him. I also invited him to the meeting tomorrow." He looked at her with sudden seriousness. "But you aren't staying here much longer, are you?"

To tell him she hadn't decided yet would feel like avoidance, so she nodded—her clenched throat kept all the words in, even if she could find the right ones. No matter how much she wanted to deceive herself, it seemed that her time with Koshmarnyk was coming to an end. She always knew their plans for the future might not work together, and since she was not willing to stay in Kaighal to be with him, she couldn't demand he abandon his goals to roam with her.

"Neither you nor Veelk are people who want to settle down." He sat down beside her, showing no disappointment at her lack of response. "But I was hoping you would like a home to return to every now and then... Even if it's an inventor's house, full of blueprints and devices, it might be nicer than a room in an inn."

Kamira allowed herself a glimmer of hope, but first she had to tell Koshmarnyk the truth. "This home... I wouldn't be able to have one in Kaighal. The Four made me an offer, and for the sake of Kaighal, I want to accept it."

He didn't hide his concern. "Does that offer require you to go to Tivarashan?"

"No." She couldn't help a smirk at the thought. If the Four wanted her back north, she'd have a much harder time deciding whether Kaighal was truly worth it. "They do want me away from Tyorane. Forever. If I leave and never return, the Four will ensure Kaighal will stay as it is, a free city," she said. "We might have pushed the demons away, but we aren't ready to stand against Tivarashan if Andalisha or one of her daughters decide it's time for Kaighal to become a part of their queendom."

She didn't mention that the deal also required her to send Fyertash away. She was hoping the demon was smart enough to know he shouldn't stay much longer so close to the lands the Four considered theirs. "And I'd rather not remind them how much of a threat I am... One dead priestess is easy enough to forget, but my presence here would likely become unnerving to them soon enough."

"So, Juamha?" he asked.

"Only if you and Veelk agree. If you want to stay here, I'll find another way," she said with sudden resolve. He wanted to stay with her and make it work in a way that would make neither of them feel like they were giving up too much, so she would be a fool to throw it away, even if it meant standing against the Four and another siege.

He shook his head. "Kaighal was never a home to me as much as it is to you, and I care for it much less than I care for you." Without any warning, he pulled her closer. He was careful not to aggravate her wound, but his embrace was firm nevertheless. "Going away, to a continent where nobody knows us, will be a pleasant change. You will have your travels, and I'll have my work, and we'll still have each other."

She smiled, leaning against him. "Juamha, then."

IT WAS late in the evening when Kamira climbed the stairs to what used to be the initiation rite chamber. She'd rather be in bed, letting her body heal, but she needed to check on Fyertash, and—if the demon was still alive—talk to him. A conversation like that was best had without any nosy archmages poking about, so Kamira waited till everyone in the Towers had retired, worn down by the defense at the walls and other events of the day.

A small lumisphere floated over her shoulder, lighting

the way and casting shadows on the walls, steps, and dark patches of blood. It would be a while before anyone had time to take care of this damage and the initiation rite chamber itself. Since it would no longer serve the purpose high mages intended it for, Kamira allowed herself to dream of removing the remainder of the walls and shaping it into a terrace everyone could visit. It could also be the place to meet the arcanists' demonic allies in the future, if any more crossed over the human world. But the decision—and the works to follow—would not belong to her.

The door at the top of the stairs looked the way she had left it, so she stepped inside the ruined chamber. If Fyertash didn't want visitors, he could have closed it, and announcing herself made little sense when the lumisphere's glow must have already warned him that an arcanist was coming... unless the demon had succumbed to his wounds and died.

The dark shape of Myrkan's body, now that the ice had melted, slumped on the floor in an awkward position, was the first thing that drew her attention, and as if responding, the scratches on her back ached, reminding her of the dangerous battle.

Fyertash wasn't where she'd left him. He was squatting at the edge of the chamber, in the spot where the wall had collapsed in its entirety, and his silhouette stood out against the starry sky as he watched the city and the port at the bay, but he turned his head toward her when she entered.

"Kamira," he said as both greeting and acknowledgment. This must have been the first time he'd used her name. "I assume Derazin is dead." His wings, though still misshapen, looked like they were healing.

"Slain by Veelk," she replied.

As he turned to her and the moon illuminated his face, his satisfaction was unmissable. "Veranesh will deal with both of them once they're reborn in Yalarethe, but that's not our concern, so my work here is done. I hope you'll manage to survive on your own without my assistance, at least for a while."

She understood. "You're leaving."

"Soon, yes. There are matters on the other continent I have to see to." With a motion of his claw, he indicated for her to come closer. "When we left there, we were expecting at least a few more yalari to join us in time. It might be that they've become aware of Uganel's destruction and chose not to cross over."

"Or they did, but they never came here," she finished for him as she approached.

He confirmed with a nod. "It's unlikely, but I'd rather know for sure than be ambushed in the future when they're ready to strike."

Kamira found a piece of broken wall to sit on. With Fyertash's size, she'd have to look up anyway, and her body demanded rest. "You mentioned trouble that accompanied your summoning... crossing." If Fyertash was about to leave, she would try to get as much knowledge from him as she could.

For a heartbeat or two, he regarded her with thoughtful curiosity, and she was certain he'd find a way to wriggle out of the question, but he said, "The humans who performed the ritual sought to bind us. To force us to do their bidding as if we were some mere asayalari. Arujhan decided they should be taught a lesson, and as you can imagine, there was quite a lot of killing involved until he was satisfied and only the obedient humans were still alive. When we left, we took some of the pactees with us to aid us in the siege and convince others to make pacts with us, but some stayed behind, in their circle, preparing for more summoning, should it be needed. They claimed the ritual required preparations, and they wanted to protect the book."

"What book?" She knew she was taking his bait.

A sly smile came to his lips. "The one that contains detailed instructions on how to bring a kanyalari to this world... and I suppose many other rituals of the past. Would you like me to fetch it for you?"

Kamira didn't even try to hide her reaction. Such a book had to be old, possibly even from before the Cataclysm. To glean secrets of the past and even find ways to make arcane arts into what they once were... The possibilities were there; Atissa's experiments with the healing circle had already proven it.

She looked Fyertash in the eye. Just because she was enthralled by the idea, it didn't mean she'd lost her wit. "And why are you so eager to get it for me?"

The demon huffed in amusement. "I made a deal with Veranesh. I'm to watch over you, but you neither want me to nor need me to. If you send me on an errand instead..." He let his voice fade. "I think Veranesh would show some understanding for why I'm not your shadow."

"Isn't finding whether other yalari crossed over task enough?" she asked. "I'd think they pose more threat to me than a book."

"For a moment I thought you didn't want it, but what you don't want is me getting my hands on it."

"Will I be racing you for it?"

There was a slight pause as he regarded her in thought. "No," he said. "By killing Myrkan on your own, you proved your worth, and I'd rather not make an enemy of you." He looked to the side, toward another tower visible through a destroyed window on the opposite side of the chamber. "My pactee, though, might not share my perspective."

Kamira inspected him with rising curiosity. It seemed unusual for a demon like Fyertash to speak so openly about how the man he had a pact with could be a threat to her, and she took it as a sign of goodwill and honesty.

"I'll handle Irtan. I'm sure we can come to an agreement." No matter how unnerving the old man was, he was also reasonable. She doubted he wanted her dead—likely only removed, and she could give him that without bloodshed.

"I hope you're right. He's a good pactee."

She had to smile. Irtan and Fyertash were a perfect match, both sly and cunning, but without the maliciousness that often marked power-thirsty men and women. It didn't escape her either that the demon assumed she'd be victorious in any confrontation with the old archmage.

"I'll stay around for a few days longer," Fyertash added. "Once you see to the matters of the city, see me again. I'll share what I know about the books and the pactees who guard it."

Fyertash certainly knew of ways to end a conversation, and she didn't try to push. Regardless of their mutual goals in the recent past, the demon would share with her only what he wanted, and when he wanted to. He also beat her with experience when it came to games, so she wouldn't be able to manipulate him even if she wanted.

"I will." Kamira glanced at Myrkan's body. "And what of him?" Despite her bold claims during the battle, she had little desire to make the demon into some kind of a display.

"Once my wings are fully healed, I'll carry him out into the sea. The body will fall apart soon enough, but it would be better if no one witnessed it."

On that, she agreed. The fewer people who knew, the fewer inconvenient questions they could ask, and Kamira would rather not make them aware of the complexities of demons' life cycles and the destruction spell. Undoubtedly, someone like Irtan would have already started piecing information together, but it didn't mean she had to make it easy for him.

"Thank you. Take your time resting," she said, leaving. "I'll speak to you soon."

~

Kamira walked down the stairs, considering the next steps. There were few things she had to see to before she left the city, but then she would finally be free. Her heart longed for the road with the strength she hadn't expected. Just her and Veelk, and an adventure, a discovery, or trouble… or everything at once, if their past travels were to foretell the future. But things would be different now, with Koshmarnyk waiting for her in whichever place he decided to settle. Somehow, she knew she wouldn't miss Kaighal that much.

She still had to talk to Veelk, but the short conversation they had in the streets the other day had reassured her that he wouldn't be opposed to leaving Tyorane and roaming Juamha for a change. Unless he decided to return to his tribe, it likely made little difference to him where they traveled, as long as there were battles to be had, coins to be earned, and beautiful girls to catch his attention.

That last thought gave her pause. Upon his return, Veelk had seemed much less flirtatious. Perhaps it was because she hadn't gotten to see him in the inn where he was staying and away from battle, but it could be that the almost dying in the desert had changed something in him.

She sighed. Too bad Opyr had sent Lefna away. Kamira couldn't blame the innkeeper for wanting to keep his daughter safe, but Lefna's presence could have soothed Veelk's mood.

At the same time, this all explained why Veelk was eager to leave Kaighal. Nothing would be the same in the city after what they'd both done, and they couldn't return to their old life easily.

As Kamira descended, the lumisphere's light fell onto a small-framed figure waiting at the point where the stairway opened to the side corridor.

Archmage Irtan offered his usual jovial smile as she approached. "Adept Koshmarnyk told me you were talking to my pact demon."

Kamira nodded. If the old man wanted to attack, he wouldn't have waited in the open, casually leaning against the banister, away from the wall and bloodstained floor marking Pelina's earlier trouble.

"Would you accept an invitation to my quarters?" Irtan asked. "I believe we have things to talk about."

She indicated for him to lead the way. If he truly wanted to talk, she wouldn't turn him down... And if it was a trap she was walking into, the sooner it was sprung, the better.

They made it through the corridors and stairways in silence. Irtan lived in the same chambers he had back when she was still a student—in the highest tower, on the topmost floor. Such a journey up, sometimes several times a day, must be straining, but the old man never complained. Whether it was the illusory solitude, the view, or the prestige of living above any other human, she didn't know, and she doubted Irtan would tell her.

As they entered the candlelit room, Irtan invited her to sit in a chair and poured wine from a carafe. The room was larger than she'd thought, given the limited space at the top of the tower, which suggested that both his bedroom and the apprentice room were rather small.

"It's not poisoned." Irtan handed her a cup. "But I'll take no affront if you decide not to drink," he added with a slight smile, as if acknowledging she had no reason to trust him.

Without hesitation, Kamira took a sip. If she survived the Thorns' poison orb, she doubted whatever the old man would put in the cup could hurt her. The wine tasted great, not too sweet, and with an impressive balance of flavors. It seemed perfect for a meeting like this.

Irtan's expression didn't change, but Kamira could swear he was pleased with her lack of fussing over the offered drink. He sat in the armchair on the opposite side of a small table. There were two more empty chairs, suggesting that when the first three archmages met, it was in Irtan's quarters.

"I know you despise games, so I won't waste your time," he said. "We both know the title of the first archmage of Kaighal is mine."

Kamira leaned back in her chair. "Do you expect me to simply step down?" she asked, amused. She might have her own plans, but she wanted to hear Irtan's ideas first.

"I was wondering whether you would, after the siege ended, but no, it wouldn't be good for arcanists," Irtan replied. "The woman who brought the high magic down and had two demons at her command, because that's undoubtedly how they'll talk about you—even though it was Veranesh who gave orders to both you and Fyertash—can't be reduced to being the cause of some minor turmoil in history. If you merely stepped down, people would settle into the old ways again, perceiving arcanists as they perceived high mages, and nothing would change.

Corruption and politics would return to the Towers as if they had never left."

Kamira remained silent, waiting. Until now, she'd considered his decision to become an arcanist nothing but another power play, and she hadn't expected Irtan to admit the high mages' shortcomings so openly.

"What I offer you is the title of *the* archmage. It's what people call you anyway," Irtan continued. "With arcane magic not being perceived as evil anymore, there will likely be more Towers built, both in Tyorane and Juamha. It would be beneficial if there was one archmage to oversee all of them, keeping an eye on the first archmages and ensuring they cooperate. One archmage to have a say in all the Towers, yet never having to bother to reside in any."

"That's assuming the first archmages would be willing to share any information with me," Kamira replied. She liked what Irtan was offering her: freedom to do whatever she wanted without being forced to stay in Kaighal or any other city, at the same time giving her the means to get involved in anything she deemed important or interesting.

Irtan shrugged. "Some things won't change, no matter how hard we try. But I'm sure you will be able to force any archmage to step down if you find them... uncooperative."

"You're quite confident that I'll take your offer, aren't you?" she asked.

"You would have told me already if I was wrong, and this wasn't something you wanted," Irtan replied. "But if it was power you craved, you would have long returned to Tivarashan, using the skills you mastered under Tijhran's tutelage to climb the ranks in the Temple. Who knows, maybe you would even be the one to besiege Kaighal and conquer it for your queen. Yet you remained a wandering arcanist for years, and I believe your encounter with

Veranesh was a chance one rather than the result of some revenge-driven plan."

She nodded. As Irtan said himself, she hated games, and with the old archmage offering an interesting solution to their power struggle, there was no reason to delay. "I like your offer. But Kaighal will always remain the new seat of arcane arts, so from now on, things are going to be a little different around here. If you agree to what I have in mind, you'll get your precious title back. If you don't"—Kamira looked him in the eye—"then I suppose you'll die in a duel."

Irtan chuckled. "Now you're the one being confident. But let's keep this amicable. You listened to my offer, so it's time I listened to yours. I'm sure we can do better than high mages did and find a solution that will satisfy us both."

He leaned back in his chair, just like she did not so long ago, and let her speak.

19

The meeting was to be held in one of the classrooms, and Kamira had students replace the benches and chairs with comfortable armchairs, setting them up in a semicircle. The plain room with the rules of high magic still hanging on the walls in complex charts was hardly a worthy place, but with the initiation rite chamber destroyed, Kamira had little choice. Her own quarters were too small, and the Towers lacked other vast rooms suitable for grand meetings. She had no doubt that with the changes to come, Irtan would take care of that to ensure that the right image of the Towers persevered.

She took her seat, the one that would face everyone else, and waited.

The door opening made her flinch. She'd had to deal with too many assassins recently to ignore caution, but as soon as the large figure pushed it wide open, she relaxed.

Veelk closed the door behind him and made his way to her, ignoring chairs and sitting down cross-legged nearby, with his repaired keshal beside him on the floor, as if he expected the peaceful meeting to erupt into bloodshed. In any other circumstances, she'd make light of his caution, but with too many assassins recently, she couldn't blame him for being on the lookout for more trouble.

"I hope we're here to hear you announce that you're leaving, and not that you're going to rebuild the Towers bigger and better," he said. "The old man seems capable enough to oversee the masonry tasks without your directions."

She chuckled. "How does Juamha sound?"

He gave her a wide grin, comforting and joyful. "Like a place that could use a bit of our presence. We've caused enough trouble on this continent and not enough on the other." He looked at her with curiosity. "Anyone else going?"

"Nyk—" she knew he was asking about the adept— "though he won't be traveling with us once we get there."

"The demon?"

Kamira glanced at the door, but no one was coming. Nevertheless, some information required caution. "Fyertash will be leaving Kaighal, but he has his own matters to see to."

"It'd be better if we killed him," Veelk muttered. "Kinyal doesn't need demons. We have enough problems with humans."

She chuckled, choosing not to argue. Veelk's perspective was a pragmatic one, and any other time she'd agree with him, but there could be more demons lurking in the human world, and having one that was somewhat on their side was beneficial. Besides, Fyertash had saved Veelk's life, and he did help her defeat Myrkan. For that alone, he deserved to be treated like an ally... at least until he decided that his own goals were more important and turned on her or any of her friends.

"What about Zelna and Mawi?" she steered the conversation toward safer topics.

Veelk shook his head. "They'll be heading back home in a while. Mawi wants to know more about Kaighal's history, so he'll be scouring the Towers and the city council's libraries, but after that..." He shrugged. "They long for the tribe's ways."

The door opened again, and Irtan entered, accompanied by Varessa and Pelina. The young woman walked slowly and with caution, but no pain marked her expression. Her quick recovery was proof that healing magic could become very powerful and change the tides of more than one war.

"Archmage," Irtan said in his usual jovial manner, as if he hadn't spent half of the previous night bargaining with her.

Varessa and Pelina repeated his greeting, and Kamira indicated the armchairs. As she expected, they sat all together, but Pelina took the chair behind the two archmages. If Irtan wanted her to become an archmage in the future—and likely his successor, judging by how adamantly he'd demanded Pelina remain under his tutelage the previous night—he had to work on her confidence.

Not long after, Koshmarnyk entered, leading Adept Davshil. The circles around Davshil's eyes and his worried expression told Kamira enough of how much he had to deal with back in Gildya. Even though she felt sorry for the poor adept, who unexpectedly had to handle all Gildya's matters on his own, it also meant that he could be more willing to listen to her plan.

They sat down, opposite the archmages, as if the decades of rivalry forced such behavior even now. More people walked in. Kamira barely recognized their faces, and their names escaped her, but she knew they came from the city council, and she gave them a warm, welcoming smile. For too long Kaighal had been a battlefield between Gildya and the Towers, with both sides ignoring the common residents of the city and their representatives.

They responded with restraint, and their expressions suggested they didn't trust her friendliness.

With everyone having taken their seats, Irtan shifted in his. "Are we expecting anyone else, archmage?"

She nodded. There were more armchairs than necessary, because she'd rather have empty seats than make anyone coming in late unwelcome, but there was still at least one she'd be happy to see in the meeting.

As if on a cue, King Allyv walked through the door. His composed and mature expression contrasted with the features of a barely mature man, but she would make sure no one dismissed his input.

"Apologies for keeping everyone waiting, archmage," Allyv said respectfully. "I had a hard time convincing my guards that they didn't have to accompany me to the meeting. With your permission, though, they will guard the entrance to this room."

"With all that's happened recently, I think we'll all welcome this additional protection," she replied. Allyv must be well aware that with two powerful archmages and two equally powerful mage killers present, the participants were in no danger, but there was no reason to upset his personal guards. It wouldn't hurt anyone if they stood outside.

While Allyv took one of the free chairs, she stood up.

"The siege is over now, even if we still have people hunting for scattered demonlings and the few rogue arcanists that managed to flee," she said. "So I think it's time to talk about the future of Kaighal."

She looked around at suddenly tense expressions. Most

were clearly waiting for her to assert even more power now that she was the city's hero—even if defeating two demons wasn't only her doing.

"I think the city has been divided for too long. With the fall of the high mages, and the demise of Gildya's leaders, we have an opportunity to build something new. To create one council to decide the matters of Kaighal."

As she'd expected, Davshil shifted uneasily, and so did the city's representatives.

"The council would have three representatives of each former faction. Three adepts from Gildya, three archmages from the Towers, and three council members from the city," she continued before they could voice objections based on their assumptions. "The first archmage of the Towers will always be the one to lead the council, but all other members will be chosen at each faction's discretion," she said with confidence, counting that they wouldn't be foolish enough to argue. She was the one who'd saved Kaighal and faced a demon. If they disagreed, she could take all the power for herself or establish the arcanists as the sole rulers of the city, taking everything from them.

Silence fell in the room as people looked at each other. Their expressions made it clear they didn't like the changes, but all of them were hoping someone else would be the one to voice objections.

Kamira gave them the time to realize changes were inevitable, and if they wanted to have a say in the future, they had to agree. Then she looked at Davshil. "It's also time to bring Gildya and the Towers closer together. You've seen already what we can achieve together."

"That's a bold move, archmage," the adept replied nervously. "I like the idea of one council, but to make any other concessions... With Gildya being weakened as it is, it would hardly be an equal partnership. I will not agree to my fellow adepts becoming the archmages' laborers."

"It's not something that will happen overnight," she agreed. "But this is the future I'd like to see everyone working toward. I'm certain that Archmage Varessa could arrange for exchange of knowledge and students, and it wouldn't be hard to share libraries and classrooms, letting the change come gradually. And having one council would ensure that adepts and arcanists are treated equally."

Varessa nodded and smiled at Davshil. "I'll be happy to make arrangements that would bring us closer."

The adept nodded nervously, but he didn't look convinced. "Perhaps something can be done, but that will have to wait until order is restored to Gildya."

"As soon as the new council forms, feel free to ask for any aid you need," Kamira said. The adept needed some reassurance or, in his anxious state, he'd reject the idea out of ungrounded fear. Even though she felt tempted to exercise her powers as the first archmage and actual leader of Kaighal to make him agree, forcing changes on people seemed like a bad idea if one wanted to make the city better. If they left her no choice, she'd use her position to push them in the right direction, but if they were willing to find a way, it wasn't necessary.

With that thought, she turned to the city's representatives. "I want the matters of common people heard, because Kaighal isn't only for adepts and arcanists. Would you agree to dissolve the city council in return for ensuring that all Kaighalans' voices are being heard? Instead of learning of the decisions having been made, you could have your say in them."

The three men and two women looked at each other hesitantly, but in the end, they all nodded, as Kamira expected. It was better to have fewer seats where it mattered than more seats in a puppet council that mostly enacted Gildya's and the archmages' decisions. They must have thought that if they didn't agree, she'd exclude them, a joint council of archmages and adepts would rule the city, and nothing would change.

She allowed herself a smile. Everyone had agreed to form one council, so other issues could become Irtan's problem for some time when she wasn't around. Just one more thing remained.

Kamira looked at the young king.

"King Allyv, the Towers and the whole of Kaighal recognize your effort in helping to defend our city," she said with genuine appreciation. If the city's defense had been entirely on her, Kaighal would have likely fallen long before Ervan's betrayal threatened it. "I've heard of your wise decisions that helped to keep the demonlings out of the streets, and ensured that our defense didn't crumble. You and your people were already welcome in our city, but now Kaighal owes you for your deeds. If you want to make the city your home, the new council will do its best to help the Devanshari in this goal. But if you'd rather reclaim your real home, I'm prepared to personally aid you."

Allyv didn't even try to control his reaction, his face expressing desperate hope. "Can... can this truly be done?"

"The demons that invaded Devanshari all came over here. There might be some smaller ones left, and rogue arcanists and brigands wandering the lands, but Veelk and I will be heading to Juamha soon, and we'll be happy to help in reclaiming the capital of your land. Adept Koshmarnyk will be going with us, so that he can blend stones with any survivors over there who are suffering from magic withdrawal."

It didn't escape her that Davshil gave Koshmarnyk a forlorn glance. Apparently, they hadn't had a chance to talk about it.

"That's very generous of you, archmage, adept." Allyv gave Koshmarnyk a nod. "I feel like I owe you, not the other way around. The citizens of Kaighal welcomed us and helped us when we arrived, beaten and struggling, and aiding the defense was nothing more than trying to help protect our new home." He swallowed. "I'm sure many of my people would like to return to Devanshari and rebuild, but I worry what future waits for them. Even if the demons are gone, there are many others who would prey on those who can't defend themselves. With our hajihali gone and our people decimated, we could become an easy mark."

Kamira hid her smile. It seemed that, unknowingly, Allyv had given her a perfect opportunity to discuss the topic she'd had in mind all along. "That's why I'd also like to discuss with you the possibility of establishing the Towers and Gildya in the new, rebuilt Devanshari. They would provide magic and inventions to keep your people safe. Of course, they would not be exempted from your rule, Your Highness, but within, they'd govern their own affairs. It will be up to you to decide whether to invite the three archmages and three adepts to become your advisers, or form a council similar to the one we just created in Kaighal."

Allyv shifted uneasily, and she didn't blame him. Her proposal would bring changes to Devanshari, and the city and the kingdom they rebuilt would be much different from the one they'd left behind.

She remained silent, letting him understand the reality: the artifact that had protected the Devanshari was gone, so he would either brave the changes to come and restore his kingdom, or he could forever be a refugee king to the refugee people while his old lands withered, likely annexed by Devanshari's greedy neighbors, possibly experiencing even more war as the bordering countries fought for rule over the abandoned domain.

She couldn't help her curiosity. Allyv seemed to have embraced his role as his people's leader, but she wouldn't put it past him to desire the quieter position of the asylum head rather than shouldering all the struggles a king crowned in difficult times would have to bear.

"Will the demon be coming as well?" he asked.

"I haven't spoken to him yet," Kamira lied smoothly, and she could swear Irtan's eyebrow arched ever so slightly.

Fyertash had his own plans, but if she could convince him to spare some time, it could be of benefit if he accompanied them during the sea journey and perhaps stayed for a while. Allyv and his people had to change their mindset about demons, if only for the sake of the arcanists that would reside in the Devanshari Towers. Wrongs had been done, and lives had been lost, but building a future on hate would turn them all into dangerous fanatics.

"If he chooses to accompany us," Kamira continued, "his aid will be of great help. Not only would he stand by us to fight against any demon, small or large, we would encounter, but with his strength, he could support the rebuilding efforts as a means of retribution for what his brethren did."

Undoubtedly, Fyertash would hate the idea, but if he wanted to stay among humans, he had to make allies. One wandering arcanist, not even his pactee, would not do.

"His presence will also make any enemies of the Devanshari think twice before they decide to attack the kingdom," she added.

Allyv closed his fists, and for a blink, his face resembled

that of Ryell when he fought overwhelming hatred. Then the young king's expression smoothed out. "It won't be easy for us, archmage," he said with a trace of sadness.

She bent her head in a respectful bow. "I appreciate that. I'll do everything in my power to help ease the brunt of the changes to come."

He relaxed, and a faint smile came to his face. "Then it is settled. I'm sure my people will be happy at the prospect of returning home, though some might choose to stay and make Kaighal their home. If any arrangements are to be made, I'll speak with the new council."

As silence fell, Kamira looked around. "With all the important matters discussed and a new course set for all of us, I have an announcement to make. As I'll be traveling to Juamha, I won't be able to lead the Council of Kaighal or oversee the daily matters of the Towers. Therefore, I'll be passing the title of first archmage of Kaighal to Irtan, who has already proven his capability to lead with caution and reason rather than emotions and brashness. From now on, he'll be the one to make decisions, and you can ask him any questions you have."

Irtan listened to her speech with a neutral expression, and when she finished, he gave her a short nod, suitable for someone who accepted his new duties but didn't crave the power that came with them. It must have been easy for him to keep a straight face after their lengthy discussion the previous night, but she appreciated it nevertheless.

"What happens upon your return?" asked the woman sent from the city council.

Kamira didn't hesitate with her reply, even though she knew she'd never return. "I keep the title of the archmage, one that is not bound to any of the Towers we hope to build, so I'll have the right to influence the decisions arcanists make for themselves, but my power ends there. If the Council of Kaighal wishes to allow me to sit in their meetings, I'd appreciate it."

The councilwoman relaxed visibly. She must remember the power struggles between high mages and their constant clashes with Gildya, and worried that Kamira would try to wrest the title back from Irtan.

"This concludes the meeting," Kamira said. "First Archmage Irtan." She stepped to the side.

Irtan stood up and walked over to her. "We will meet again in ten days," he said. "That should be enough time for the Towers, Gildya, and the city to choose their three council members. It will also allow us to see to a proper farewell to the archmage who saved Kaighal before we start changing things around," he finished with a jovial smile.

With his announcement, everyone stirred. The representatives of the city council left first, so deep in conversation that all they offered Kamira was quick nods, and Allyv followed them. Undoubtedly, he wanted to share the news with his people. Davshil left shortly after, as soon as Koshmarnyk reassured him that he'd visit Gildya later to discuss arrangements for the new Gildya in Devanshari.

"With your leaving, we're short an archmage for the council," Varessa said. "I'd hate to give the title to one of the previous ones without merit. With Irtan in the lead again, some might see it as returning the Towers to what they were before."

Kamira appreciated that Varessa didn't bring it up during the meeting with others. Even if Veelk and Koshmarnyk lingered in the room, now in a quiet conversation to the side, no other outsiders had to learn of the Towers' inner matters. As much as she wanted to see a unified Kaighal, this was a long process, and Irtan was right to negotiate some freedom for all the factions. They needed time to come closer.

"You could give the title to a promising arcanist instead," she replied. "She's brave, she almost gave her life to fulfill her task, and she likely knows more about arcane magic than you."

With a smirk, Varessa glanced back at Pelina, making it clear she knew whom Kamira had in mind. "People will talk."

"People always talk." Kamira shrugged. Varessa probably didn't like the idea of making Pelina an archmage simply because she was Irtan's student. But with his age advancing, he needed a successor—one not corrupted by the high mages' ways—and if Varessa wasn't going to go after the first archmage position herself, Pelina seemed like a perfect candidate. She still had years, if not decades, to learn, because Irtan would likely cling to life, so there would be no rush.

"Come, my dear." Irtan took Varessa by the arm. "We shouldn't bother *the* archmage with such menial problems. We can discuss it later, on our own."

With some reluctance, she nodded. "I'll see you before you leave," she said to Kamira.

Before they both left, Irtan shot her an amused glance, but it was a friendly one, and she allowed herself her first true breath of relief.

It was all done. She'd cleaned up the mess she caused, and the mess that high mages made was Irtan's to handle. She was free.

There was still the matter of sending a message to the Four to ensure her bargain with them stood, discussing travel plans with Allyv, and some packing, but before that, she could finally indulge in getting some rest. She allowed that relief to show on her face.

"That calls for a celebration," Veelk said. "Best food and wine Kaighal has to offer. After all, we might not be eating well for quite a while."

Kamira couldn't help a chuckle. She should have expected that Veelk's idea of resting would be much different from hers, but a carefree day among close friends sounded wonderful. "You're paying for it," she replied, because he could announce otherwise.

"The heroes of Kaighal should dine for free," Veelk replied. "Well, at least I should for single-handedly dealing with a demon."

"I killed one too," she added.

He gave her a doubtful one-over. "Hardly. You had another demon to help you in your fight, and you *still* managed to get seriously wounded and all beaten up. You clearly haven't learned a thing about fighting in our years together."

"Why would I?" Kamira replied, heading to the door. With all the burden of responsibility gone, at least for a little while, and with the prospect of more travels and adventures, her mood had finally lifted. "I have you to do the fighting."

She didn't hide her amusement as she left the room quickly, making sure Veelk had no chance for a retort. Some battles could be won, but this one she preferred unresolved while she still had the upper hand.

～

KAMIRA HESITATED before approaching the door to Atissa's rooms. It would have been easier if she'd sent Veelk, but even if she had, she couldn't avoid a similar conversation later, likely in less favorable circumstances and with less privacy.

With that, she knocked on the door.

"Come in!" Atissa's voice came muffled from inside, so Kamira let herself in.

The room looked much cleaner than the last time Kamira had seen it, with most of the blood scrubbed off, and only a few darker stains still marking the wood.

Atissa was on her knees, with a small lumisphere hovering over her. Chalk markings covered the floor, and the chisel in her hand suggested that she was busy reinforcing the lines—a usual practice for arcanists who worked with circles regularly in their own homes.

When she saw Kamira, she got up. "Archmage."

"I have an offer to make," Kamira said softly. With the history between them, it made no sense to bother with small talk.

"Have a seat." Atissa brushed some chalk off her clothes and pointed at one of the armchairs. "I still have some wine, if you want any."

"No, let's just talk. I'm sure this situation makes you as uncomfortable as it makes me."

Surprise flashed on Atissa's face, and she nodded. They both sat down.

"Have you heard that I'm leaving?" Kamira asked. The conversation was hers to lead.

"Yes." A slight grimace accompanied Atissa's quiet response. "Irtan has his power again."

"And you're his rival's daughter." Some bluntness was necessary. "More so, no matter what you do, people around here might always remember you as Yoreus's child, seeking hidden meanings in your good deeds and sacrifices."

Atissa curled her lips downward. "It's not like I have anywhere else to go."

"Both Tivarashan and the Western Kingdom would welcome a healer," Kamira replied. "And... you could also go with us. The Devanshari will need healers, and they already know you as someone who helped them in the past. They don't care if you're a former archmage's daughter. You could build a truly new life."

A spark flashed in Atissa's eyes, but it died quickly. "Why would you offer it to me?"

Kamira didn't blame her for being suspicious. Archmages always played with each other and used everyone else in their games. Powerless, Atissa was nothing but a pawn, and having seen and partaken in her father's plots, she must be aware of that.

"Unless you leave for the west, you'll always be stuck between me and Irtan," Kamira said. "But here, he'll haunt your every move, and you'll always be watched. Over there... I won't be staying in Devanshari long. I will return every now and then, so you'll see me and Veelk around, but I have no need to keep an eye on you. Adept Koshmarnyk is planning to help with the rebuilding and settle there, but I thought you wouldn't mind his presence much." She allowed herself a smile. "As to why I would do it... I suppose keeping the only arcane healer away from Irtan has its appeal." In truth, she cared little for it, having made the deal with the old archmage already, but it could be something Atissa would understand.

"With the books from the hidden library, he'll have his own healers soon enough," Atissa replied grimly.

"No, he won't." Kamira couldn't resist the cheerful note in her voice. "He wanted his title back more than the books. They're yours, wherever you decide to take them." Her expression softened. "What happened between me and your father... You shouldn't have suffered for it. I can't give you your old life back, but I can offer you a new one. What you do with it... it's up to you, and only you."

She stood up. With that, there was nothing else to say, and to convince Atissa would mean forbidding her to make her own decisions, whatever they might be.

"We're leaving tomorrow, at dawn. Pack what you'll need for the journey, and I'll make sure Irtan sends the rest once we settle." Kamira would also make sure he'd see to whatever was left of Atissa's home in the woods, but that could wait. "If you want more time to think, you'll have to make your own way to Juamha, but I'll make sure a warm welcome will wait for you no matter when you decide to arrive."

She was heading for the door when Atissa's voice stopped her.

"Archmage."

Kamira looked over her shoulder.

"Thank you. I appreciate your offer."

20

The morning was cloudless, and the breeze from the sea brought the promise of a new beginning. Kamira wasn't particularly fond of sea travel, but a few weeks on a ship were a small price to pay for a new beginning.

Veelk stood beside her, his keshal strapped at his back, and a travel pack slung across his body. By the pier, Koshmarnyk was overlooking men loading up crates sent from Gildya.

"I'm surprised you actually got up so early," Veelk said. "I was certain we'd have to wait for you at least till noon."

She chuckled and didn't remind him that he wasn't an early riser either. Being up at dawn meant quieter departure with fewer onlookers, but it also showed how eager both of them were to leave. With everything that had transpired, Kaighal stopped being the safe and quiet haven, so it was time to find a new one.

Irtan, Varessa, and Pelina had accompanied Kamira from the Towers, but now they were engaged in a quiet discussion with Davshil, likely about the future cooperation between the Towers and Gildya.

Veelk nudged Kamira. "It seems that even your compatriots want you gone."

She looked where he pointed. Far away from the pier, in the shade of a narrow alley, stood a Tivarashan woman. Middle-aged, with her hair neatly tied and her clothes those of a merchant's wife, she drew no attention to herself. But as she shifted in her stance, a medallion on her chest caught a ray of the morning sun.

Kamira knew that shape. The Temple of the Four had come to make sure the bargain was sealed.

The woman smiled and nodded, then turned and left, though Kamira had no doubt that after delivering this simple but clear message from the Four—one the messenger likely didn't understand herself—the priestess would stay hidden, watching, until the ship disappeared on the horizon, to ensure that Kamira had truly left the city. Demons weren't the trusting kind, and the people who worshiped them often had a similar approach.

"I sure won't be missing them," Kamira muttered.

Veelk laughed, and his voice sounded just like she remembered, confident and carefree.

Allyv appeared on board and headed straight for Kamira. "Archmage. The captain says we're ready when you are."

Only one ship was heading for Juamha, with but a handful of Devanshari on it, mostly men. They wanted to make sure the land was indeed safe before allowing their families' return. Allyv didn't seem disappointed, but Kamira couldn't shake the feeling he had been hoping for more people to join him on their journey back.

At least Fyertash had agreed to alter his plans and help the Devanshari. He'd done so with his usual slyness and nonchalance, but this once, she didn't mind his attitude.

Allyv's people had to get used to the demon's presence, but it didn't mean they should start trusting him.

"I'll be there soon," she replied.

All they had left were the goodbyes, and she didn't foresee any long ones. Irtan would be happy to see them both off, she was never close with Varessa, and Pelina... The conspiracy against the high mages that tied them together had already ended. No matter what fondness Pelina might have toward her, it was Irtan who'd become her teacher and mentor. If Kamira was to meet Pelina in the future, the timid and loyal woman would be gone, replaced but a confident arcanist... likely an archmage already. After all, she'd suggested Pelina for the position herself, and Irtan certainly wouldn't oppose it.

Two figures appeared in the street leading to the heart of the city. Mawi's step was springy, and his expression cheerful, making Kamira wonder if all in Veelk's tribe were so eager to smile, but Zelna's grouchy face reassured her that grinning didn't run in the family. The warrioress walked toward the pier with her fist covering huge yawns. It seemed that sleeping in *did* run in the family.

"Archmage, it was a pleasure to meet you," Mawi said while Zelna closed her brother in a tight embrace.

Kamira could swear some bones in Veelk's body cracked, but he returned the hug with similar strength.

"Likewise," she replied, shaking Mawi's hand.

Zelna gave her an evaluating look. "You're still a little scrawny, but you're truly worthy to be my brother's travel companion. Make sure he doesn't do anything foolish."

Veelk's expression was pure innocence, and Kamira chuckled. As Mawi and Zelna stepped to the side, the three archmages approached while Davshil headed for Koshmarnyk.

"Archmage," Irtan said with a hint of amusement. "We'll be looking forward to the news of the new Towers in Devanshari."

"I'm sure you will," Kamira replied.

His expression changed, softness replacing his usual joviality. "Archmage Tijhran would be proud of you."

Kamira swallowed, letting a slight bow of her head conceal the sudden tears gathering. When she looked up, her eyes were dry again.

Varessa gave her a simple nod, but Pelina showed less restraint. She took a step forward and hugged Kamira. "I'll keep an eye on Archmage Irtan for you," she said cheerfully, ignoring that said archmage stood right beside her. "Safe journeys."

There were no more goodbyes left, as Davshil finished his conversation with Koshmarnyk and gave Kamira but a nod in passing. She hoped that, under his leadership, Gildya would once more become a place of invention rather than politics, and since Adept Ervan took poison while imprisoned, the matter of his judgment and punishment had resolved itself, so the past could be left behind.

Kamira was about to turn away from the city when someone rushing down the street caught her attention. But, of course, Veelk recognized the small-framed figure first.

"After all, you did convince her," he said, impressed.

Atissa was running toward them, her hair wild and her face reddened. The bag she had slung over her shoulder looked heavy, and she had two more books in her arms.

"Archmages," she said to Irtan and Varessa, and gave Pelina a warm smile. Then she turned to Kamira. "Archmage," she said with more respect. "I decided to take your offer."

"I'm sure we have a spare cabin on the ship," Kamira

replied. "Adept Koshmarnyk will make sure you're comfortable."

Atissa rushed off toward him, and Kamira looked at Veelk. "It's time for us as well." It didn't escape Kamira that her friend's attention was on Atissa, but this once, she kept her comments to herself. Whatever there could be growing between them, it deserved time to grow undisturbed.

They walked to the ship without any rush.

"Ready to become the Wandering Queen of Arcanists?" Veelk teased.

Kamira chuckled. "I might have made a bad bargain. I could have became a Tivarashan queen," she said, remembering Prince Jalyn's offer.

"Now that's a story I haven't heard yet," Veelk replied. "What other kinds of trouble have you gotten yourself into when I wasn't around?"

She smiled. "I'll tell you all about it."

Stories would fill their journey with laughter, and then there was Juamha. A whole continent of opportunities, with an ancient book to chase down, and a circle of powerful arcanists to find. Adventures, travels, and... a home as well, she realized, as Nyk wrapped his arm around her as soon as she embarked.

She brushed the crystal nightflies, battered but still coiled around her forearms. One day, perhaps, she would reach out to Veranesh and figure out how much she'd really changed, but for now, she'd enjoy the simpler threats and plots of the human world.

With Veelk—and now also Koshmarnyk—by her side, she'd survive everything and anything Juamha threw at her.

THANK YOU FOR READING

Thank you for reading! If you enjoyed the book, please consider leaving a review.
If you'd like to know how Kamira and Veelk met, sign up for the author's newsletter and receive your complimentary copy of Scourges, Spells, and Serenades – a collection that contains two stories featuring Kamira and Veelk as well as other short stories:
authorjm.com

Check out Joanna's new contemporary fantasy series:

Shadows of Eireland

WILL KAMIRA AND VEELK RETURN?

When I announced Demon Siege, the fourth book in the Pacts Arcane and Otherwise series, I called it the final one. It certainly wraps up the story arc that revolved around the demon imprisoned under the desert, leaving no major plots unresolved, so it will provide the satisfying read of a completed series. At the same time, with the world of Kinyal complex and vast, there could many more stories told, those involving Kamira and Veelk as well as other characters and other places.

Will Kamira and Veelk return?

The simple answer is: they could. But that's up to numbers, and I'll be honest with you: they don't look good enough for the adventurous duo. Kamira and Veelk have devoted fans, and I'd love to offer them more of their stories, but the business side of publishing is merciless, and the numbers have to add up. As I'm my own publisher, the cost of editing and covers is on me, and I have to make the harsh decision based on the sales. In a series where you have to start at book 1 to make sense of the story, the follow up books can only appeal to fans which means that there has to be enough of them to keep any series going.

If you ever were upset by a publisher cutting the series before its conclusion, I feel for you: it's frustrating and often damages your trust. At the same time, I understand the other side as well. I'm not a big publisher, so I could afford to take the risk with the series and deliver my promise to the readers: to finish the full story arc for a satisfying read, but if I want to continue writing and publishing books, I need to let Kamira and Veelk go, at least for a time being.

The mundane reality is that publishing requires investing—at minimum—in covers and editing, which means the previous books have to earn enough to first cover their own costs and then to ensure an investment into the future installments. Without it, no series can continue.

So... Is this a definite end?

No. You can help bring Kamira and Veelk back on another adventure by sharing your enthusiasm for the series. If your trust toward unfinished series was damaged in the past and you were holding off getting Pacts Arcane and Otherwise, you can now be certain you'll be able to read the whole story.

If you already have the books, you can help spread the word about them: any post on social media, any review left on Goodreads (even as simple as one sentence telling why you enjoyed the book), StoryGraph, Readerly, or online stores, and any mention to other fantasy fans might help to get the cruel numbers in favor of Kamira and Veelk. You can also recommend the series to your library: the books are available in many library systems both in paperback and ebook (including Overdrive, Libby, Hoopla). It might seem counter-intuitive since library books can be checked out for free, but many readers take a chance on new authors this way and become fans.

What's next?

I'm keeping my fingers crossed that Pacts Arcane and Otherwise will find enough fans to grow into a bigger series, but in the meantime, you can check out my new series, Shadows of Eireland. If contemporary fantasy set in Dublin with a not so epic scope of story is something you might enjoy, the preorder for book 1 in the series is now available as well as sample chapters. As always, you can expect some fun characters, friendly banter, and a promise of an ending that might make you smile. What's more, the books in this series are more stand alone, so you can dive into book 1 without feeling the story is unfinished.

ABOUT THE AUTHOR

Joanna might be a bit too cautious to do anything even remotely daring or dangerous herself, so she writes about daring adventures and dangerous magic instead. Yet, she found enough courage to abandon her life in Poland and move to Ireland, and then some years later, she abandoned her life in Ireland to move over to the US. She's determined to settle there, once she finally chooses which state to reside in.

When she's not writing or thinking about writing, she plays video games or makes amateur art. She lives the happy life of a recluse, surrounded by her husband, a stuffed red monkey, and a small collection of books she insisted on hauling across two continents.

You can find the full list of her publications and more about her at:

http://authorjm.com

and connect with her via social media:

facebook.com/AuthorJMac

instagram.com/authorjmac

indiepocalypse.social/@AuthorJMac

bsky.app/profile/authorjmac.bsky.social

threads.com/@authorjmac

x.com/AuthorJMac

goodreads.com/authorjmac

bookbub.com/authors/joanna-maciejewska

ACKNOWLEDGMENTS

I have a little secret to share: I've been delaying writing this section. To write the acknowledgements in the last book of a series feels... well, final, and I still don't feel ready to let this series go.

But it's time to acknowledge all the support I've had over the years writing Pacts Arcane and Otherwise, and none of the books would have happened without my husband, Inq. He helped me with plot holes, world building problems, and—most of all—with battles. Without him, you could have been reading a chaotic gibberish of a flurry involving weapons and limbs or a one sentence account of Veelk having killed the demon.

I'm also gifted with a lot of wonderful friends who offer feedback, support, and companionship: Piotr Schmidtke, Mariusz Kubiński, Kamil Jach, Joanna Kończak, Joanne White, and L.A. McGinnis. An author can't forget about her fans either, and I've been grateful for many people who expressed their love for my books: C.M., Barb, Jan to name but a few, and wonderful reviewers like Raven or Heather. A special shoutout goes to my guildmates—Fez, Mech, and Saz—who not only keep me company in an online game we play together, but who also show their enthusiasm for my writing. Thank you all!

This book wouldn't be complete without its cover and edits, so my words of gratitude also go to my designer, Jake, and my editor, Arran.